D0480901

PATTERSON

THE JESTER

AND

ANDREW GROSS

headline

First published in Great Britain in 2003
by HEADLINE BOOK PUBLISHING

First published in paperback in Great Britain in 2004
by HEADLINE BOOK PUBLISHING

This edition published in 2011
by HEADLINE PUBLISHING GROUP

3

Cataloguing in Publication Data is available from the British Library

ISBN 978 0 7553 4946 3

Printed and bound in Great Britain by Clays Ltd, St Ives plc

Headline's policy is to use papers that are natural, renewable and
recyclable products and made from wood grown in sustainable forests.
The logging and manufacturing processes are expected to conform
to the environmental regulations of the country of origin.

HEADLINE PUBLISHING GROUP
An Hachette UK Company
338 Euston Road
London NW1 3BH

www.headline.co.uk
www.hachette.co.uk

THE JESTER

ACKNOWLEDGEMENTS

The authors would like to acknowledge that *The Jester* is, in all ways, a work of fiction, an entertainment, and while painstaking care has been paid to historical detail and times, now and then a fact has been stretched or a truth bent for the sake of the story.

Thanks to H.D. Miller of Yale University for his scholarly yet always anecdotal reading of the manuscript. And also to Mary Jordan, who kept this project on the right track at all times.

And most of all, to Sue and Lynn, whose warmth and laughter and spirit found their way on to many pages of this book. And to our kids, Kristen and Matt and Nick and Jack, in the hope that the sound of laughter will never fail to be a guiding companion and a cherished friend in their lives.

PROLOGUE

THE FIND

Wearing a brown tweed suit, and his customary dark tortoiseshell sunglasses, Dr Alberto Mazzini pushed through the crowd of loud and agitating reporters blocking the steps of the Musée de l'Histoire in Blois.

'Can you tell us about the artefact? Is it real? Is that why you're here?' a woman pressed, shoving a microphone marked CNN in his face. 'Have tests been performed on the DNA?'

Dr Mazzini was already annoyed. How had the press jackals been alerted? Nothing had even been confirmed about the find. He waved off the reporters and camera operators.

'This way, *Dottore*,' one of the museum aides instructed. 'Please, come inside.'

A tiny, dark-haired woman in a black trouser suit was waiting for Mazzini. She looked to be in her mid-forties, and appeared almost to curtsy in the presence of this prestigious guest.

'Thank you for coming. I am René Lacaze, the director of the museum. I tried to control the press, but . . .' she shrugged, 'they smell a big story. It is as if we've found an atom bomb.'

'If the artefact you've found turns out to be authentic,' Mazzini replied flatly, 'you will have found something far greater than a bomb.'

As the national director of the Vatican Museum, Alberto Mazzini had lent the weight of his authority to every important find of religious significance that had been unearthed over the previous thirty years: the etched tablets presumed to be the work of the disciple John, dug up in western Syria; the first Vulgate Bible. Both now rested among the Vatican treasures. He had also been involved in the investigation of every hoax, hundreds of them.

René Lacaze led Mazzini along the narrow fifteenth-century hall inlaid with tiles of heraldic designs.

'You say the relic was unearthed in a grave?' Mazzini asked.

'A shopping mall . . .' Lacaze smiled. 'Even in Blois, construction goes on night and day . . . The bulldozers dug up what must have been a crypt. We would have missed it completely had not a couple of the sarcophagi split open.'

Ms Lacaze escorted her important guest into a small elevator and then up to the third floor. 'The grave belonged to some long-forgotten duke who died in 1099. We did acid and photoluminescence tests immediately. Age-wise, it's right on. At first we wondered, why would a precious relic from a thousand years earlier *and half the world away* be buried in an eleventh-century grave?'

'And what did you find?' Mazzini asked.

'It seems our duke went to fight in the Crusades. We know he sought valuable relics from the time of Christ.' They finally arrived at her office. 'I advise you to take a breath. You are about to behold something truly extraordinary.'

The artefact lay on a plain white sheet across an examiner's table, as humble as such a precious thing could be.

Mazzini finally removed his sunglasses. He didn't have to hold his breath. It was completely taken way. *My God, this is an atom bomb!*

'Look closely. There is an inscription.'

The Vatican director bent over it. Yes, it could be. It had all the right markings. The inscription was in Latin. He squinted close to read. *'Acre, Galilee . . .'* He examined the artefact from end to end. The age fitted the markings. It also corresponded to descriptions in the Bible. Yet how had it come to be buried here? 'All this, it does not really prove anything.'

'That's true, of course,' René Lacaze shrugged, 'but, *Dottore*, I am from here. My father is from the valley, my father's father, and his. There have been stories here for hundreds of years, long before this grave tumbled open, stories every schoolchild in Blois was raised on. That this holy relic was here, in Blois, a thousand years ago.'

Mazzini had seen a hundred purported relics like this, but the tremendous power of this one gripped and unnerved him. A reverent force gave him the urge to kneel on the stone floor. Finally, that's what he did – as if he was in the presence of Jesus Christ.

'I waited until your arrival to place a call to Cardinal Perrault in Paris,' said Lacaze.

'Forget Perrault.' Mazzini looked up, moistening his dry lips. 'We are going to call the Pope.'

Alberto Mazzini couldn't take his eyes off the incredible artefact on the plain white sheet. This was more than just the crowning moment of his career. It was a miracle.

'There's just one more thing,' said Ms Lacaze.

'What?' Mazzini mumbled. 'What one more thing?'

'The local lore, it always said a precious relic was here, though never that it belonged to a duke, but to a man of far humbler origins.'

'What sort of lowborn man would come into such a prize? A priest . . .? Perhaps a thief . . .?'

'No.' René Lacaze's brown eyes widened. 'Actually, a jester.'

PART ONE

THE ORIGINS OF COMEDY

Chapter One

Veille du Père, a village in southern France, 1096.

The church bells were ringing. Loud, quickening peals – echoing through the village in the middle of the day.

Only twice before had I heard the bells sounded at midday in the four years since I had come to live here. Once, when word reached us that the King's son had died. And the second, when a raiding party from our lord's rival in Digne swept through the place during the wars, leaving eight dead and burning almost every house to the ground.

What was going on?

I rushed to the upstairs window of the inn I looked after with my wife, Sophie. People were running into the square, still carrying their work tools. 'What's going on? Who needs help?' they shouted.

Then Arnaud, who farmed by the river, galloped over the bridge aboard his mule, pointing back towards the road. 'They're coming! They're almost here!'

From the east I heard a loud chorus of voices, seemingly raised as one. I squinted through the trees and felt my jaw drop. 'Jesus, I'm dreaming,' I said to myself. A pedlar with a cart was considered an event here! I blinked at the sight, not once, but twice.

Jammed along the narrow road into the village, stretching out as far as the eye could see, was the greatest multitude I had ever seen!

'Sophie, come quick, *now!*' I yelled.

My wife of three years hurried to the window, her golden hair pinned up for the workday under a white cap. 'Mother of God, Hugh . . .'

'It's an army,' I muttered, barely able to believe my eyes. 'The army of the Crusade.'

Chapter Two

Even in Veille du Père word had reached us of the Pope's call. We had heard that masses of men were leaving their families, taking the Cross, as nearby as Digne. And here they were – the army of Crusaders marching through Veille du Pere!

But *what* an army! More of a rabble, like one of those multitudes prophesied in Isaiah or John. Men, women, children, carrying clubs and tools straight from home. And it was vast – thousands of them! Not fitted out with armour or uniforms, but shabbily, with red crosses either painted or sewn on to plain tunics. And at the head of this assemblage – not some trumped-up duke or king in crested mail and armour, sitting imperiously atop a massive charger, but a little man in a monk's homespun robe, barefoot, bald, with a thatched crown, sitting atop a mule.

I shook my head. 'It is their awful voices the Turks will turn and run from, not their swords.'

Sophie and I watched as the column crossed the stone bridge on the outskirts of our town: young and old, men and women, some carrying axes and mallets and ancient swords, some old knights parading in rusty armour; carts, wagons, tired mules and plough horses. Thousands of them.

Everyone in town stood and stared. Children ran out and danced around the approaching monk. No one had ever seen anything like it before. *Nothing ever happened here!*

I was struck with a kind of wonderment. 'Sophie, tell me, what do you see?'

'Either the holiest army I've ever seen, or the most stupid. In any case, it's the worst equipped.'

'But look, not a noble anywhere. Just common men and women. *Like us.*'

Below us, the vast column wound into the square and the strange monk at its head tugged his mule to a stop. A shabby, bearded knight helped him slide off. Father Leo, our priest, went up to greet him. The singing stopped, weapons and packs were laid at ease. Everyone in our village was pressed around the tiny square to listen.

'I am called Peter,' the monk spoke in a surprisingly strong voice, 'called by His Holiness Urban to lead an army of believers to the Holy Land to free the Holy Sepulchre from the heathen hordes. Are there any believers here?'

He was pale and long-nosed, resembling his mount, and his threadbare brown robes had holes in them. Yet, as he spoke, he seemed to grow, his voice rising in power and conviction.

'The lands of Our Lord's great sacrifice have been defiled by the infidel Turk. Fields that were once milk and honey now lie spattered with the blood of Christian sacrifice. Holy churches have been burned and looted, sainted sites destroyed. The holiest treasures of our faith, the bones of saints, have been fed to dogs; cherished vials, filled with drops of the Saviour's own blood, poured into heaps of dung like spoiled wine.'

'Join us,' many from the ranks called out loudly. 'Kill the pagans, and sit with the Lord in Heaven.'

'For those who come,' the monk named Peter went on, 'for those who put aside their earthly possessions and join our Crusade, His Holiness Urban promises unimaginable rewards: riches, spoils, and honour in battle; his protection for your families who dutifully remain behind; and eternity in Heaven at the feet of Our grateful Lord. And, most of all, freedom. Freedom from all servitude upon your return. Who will come, brave souls?' The monk reached out his arms.

Shouts of acclamation rose throughout the square. People I had known for years shouted: '*I* . . . I will come!'

I saw Marc, the miller's elder son, just sixteen, throw up his hands and hug his mother. And Jules, one of our smiths, who could crush iron in his hands, kneel and take the Cross. Several people, many of them just boys, ran to get their possessions, then merged with the ranks. Everyone was shouting, '*Deus vult!*' God wills it!

Inside, my own blood surged. What a glorious adventure awaited. Riches and spoils picked up along the way. A chance to change destiny in a single stroke. I felt my soul spring alive. I thought of gaining our freedom, and the gold I might find on the Crusade. For a second I almost raised my hand and called out, 'I will come! I will take the Cross.'

But then I felt Sophie's hand pressing on mine. I lost my tongue.

In minutes, the procession started up again, the ranks of farmers, masons, bakers, maids, whores, jongleurs and outlaws, hoisting their sacks and makeshift weapons, swelling in song. The monk Peter mounted his mule, blessed the village with a wave, then pointed west.

I watched them with a yearning I thought had long been put behind me. I had travelled in my youth. I'd been brought up by goliards, monks who entertained from town to town. And there was something that I missed from those days. Something my life in Veille du Père had stilled but not completely put aside.

I missed being free, and even more than that, I wanted freedom for Sophie and the children we would one day have.

Chapter Three

Two days later, other visitors came through our village.

There was a ground-shaking rumble from the west, followed by a cloud of gravel and dust. Horsemen were coming in at a full gallop! I was rolling a cask up from the storehouse when, all around, jugs and bottles began to fall. Panic clutched at my heart. A devastating raid by marauders just two years before flashed through my mind. Every house in the village had been burned or sacked.

There was a shriek, and a shout. Children, playing ball in the square, dived out of the way. Eight massive warhorses thundered across the bridge into the village centre and on their riders, I saw the green and gold colours and eagle of Baldwin, our liege lord.

The party of horsemen pulled to a stop in the square. I recognized the knight in charge as Norcross, our liege lord's chatelain, his military chief. He scanned our village from atop his mount and remarked for everyone to hear, 'This is Veille du Père?'

'It must be, my lord,' a companion knight replied with an exaggerated sniff. 'We were told to ride west until we caught the smell of shit, then head directly for it.'

Their presence here could signal only harm. I began to make my way slowly towards the square with my heart pounding. Anything might happen. *Where was Sophie?*

Norcross dismounted, and the others followed, their chargers snorting heavily. The chatelain had dark, hooded eyes that flashed only a sliver of light, like an eighth moon, and a trace of a thin, dark beard.

'I bring greetings from your lord, Baldwin,' he said for all to hear, stepping into the centre of the square. 'Word has reached him that a rabble passed through here a day or two ago, some babbling priest at the head.'

As he spoke, his knights began to fan out through town. They pushed aside women and children, sticking their heads into houses as if they owned them. Their haughty faces read: Get out of my way, scum. You have no power. I can do anything I want.

'Your lord asked me to impress upon you,' Norcross declared, 'his hope that none of you were swayed by the ravings of that religious crank. His brain's the only thing more withered than his dick.'

Now I realized what Norcross and his men were doing here. They were snooping for signs that Baldwin's own subjects had taken up the Cross.

Norcross strutted around the square, his narrow eyes ratcheting from person to person. 'It is your lord, Baldwin, who demands your service, not some moth-eaten crank. You are pledged and honour-bound to *him*. Next to his, the Pope's protection is worthless.'

I finally caught sight of Sophie, hurrying from the well with her pail. Beside her was the miller's wife, Winnie, and their daughter, Amiée. I motioned with my eyes for them to stay clear of Norcross and his bullies.

Father Leo spoke up. 'On the fate of your soul, knight,' the priest said, stepping out, 'do not defame those who now fight for God's glory. Do not compare the Pope's holy protection to yours. It is blasphemy.'

Frantic shouts rang out. Two of Norcross's knights returned to the square dragging Georges the miller and, behind him, his younger son, Alo, by the hair. The knights threw both in the middle of the square.

I felt a hole in the pit of my stomach. *Somehow they knew . . .*

Norcross seemed delighted. He went and cupped the face of the cowering boy in his massive hand. 'The Pope's protection, you say, eh, priest?' he chuckled. 'Why don't we see what his protection is truly worth?'

Chapter Four

Our powerlessness was so obvious and shameful to me. The iron of Norcross's sword jangled as he made his way to the frightened miller. 'On my word, miller,' Norcross smiled, 'only last week did you not have *two* sons?'

'My son Marc has gone to Valcluese,' Georges said, and looked towards me. 'To study the metal trade.'

'The metal trade . . .' Norcross nodded, bunching his lips. He smiled as if to say, I know that is a pile of shit.

Georges was my friend. My heart went out to him. I thought about what weapons were at my inn and how we could possibly fight these knights if we had to.

'And with your stronger son gone,' Norcross pressed on, 'how will you continue to make your allotment to the duke, your labour now depleted by a third?'

Georges's eyes darted about. 'It will be made easily, my lord. I will work that much the harder.'

'That is good,' Norcross nodded, stepping over to the boy. 'In that case, you won't be missing *this* one too much, will you?' In a flash, he hoisted the nine-year-old lad up like a sack of hay.

He carried Alo, kicking and screaming, towards the mill.

As Norcross passed the miller's cowering daughter, he winked at his men. 'Feel free to help yourself to some of the miller's lovely grain.' They grinned, and dragged poor Amiée, screaming wildly, inside the mill.

Disaster loomed in front of my eyes. Norcross took a hemp rope and, with the help of a cohort, lashed Alo to the staves of the mill's large wheel, which dipped deeply beneath the surface of the river.

Georges threw himself at the chatelain's feet. 'Haven't I always been true to our lord Baldwin? Haven't I done what was expected?'

'Feel free to take your appeal to His Holiness,' Norcross laughed, lashing the boy's wrists and ankles tightly to the water wheel.

'Father, Father . . .' the terrified Alo called out.

Norcross began to turn the wheel. To Georges and Winnie's frantic shrieks, Alo went under. Norcross held it for a few seconds, then slowly raised the wheel. The child appeared, wildly gasping for air.

The despicable knight laughed at our priest. 'What do you say, Father? Is this what you expect from the Pope's protection?' He lowered the wheel again and the small boy disappeared completely. Our entire town gasped in horror.

I counted close to thirty heart-stopping seconds. 'Please,' Winnie begged on her knees. 'He's just a boy.'

Norcross finally began to raise the wheel. Alo was gagging and coughing water out of his lungs. From behind the mill door came the sickening cries of Amiée. I could scarcely breathe myself. I had to do something – even if it sealed my own fate.

'Sir,' I stepped towards Norcross, '*I* will help the miller increase his allotment by a third.'

'And who are *you*, Carrot-top?' The glowering knight turned and fixed on my shock of bright red hair.

'Carrots too, if my lord wants.' I took another step. I was prepared to say anything, whatever gibberish might divert him. 'We'll throw in two sacks of carrots!'

I was about to go on – a joke, nonsense, anything that came into my head – when one of the henchmen rushed up to me. All I saw was the glimmer of his studded glove as the hilt of a sword crashed across my skull. In the next breath I was on the ground.

'Hugh, Hugh!' I heard Sophie scream.

'Carrot-top here must be keen on the miller,' Norcross jeered. 'Or the miller's wife. By a third more, you say. Well, in my lord's name I accept your gift. Consider your allotment raised.'

At the same time he lowered the wheel. I heard a struggling, choking Alo go under one more time.

Norcross shouted, 'If it's fight you want, then fight for the glory of your liege when called upon. If it's riches, then attend harder to your work. But the laws of custom are the laws. You all understand the laws, do you not?'

Norcross leaned against the wheel for the longest time. An anguished plea rose from the crowd: 'Please . . . let the boy up. Let him up.' I clenched my fist, counting while Alo remained under. *Twenty . . . thirty . . . forty.*

Then Norcross's face split into an amused smile. 'Goodness . . . do I forget the time?'

He slowly raised the wheel. When Alo broke the surface, the boy's face was bloated and wide-eyed. His small jaw hung open, lifeless.

Winnie screamed and Georges rolled over on the ground and began to sob.

'What a shame,' Norcross sighed, leaving the wheel aloft and Alo's lifeless body suspended high. 'It seems he wasn't cut out for the miller's life after all.'

A silence ensued, a terrible moment that was empty and gnawing. It was broken only by Amiée's whimpers as she emerged weak-kneed from the mill.

'Let us go.' Norcross gathered his knights. 'I think the duke's point is adequately driven home.'

As he made his way back across the square, he stopped over me and pressed his heavy boot into my neck. 'Do not forget your pledge, Carrot-top. I will be looking especially for *your* allotment.'

Chapter Five

That terrible afternoon changed my life. That night, as Sophie and I lay in bed, I couldn't hold back the truth from her. She and I had always shared everything, good and bad. We were lying as one on the thatched mattress in our small quarters behind the inn. I gently stroked her long golden hair, which fell all the way down her back. Every time she moved, every twitch of her nose, reminded me how much I loved her, how I had since the first time I had set eyes on her.

It was love at first sight for us. *At ten!*

I had spent my youth travelling with a band of goliards, given to them at a young age when my mother died, the mistress of a cleric who could no longer hide my presence. They raised me as one of their own, taught me Latin, grammar, logic, but most of all, how to perform. We travelled the large cathedral towns, Tours, Cluny, Le Puy, reciting our irreverent songs, tumbling and juggling for the crowds. Each summer, we passed through Veille du Père. I saw Sophie there at her father's inn, her shy blue eyes unable to hide from mine. And later, I noticed her peeking at a rehearsal – I was sure, *at me* . . .

I swiped a sunflower and went up to her. 'What goes in all stiff and stout, but when it comes out it's flopping about?'

She widened her eyes and blushed. 'How could anyone but a devil have such bright red hair?' Then she ran away. 'A cabbage,' I was about to say.

Each year when we returned, I came bearing a sunflower, until Sophie had grown from a gangly girl into the most beautiful woman I had ever seen. She had a song for me, a teasing rhyme:

> A maiden met a wandering man
> In the light of the moon's pure cheer,
> And though they fell in love at that first sight,
> It was a love that was borne for tears.

I called her my princess, and she said that I probably had one in every town. But in truth, I did not. Each year I promised I would come back, and I always did. One year, I stayed.

The three years we'd been married had been the happiest I had known. I felt secure for the first time in my life. And deeply in love.

But as I held Sophie that night, something told me I could no longer live like this. The rage that burned in my heart from that day's horror was killing me. There would always be another Norcross, another tax or allotment levied upon us. Or another Alo . . . One day, the boy strung up on that wheel could be our own.

Until we were free.

'Sophie, I have something important to talk to you

about.' I snuggled into the smooth curve of her back.

She had nearly drifted off to sleep. 'Can't it wait, Hugh? What could be more important than what we've just shared?'

I swallowed. 'Raymond of Toulouse is forming an army. Simon the carter told me. They leave for the Holy Land in a few days.'

Sophie turned in my arms and faced me with a blank unsure look.

'I have to go,' I said.

She sat up, almost dumbfounded. 'You want to take the Cross?'

'Not the Cross. I wouldn't fight for that. But Raymond has promised freedom to anyone who joins. *Freedom*, Sophie . . . You saw what happened today.'

She straightened. 'I *did* see, Hugh. And I saw that Baldwin will never free you from your pledge. Or any of us.'

'In this he has no choice,' I protested. 'Raymond and Baldwin are aligned. He has to accept. Sophie, think of how our lives could change. Who knows what I might find there. There are tales of riches, just for the taking. And holy relics, worth more than a thousand inns like ours.'

She turned her eyes from me. 'You're leaving because I have not given you a child.'

'I am not! You mustn't think that, not even for a second. I love you more than anything. When I see you each day, working around in the inn, or even amid the grease and smoke of the kitchen, I thank God how lucky I am. We were meant to be together. I'll be back before you know it.'

She nodded unconvincingly. 'You are no soldier, Hugh. You could die.'

'I'm strong. And agile. No one around can do the tricks I do.'

'No one wants to hear your silly jokes, Hugh, but me,' Sophie sniffed.

'Then I'll scare the infidels off with my bright red hair.'

I saw the outline of a smile from her. I held her by the shoulders and looked in her eyes. 'I will be back. I swear it. Just as when we were children. I always told you I'd return. I always did.'

She nodded, a bit reluctantly. I could see how scared she was, but so was I. I held her and stroked her hair.

Sophie lifted her head and kissed me, a mixture of ardour and tears.

A stirring rose in me. I couldn't hold it down. I could see in Sophie's eyes that she felt it too. I held her by the waist and she moved on top of me. Her legs parted and I gently eased myself inside. My body lit with her warmth.

'My Sophie . . .' I whispered.

She moved with me in perfect rhythm, softly moaning with pleasure and love. How could I leave her? How could I be such a fool?

'You'll come back, Hugh?' Her eyes locked on mine.

'I swear. In a year.' I reached and wiped away a glistening tear from her eye. 'Who knows,' I smiled, 'maybe I'll come back as a knight, with untold treasure and fame.'

'My knight,' she whispered. 'And I, your queen . . .'

Chapter Six

The morning of the day I was to leave was bright and clear. I rose early, even before the sun. The villagers had bid me farewell with a festive roast the night before. All the toasts had been made and goodbyes said.

All but one.

In the doorway of the inn, Sophie handed me my sack. In it was a change of clothes, bread to eat, and a hazel twig to clean my teeth. 'It may be cold,' she said. 'You have to cross the mountains. Let me get your skin.'

I stopped her. 'Sophie, it's June. I'll need it more when I come back.'

'Then I should pack some more food for you.'

'I'll find food.' I pumped out my chest. 'People will be eager to feed a Crusader.'

She stopped, and smiled at my plain, flax tunic and calfskin jerkin. 'You don't look like much of a Crusader.'

I stood before her, ready to leave, and smiled too.

'There's one more thing,' Sophie said with a start. She hurried to the table by the hearth. She came back a moment later with her treasured comb, a thin band of beechwood painted with flowers. It had belonged to her mother. Other than the inn, I knew she valued it more than anything in her life. 'Take this with you, Hugh.'

'Thank you,' I tried to joke, 'but where I'm going a woman's comb may be looked at strangely.'

'Where you're going, my love, you will need it all the more.'

To my surprise, she snapped her prized comb in two. She handed half to me. Then she held her half out and we touched the jagged edges together, neatly fitting it back into a whole.

'I never thought I would ever say goodbye to you,' she whispered, doing her best not to cry. 'I thought we would live out our lives together.'

'We will,' I said. 'See . . .' One more time, we fitted the combs together and made a whole.

I drew Sophie close and kissed her. I felt her thin body tremor in my arms. I knew she was trying to be brave. There was nothing more to say.

'So . . .' I took a breath and smiled.

We looked at each other for a long while, then I remembered my own gift. From my jerkin pocket I took out a sunflower. I had gone into the hills to pick it early that morning. 'I'll be back, Sophie, to pick sunflowers for you.'

She took it, her bright blue eyes moist with tears.

I threw my pouch over my shoulder and tried to drink in the last sight of her beautiful, glistening eyes. 'I love you, Sophie.'

'I love you too, Hugh. I cannot wait for my next sunflower.'

I started towards the road. East, to Toulouse. At the stone bridge on the edge of town, I turned and took a long last look at the inn. It had been my home for the past three years, the happiest days of my life.

I gave a final wave to Sophie. She stood there, holding the sunflower, and reached out the jagged edge of her comb one last time.

Then I did a little hop, like a jig, to break the mood, and started to walk, spinning round to catch her laugh.

Her golden hair down to her waist. That brave smile. Her tinkling, little-girl laugh.

It was the image I carried for the next two years.

Chapter Seven

A *year later, somewhere in Macedonia.*

The heavy-bearded knight reared his mount over us on the steep ridge. 'March, you princesses, or the only Turkish blood you'll get to spill will be at the end of a mop.'

I put my shoulder into the wheel. *March . . .* We had been marching for eight months now – months so long and gruelling, so lacking in all provision, I could mark them only by the sores oozing on my feet, or the lice growing in my beard.

We had marched across all of Europe, through the Alps and Maritimes – at first, in tight formation, cheered in every town we passed through, our tunics clean, with bright red crosses, helmets gleaming in the sun.

Then, into the craggy mountains of Serbia – each step slow and treacherous, every ridge ripe with ambush. I watched as many a loyal soul, eager to fight for the glory of God, was swept screaming into vast crevasses or dropped in their tracks by Serb or Magyar arrows months before the first sign of a Turk.

All along we were told Peter's army lay months ahead of us, slaughtering infidels and hoarding all the spoils, while our nobles fought and bickered amongst themselves and the rest of us trudged like beaten livestock in the blistering heat or cold, and bargained for what little food there was.

I'll be back in a year, I had promised Sophie . . . Now that was just a mocking refrain in my dreams. And so was *our* song . . . 'A maiden met a wandering man/In the light of the moon's pure cheer.'

Along the way, I made two lasting friends from among the ranks. Nicodemus, an old Greek, was schooled in sciences and languages, and managed to keep up his steady stride despite the heavy satchel flung across his back, crammed with the tracts of Aristotle, Euclid and Boethius. *Doctor*, we called him. Nico had made pilgrimages to the Holy Land and knew the language of the Turk, and spent many hours on the march teaching me. He had contracted on to the quest as a translator, and because of his white beard and moth-eaten robe, he had the reputation for being a bit of a soothsayer too. But every time a soldier moaned, 'Where the hell are we, Doctor?' and the old Greek muttered, 'Near . . .' his reputation as a seer suffered.

There was also Robert with his goose, Hortense, who sneaked into our ranks one day as we passed through Apt. Fresh-faced and chattering, Robert claimed to be sixteen, but it didn't take a seer to divine that he was lying.

'I've come to carve the Turks,' he boasted, brandishing a makeshift knife.

I handed him a stick that would be good for walking. 'Here, start with this,' I laughed. From that moment on, he and the goose were our mascots.

It was June when we finally came out of the mountains.

'Where are we, Hugh?' Robert moaned, as another interminable valley loomed before our eyes.

I tried to sound upbeat. 'By my calculations, a left at the next ridge and we should see Rome. Isn't that right, Nico? This was the pilgrimage to St Peter's we signed up for, wasn't it? Or, shit, was it the Crusade?'

A ripple of tired laughter snaked through the exhausted ranks.

Nicodemus started to answer, but everyone shouted him down.

'We know, Doctor, we're *near*, right?' smirked Mouse, a diminutive Spaniard with a large, hooked nose.

Suddenly, I heard shouting from up ahead. Nobles on horseback whipped their tired mounts and rushed towards the front of the procession.

Robert bolted ahead. 'If there's fighting, Hugh, I'll save you a spot.'

All at once, my own legs seemed to comply. I grabbed my shield and ran after the boy. Ahead of us was a wide gulf in the mountains. Hundreds of men were gathered there, knights and soldiers.

For once, they were not defending themselves. They were shouting, slapping each other on the backs, thrusting their swords towards heaven and hurling their helmets into the air.

Robert and I pushed our way through the crowd and peered out over the edge.

Off in the distance the grey outline of hills narrowed to a sliver of shining blue. 'The Bosporus,' people shouted. 'The Bosporus!'

'Son of Mary,' I muttered. We were here!

A jubilant roar went up. Everyone pointed towards a walled city nestled into the isthmus edge. *Constantinople*. It took my breath away, like nothing I had ever seen before. It seemed to stretch out for ever, glinting through the haze.

Many knights kneeled in prayer. Others, too exhausted to celebrate, simply bowed their heads and wept.

'What's going on?' Robert looked around.

I too kneeled down, and took a handful of earth to mark the day and placed it in my pouch. Then I hoisted Robert into the air. 'You see those hills over there?' I pointed across the channel.

He nodded.

'Sharpen your knife, boy. Those are Turkish!'

Chapter Eight

For two weeks we rested outside the gates of Constantinople.

Such a city I could not have imagined in all my life: with its massive, glittering domes and hundreds of tall towers, Roman ruins and temples, and streets paved with polished stone. Paris could have fitted ten times within its walls!

And the people . . . Crowding the massive walls, roaring with cheers. Clad in colourful, light cottons and silks, in hues of crimson and purple I had never seen. Every race was represented: European, black slaves from Africa, yellow from China. And people of no stench, who bathed and smelled of perfume, dressed up in ornate robes. Even the men!

I had travelled across Europe in my youth and had played in most of the large cathedral towns, but never had I seen a place like this! Gold was like tin here. Stalls and markets were crammed with the most exotic goods. I traded for a gilded perfume box to take back home for Sophie. 'A relic, already!' Nico laughed. New aromas entranced me – cumin and ginger – and fruits I had never tasted before: oranges and figs.

I savoured every exotic image, thinking of how I would describe it all to Sophie back home. We were hailed as heroes and we had fought no one. If this was how it would be, I would return both sweet-smelling *and* free!

Then the knights and nobles rallied us: 'Crusaders, you are here for God's work, not for silver and soap.' We said our goodbyes to Constantinople, crossing the Bosporus on wooden pontoons.

At last, we stood in the land of the dreaded Turk!

The first fortresses we encountered were empty and abandoned; towns scorched and plundered dry.

'The pagan is a coward,' the soldiers mocked. 'He hides in his hole like a squirrel.'

We spotted red crosses painted everywhere, pagan towns now consecrated in the name of God. All signs that Peter's army had been through.

The nobles pushed us hard. 'Hurry, you lazy slackers, or the little monk will take all the spoils.'

And we did hurry, though our new enemy became the blistering heat and thirst. We baked like hogs in our heavy armour, though we sucked our water skins dry. The pious among us dreamed of our holy mission; the nobles, no doubt, of relics and glory; the innocent, to prove finally their worth.

At Civetot we had our first taste of the enemy. A few straggling horsemen, turbaned and cloaked in robes, ringed our ranks, lofting some harmless arrows at us, then fleeing into the hills, like children after hurling stones.

'Look, they run like grandmothers,' Robert cackled.

'Send Hortense after them.' I squawked about like a chicken. 'No doubt they are cousins of your goose.'

Civetot seemed deserted, an enclave of stone dwellings on the edge of a dense wood. We needed water badly. And no one wanted to delay in our rush to catch up with the army of Peter.

On the outskirts of town, a grim odour pressed at my nostrils. Nicodemus glanced at me. 'You smell it, don't you, Hugh?'

I nodded. I knew the stench, from burying the dead, one or two, but this was magnified a thousand times. At first I thought it was just slaughtered livestock, or offal, but as we got closer, I saw that Civetot was smoking like burning cinders.

As we entered the town there were corpses everywhere. A sea of naked body parts: heads severed and gawking, limbs cut off and piled like wood, blood drenching the parched earth, men and women hacked up like diseased stock, torsos naked and disembowelled, heads charred and roasted, hung up on spears. Red crosses smeared all over the walls – *in blood*.

'What has happened here?' a soldier muttered.

Some puked and turned away. My stomach felt as empty as a bottomless pit.

Out from the trees, a few stragglers appeared. Their clothing was charred and tattered, their skin dark with blood and filth. They all bore the wide-eyed, hollow look of men who have seen the worst atrocities and somehow lived. It was impossible to tell if they were Christian or Turk.

'Peter's army has crushed the infidels,' Robert rang out.

'They've gone ahead to Antioch.'

But not a man among us cheered.

'This *is* Peter's army,' Nicodemus said grimly. 'What remains of it.'

Chapter Nine

The few survivors huddled around fires that night, sucking in precious food, and told of the fate of Peter the monk's army.

There were some early successes, they recounted. 'The Turks fled like rabbits,' an old knight said. 'They left us their towns, their temples. "We'll be in Jerusalem by summer," everyone cheered. We split up our forces. A detachment, six thousand strong, pushed east to seize the Turkish fortress at Xerigordon. Rumour had it some holy relics were held ransom there. The balance of us stayed behind.

'After a month, word reached us that the fortress had fallen. Spoils and booty were being divided up among the men. St Peter's sandals, we were told. The rest of us set out for there, eager not to miss out on the loot.'

'It was all lies,' said another in a parched, sorry voice, 'from infidel spies. The detachment at Xerigordon had already perished – not by siege, but by *thirst*! The fortress lacked all water. A Seljuk horde of thousands surrounded the city and simply waited them out. And when our troops finally opened the gates in desperation, mad with thirst, they were overrun and slaughtered to a man. Six thousand, gone. Then the devils set their sights on us.'

'At first, there was this *howl* from the surrounding hills,' another survivor recounted, 'of such chilling proportion that we thought we had entered a valley of demons. We stood in our tracks and scanned the hills. Then suddenly, daylight darkened, the sun blocked by a hail of arrows.

'I will never forget that deafening *whoosh*. Every next man clutching at his limbs and throat, falling to his knees. Then turbaned horsemen charged – wave after wave, hacking away at limbs and heads, and our ranks were shredded. Hardened knights fled terror-stricken back to camp, horsemen at their tails. Women, children, feeble and sick, unprotected – chopped to bits in their tents. The lucky among us were slain where they stood, the rest were seized, the women raped, cut apart, limb by limb. What's left of us, I am sure, were spared just so we could bear the tale.'

My throat went dry. Gone . . . All of them? It could not be! My mind flashed back to the cheerful faces and joyous voices of the monk's army as it marched through Veille du Père. Marc, the miller's son. Jules, the smith . . . All the young, who had so eagerly joined up. Was there nothing left of them?

A nauseating anger boiled up in my stomach. Whatever I had come for – freedom, fortune – all that left me as if it were never there. For the first time, I wanted to fight not just for my own gain, but to kill these curs. *To pay them back!*

I stood up and ran, leaving Robert and Nico, passing the fires, to the edge of the camp.

Why did I ever come to this place? I had walked across all

of Europe, fighting for a cause in which I didn't even believe. The love of my life, all that I held true and good, was a year's march away. *How could all those faces – all that hope – be gone?*

Chapter Ten

We buried the dead for six days straight. Then our dispirited army headed further south.

In Caesarea, we joined forces with Duke Robert of Flanders, and Bohemond, a heralded Norman fighter. They had recently taken the port of Nicea. Our spirits were bolstered by the tales of Turks fleeing at full run, their towns now under Christian flags. Our once-fledgling troop had now become an army forty thousand strong.

Nothing lay in our path towards the Holy Land, except the Muslim stronghold of Antioch. There it was said that believers were being nailed to the city's walls, and that the most precious relics in all of Christendom, a shroud stained by the tears of Mary, and the very lance that pierced the Saviour's side on the Cross, were being held for ransom.

Yet nothing so far could prepare us for the hell we were about to face.

First it was the heat, the most hostile I had ever felt in my life. The sun became a raging, red-eyed demon we, never sheltered, grew to hate and curse. Hardened knights, praised for valour in battle, howled in anguish, literally boiling in their armour, their fingers blistered at the touch.

Men simply fell as they marched, overcome, and were left, uncared for, in the place where they lay.

And the thirst . . . Each town we got to was scorched and empty, run dry of provision by the Turks themselves. What little water we carried we consumed like drunken fools. I saw once-proud men, now clearly mad, guzzle their own urine as if it were ale.

'If this is the Holy Land,' the Spaniard Mouse spit drily, 'God can keep it.'

Our bodies cried, yet we trudged on; our hearts and wills, like the water, slowly depleting. Along the way, I picked up a few Turkish arrow and spearheads that I knew would be worth much back home. I did my best to try to cheer the men, but there was little anywhere to find amusing.

'Hold your tears,' Nico warned, keeping up with his shuffling stride. 'When we hit the mountains, you will think *this* was Paradise.'

And he was right. Jagged mountains appeared in our path, chillingly steep and dry of all life. Narrow passes, barely wide enough for a cart and a horse, cut through the rising peaks. At first, we were glad to leave the inferno behind, but as we climbed, a new hell awaited.

The higher we got, every step became slow and treacherous. Sheep, horses, carts overladen with supplies had to be dragged single file and pulled up the steep way. A mere stumble, a sudden rockslide, and a man disappeared over the edge, sometimes dragging a companion along with him.

'Press on,' the nobles pushed. 'In Antioch, God will reward you.'

But every summit we cleared brought a new peak, each

trail more nerve-racking than the last. Knights trudged humbly, their chargers useless, dragging their armour alongside foot soldiers like Robert and me.

Somewhere in the heights, Hortense disappeared, her feathers left in a cart. It was never known what became of her. Many felt the nobles had themselves a meal at Robert's expense. Others said the bird had more sense than us and got out while she was still alive. The boy was heartbroken. That bird had walked across Europe with him! Many felt our luck had run out along with hers.

Yet still we climbed, one step at a time, sweltering in our tunics and armour, knowing that on the other side lay Antioch.

And beyond that, the Holy Land. Jerusalem!

Chapter Eleven

'Tell us a story, Hugh?' Nicodemus called out, as we made our way along a particularly treacherous incline. 'The more blasphemous the better.'

The trail seemed cut right out of the mountain's edge, teetering over an immense chasm. One stumble, one false step was all that separated us from grisly death. I had latched myself to a goat, and placed my trust in its measured step to pull me further on.

'There is the one about the convent and the whorehouse,' I said, delving back to my days as an innkeeper. 'A traveller is walking down a quiet road when he notices a sign scratched on to a tree: "Sisters of St Brigit Convent, House of Prostitution, two leagues".'

'Yes, I saw it myself,' a soldier remarked, 'a ways back on that last ridge.' The peril of the climb was broken by a few welcome laughs.

'The traveller assumes it is a joke,' I went on, 'and continues along. Soon he comes to another. "Sisters of St Brigit, House of Prostitution, one league". Now, his curiosity is aroused. Then there is a third. This time: "Convent, Brothel, Next Right".

'Why not? the traveller thinks, and turns down the road until he arrives at an old stone church marked "St Brigit". He steps up and rings the bell and an abbess answers: "What may we do for you, my son?"

' "I saw your signs along the road," the traveller says.

' "Very well, my son," the abbess replies. "Please, follow me."

'She leads him through a series of dark, winding passages where he passes many beautiful young nuns who smile at him.'

'Where are these nuns when *I* am in need?' a soldier behind me moaned.

'At last the abbess stops at a door,' I went on. 'The traveller goes in and is greeted by another comely nun who instructs him, "Place a livre in the cup". He empties his pockets, excitedly. "Good enough," she says. "Now, just go through that door."

'Aroused, the traveller hurries through the door, but finds himself back outside, at the entrance, facing another sign. "Go in peace," it reads, "and consider yourself properly screwed!" '

Rounds of laughter broke out from all around.

'I don't get it,' Robert said, behind me. 'I thought there was a brothel?'

'Never mind.' I rolled my eyes. Nico's trick had worked. For a few moments, our burden seemed bearable. All I wanted was just to get off this ridge.

Suddenly I heard a rumble from above. A slide of rock and gravel hurtled down at us. I reached for Robert and pulled the boy towards the mountain face, gripping the sheer stone, as huge rocks crashed around us, missing me by the width of a blade, bouncing over the edge into oblivion.

We gazed at each other with a sigh of relief, realizing how close we had come to death.

Then I heard a mule bray from behind, and Nicodemus trying to settle it. 'Whoa . . .' The falling rocks must have frightened it.

'Steady that animal,' an officer barked from behind. 'It carries your food for the next two weeks.'

Nicodemus grasped for the rope. This time the animal's hind legs spun, trying to get a purchase on the trail.

I lunged for the harness round its neck, but the mule bucked again and stumbled. Its feet were unable to hold the trail. Its terrified eyes were aware of the danger, but the stone gave way. With a hideous bray, the poor creature toppled over the edge and fell into the void.

As it did, it caused a terrible reaction, pulling along the animal behind it to which it was tied.

Before I could call out, I saw disaster looming. '*Nico!*' I shouted.

But the old Greek was too slow and laden with gear to get out of the way, and he stumbled in his long robe.

'Nico!' I screamed, seeing the old man slipping near the edge. I lunged towards him, grasping for his arm.

I was able to firm my grip on the strap of leather satchel slung over his shoulder. It was all that kept him from plunging over the edge to his death.

The old man looked up at me and shook his head. 'You must let go, Hugh. If you don't, we'll both fall.'

'I won't. Reach up your other hand,' I begged. A crowd of others, Robert among them, had formed behind me. 'Give me your hand, Nico.'

'My dream was true, Hugh,' Nicodemus said, almost calmly. 'Go home, son. Find your queen.'

I searched his eyes for panic, but they were clear and sure. I wanted to say, 'Hold on, Doctor. Jerusalem is near,' but the weight of the satchel slid out of my grasp. Nicodemus, his white hair and beard billowing in the draught, fell away from me.

'*No . . .!*' I lunged, grabbing, calling his name.

In a second he was gone. We had marched together across Europe, but for him it was never far, *always near . . .* I had never known my father, but the grief emptying from me showed that Nicodemus was as close to a father as I'd ever had.

A knight pushed up the trail, grumbling about what the hell was going on. I recognized him as Guillaume, a vassal of Bohemond, one of the nobles in charge.

He peered over the edge and swallowed at the grisly sight. 'A soothsayer who couldn't even predict his own death?' he spat. 'No great loss.'

Chapter Twelve

For days to come, the loss of my friend weighed greatly upon me. We continued to climb; at each step, all I saw in my path was the wise Greek's face.

Without my noticing it at first, the trails began to widen. I realized we were marching through valleys now, not peaks. We were heading down. At the feel of level ground, our pace quickened, and the ranks swelled with anticipation of what lay ahead.

'I've heard from the Spaniard there are Christians chained to the city's walls,' Robert said as we marched. 'The sooner we get there, the sooner we can set our brothers free.'

'Your friend's an eager one, Hugh,' Mouse called from behind. 'You'd better tell him that just because you're first at the party doesn't mean you get to sleep with the mistress of the house.'

'He wants a fight,' I defended Robert, 'and who can blame him? We've marched a long way.'

From behind came the clatter of a warhorse galloping upon us. 'Make way!'

We scattered off the trail and turned to see Guillaume,

the same arrogant bastard who'd mocked Nico after his death, in full armour astride his large charger. He nearly knocked men down as he indifferently charged through our ranks.

'That's who we fight for, eh?' I bowed sarcastically, with an exaggerated flourish.

We soon came to a wide clearing between mountains. A good-sized river lay in the column's path.

Up ahead, I heard nobles disagreeing on the proper spot to ford. Raymond, our commander, insisted that the scouts and maps suggested a point two leagues to the south. Others, eager to show our face to the Turks, the stubborn Bohemond among their ranks, argued against losing a day.

Finally, I saw Guillaume shoot from the crowd. 'I will make you a map,' he shouted to Raymond. He jerked his charger down the steep bank to the shore and led the mount in.

Guillaume's horse waded in, bearing the knight in full chain mail. Men lined the shore, either cheering, or laughing at his attempt to show off in front of nobility.

Halfway across, the water was still no higher than the horse's ankles. Guillaume turned round and waved, a vain smile visible through his moustache. 'Even my mother's mother could cross here,' he called. 'Are the mapmakers taking notes?'

'I never knew that a peacock would so take to water,' I smirked to Robert.

Suddenly, in the middle of the river, Guillaume's mount seemed to stumble. The knight did his best, but in his full armour and with unsteady footing he couldn't hold the horse. He fell facefirst into the river.

The troops along the shore burst into laughter, jeers, catcalls and mock waving.'Oh, *mapmakers*,' I laughed above the din, 'are you taking notes?'

The raucous laughter continued for a time, as we waited for the knight to re-emerge. But he did not.

'He stays under out of shame,' someone sniggered. But soon we understood it was not embarrassment, but the weight of Guillaume's armour that prevented him from pulling himself up.

As this became clear, the hooting on shore ceased. Another knight galloped into the water and waded out to the spot. A full minute passed before the new rider was able to reach the area. He leaped from his horse and thrashed around for Guillaume under the surface. Then, raising the knight's heavy torso, he shouted back, 'He is drowned, my lord.'

A gasp escaped from those on shore. His supporters bowed their heads and crossed themselves.

Just a few days before, the same Guillaume had stood behind me after Nicodemus had been swept off rocky cliffs to his death.

I looked at Robert, who shrugged with a thin smile. 'No great loss,' he said.

Chapter Thirteen

W e came to a high ridge overlooking a vast, bone-white plain and there it was: Antioch!

A massive, walled fortress, seemingly built into a solid mound of rock, larger and more formidable than any castle I had ever seen back home. The sight sent a chill shooting through my bones.

The fortress was built on a sharp rise. Hundreds of fortified towers guarded each length of an outer wall that appeared ten feet thick! We had no machines to breach such walls, no ladders that could even scale their height. It seemed impregnable.

Knights took off their helmets and surveyed the city in awe. A few crossed themselves. I know the same sobering thought pounded through each of our minds: *we had to take this place!*

'I don't see any Christians chained to the walls.' Robert squinted into the sun, sounding almost disappointed.

'If it's martyrs you're looking for,' I promised grimly, 'don't worry, you'll have your pick.'

One by one, we continued along the ridge and down the narrow trail. There was a feeling that the worst was over, that whatever God had in store for us, surely the coming battles could test us no more than what we had already faced. The talk was again of treasure and glory.

Stumbling on a ledge, my eye was caught by a faint glimmer from under a rock. I bent down to pick up the shining thing and could not believe it.

It was a scabbard, from some kind of dagger. Very old, I was sure. It had a carved, rusted hilt like bronze, with some engraved writing that I could not understand.

'What is it?' Robert asked.

'I don't know.' I wished Nico were there. I knew he would be able to interpret the writing. 'Maybe the language of the Jews . . . God, it looks old.'

'Hugh's rich,' Robert shouted. 'My friend is rich! Rich, I say!'

'Quiet,' a soldier hushed him. 'If one of our illustrious leaders hears you, you won't have your treasure for long.'

I placed the scabbard in my pouch, which was starting to fill up. I felt like a man who had just claimed the richest dowry. I couldn't wait to show it to Sophie! Back home, a prize like this could buy us food for a winter. I couldn't believe my good luck.

'Up here, the relics fall out of trees,' Mouse grumbled from behind, 'if there *were* any fucking trees.'

For the first time the thought of Nico had drifted from my mind. The trail we walked was flat and manageable. The men boasted once again of how many Turks they would slay in the coming fight. After my discovery, thoughts of treasure and spoils seemed alive and real. Maybe I *would* be rich.

Suddenly the column came to a halt. Then – eerie silence.

As far as the eye could see, the trail ahead was lined with

large, white rocks, spaced at intervals equal to a man's height. Each rock was painted with a bright, red cross.

'The bastards are welcoming us,' someone said. *Mocking* us was more like it. The rows of red crosses sent a shiver right through me.

Robert ran ahead to hurl one of the rocks towards the walls, but as he got close, the boy stopped in his tracks. Other knights who had reached the rocks kneeled and crossed themselves.

They were not rocks at all – but skulls.

Thousands of them!

Chapter Fourteen

There were fools among us who believed that Antioch would fall in a day. On that first morning, we lined up, many thousands strong, a sea of white tunics and red crosses massing against the eastern wall.

Heaven's army, if I truly believed.

We focused on the eastern gate, a buttress of grey rock spilling over with defenders in white robes and bright blue turbans at every post. And higher up, the towers, hundreds of them, each manned with archers, their long, curved bows glinting in the morning sun.

My heart pounded under my leather tunic. At any moment, I knew I would have to charge, but my legs seemed rooted to the ground, set in stone. I muttered Sophie's name, as if in a prayer.

Next to me in line, young Robert looked fit and ready, his smooth, innocent face hidden under the flat rim of his helmet. 'Are you ready, Hugh?' he asked with an eager smile.

'When we charge, stay by me,' I instructed him. I was twice the boy's size. For whatever reason, I had sworn in my heart to protect him.

'Don't worry, God will watch over me.' Robert seemed assured. 'And you too, Hugh, even if you try to deny it.'

A trumpet sounded the call to arms. Raymond and Bohemond, in full armour and mail, galloped down the line on their crested mounts. 'Be brave, soldiers. Do your duty.' They urged. 'Fight with honour. God will be at your side.'

Then all at once a chilling roar rose up from behind the city walls – the Turks, taunting and mocking us. I fixed on a face above the main gate. Then the trumpet sounded again. We were at a run.

I know not what went through my mind as, in formation, we advanced towards the massive walls. I do know I made one last prayer to Sophie. And to God, for Robert's sake, to watch over us.

But I know I ran, swept up in the tide of the charge. From behind, I heard the *whoosh* from a wave of arrows shoot across the sky, but they fell against the massive walls like harmless sticks, clattering to the ground.

As we came into range a volley of arrows shot back from the towers in return. I held my shield aloft as they ripped into us, thudding and clanging into shields and armour all around. Men fell, clutching at their heads and throats. Blood spurted from their faces and gruesome gasps escaped from their wretched mouths. The rest of us surged ahead, Robert still at my side. In front of us, I saw the first battering ram approach the main gate. Our division captain ordered us to follow. From above, heavy rocks and fiery arrows rained down on us. Men screamed and toppled over, either pierced or trying to beat out flames from their bodies.

The ram pounded into the heavy gate, a solid bronze barrier the height of three full men. It bounced off with the effect of a pebble tossed against a wall. The team reversed and rammed again. Foot soldiers were hurling their lances up at the defenders, but they fell halfway up the walls and, in return, brought down volleys of spears and Greek fire, molten pitch. Men writhed on the ground, kicking and screaming, their white tunics ablaze with tar. Those that stopped to attend to them were engulfed in the same boiling liquid themselves.

It was a slaughter: men who had travelled so far, endured so much – God's call beating in their hearts – cut down like limbs of trees. I saw poor Mouse, an arrow piercing his throat so completely that his hands gripped it on both sides, fall to his knees. Others toppled over him. I felt sure I would soon die too. One of the ram carriers fell over. Robert picked up his place. Soon they were battering again at the wooden gates, but without result.

A wave of arrows and stones and burning pitch rained down on us from all directions. It was only luck to avoid death at any point. I searched the walls for archers or pitch, and to my horror, spotted two large Turks preparing to tip a vat of bubbling tar upon those manning the ram. As they readied, I bolted into Robert, knocking him off his post and flush against the wall, just as a sulphurous black wave engulfed his ram-mates. They all shrieked, buckling to their knees, tearing at their sizzling faces and eyes, an odious smell exuding from their flesh.

I pressed Robert up against the wall, for a moment out of harm's way. All around us, our ranks were being shredded. Soldiers fell to their knees and moaned. Battering rams were tossed and abandoned. I could not tell whose tunic bore its crimson cross or whose was red with blood.

Suddenly, the assault turned into a rout. Crusaders, hearing the alarm, turned and fled from the walls. Arrows and spears followed them, dropping them as they fled.

'We've got to get out of here.'

I gripped Robert, dragged him from the wall and we ran with all our might, I praying as I did that my back would not be ripped apart by a Saracen arrow.

As we fled, the mighty fortress gate opened and, from within, horsemen appeared, dozens of turbaned riders flashing long curved swords. They swept towards us like hunters chasing hares, yelping mad cries that I recognized as 'Allah akbar' – God is great.

In spite of being outnumbered, there was no option for us but to stand and fight. I drew my sword, resolved that any breath might be my last, and hacked away at the first wave of horsemen.

A dark-skinned Saracen whirred by and the head of a man next to me shot off like a kicked ball. Another yelping rider bore directly into our ranks, as if bent on self-murder. We pounced on him and hacked him bloody. One by one, the small group of men we had attached ourselves to began to thin. Others, beseeching God, were split open by the Turks as they swooped by.

I grabbed Robert again by the tunic and dragged him further away. In the open, I saw a horseman hurtling directly towards us at full speed. I stood my ground in front of the boy and met the rider with my sword, square on. If this was it, then so be it. Our weapons came together in a mighty clang, the impact shaking my entire body. I looked down, expecting to see my legs split from my torso, but, thank God, I was whole. Behind me, the Saracen warrior had fallen off, horse and rider surrounded by a cloud of dust. I leaped on him before he had a chance to recover, plunging my sword into his neck and watching a flow of blood rush out of his mouth.

Before this day I had never taken a life, but now I hacked and slashed at anything that moved as if I had been bred for it.

Every second, more horsemen stormed out of the gates. They swept up on fleeing troops and cut them down where they stood. Blood and gore soaked the ground everywhere. A wave of our own cavalry went out to meet them, only to be overcome by the sheer numbers they faced. It seemed as if our whole army was being decimated.

I pushed Robert through the smoke and dust in the direction of our own ranks. We were now out of arrow range. Men were still moaning and dying on the field, Turks hacking at them.

For the first time, I noticed that my own tunic and arms were smeared with blood, whose I did not know. And my legs stung from the spray of molten pitch. Though I had seen many men fall, in a way I was proud. I had fought bravely. And Robert, too. And I had saved him, as I had vowed. Though I wanted to weep for my fallen friends, Mouse among them, I fell to the ground, happy just to be alive.

'I was right, Hugh.' Robert turned to me, grinning. 'God did protect us after all.'

Then he lowered his head and puked his guts on the field.

Chapter Fifteen

I t happened just that way nearly every day.

Assault upon assault.

Death after meaningless death.

The siege took months. For a while, it seemed as if our glorious Crusade would end in Antioch, not Jerusalem.

Our catapults flung giant missiles of fiery rock, yet they barely dented the massive walls. Wave after wave of frontal attacks only mounted the dead.

Finally, we constructed enormous siege engines, as tall as the highest towers. But the forays were met with such fierce resistance from the walls that they became fiery graveyards for our bravest men.

The longer Antioch survived, the lower our spirits fell. Food was down to nothing. All the cattle and oxen had been butchered; even the dogs had been slain. Water was as scarce as wine.

All the time, rumours reached us of Christians inside the city being tortured and raped, and holy relics desecrated.

Every couple of days, a Muslim warrior would hurl some urn down from the towers and it would shatter on the ground, spilling blood. 'That is the blood of your useless

Saviour,' he would laugh. 'See how it saves you now.' Or, lighting a cloth afire and tossing it to the earth: 'This is the shroud of the whore who gave him life.'

At intervals, Turk warriors made forays outside the city walls. They charged our ranks as if on a holy mission, yelping and hacking at those who met them, only to be surrounded and chopped to bits. They were unafraid, even heroic. It made us realize even more how they would not easily give in.

Those captured were sometimes handed over to a fearsome group of Frank warriors called Tafurs. Barefoot, covered in filth and sores, the Tafurs were distinguished by the ragged sackcloth they wore as uniforms and by the ferocious savagery with which they fought. Everyone was afraid of them. Even us.

In battle, these Tafurs fought like possessed devils, wielding leaded clubs and axes, gnashing their teeth as if to devour the enemy alive. It was said they were disgraced knights who followed a secret lord, and had taken vows of poverty until they could buy back their favour in God's eyes.

Infidels unlucky enough not to be killed on the field of battle were handed to them like scraps to dogs. I watched with disgust as these swine would disembowel a Saracen warrior in front of his own eyes, stuffing his entrails into his mouth as he died. Or rub fat over the bodies of those captured, cloak them in the skins of animals and throw them to dogs to be torn limb from limb. This happened, and much worse, so help me.

These Tafurs had allegiance to no lord we knew of and, to most of us it seemed, no God either. They were marked by a cross burned into their necks, which spoke not so much of their religious fervour as of their urge to inflict pain.

The longer the dreadful siege went on, the further away I felt from anything I knew. It was now a year and a half since I'd been gone from home. I dreamed about Sophie every night, and often during the day: that last image of her, watching me leave, her brave smile as I hopped down the road.

Would she even know me now, bearded, thin as a pole and blackened with grime and enemy blood? Would she still laugh at my jokes, and tease me for my innocence after what I had seen and knew? If I brought her a sunflower, would she kiss my bright red hair, now that it was filled with gore and lice?

My queen . . . how far away she seemed right now . . .

' "A maiden met a wandering man",' I sang our song in the quietest voice before I slept each night,' "In the light of the moon's pure cheer".'

Chapter Sixteen

The word spread like fire from battalion to battalion. 'Get ready . . . Full battle gear. We're going in, *tonight!*'

'Tonight, another charge?' Weary and frightened soldiers around me moaned in disbelief. 'Do they think we can see at night what we cannot even shoot during the day?'

'No, this time it's different,' our captain promised. 'Tonight you'll go to sleep fucking the Emir's wife!'

The camp sprang alive. There was a traitor inside Antioch. He would give up the city. Antioch would finally fall. Not from its walls crumbling, but from treachery and greed.

'Is it true?' Robert asked, hastily fitting on his armour and boots. 'Do we finally get to pay them back?'

'Sharpen that knife,' I told the eager lad.

Raymond ordered the army to break camp, giving the appearance we were heading for a raid elsewhere. We pulled right back as far as the river Orontes. Then, under the cover of night, we held, until close to dawn. The signal was spread. *Everyone be ready . . .*

Under the shield of darkness, we quietly crept back within sight of the city walls. A sliver of orange light was just breaking over the hills to the east. My blood was surging. Today, Antioch would fall. Then it was on to Jerusalem. *Freedom.*

As we waited for the word I put my hand on Robert's trembling shoulder. 'Nerves?'

The boy shook his head. 'I fear not.'

'You may have started the day still a boy, but by its end, you'll be a man,' I told him.

He grinned back sheepishly.

'I guess we'll both be men,' I winked.

Then a torch waved over the north tower. That was it! Our men were inside. 'Let's go!' the nobles shouted. 'Attack!'

Our army charged – Frank, Norman, German, Tafur side by side, with one purpose, one mind. 'Show them whose God is One,' the leaders cried.

Our battalions headed towards the tower, where ladders were hoisted against the walls and wave after wave of men climbed over. The sound of shouts and vicious fighting erupted from inside. Then all at once, the big bronze gates opened right in front of our eyes. But instead of attacking Muslim horsemen streaking out, our own conquering army spilled in.

We made our way helter-skelter through the streets. Buildings were torched. Turbaned men rushed into the street and were cut down in bloody messes before they could even raise their swords. Cries of 'Death to the pagans!' and *'Deus vult!'* – God wills it – echoed everywhere.

I ran in the pack, with no great malice towards the enemy, but ready to fight whomsoever confronted me. I saw one defender cut in half by a mighty axe blow. Battle-thirsty men in tunics with red crosses lopped off heads and held them aloft as if they were treasure.

In front of us a young woman ran out of a burning house, screaming. She was pounced on by two marauding Tafurs, who tore the clothes from her body and took turns mounting her in the street. When they were done, they ripped a bronzed bracelet from her wrist and bludgeoned her lifeless.

I stared in horror at her bloody shape. I kneeled, and from her clutched fist I took a cross. *Good Lord, she was Christian.*

A moment later from the same building, a fiery-eyed Turk, maybe her husband, charged at me with a scream. I stood paralysed, my sword trapped at the side. An image of my own death rose in my mind. All I could think to utter was, 'It was not me . . .'

But just as the man's spear was inches from my throat, his rush was intercepted by Robert, thrusting his sword through the Turk's chest. The man staggered, his eyes horrifically wide. Then he toppled on to his wife, dead.

I blinked back an amazed stare. I turned to Robert with a sigh of relief.

'See, it's not just God who watches over you,' he winked, 'it's me.'

He had just uttered these words when another turbaned warrior charged towards him, brandishing a long blade. The boy's back was turned and I saw I could not get there in time. He was tugging on his sword, but it remained stuck in the dead Turk's chest. His face was still lit in that innocent grin.

'Robert!' I screamed. '*Robert!*'

Chapter Seventeen

The attacker hurtled into him and swung his sword with both hands. I had only an instant to intercede. I tried to pivot round Robert, but I was blocked. All I could do was scream, 'No!'

The blade caught Robert just below the throat. I heard the sound of bones cracking and his shoulder fell away from his body as the massive blade lodged deep in his chest, seeming to split him in two.

At first I stared in horror. It was as if the boy saw that he was powerless to stop his own death, and instead of turning to face his attacker, turned towards me. I will carry that expression with me for the rest of my life.

Then, gaining hold, I lunged, piercing the Turk with my sword. I ran him through again as he fell. On the ground, I hacked at him, as if my ardour could bring back my friend.

Then I kneeled beside Robert. His body was asunder, but his face was still as boyish and smooth as when he had first joined our ranks, his goose comically trailing behind. My eyes fought back tears. *He was just a boy* . . . All around me, madness and lunacy boiled out of control. Red-crossed soldiers stormed through the streets, running from house to house, looting, burning. Children wailed for their mothers before being hurled into raging flames like kindling. Tafurs, mad with greed, slaughtered Christian and infidel alike, stuffing anything of value into their filthy robes.

What kind of God inspired such horror? Was this God's fault? Or man's?

Something snapped in me. Whatever I thought I was fighting for, whatever dream of freedom or wealth had brought me here, burst. And there was nothing in its place. I did not care about Antioch. Or freeing Jerusalem. Or freeing myself. I only wanted to go home. To see Sophie once more. To tell her I loved her. I could deal with the harshness of laws and taxes and the wrath of our lord, if only I could hold her one more time. Nicodemus had been right. I had come here to set myself free. *Now I was free.* Free of my illusion.

My comrades went on, but I remained, consumed with grief and rage. I did not know where I was going, just that I could no longer fight in their ranks. I staggered around, wandering the burning city, passing from horror to horror. Carnage and screams were everywhere. The streets ran ankle-deep with blood.

I came upon a Christian church – *Sanctum Christi . . .* St Paul's. It almost seemed funny to me, *this . . .* this old tomb was what we were fighting for. This empty block of stone was what we came to set free.

I wanted to lash at the church with my sword. It was a host of lies. I finally staggered up the steep stone steps in a fit of rage.

'God wills *this*?' I screamed. 'God wills this *murder*?'

Chapter Eighteen

I had no sooner stepped inside the dark, cool nave of the church when I heard a cry of anguish coming from the front. This madness just wouldn't stop!

On the steps of the altar, two black-robed Turks hovered over a priest, pummelling him with kicks, cursing him in their tongue, while the fearful prelate did his best to defend himself with a rough, wooden staff.

A moment before, I had hesitated. A friend had died. I had no fealty to this priest, but this time, I charged full force towards the assault.

I ran with my sword drawn and a loud cry, just as one of the attackers thrust a dagger into the belly of the priest. The other infidel turned, and I leaped upon him. The blade of my sword penetrated his side. The Turk let out a chilling howl.

The other assailant rose and faced me, thrusting the dagger that was still fresh with the priest's blood. He lunged, spitting words I recognized. *'Ibn Kan . . .'* – Son of Cain.

I pivoted aside, and brought my sword over the back of his neck. It sheared through him as if severing a weak limb from a tree. The Turk fell to his knees, his head rolling away from him. Then he toppled forward, landing on what would have been his face.

I stood, transfixed by the awful corpses of the Saracens. I no longer knew what was inside of me. *What was I doing here? What had I become?*

I went to the fallen priest, to help if I could. As I kneeled beside him his eyes grew cloudy. He exhaled a final breath. The useless wooden staff fell from his hand.

Too late . . . I was no hero, only a fool.

Just then, I heard a rustling behind me. I spun to see a third attacker, this one bare-chested and monstrous, the size of two men. Seeing his comrades slain, he rushed towards me, his sword poised for attack.

In that instant I saw my futility. This assailant was a bear of a man with massive arms nearly twice the thickness of mine. I could no more hold him off than I could a hurricane. As he charged I raised my sword, but the Turk's stroke was so strong it knocked me backwards over the dead priest. He charged at me once more, his eyes focused and fierce. This time, my sword flew out of my hands, clattering across the church floor. I lunged after it, but the Turk intercepted me with a vicious kick that sucked the air out of my belly.

I was going to die . . . I knew it. There was no way to defeat this horrible monster. In a last effort, I reached for the priest's wooden staff. The smallest hope flashed through my mind: maybe I could whack it across his ankles.

But my attacker merely took a giant step, pinning the staff uselessly under his sandals. I peered into the bastard's black eyes. I was helpless. Above me, his blade caught the glint of a torch.

What profound images filled my mind as I tensed waiting for the blade to fall? It did not occur to me to pray, to ask God for the remission of all my sins. No, God had taken me where I belonged. I bid farewell to my sweet Sophie. I felt I had shamed myself, to leave her this way. She would never know how I died, why, or where, or that I was thinking of her at the end.

But what did flash through my brain was the incredible irony of it all. Here I was, dying in front of an altar of Christ, on a holy crusade that I never really believed in.

I didn't believe . . . Yet I was dying for this cause anyway.

As I looked at my murderer, my fear left me. So did my urge to resist. I peered into the Turk's vengeful eyes. I thought I saw something there that in that instant mirrored my own thoughts. The strangest urge took hold of me. I could not hold it back.

I didn't pray, or close my eyes, or even beg for my life.

Instead, I began to laugh.

Chapter Nineteen

The Turk's sword hovered over me. At any second he would strike the final blow. Yet all I could do was laugh.

At what I was dying for. At the total ridiculousness of it all. At the precious *freedom* I was about to be granted at last.

I looked in his hooded eyes, and though I knew it was probably my last breath, I simply could not hold back. *I just laughed . . .*

My attacker hesitated, his sword poised above my head. He must have thought he was about to dispatch a complete idiot to the Almighty. He blinked back at me, his brows arched, confused.

In his own tongue, which Nicodemus had taught me, I searched my mind for something to say. *Anything* at all.

'This is your last warning,' I said to him. 'Are you ready to give up?' Then I burst out laughing once again.

The massive Turk, his fiery eyes like coals, leered over me. I waited for the deathblow. Then I saw his glare relax into the slightest inkling of a smile.

Choking back the laughter, I stammered, 'The thing is . . . I'm not even a believer.'

The giant man hesitated. I didn't know if he would speak

or strike. His mouth curved into a sheepish grin. 'Nor am I.'

His sword still quivered menacingly over my head. I knew any moment could be my last. I raised myself to my elbows, looked him in the eye and said, 'Then, one non-believer to another, you must kill me,' I said, 'in the name of what we do *not* embrace.'

Slowly, almost inexplicably, I saw the hostility on his face begin to fade. To my utter amazement, the Turk lowered his sword. 'We're too few as it is,' he nodded. 'No reason to make one less.'

Was this possible? Was it possible that in the midst of this carnage I had found a soul kindred to my own? I looked in his eyes. This beast that only a moment before was set to chop me in two. I gazed deeply in his eyes. I saw something that in this whole bloody night I had not seen before: virtue, humour, a human soul . . . I couldn't believe it. *Please God*, I finally prayed, don't let this be some kind of cruel trick.

'Is this true? You're going to let me go?' My fingers slowly relaxed from the priest's staff.

The Turk took a measuring look in my eyes, then he nodded.

'You probably thought you were ridding the world of a complete madman,' I said.

'The thought occurred,' he grinned.

Then my mind fixed on the danger of the moment. 'You had better go. Our forces are all around. You are at risk.'

'Go?' The Turk seemed to sigh. 'Go where?' There was something in his face – no longer hatred or the urge to kill. It was more like resignation.

At that moment, loud footsteps burst through the outer

door. I heard voices. Soldiers stormed into the church. They were not wearing crosses, but filthy robes. Tafurs.

'Get out of here,' I urged him. 'These men will show you no mercy.'

He took a look at his assailants. Then he merely winked at me. He started to laugh himself, then turned to face their charge.

The Tafurs came upon him with their knives and awful clubs.

'*No!*' I screamed. 'Spare this man. Spare him!'

He managed to kill the first one with a mighty sweep of his sword, but then was overwhelmed, consumed in heavy blows and disembowelling slashes, never once crying out, until his powerful body resembled some hideous slab of meat and not the noble soul he was.

The leading Tafur delivered one more blow to the bloody mound, then he delved through the Turk's robes, looking for something of value. Finding nothing, he shrugged to his comrades. 'Let's search the fucking crypt.'

It took everything I had not to leap on the Tafurs myself, but these savages would surely kill me.

They passed by on their way to loot the church. I was trembling with horror.

The lead vermin ran the blade of his sword across my chest, as if he was evaluating whether to leave me in the same condition as the Turk. Then he sneered, amused. 'Don't look so sad, redhead. You are free!'

Chapter Twenty

I was *free*, the Tafur said. *Free!*

I started to laugh once more. The irony was bursting through my sides. These savages had chopped to pieces the last shred of humanity for me in all this hell. Now . . . they were setting me free!

If the Turk had not hesitated just a moment ago, I'd be dead myself. It would be *me* in that pool of blood that was leaking across the stones. Yet he'd spared me. In all this madness I had found a moment of clarity and truth. This Turk, whose name I did not even know. We'd touched souls. And this vermin had laughed that I was free.

I struggled to my feet. I stepped over the body of the man who had spared me and looked, horrified, at his bloody robes. I kneeled down and touched his hand. *Why . . .?* I could walk out of this church. I could be cut down as soon as I stepped out on the street, or I could live for years, a full life. To what end?

Why did you spare me? I looked into his dull, still eyes. *What did you see?*

It was laughter that had saved me. Laughter that had somehow touched the Turk. I had been only a breath away from death and yet instead of panic and fear, laughter had entered my soul. It had saved my life. Amid all this fighting, I had simply made him smile. Now he was gone and I was here. A calm came over me. You are right, Tafur . . . I am finally free.

I had to get out of there. I knew I could no longer fight. I was a different man from a moment ago. This cross on my tunic meant nothing to me. In a fit of anger, I stripped it from my chest. I had to go back. I had to see Sophie again. What else could matter? Nico had told me as much. I was a fool to have left her. *For freedom . . .?* Suddenly the truth seemed so clear. A child could have seen it.

It was only *with* Sophie that I felt truly free!

I wanted to take something from the church with me, something from this moment that I would affix to the rest of my life. I leaned over the dead Turk. The poor warrior was empty of anything – a ring, a memento.

I heard voices outside. It could be anybody – infidels, raiders, Tafurs hunting for spoils. I looked around. *Please, something.*

I went back to the priest. I lifted the staff that had been in my hands when the Turk spared my life. It was a rough, gnarly stick of wood, maybe four feet long, and thin. But I held it and it seemed strong. It would be my friend when I crossed the mountains again. It was my companion. I vowed to carry it with me wherever I went for the rest of my life.

I looked at the fallen Turk and whispered a last goodbye. 'You're right, my friend, we are too few as it is.'

I gave him a last wink and went to the church door.

On my way I noticed a crucifix on the church altarium. It

appeared to be gilded, and decorated with what looked like rubies. I pulled it off the bars and stuffed it into my pouch. I had earned this much. A golden cross.

The cries of more men dying hit me as I stepped outside. Mayhem was still rampant in the streets. The conquering throng had gone deeper into Antioch, cleansing the city of anything infidel. Bloody corpses were scattered everywhere. A few latecomers in clean armour rushed by me, eager to share the spoils.

I heard the awful cries of death further up the hill, but I wasn't going there. I put the priest's staff to the ground and took a step – the other way.

Away from the senseless killing and my comrades in arms. Back towards the city gates.

I would never see Jerusalem in this lifetime.

I was heading home to Sophie.

PART TWO

BLACK CROSS

Chapter Twenty-One

I t took six months for me to find my way home.

After Antioch, I headed east, towards the coast. I wanted to get as far away from my murderous army as I could. I stripped out of my bloody armour and donned the robes of a pilgrim whose corpse I had stumbled upon. I was a deserter. All promises of protection made by the Church were now revoked.

I travelled by night, crossing the barren mountains to St Simeon, a port held in Christian hands. There, I slept on the docks like a beggar, until I finally managed to convince a Greek captain to let me board his ship to Malta. From there, I traded my way on to a Venetian cargo ship, carrying sugar and spun cloth back to the republic. *Venice* . . . it was still many months' trek from my little village.

I earned my passage recalling my old days as a jongleur, reciting tales of the legendary Roland and entertaining the crew at their meals with raucous jokes. No doubt, the crew had their suspicions of me. Deserters were everywhere, and why else would an able, penniless man be running from the Holy Land?

Every night I had dreams of Sophie, of bringing something precious back to her. Of her golden braids, her delicate laugh. I kept my eyes fixed on the western horizon, her image like a soft trade wind drawing me home.

When we reached Venice, my heart leaped to place my foot on the earth that would eventually lead to Veille du Père.

But I was thrown in gaol, turned in by the suspicious captain for a fee. I barely had the time to hide my pouch of valuables on the quay before I was tossed into a narrow, stinking hole filled with thieves and smugglers of all nationalities.

The guards all called me Jeremiah – a crazed-looking man in a tattered robe, who clung to his staff. I did my best to keep my good humour and pleaded with my gaolers that I was only trying to get home to my wife. 'A lice-filled beast like you has a wife?' they laughed.

But luck had not run out for me yet. On All Saints' Day, a local lord paid for the release of ten prisoners as forgiveness for an offence. One died during the night, so they chose the affable, crazy Jeremiah to round up the number. 'Go back to your wife, Frenchie,' the gaoler laughed as they handed me my staff. 'But first, I advise you to have a bath.'

That very night I found the pouch with my valuables where I had hidden it, and began to walk west, across the marshy road to the mainland. *Towards home.*

I headed across Italy. Every town I came to, I told tales at the local inn for a meal of bread and ale. Local farmers and drunks listened spellbound to my account of the siege of Antioch, the ferocity of the Turks, and my friend Nicodemus's untimely end.

I climbed through the smaller hills and then the Dolomites. Winter set in. The winds blew cold and strong. It took a full month to cross the mountains. But finally, as I descended from the peaks, the language that greeted me in the snow-filled towns was French. *French!* My heart leaped, knowing I was near my home.

The towns became familiar: Nîmes, Montpellier, Tours . . . Veille du Père was only days away. *And Sophie.*

I started to worry about how it would be. Would she even recognize me from the haggard mess I had turned into? So many times, I would picture her face as I stood in front of her for that first time. She would be at the urn, heating soup or making butter, wearing her pretty, patterned smock, her golden braids peeking through her white cap. 'Hugh,' she would gasp, too stunned to move. Just *Hugh*, not another word. Then she would leap into my arms and I would squeeze her tight. She would touch my face and hands to make sure I was no apparition, then smother me in kisses. One look at my face, my rags and sore, bare feet and Sophie would know immediately what I had been through. 'So . . .' she would do her best to smile, 'you have not quite returned a knight after all?'

It was in a damp rain that I finally reached the outskirts of Veille du Père. I went down on my knees.

Chapter Twenty-Two

Those last miles, I almost ran the entire distance. I began to recognize roads I had travelled, sights I was familiar and comfortable with. I tried to put aside everything bad that had happened to me: the deaths of Nico and Robert, and Antioch. All of the misery seemed so distant now. I was home.

My plight was over. I had arrived, no knight or squire, not even a free man. Yet I felt like the wealthiest noble in all the world.

I spotted the familiar, bubbling stream and stone wall that bordered it that led to town. Arnaud's barley field came into view. Then a bend I knew so well, and our wooden bridge up ahead.

Veille du Père . . .

I stood there, like a beggar at a feast, for just a few moments to take it in. My mind was filled with everything that had taken place: the horrors I had put behind me, the many miles and months I had travelled, dreaming only of Sophie's face, her touch, her smile.

How I wished it was July and I could walk in bearing a sunflower. I searched out the square. Familiar faces, doing their work. It all seemed just as I remembered. Odo, the smith who worked with Jules, Georges . . . Father Leo's church.

Our inn . . .

Our inn! I fixed on it in horror. No, it could not be . . .

In the blink of an eye, I knew that everything had changed.

Chapter Twenty-Three

My legs bolted towards the village square – the pallor of a ghost stamped upon my face.

Children stared at me, then ran towards their houses. 'It is Hugh. Hugh DeLuc. He's back from the war,' they shouted.

All that could have seemed familiar about me was my mane of red hair. People rushed up to me. Neighbours whom I had not set eyes upon in two years, their faces caught between shock and joy. 'Hugh, praise God, it is you.'

But I pushed past them, barely acknowledging them. I was drawn on a direct path towards our inn. Our home . . . My heart sank as I came to the spot and fixed on it. The blood had drained from my face.

A burned-out hole was left where our inn had once been.

A single, charred support post stood among the cinders, which had held up a two-storey house, built by the hands of my wife's father.

Our inn had been burned to the ground.

'Where is Sophie?' I muttered, first to the charred ruins of our house, then to faces in the gathered crowd.

I went from person to person, sure that at any moment I

would spot her coming back from the well. But everyone stood silently.

My heart began to beat insanely. *'Where is Sophie?'* I shouted. 'Where is my wife?'

Sophie's older brother, Mathieu, finally pushed out of the crowd. Fixing on me, his expression shifted – from surprise to a look of deep concern. He stepped forward, hurling his arms around me. 'Hugh, I can't believe it. Thank God, you've come back.'

I knew the worst had happened. I searched his eyes. 'What's happened, Mathieu? Tell me, where is my wife?'

A look of deep sorrow came on to his face. Oh God . . . I almost did not want him to tell me the rest. He led me by the arm to the remains of our home. 'There were riders, Hugh. Ten, twelve . . . They swept in, in the dead of night, like devils, burning everything they could. Black crosses on their chests. They wore no colours. We had no hint of who they were. Just the crosses.'

'Riders?' My blood was frozen with dread. 'What riders, Mathieu? What did they do to Sophie?'

He placed a hand gently upon my shoulder. 'They burned three dwellings in their path. Simon the carter, Sam, old Arnaud, their wives and children were killed as they fled. Then they came to the inn. I tried to stop them, Hugh, I did,' he cried.

I seized him by the shoulders. 'And Sophie?' I knew the worst had happened. *No, this could not be. Not now . . .*

'She's gone, Hugh.' Mathieu shook his head.

'Gone?'

'She tried to run, but the men took her inside. They beat her, Hugh . . .' He pursed his lips and bowed his head. 'They did worse. I heard her screams. They held me as they beat and raped her. Knights tore up the place, ripping it post by post. Then they dragged her out. She was barely alive. I was sure they would leave her to die, but the leader threw her over his horse while the others released their torches. It was then that . . .'

I could barely hear him. A distant voice was echoing, *No, this cannot be!* My eyes welled up with tears. 'It was then that *what*, Mathieu?'

He bowed his head. 'They dragged her away, Hugh. I know she is dead.'

All strength drained from my legs. I sank to my knees. Oh God, how could this have happened? How could I have left her to this fate? My Sophie gone . . . I gazed upon the charred ruins of my former life.

'Norcross did this, didn't he? Baldwin?'

'We do not know for certain.' Mathieu shook his head. 'If I did, I would go after them myself. They were beasts, but faceless ones. They wore no crests. Their visors were down. Everyone ran to the woods for cover. Yours was the only house . . . they entered. It was as if they came for you.'

For me . . . Those bastards . . . I had fought two years for Baldwin's own liege. I had marched across half the world and seen the worst things. And still, they took from me the one thing I loved.

I grabbed the dust from the fire and let it slip through my fists. 'My poor Sophie . . .'

Mathieu kneeled down beside me. 'Hugh, there's more.'

'*More?* What could be more?' I looked in his eyes.

He put a hand on my face. 'After you left, Sophie had a son.'

Chapter Twenty-Four

Mathieu's words hit me like a stone wall, collapsing over me. *A son . . .*

For three years Sophie and I had tried to conceive, with no result. We had wanted a child more than anything. We even spoke of it that last night we were together. I had left her, and never even knew I had a son . . .

I turned towards Mathieu with a flicker of hope.

'He is *dead*, Hugh. He was only six months old. The bastards killed him that same night. They tore him from Sophie's arms as she tried to flee.'

A wall of tears rushed at my eyes. A son . . . a son I would never know or hold. I had been through the fiercest battles, the worst of all horror. But nothing could prepare me for this.

'How?' I muttered. 'How did my son die?'

'I can't even say it.' Mathieu's face was ashen. 'Just believe me when I say that he is dead.'

I repeated my question, this time my eyes fixed upon his. '*How?*'

His voice was so quiet. 'As he drew Sophie's lifeless body over his mount, the leader smirked, "We have no room for such a toy. Toss him in the flames." '

I felt a pressure building up, an anger clawing at me as though my insides were ripping through my skin. God had smiled on us, after all this time. He had blessed us with a son. Now, He spat at me with the sharpest mockery.

How could I have left them? How could I still be alive if they were dead?

I looked at Mathieu and asked, 'What was his name?'

He swallowed. 'She named him Philippe.'

I felt a lump catch in my throat. Philippe was the name of the goliard monk who had raised me. It was her tribute to me. Sweet Sophie, you are gone. My son too . . . I felt the urge to die right here, amid the charred ash, the ruins of my old life.

'Hugh,' Mathieu lifted me up, 'you have to come.' He led me up the trail to a knoll above the town. A small slate stone marked my son's grave.

I sat down on the hard earth, under a shroud of tall poplars. 'Philippe DeLuc, son of Hugh and Sophie', was scratched into the stone. 'Year of our Lord, 1098'.

I lay my head on the cold, bare earth and wept. For my sweet Philippe, who I would never see, not even once in my life. For my wife, who was surely dead.

Was this why I was spared? Was this why the Turk had not swung his murderous sword? So I would live to see all that I loved lost? Was this why the laughter had saved me? So God could laugh at me now?

I took off my pouch that contained the things I had brought back for Sophie: a perfume box, ancient coins, the jewelled scabbard, the golden cross – and I dug a hole next to my baby's grave. I gently placed my 'treasures' in it. They were worthless to me now. 'They belong to you,' I whispered to Philippe. *My sweet baby*.

I smoothed out the earth and once more lay my head against the ground. I'm so sorry, Philippe and Sophie . . . Slowly, my grief began to harden into rage. I knew Baldwin had ordered this. And Norcross had carried it out. But why? Why?

I'm just an innkeeper, I thought. I am nothing. Just a serf. 'But a serf who will see you dead.'

Chapter Twenty-Five

A crowd gathered around as Mathieu and I came back into town. Father Leo, Odo, my friends – everyone wanted to comfort and bless me. And hear of my two years in the war.

But I pushed past them. I had to go to the inn, its ruins . . . Amid the rubble, I sifted through the charred wood and ash, searching for anything that breathed of her, my Sophie – a piece of cloth, a mirror, a last memento of what I had lost.

'She spoke of you all the time, Hugh,' Mathieu told me. 'She missed you terribly. We all thought you were lost in the war. But not Sophie.'

'You are certain, brother, that she is dead?'

'I am,' he replied. 'When they took her she was already more dead than alive.'

'But you did not actually see her die? You don't know for sure?'

'Not for sure. But I beg you, brother, not to cling to false hope. I'm her flesh and blood. And I damn well pray she *was* dead as they dragged her out of here.'

I met his eyes. 'So she may *not* be dead, Mathieu?'

He looked at me quizzically. 'You must accept it, Hugh. If she was not then, I'm certain she was within minutes. Her body could be strewn somewhere along the road.'

'So you searched the road? And did you find her? Has anyone travelling from the west in the past weeks come upon her remains?'

'No, no one.'

'Then there's a chance. You say she never doubted me, that she knew I would return. Well, I do the same for her.'

I found myself walking in the part of our home where the living space had been. Everything was cinder – our bed, a linen chest. On the floor, I noticed something reflecting light.

I dropped to my knees, swept away ash. My heart almost exploded with joy. Tears welled in my eyes.

It was Sophie's comb. Her half of the one she'd placed in my hand the day I left. It was charred, broken; it almost crumbled in my hand. But in my blood, I felt her!

I held it up, and from my pouch, hastily removed the other half. I fitted them together and they melded seamlessly. In that moment, Sophie came alive to me – her eyes, her laugh – as vibrantly as when I had last seen her.

'These knights, Mathieu, they didn't leave her to die in the same flames as my son. They took her for a reason.' I looked up at him, holding the comb aloft. 'Perhaps it is not such a false hope after all.'

Outside, my old friends Odo and Georges the miller were waiting.

'Give us the word, Hugh,' Georges said, 'and we will hunt the bastards with you. We've all suffered. We know who is responsible. They deserve to die.'

'I know.' I put my hand on the miller's shoulder. 'But first, I must find Sophie.'

'Your wife is dead,' Odo replied. 'We saw it, Hugh, though it seems more nightmare than real.'

'You saw her dead?' I waited for the smith to answer.

I looked at Georges. 'Or you?'

They both shrugged guiltily. They glanced towards Mathieu for support.

'Sophie lives as my own Alo lives,' the miller swallowed, 'in Heaven.'

'For you, Georges, but not for me. Sophie still lives on this earth. I know it. I can feel her.'

I picked up my staff and slung a skin of water round my neck. I headed towards the stone bridge.

'What are you going to do, Hugh, jab them with that stick?' Odo hurried by my side. 'You are just one man with no armour or sword.'

'I'm going to find her, Odo. I promise, I'll find Sophie.'

'Let me get you some food,' Odo pleaded. 'Or some ale. You still drink ale, don't you, Hugh? The army didn't cure you of that? Next I'll hear you've been going to church on Sundays.'

From his guarded look, it was clear he thought he would never see me again.

'I will bring her back, Odo. You'll see.'

I took my stick and headed into the woods, towards Tours.

Chapter Twenty-Six

I ran in a blind haze, in the direction from which I had come. Towards my liege's castle at Tours.

Grief tore at me like wild dogs. My son had died because of me. Because of my stupid folly. Because of my foolishness and pride.

As I ran, the swell of bitterness surged inside. The thought of that bastard Norcross, or any of his henchman, having my poor Sophie . . .

I had fought for these so-called nobles in the Holy Land, while they raped and slaughtered in the name of God. I had marched and killed and followed the Pope's call. And this was my wage. Not freedom. Not a changed life, but misery and scorn. I had been a fool to trust the rich.

I ran, on and on. Then, exhausted and blind with rage, I stumbled, my sores covered in dirt.

I had to find Sophie. *I know you are alive. I'll make you well. I know how you've suffered.*

At every turn, I prayed I would not stumble over her body. Each time I didn't gave me hope she was alive.

After a day of wandering, I looked around and realized I didn't know where I was. I had neither food nor water. All that pushed me on was rage. I checked the sun. Was I west or north? I had no idea.

But still I ran. My legs became like heavy irons. I was dizzy and my stomach ached for food. My eyes were glazed over with tears. Yet, I ran.

Passers-by on the road looked at me as if I were mad. A madman with his staff. 'Tours . . .?' I begged them.

They scurried to get out of the way. Pilgrims, merchants, even outlaws let me pass for the fury and madness in my eyes.

I knew not if one day or two had passed. I ran until my legs finally gave out. As I came to my senses, darkness clung to me all around. The night was terribly cold and I was shivering. Ominous sounds hooted from the brush.

From deep in the woods, I heard the rushing water of a stream. I clawed my way off the road and into the woods and followed the sound.

Suddenly, I stumbled. I grasped for a bush, but my hand slipped. I clawed for anything to hold, a vine, a branch. The ground disappeared under my feet. Jesus . . . I was falling.

Let it come. I deserve it. I will die out here in the night.

I called to Sophie as I hurtled out of control down a ravine.

My head smacked against something hard. I felt a warm and viscous fluid fill my mouth. 'I'm coming,' I said, one more time.

To Sophie.

To the howling darkness . . .

Then the world went black, and that was much better, thank you Lord.

Chapter Twenty-Seven

I came to – not to the rush of water, or anything heavenly, but to a low, dangerous rumbling sound.

I blinked open my eyes. It was still night. I had fallen into a deep ravine, far below the level of the road. My back was twisted against a tree and I could barely move. A wound ached horribly on the side of my head.

Again, I heard the deep rumbling from inside the woods. 'Who's there?' I called. 'Who is it?'

There was no reply. I focused on the spot in the darkness, trying to make out any shape. Who would be out here in the night? Not anyone I wanted to meet.

Then I focused on a set of eyes. Eyes not human at all – but large as prayer stones: yellow, narrow, fuming. My blood froze.

Then it moved! I heard the brush crush under its feet. The thing took a step out of the forest and came clear.

Dark, hairy . . .

Blessed Jesus Christ! It was a boar! Not twenty feet away!

Its yellow eyes were trained on me, inspecting me as if I were its next meal. I heard a snort. Then it was deathly still.

The thing was about to charge! I was certain of it.

I tried to clear my head. I could not possibly fight such a beast. And with what? Its breadth alone was twice mine. It could slash me to pieces with its sharp tusks.

My heart was pounding – the only sound I heard other than the beast's low growl. It took another step towards me. The boar's murderous eyes, deliberate and tracking, never left my own.

God help me, what could I do? I couldn't flee. It would run me down in my first steps. There was no one to shout to for help.

I searched for a strong tree to climb, but I didn't want to move, to set it off. The beast seemed to study me, bucking its head, snorting its deadly intent. I could smell its fierce, hot breath, the blood from past conflicts matted in its hair.

I grabbed the knife at my belt. I didn't know if it would snap against the beast's hard coat.

The boar snorted, twice, and flashed its teeth at me, its jowl red and dripping. I knew I did not want to die. Not like this . . . Please, God, I prayed, do not make me fight this thing.

I felt so incredibly alone.

Then with a last deep snort, the beast seemed to understand that – and it charged.

All I could do was leap behind a tree, barely escaping the first violent gnash of its fearsome teeth.

I stabbed wildly at it, tearing at its face and neck, anything I could do to repel its snarling jaws. The beast lunged viciously. It came again and again. I clawed with my knife, backing round the tree. The boar's jaw ripped into my thigh and I cried out. The air emptied from my lungs.

Good Lord, I was pierced!

I had no time to inspect my wound. The beast slammed into me again, this time goring my abdomen. I screamed in pain.

I kicked at it and slashed my blade. The creature backed and lunged. Its terrible teeth clamped on my thigh and it shook its head as if to tear my leg out of it socket.

I kicked myself away from the boar. I tried to run, but my legs had no strength. Blood was spattered everywhere.

Somehow I limped across the clearing, my strength nearly sapped. My abdomen felt as if it were on fire. I was done here. I fell to my side and backed myself against another tree, waiting for the end to come.

Beside the tree, I saw my staff. It must've toppled there in my fall. I reached for it, though it wasn't much of a weapon.

I stared at the angry, snorting boar. 'Come at me, offal. Come at me! Finish what you started.'

My mind flashed to the Turk who had spared me, a world away. This time no laughter would save the day. I held the staff like a spear. 'Come at me,' I spat at the boar again. 'Kill me. I am ready. Kill me.'

As if to oblige, the beast made another charge.

My breath was still. I offered no defence, except to raise the staff at the shape flying towards me. Harnessing my remaining strength, I thrust the staff with all my might into its eyes.

The beast let out a blood-chilling cry. I had actually hurt it. The staff stuck in one eye. The boar staggered and shook its head madly, trying to free itself.

I grabbed my knife and, with whatever strength I had, stabbed wildly at its throat and face, at anything I could strike.

Blood seeped out of its fur, each knife-thrust striking home. The creature's growls diminished. It stumbled on its hind legs, still swinging its head to free the rod, while I continued to slash, tearing at its coat.

The beast's blood mixed with my own. Finally, it fell on its hind legs. I took the staff and forced it deeper into the boar's skull. A dying snarl came out of its awful tooth-filled mouth.

With a crash, the monster fell on its side. I just kneeled there, depleted of strength. And amazed. I let out an exhausted shout.

I had won!

But I was badly wounded. Blood ran freely from my stomach and thigh and neck. I had to get out of the ravine, or I knew I would die there.

Sophie's face appeared in my mind. I know I smiled; I reached out to touch her. 'Here is the way,' she whispered. 'Come to me now.'

Chapter Twenty-Eight

At first it was quiet, like any sleeping town. The dark riders edged their panting mounts close to the edge. A few thatched cottages with post fences, animals sleeping in their sheds – that was all there was.

This would be easy, mere sport for such men. The leader sniffed, shutting his face plate, which bore the symbol of a black Byzantine cross. He had chosen only men who killed for pleasure, who hunted for spoils, like others hunted for meat. They wore the darkened armour of battle, no crests, visors down. No one knew who they were. They strapped on their weapons – war swords, axes and maces. They looked at him, eager, thirsty, ready.

'Have your fun,' Black Cross sniffed, a hint of laughter coming through his command. 'Just let us not forget why we are here. Whoever finds the relic will be a rich man. Now, ride!'

The night was split asunder by the explosion of charging hoofs.

The clang of a warning bell sounded. Too late! The first thatched dwellings went up in flames. The sleeping town came alive.

Women screamed and ran to protect their children. Aroused townspeople struggled out of their homes to save themselves, only to be struck down by lances, or trampled in the mêlée as the armed riders stormed by.

These pathetic peasants, Black Cross mused, they run and die like swatted flies, protecting their tiny clumps of shit. They think we are invading soldiers, come to take their cattle and steal their bitches. They do not even know why we are here!

Fire and mayhem raging, Black Cross trotted unconcerned through the street to the large stone house, the best in the town. Five of his riders followed.

Sounds of panic rang out from inside – a woman screaming, the noise of children being roused from bed.

'Break it down,' Black Cross nodded to a cohort. A single axe blow shattered the door.

A man wearing a white and blue shawl, with long grey hair and a heavy beard, appeared in the doorway. 'What do you want here?' the cowering man asked. 'We've done no harm.'

'Get out of my way, Jew,' Black Cross barked.

The man's wife, in a woollen shawl, rushed out and spoke fearlessly. 'We are peaceful people,' she said. 'We will give you whatever you want.'

Black Cross yanked the woman away and pinned her by her throat to the wall. 'Show me where it is,' he spat. 'Show me, if you have any regard for his life.'

'Please, the money is in the courtyard,' the panicked husband whined. 'In a chest under the drinking trough. Have it. Take what you will.'

'Search the house,' Black Cross screamed at his men.

'Rip down every wall. Just find it.'

'But the money . . . I told you—'

'We did not come for money, filth,' Black Cross leered. 'We are here for the jewel. Christendom's precious relic.'

His henchmen stormed inside. They found an old man, his arms around two cowering children. A boy, perhaps sixteen, already with the locks of his race, and a girl, maybe a year younger, with dark, trembling eyes.

'What do you mean?' the father crawled on his knees. 'I am a merchant. We have no jewels. No relics!'

Timber by timber, the house was torn apart. The raiders smashed their swords into walls, dug with axes at stone, tore through chests and cupboards.

Black Cross pulled the husband up by the throat. 'I will not trifle any longer. *Where is the treasure?*'

'I beg you, we have no jewels,' the trembling man gagged. 'I trade in wool.'

'You trade in wool,' Black Cross nodded, glancing at his young son. 'We shall see.' He took out a knife and pressed it against the boy's throat. The child flinched, revealing a line of blood. 'Show me the treasure, unless you want your son to die.'

'The hearth . . . there are tiles underneath the hearth.' The father bowed his head in his hands.

In a rush, two of the knights ran to the fireplace and, using axes and hilts, crashed through the floor tiles, unearthing a secret space. From it, they raised a chest, and inside were coins, necklaces, brooches of gold and silver. And finally, a large gorgeous ruby, the size of a gold coin, set in a gilded, Byzantine-style setting. It shimmered with a luminous glow. The knight held it aloft as if it was a cherished prize.

'You have no idea what you hold,' the Jew blinked back tears.

'Don't I?' Black Cross grinned. 'It is the seal of Paul. Your race is unworthy even to hold it. You will steal from Our Lord no more.'

'I did not steal. It is you who does that. It was sold to me.'

'Sold, not stolen?' Black Cross's eyes glimmered. He turned back to the son. 'Then it is only a small loss, compared to what your race has taken from us.'

In the same instant, he pushed his knife into the boy's gut. A gasp emerged; his eyes grew wide and blood dribbled from his mouth. All the while, Black Cross smirked. The filth was choking, and at the same time, trying to pray.

'Nefrem . . .' The merchant and his wife screamed. They tried to rush to their son, but were held back by other raiders.

'Burn the place,' Black Cross said. 'Their seed is dead. They can foul the earth no more.'

'What of the daughter?' the knight enquired.

Black Cross yanked the girl towards him and looked at her, measuringly. She was a pretty specimen. He ran his gloved hand along the smooth skin of her cheek.

'Such a pretty pelt, wool merchant . . . I wonder what it's like to be wrapped in such a cloth. Why don't you tell me?'

'Please, you have taken everything,' the father begged. 'Leave us our child.'

'I'm afraid not.' Black Cross shook his head. 'I must have her later. And no doubt, the duke's mule cleaner will want to do the same. Take her with us.' He threw the girl to a knight.

In a flash, she was carried out of the house, screaming in horror and fear. Torches were swept around the walls.

'Don't be so sad, Jew,' Black Cross addressed the sobbing man. He tossed a coin at him from the chest of treasure. 'As you say, I do not steal your daughter, I buy her.'

Chapter Twenty-Nine

'**I**s he dead?'

A voice crept through the haze. *A woman's voice* . . . I opened my eyes, but I couldn't see a thing. Only a shifting blur.

'I don't know, my lady,' another said, 'but his wounds are grave. He doesn't look far from death.'

'Such unusual hair . . .' remarked the first.

I blinked, my brain slowly starting to clear, as if a shimmering veil reflecting in my sight was lifting. *Was I dead?* There was a lovely face leaning over me. Yellow hair, braided densely, tumbling from under a brocaded, purple cloak. She smiled. It warmed me, like the sun.

'Sophie,' I muttered. I reached to touch her face.

'You are hurt,' replied the voice, like the delicate trill of ringing glass. 'I'm afraid you mistake me for someone else.'

My body felt no pain. 'Is this Heaven?' I asked.

The woman smiled again. 'If Heaven is a world where all wounded knights resemble vegetables, then, yes, it must be.'

I felt her hands cradle my head. I blinked again. It was

not Sophie, but someone lovely, speaking High French, the accent of the north. *Paris.*

'I still live,' I uttered with a sigh, my head falling back in her arms.

'For the moment, yes. But your wounds are serious. We must get you to a physician. Are you from here? Do you have family?'

I focused on her questions. *Where am I?* I was heading to Tours. It was all too fuzzy and painful. I just said, 'No.'

'Are you an outlaw?' the second woman's voice intoned from above.

I struggled to see a lavishly robed lady, clearly noble, atop a magnificent white charger.

'I assure you, ma'am,' I did my best to smile, 'I am benign.' I saw my shirt was matted with blood. 'Regardless of how I look.' Sharp pain lanced my stomach and thigh. I had no strength. With a gasp I fell back once more.

'Where do you head, Monsieur Rouge?' the golden-haired maiden asked.

I had no idea where I was or how far I had travelled. Then I remembered the boar. 'I head to Tours,' I said.

'To Tours!' she exclaimed. 'Even if we could take you, I fear you will die before you reach Tours.'

'*Take* him?' the older lady questioned. 'Look at him. He is covered with the blood of who knows whom. He smells of the forest. Leave him, child. He will be found by his own kind.'

I wanted to laugh. After all I'd been through, my life was being bargained for by a couple of bickering nobles.

I replied in my finest accent with as much of a smile I could muster. 'No need to fret, madame. My squire should be arriving at any moment.'

Then the young maiden winked at me. 'He seems harmless. You are *harmless*, aren't you?' She looked into my eyes. A lovelier face I hadn't stared at in a long time.

'Only to you,' I smiled faintly.

'See,' she said. 'I vouch for him.'

She tried to lift me, appealing to two guards in bucket helmets and red tunics for help. They glanced towards their lady, the older of the women.

'If you must,' the grand lady sighed. She waved and the guards responded. 'But he is your charge. And if your concern is so great, child, you will not mind giving up your horse.'

I tried to push myself to my feet, but my strength was not there.

'Do not struggle, Redhead,' the blonde-haired maiden said.

One of the accompanying guards, a big, hulking Moor, lifted me by the arms and legs. The lady was right. My wounds were severe. If I slipped back into unconsciousness, I didn't know if I would ever wake up.

'Who saves me,' I asked her, 'so I will know who to bless in Heaven should I pass on?'

'Your own smile saves you, Redhead,' the maiden laughed. 'But should the Lord not feel as favourably . . . I am called Emilie.'

Chapter Thirty

I awoke, this time with a sense of peace and the warmth of a fire about me. I found myself in a comfortable bed, in a large room with stone walls. A bowl of water sat on a wooden table to my right.

Above me, a bearded man with wide eyes, dressed in a scarlet robe, shot a satisfied grin to a portly priest at his side.

'He wakes, Velloux. You can go back to the abbey now. It seems you are out of a job.'

The priest lowered his flabby face in front of mine. He shrugged. 'You have done well, Augustus . . . on the *body*. But there is also the matter of the soul. Perhaps there is something this blood-spattered stranger would like to confess.'

I wet my lips, answering for myself. 'I am sorry, Father. If it's a confession you're looking for, you might get a better one out of the boar who attacked me. Certainly a better meal.'

This made the physician laugh. 'Back among us for only a second, Velloux, and he's sized you up.'

The priest scowled. It was clear he didn't like being the

brunt of mockery. He threw on a floppy hat. 'Then I'm going.'

The priest left, and the kindly-looking physician sat beside me. 'Don't mind him. We had a bet. Who got you – he or I.'

I raised myself up to my elbows. 'I'm glad to have been the subject of your sport. Where am I?'

'In good hands, I assure you. My reputation is that I've never lost a patient who wasn't truly sick.'

'And where do I fit in?'

He shrugged. 'You, sir, I'm afraid, are truly *very* sick.'

I forced a weak smile. 'I meant the place, sir. Where have I been taken?'

The physician gently patted my shoulder. 'I knew that, boy. You are in Blois.'

Blois . . . My eyes widened in shock. Blois was among the most powerful duchys in France – three times the size of Tours. Blois was also a four-day ride from Tours, but north, in the furthest region of the province. How had I ended up here?

'How long have I been in Blois?' I finally asked.

'Four days here. Two more along the way,' the physician said. 'You cried out many times.'

'And what did I say?'

Augustus wrung out a cloth from the bowl and placed it across my forehead. 'That your heart is not whole, though not from any boar wound. You carry a great burden.'

I did not try to disagree. My Sophie lay somewhere – *at Tours*. I still felt her alive.

I pushed myself up. 'You have my thanks for attending my wounds, Augustus. But I have to go.'

'Whoa,' the physician held me back, 'you are not yet well enough to go. And do not thank me. I merely applied the salve and cauterized the wounds. It is the Lady Emilie who deserves your thanks.'

'Emilie . . . yes . . .' Through the haze of my memory I brought back her face. I had thought she was Sophie. All at once, flashes of my journey here came to me. The Moor had carried me. He'd constructed a harness. The lady had given up her own mount for me, and walked behind.

'Without her, pilgrim,' the physician nodded, 'you would have died.'

'You are right, I truly owe her thanks. Who is this lady, Augustus?'

'A soul who cares. And a lady-in-waiting at the court.'

'Court . . .?' My eyes opened wide. 'What court do we speak of? You said you were commanded to my care. By whom? Who is it that you serve?'

'Why, the Duchess Anne,' he replied, 'wife of Stephen, Duke of Blois, second cousin to the King, who is away on the Crusade.'

Every nerve in my body seemed to leap to attention. I could not believe it. *I was entrusted to the personal care of a cousin to the King of France . . .*

The doctor smiled. 'You have done well, boar-slayer. You rest in their castle now.'

Chapter Thirty-One

I sat up in bed, confused and shocked.

I did not deserve this. I was no knight, no noble. Just a commoner. And a lucky one at that – fortunate not to have been ripped to shreds by a beast. My ordeal came back to me – my wife and child. More than six days had elapsed since I set out to find Sophie.

'Your care is most appreciated, Augustus, but I must leave. Please thank my gracious host for me.'

I limped up out of bed, but got no further than a couple of painful steps. There was a knock at the door. Augustus went to see who was there.

'You may thank the lady yourself,' he said. 'She has come.'

It was Emilie, adorned in a dress of linen decorated with golden borders. Dear God, I had not been dreaming. She was as lovely as the image from my dreams. Her eyes shimmered soft and green.

'I see our patient is up!' Emilie exclaimed, seemingly delighted. 'How is our Red today, Augustus?'

'His ears are uninjured. So is his tongue,' the physician said, prodding at me.

I didn't know whether to bow or kneel. I did not speak to

nobles directly, unless addressed. But something made me look into her eyes. I cleared my throat. 'I would be dead if not for you, lady. There is no way I can express my thanks.'

'I did what anyone would do. Besides, having vanquished your boar, what a shame it would have been if you had become the dinner of the next beast who stumbled by.'

Augustus pushed over a stool and Emilie sat down across from me. 'If you must show gratitude, you can do so by permitting me a few questions.'

'Any,' I said. 'Please ask . . .'

'First, an easy one. What is your name, Redhead?'

'My name is Hugh, lady.' I bowed my head. 'Hugh DeLuc.'

'And you were on your way to Tours, Hugh DeLuc, when you encountered the boorish boar?'

'I was, my lady. Though the physician has pointed out my direction was slightly askew.'

'So it would seem,' Lady Emilie smiled. This surprised me. I had never met a noble with a very keen sense of humour, unless it was a cruel one. 'And on this journey, you set out alone? With no food or water, or proper clothes?'

I felt a lump in my throat – not from nerves, but because of what must have seemed my enormous stupidity. 'I was in haste,' I said.

'Haste?' Emilie nodded, with polite jest again. 'But it seems, if I recall my physics, that no matter how fast you travelled, if it be the wrong direction it would only widen the distance to your goal, no?'

I felt like an idiot. I'm sure I blushed. 'In haste, *and confused*,' I replied.

'I would agree.' She widened her eyes. 'And the purpose

of such haste . . . and confusion, if you don't mind . . .?'

All at once my being ill at ease shifted. This was not a game and I was not a toy for amusement, no matter how much I owed to her.

Emilie's expression shifted as well, sensing my unease. 'Please know I do not mock you. You cried out in anguish many times during the trip. I know you carry a heavy weight. You may be no knight, as you say, but you are surely on a mission.'

I bowed my head. All the lightness of this moment fled from me. How could I speak of such horrors? And to this woman who did not know me? My throat went dry. 'It is true. I do have a mission, lady. But I cannot speak of it.'

'Please speak, sir – ' I couldn't believe it. She addressed *me* as *sir* – 'you are troubled. I do not belittle you at all. Perhaps I can help.'

'I am afraid you cannot help,' I said, and bowed my head. 'You have helped too much already.'

'You may trust me, sir. How can I prove it more than I already have?'

I smiled. She had me there. 'Just know, these are not the tales of a noble, the kind you are no doubt used to hearing.'

'I do not seek entertainment,' she replied, her eyes firmly on mine.

My experience with those highborn had taught me to beware always of their taxes and random killing and total indifference to our plight. But she seemed different. I could see compassion in her eyes. I'd felt it in that first glance as I lay near death.

'I'll tell it to you, lady. You have earned that. I only hope it does not upset you.'

'I assure you, Hugh,' Lady Emilie smiled, 'if you have not already noticed, you will find my tolerance for facing the upsetting to be quite *high*.'

Chapter Thirty-Two

So I told it to her. *Everything.*

Of Sophie, and my past life in our village. Of my journey to the Holy Land, the terrible fighting there. Of my moment with the Turk . . . How I was saved, freed, to come back, to see Sophie again.

Then I told Emilie of the horrible truth that I'd found upon my return.

My voice cracked, my eyes welled every time it came to mind. It was why I had wandered the woods like a madman when they had come upon me. *Why I had to get to Tours . . .*

All the while, Emilie seemed riveted by my tale, never once interrupting. I knew that much of what I said must have torn asunder the fantasies of her upbringing. Yet never once did I feel her react as a spoiled noble. She did not question my desertion from the army, nor take offence at my anger towards Norcross and Baldwin. And when I came to why I so desperately needed to get to Tours, her eyes glistened.

'Indeed I understand, Hugh.' She leaned forward, placing a hand upon mine. 'I see that you have been truly wronged.

You must go to Tours, and find your wife. But what do you intend to do, go there as one man? Without arms or access to the duke's circle? Baldwin is well known here for what he is: a self-serving goat who sucks his own duchy dry. But what will you do, call him out on the field of combat? Challenge him? You will only get yourself tossed into a cell, or killed.'

'You speak as Sophie would have,' I said. 'But even if it seems madness, I have to try. I have no choice in this.'

'Then I will help you, Hugh,' Emilie whispered, 'if you will let me . . .'

I looked at her, both confused and overcome by her trust and resolve. 'Why do you do this for me? You are highborn yourself. You attend the royal court.'

'I told you the first time, Hugh DeLuc. It is your smile that saves you.'

'I think not,' I said, and dared to hold my gaze on her. 'You could have left me on the road. My troubles would have died along with me.'

Emilie averted her eyes. 'I will tell you, but not now.'

'Yet *I* have told *you* everything.'

'This is my price, Hugh. If you wish to go to other vendors, I can have you delivered back where I found you.'

I bowed my head and smiled. She was funny when she wished to be. 'Your price is agreeable, Lady Emilie. I'm truly grateful, whatever your reason.'

'Good!' she exclaimed. 'So first we must start work on a *pretext* for you, a way for you to get in. What is it you do well, other than that keen sense of direction I saw?'

I laughed at her barb, sharp as it was. 'I am one of those with skills abundant, but talents none.'

'We'll see,' Emilie said. 'What did you do in your town before the war?'

'We owned an inn. Sophie looked after the food and beds, and I—'

'Like most innkeepers, you poured the ale and kept the patrons entertained.'

'How would you know such a thing?' I asked.

'No matter. And during the war? From what I've seen, you were certainly not a scout.'

'I fought. I learned to fight quite well, actually. But I was told I was always able to keep my friends amused by my stories, and their minds off the fighting. In the most worrisome of times, they always requested my tales . . .' I told her how I grew up, travelling the countryside, reciting verses and profane songs as a goliard. And how after the war I made my way home, entertaining inn customers and pilgrims as a jongleur. 'Maybe I have a talent after all.'

'A jongleur . . .' Emilie repeated.

'It's a modest one, but I've always had the skill to make new friends.' I smiled to let her know of whom I was speaking.

Emilie blushed, then stood up. She straightened her dress and produced a demure look. 'You must rest now, Hugh DeLuc. Nothing will happen until your wounds have healed. In the meantime, I must go.'

A worry shot through me. 'Please, lady, I hope I have not offended you.'

'*Offended* me?' she exclaimed. 'Not at all.' She broke into a most wonderful smile. 'In fact, your vast talents have given me a splendid idea.'

Chapter Thirty-Three

The following afternoon, Emilie knocked on the door of the large chamber in the royal apartment of the tower. The Duchess Anne was at a table, overseeing a group of ladies-in-waiting at work on a tapestry.

'You called for me, my lady,' said Emilie.

'Yes,' Anne replied. The quintet of women stopped work and looked up for a sign to leave. 'Please, stay,' she said. 'I will speak with Emilie in the antechamber.'

The duchess motioned her into the next room, adjacent to the bedroom, where there was a large table, bowls of perfumed water and a bright, reflecting glass, a *mirror*.

Anne sat on the stool. 'I wish to speak of the health of your new red squire,' she started.

'He recovers well,' Emilie replied. 'And please, he is not my squire. In fact, he is already married, and seeks to find his wife.'

'His wife! And that was where he was heading when we found him so neatly trussed in the woods? A curious courtship,' Anne smiled. 'But, now that he is well—'

'Not quite well,' Emilie cut in.

'But now that he *recovers*, it is fitting he should be on his way. Anyway, the physician tells me he has a will to leave.'

'He has suffered great injury, madame, which he seeks to right. The author of his offence is Baldwin of Tours.'

'Baldwin?' Anne grimaced, as if she had swallowed spoiled wine. 'Surely Baldwin is no friend to this court. But this man's affairs, lowly as they are, are no concern of ours. Your heart is admirable, Emilie. You have quite surpassed what anyone might expect of you. Now I want you to let him *leave*.'

'I will not shoo him away, madame.' Emilie stood tall. 'I want to help him right this wrong.'

'Help him?' Anne looked shocked. 'Help him *what*? Regain his title? His honour? A set of clothes?'

'Please, madame, every man deserves his honour, regardless of his rank in life. This man has been horribly wronged.'

Anne came up to her. As befit her social status, her dark brown hair was combed long and over her shoulders. She was perhaps thirty, but in many ways she was like a mother to Emilie. 'My sweet Emilie, where did you get such notions?'

'You know well, my lady. You know why I came to be here, why I left Paris and my own troubles there.'

Anne placed her hand tenderly on Emilie's shoulder. She *did* love the girl. 'You are as caring, child, as you are rash. None the less, as soon as he is ready to travel he must be on his way. If my husband would hear of this, he'd come back from the Crusade and thrash me blue. This Red, does he have a profession? Some skill, other than boar-fighting?'

'I am teaching him a profession – starting today,' Emilie replied.

'But not for here, I hope. We are overburdened with hangers-on as it is.'

'No, not for here, my lady. Once he learns what I have to teach, he will be on his way. He has a wife to find. He loves her dearly.'

Chapter Thirty-Four

I rested for three more days, until most of my wounds had healed some more.

Then Emilie knocked on the door, seeming excited. She enquired as to my health. 'Are you able to walk?'

'Yes, of course I can.' I hopped out of bed to show her, though still a little impaired.

'That'll do.' She seemed pleased. 'Then come along with me.'

She marched to the door and I hurried, with a slight limp, behind her. She led me down the halls, wide and arched and adorned with beautiful tapestries, then down a steep flight of stone stairs.

'Where are we going?' I asked, pushing to keep up. It felt good to be out of my sickroom.

'To view your new *pretext*, I hope,' she smiled.

We travelled to a different part of the castle. I had never been so close to the abode of royalty before.

On the main floor there were large, great rooms, with long rows of tables and huge hearths with roaring fires, guarded by uniformed soldiers at every door. Knights milled about, in their casual tunics, trading stories and rolling dice. Mounted torches lit the halls against the winter darkness.

Then, we passed the kitchen, with an inviting smell of garlic in the air, maids and porters shuffling around casks of wine and ale.

Still we travelled, down a narrow corridor, leading beneath the ground. Here, the walls were of coarsely laid stone. The air grew stale and damp. We were in some sort of keep now, in the womb of the castle. Where was Emilie taking me? What did she mean by my 'new pretext'?

Finally, when the halls were so ill-lit and dank that the only living thing must be some slumbering beast, Emilie stopped in front of a large, wooden door.

'My new pretext is a mole,' I said with a laugh.

'Do not be rude,' she smiled, and knocked.

'Come in,' groaned a voice from deep inside. 'Come, come. Hurry before I change my mind.'

With a curious look, I followed Emilie as we stepped into a chilly room. It was more of a cell, or a dungeon, but large, candle-lit, and on the walls, shelves with what I took to be toys and props.

In the rear, on an ornately carved chair, sat a hunched man in a red tunic, green hose and a patchwork skirt.

He lowered a jaundiced eye towards Emilie. 'Come in, Auntie. May I have a lick? Just a lick would do . . .'

'Oh, *shut up*, Norbert,' Emilie retorted, though not crossly. 'This is the man I spoke of. His name is Hugh. Hugh, this is Norbert, the lord's fool.'

'Egad.' Norbert leaped out of his chair. He was squat and gnome-like, yet he moved with startling speed. He sprang up to me, placed a hand on my red hair, then swiftly pulled back. 'Do you intend to burn me, ma'am? What is he, torch or man?'

'What he is, is no fool, Norbert,' Emilie cautioned. 'I think you'll have your work cut out for you.'

I looked at Emilie with consternation. 'My *pretext* is a jester, ma'am?'

'And why not?' Emilie replied. 'You say you have a knack for amusing people. What better role? Norbert informs me that the jester at Tours is as old as vinegar . . .'

'And his wit even more sour,' the jester croaked.

' . . . And that he has lost the favour of his liege there, Baldwin. It should be no great feat for a youthful up-and-comer like yourself to gain his ear. Easier, I would think, then storming his castle in a fit of rage.'

I started to stammer. I had just come back from the war, where I had fought as bravely as any man. I was looking to avenge a misery that cut deep to my core. I thought of myself as no hero. But a *jester*? 'I can't dispute your reason, lady, but . . . I am no fool.'

'Oh, you think it's a natural thing to act this way?' The gnome-like man hopped up to me. 'Unpractised, not learned? You think, Carrot-top,' he stroked my face with his rough hands and batted his wide eyes, 'that I was never as young and fair as you . . .' He sprang back, narrowing his gaze. 'Just because you play the fool, boy, doesn't mean you must be thick inside. The lady's plan is well-conceived. *If* you have the knack to carry it out.'

'Nothing moves me more than the will to find my wife,' I insisted.

'I didn't say the *will*, boy. I said, the *knack*. The lady says you have a way about yourself. That you fancy yourself a jongleur. Jongleurs . . . oh, they can soften the blood of blushing maidens and patrons incapacitated on ale. But the real trick is, can you walk into a room filled with scoundrels and schemers, and make an ill-tempered king smile?'

I looked at Emilie. She was right. I did need some way to gain access to Baldwin's castle. Sophie, if she was alive, wouldn't be dressed up in the royal court, would she? I needed to snoop around, gain some trust . . .

'Perhaps I can learn,' I replied.

Chapter Thirty-Five

'**L**earn . . .' Norbert shook his head and bellowed with laughter. 'Learning would take years. How would you learn in a short time to do *this*?'

The gnome took a lighted candle, waved his bare hand through the flame, not once crying out, then clicked his fingers and the flame was snuffed, as if by magic. 'It's what comes natural that I need to know. So tell me, what do you do?'

'Do . . .?' I muttered.

'Do,' the jester snapped. 'What kind of student have you brought me, Auntie? Has a rock hit your head? *What do you do?* Juggle, tumble, fall down . . .?'

I looked around. I spotted a staff leaning against a table, roughly the same as mine. I winked at Norbert. 'I can do *this* . . .' I raised the staff on my hand, balancing it in the air, then lightly transferred it to a single finger. For a full minute, it stood straight on end.

'Oh, that's *goood* . . .' Norbert crooned. 'But can you do *this*?' He snatched the staff from me. In a flash, he balanced it, just as I had, upon his index finger. Then, with almost no hesitation, he flung it in the air and caught it as before with the same finger. Then again, on only one finger. 'Or *this*?' he smirked, and began to twirl the staff so fast it looked as if six sets of hands were twirling it at once. I could not even follow its path. Then he brought it to a stop and handed it to me in the same motion. 'Let me see you do that.'

'I cannot,' I stammered.

'Then this, perhaps . . .' He winked at me with his bulging eye. 'The lady said you were sprightly . . .'

In a motion that defied my eyes, this squat, curved man spun into a complete forwards somersault, then backwards again, landing precisely where he had started. My eyes widened in amazement.

'What about jokes, then? The lady said you could make me laugh. You must know some fabulous jokes.'

'I know a few,' I said.

Norbert folded his arms. 'So, go ahead, boy. Bowl me over. Make me laugh until I piss myself.'

Now, I was eager to the dare, eager to show the jester up. This I could surely do. I thought through my best inventory. 'There's the one about the peasant who is so lazy, as he watches a gold coin drop from the money bag of a knight riding by—'

'Know it,' Norbert said immediately. 'He says to his friend, "If he comes back the other way, this just might be our lucky day." '

'OK, then there's the one about the traveller and the whorehouse,' I began. 'A traveller is walking down the road—'

'Know it,' the jester interrupted again. 'The sign says, "Congratulations, you've just been screwed." '

I went through two other tales that never failed to stir a

laugh. 'Know it,' he snapped to both. He seemed to know them all. Emilie held back a laugh.

'So that's it. That's your entire repertoire?' The jester shook his head. 'Can you at least rhyme? A dour king cannot ignore, *refusedly*, a spicy tale about his wife if it is told, *amusedly*.

'This stuff is *easy*, right? Hump your back, hop around like an ape, everyone rolls over in stitches. C'mon, Red, you must have something decent. You want a pretext? Well, I want to be a patron. *I want to be a patron . . .*' he pranced around and whined like a spoiled child. 'You know, maybe on second thoughts, you would have an easier time storming Baldwin's castle than making them laugh.'

In a fit of vexation, I searched the room. This was no sport to me, no stupid audition. This was about the fate of my wife. Then in the corner of the jester's cell I spotted a ball and chain.

'*That*.' I pointed.

'What? Want to play catch?' Norbert asked haughtily.

'No, jester. Fetch me the chain.' I remembered something I had seen on the Crusade. A captured Saracen did a trick to amuse his captors; it worked so well they kept him alive.

'Bind me with it,' I said. 'Wrap it all the way around, tight as you can. I will extricate myself.'

This brought a worried look from Emilie. The chains were heavy. Wound too tight, they could squeeze the air out of a man.

'Your poison.' Norbert shrugged.

He went over and dragged the heavy chains back to me. I took several deep breaths, much as I had seen the Saracen do when he had performed the trick. Then the jester began to wrap. Slowly, heavily, the chains squeezed my breath. I lifted my arms and he wrapped chains around my shoulder. And for good luck, between my legs.

'Your rubicund friend has a knack to kill himself,' Norbert chuckled.

'Please be careful,' Emilie said.

I pushed out my chest as expansively as I could as the jester circled it with the chains. I had to enlarge myself. I had to hold my breath. I had seen this done. I had questioned the Turk myself. I only hoped I could recreate the effect now.

'Time's moving on,' Norbert said, after the chains were secure.

They felt like a crushing weight upon my shoulders. He stood back, and slowly I released the captured air from my lungs. With the slightest wiggle room developed around my chest. It was only an inch or two.

Then I was able to shift my shoulders, back and forth. Then gradually my arms. Every gruelling minute advanced like an hour. The weight of the chains pressed me to the floor. My hands were pinned behind my back, but finally, I pulled one free. Like a snake, I twisted it through an opening up around my shoulders.

Emilie gasped. The jester looked on, finally interested in me.

It took all of my strength to get an arm free. My side and legs still ached from the boar's attack. Each exertion was agony, but gradually, with the arm free, I was able to unwrap the chain. From between my legs, from under my arms, from around my chest, layer after layer came off. Then I freed my other arm.

As I kicked off the final ring, Emilie screeched a happy cry.

I doubled over, drenched in sweat. I looked up at my patron.

Norbert drummed his fingers along the side of his face. He smiled at Emilie. 'I think we can work with that.'

Chapter Thirty-Six

I studied with Norbert for nearly a fortnight, until my wounds finally healed. My days were spent juggling, tumbling, and watching him perform in front of the court; my nights with the telling and retelling of jokes and rhymes.

Step by step, I learned the jester's trade.

Much of it came easily to me. I had been a jongleur and used to entertaining. And I had always been agile. We practised forward flips and handstands; in return, I taught him the trick about the chains. A hundred times, Norbert held out his arm, like a bar, at waist height, while I strained to flip my body over it. At first, I hit my head on the straw mat over and over and groaned in pain. 'You find new ways to injure yourself, Red.' My patron would shake his head.

Then slowly, surely, my confidence began to grow. I began to clear Norbert's bar, though sometimes falling to my seat. On my last day, I made it over, my feet sticking to the precise spot from where I had sprung. I met his eyes. Norbert's face lit up in a monumental smile.

'You'll do all right,' he nodded.

At last, my education was complete. There was an

urgency to things; the image of Sophie was never far from my thoughts. If I had any hope of finding her alive, I had to go now.

At the end of our final session, Norbert dragged over a heavy wooden trunk. 'Open it, Hugh. It's a gift from me.'

I lifted the top and pulled from it a set of folded clothes. A green and red tunic. A floppy, pointed cap. A colourful patchwork skirt.

'Emilie made it,' the jester said, proudly, 'but to my design.'

I looked at the jester's garb with wariness.

Norbert grinned. 'Afraid to play the fool, eh? Your pride's your enemy then, not Baldwin.'

I hesitated. I knew I had to play the role, *for Sophie*, but it was hard to see myself wearing this outfit. I held it up to me, sizing it against my chest.

'Put it on, then,' Norbert insisted, smacking me on the shoulder. 'You'll be a chip off the old block.'

I removed a set of bells from the trunk.

'For the cap,' said Norbert. 'No liege must be sneaked up on by his fool.'

The uniform I suppose I had to wear, but there was no way I could see myself tinkling about. 'These, I must leave with you.'

'No bells?' the jester exclaimed. 'No club foot, no hunch of the spine?' Again, he slapped my shoulders. 'You are indeed the new breed.'

I put aside my own tunic and hose and slipped into the jester's outfit. Piece by piece I felt a new confidence take over my body. I had worn the robes of a young goliard, the armour of a soldier on the Crusade. Now *this* . . .

I looked myself up and down and broke into a wide smile. I felt a new man! I was ready.

'Brings tears to my eyes.' Norbert feigned growing misty. 'The lack of a limp bothers me some – a jester needs a good strut. Oh, but you will appeal to the ladies!'

I sprang into a forward flip, stuck it, and bowed with pride.

'You are done then, Hugh,' the jester said. He tugged at my tunic and skirt to adjust the fit. 'Just one thing more . . . It is not enough, boy, simply to make them laugh. Any fool can make a man laugh. Just fall on your face. The mark of a true jester is to gain the trust of the court. You may speak in rhyme, gobbledegook, in gibberish, for all I care, but somehow you must touch something true. It is not enough to win your lord's laughter, lad. You must also win his ear.'

'I'll win Baldwin's ear,' I promised. 'Then I'll cut if off and bring it back to you.'

'Good. We'll make a soup of it!' the jester roared. He pulled my hand soundly, as if trying to force me off my mark, then looked at me with some welling in his eye.

'You are sure of this, Hugh? Of going to all this risk? It would be a shame to waste this valuable teaching on a corpse. You're sure your wife lives?'

I looked into his eyes. 'I feel it with all my heart.'

He raised those bushy brows of his and smiled. 'So go, then, lad . . . *To the sails* . . . Find your beloved. You are a dreamer, boy, but heavens, what good jester isn't?' He winked and stuck out his tongue. 'Give her a lick for me . . .'

Chapter Thirty-Seven

I t was a crisp, cold morning as the sun broke through the mist, low in the sky. Emilie met me on the stone road outside the castle gate. 'You rise early, Hugh DeLuc.'

'And you, lady. I'm sorry to have brought you out on such a frosty morn.'

She smiled bravely. 'It is for a good purpose, I hope.'

'I hope so too,' I said.

She had on her brown velvet cloak, which she always wore for matins. She cinched the collar against the cold. I stood before her in my ridiculous jester's outfit. I did a sprightly hop and a jump that made her smile.

'I hear it is *you* I have to thank for the new clothes.' I bowed.

'What thanks?' she curtsied. 'A jester could not do his work without looking the part. Besides, your other clothes reeked of a particular smelly beast.'

I smiled, fixing on her soft, green eyes. 'I feel the fool in front of you, my lady.'

'Not for me. You look quite handsome, if I may say so.'

'The handsome jester – not what is normally thought of as right.'

Emilie's pupils glistened. 'Did I not tell you, Hugh, I have a penchant for not doing what is considered right.'

'You did tell me,' I nodded, smiling.

We stood and stared at each other for a long while, the space empty of words. A rush of feelings rose in my chest. This beautiful girl had done so much for me. If not for her, I would be dead, a bloody mound on the side of the road. I reached out my hand to her. There was a spark between us, a warmth against the chill of the day.

I let my hand linger longer than I could have dreamed would be allowed. She did not pull away. 'I owe you so much, Lady Emilie. I fear I owe you a debt I can never repay.'

'You owe me nothing,' she smiled with her chin raised, 'but to be on your quest and to complete it safely.'

I didn't know what else to say. For me there had only been Sophie. Each night I went to sleep with my mind dancing with a thousand images of our lives together, my hands aching to touch her skin once more. I loved my wife, and yet, this woman had done so much. *And received nothing in return*. I wanted to take her in my arms and let her know my feelings. The strongest surge swelled inside me; it gave me a trembling in every bone in my body.

'I hope with all my heart your Sophie *is* alive,' Emilie finally said.

'She is alive. I know it.'

My hands were still cupped in hers, and when I finally pulled them away, I felt a loss – but also a small object pressed in them, wrapped in a linen cloth.

'This was in your clothes,' Emilie said, 'when I first found you on the road.'

I unwrapped it. The breath froze in my chest. It was the broken comb with the painted edge I had found in the cinders of our inn. *Sophie's comb*.

Emilie's eyes were liquid and brave, her voice strong. She took my hand again. 'Go and find her, Hugh DeLuc. I truly believe that is what you were saved for.'

I nodded. I squeezed her hand in return with all my might. 'In all the world, I hope to see you again, my lady.'

'In all the world, I hope to see you again *too*, Hugh DeLuc. It pains me that you leave.'

I let her go and tossed my sack upon my back. I picked up my staff and started south, on the true road to Tours.

I took a skip and a hop, and twirled back to take a final look at her. She was still watching me and bravely smiled. I thought: with all the worlds that separated us, how had I deserved such a lovely friend?

'Goodbye,' I whispered under my breath.

I thought I saw her lips move too. '*Goodbye, Hugh . . .*'

Chapter Thirty-Eight

The armoured raiders swept down upon the sleeping manor. It was a large stone house in a neighbouring duchy, miles from the nearest town.

I will make them pay, Black Cross promised. *No man is bold enough to steal from God. Especially not the true relics of Christendom.*

At first, there was a yap of dogs as the massive chargers thundered out of the calm night. Then everything was ablaze. Torches lit up the darkness.

The horsemen set fire to the stables, horses bucking and neighing in fright. A few terrified workers who had been sleeping there ran out and were mown down by the blades of hard metal charging by.

The manor house burst alive with light. Two dark knights dismounted and crashed through the heavy wooden door with their axes. Black Cross burst inside with the rest of his men.

The knight of the manor appeared in a doorway. His name was Adhemar. All France knew of this old man, this renowned fighter, who still stood with a strength that spoke of his past. Behind him, his wife huddled in a bed gown.

The knight had donned his tunic. It bore the purple and gold fleur-de-lis of the King.

'Who are you?' Adhemar challenged the raiders. 'What do you want here?'

'A piece of gold, old man. From your last campaign,' said Black Cross.

'I am no banker, intruder. My last campaign was in service to the Pope.'

'Then it should not be so hard to remember. What we seek was plundered from a tomb in Edessa.'

'Edessa . . .?' The old knight's eyes flicked from intruder to intruder. 'How do you know of this?'

'The noble Adhemar's fame is *well* known,' Black Cross said.

'Then you also know I have fought with William at Hastings. That I wear the Gold Fleur, awarded to me by King Philippe himself. That I have defended the faith at Acre and Antioch, where my blood still lies.'

'We know *all* of this,' Black Cross smiled. 'In fact, that is why we are *here*.'

He signalled to one of his men, who bound the arms of the knight's wife. Adhemar moved to defend her, but he was pinned by the blade of a sword to his neck.

'You insult me, intruder. You show no face or colours. Who are you? Who has sent you? Tell me, so I will know you when I meet you in Hell.'

'Know *this*,' Black Cross said, and lifted his helmet, revealing a dark cross burned into the side of his neck.

The old knight fell silent with recognition.

'Take us to the shrine,' Black Cross said.

His henchmen dragged the couple through their house,

the knight's wife screaming futilely at her captors. Beyond a stone arch leading to a rear courtyard, they came upon a bronze altar with a crucifix hanging above.

'In Edessa you looted the tomb of a Christian shrine. In the reliquary, there were crosses and vestments and coins. There was also a gold box. In it were ashes. That is all we came for. Just a box filled with ash . . .'

Black Cross grabbed a war axe from one of his cohorts and raised it over the knight's head. The knight closed his eyes. As his wife shrieked, Black Cross swung the axe in a mighty arc, narrowly missing the knight, but smashing the stone floor beneath the altar. The rock crumbled under the mighty blows.

Beneath the masonry, a hidden space came into view, containing a gold ark wrapped in cloth. One of Black Cross's men kneeled and lifted it. He smashed the valuable chest as if it were a trinket, prying open the lock.

Inside, he lifted a simple wooden box. He opened the lid and gazed, awe-struck, at the dark sand inside.

'It is blasphemy that you should hold such a thing in His name,' the old knight glared.

Black Cross's eyes lit up with rage. 'Then we shall let Him decide.'

Black Cross scanned the broken chapel, his gaze coming to rest on the crucifix hanging on the wall. 'Such a spirited faith, brave knight. We must make sure such faith is recognized for all to see.'

The knight and his wife were crucified.

Chapter Thirty-Nine

My journey to Tours took five days. The first two, the road was busy with travellers – pedlars dragging their carts; workers with tools and belongings; pilgrims hurrying back home before the teeth of winter set in.

By the third day, the villages grew smaller, and so did the traffic.

By the fourth, at dusk, I huddled in the cold after a stingy meal of bread and cheese. I could not rest. Tours was but a good day's walk away, and the anticipation of reaching there and finding Sophie beat through my blood like a restless drum.

I decided to travel a bit further until darkness set in completely.

I heard voices up ahead, then shouts, and a woman's cries. In a short distance, I came upon a merchant family – father, wife and son – being attacked by two robbers.

One of the scavengers grabbed a prize, a ceramic bowl or something. 'Look what I have, Shorty. A piss-bowl.'

'Please,' the merchant begged, 'we have no money. Take the wares if you must.'

The one called Shorty sneered. 'Let's have a trade. You can have your piss-bowl back for a stab at your wife.'

The blood stiffened in my veins. I did not know these people – I had my own pressing needs in Tours – but I couldn't stand by and watch them be robbed or possibly murdered.

I put down my pack and crept closer. Finally I stepped out from behind my cover.

Shorty's eyes fell upon me. He was stumpy and barrel-chested, balding on top, but very muscular. In my outfit, I knew I made a ridiculous sight.

'Let them be,' I said. 'Leave them and go,'

'What do we have here?' The fierce outlaw grinned toothlessly. 'A May Day ornament come out of the woods.'

'You heard the man.' I came closer with my staff. 'Take what you have. You can sell it in the next town. That's what I would do.'

Shorty stood up, hardly about to buckle in to a threat delivered by one in a jester's suit. 'What I would do, eh, fine fellow . . . What I would do is run off now. Your bad jokes aren't needed here.'

'Let me try another,' I said, stepping forward. 'How about this one? Name the sexual position that produces the ugliest children.'

Shorty and his partner shared looks, as if they could not believe what was going on.

'Don't know, Shorty?' I gripped my staff. 'Well, why don't we just ask your mother?'

The tall one grunted a slight laugh, but Shorty cut him silent. He lifted his club above his shoulders. I watched his eyes grow narrow and mean. 'You really are a fool, aren't you?'

Before the words had left his mouth, I swung my staff. It cracked him firmly in the mouth and sent him reeling. He grabbed his jaw, then raised his weapon. Before he could swing it, I sprang forward again and whacked my stick across his shin, doubling him over in extreme pain. I rapped his shin again and he screamed.

The other came at me, but as he did, the merchant rushed forward and thrust his torch into the outlaw's face. His entire head was engulfed in seconds. The man howled, and smacked at his head to douse the flames. Then his clothing caught fire, and he fled into the woods, screaming, followed by Shorty.

The merchant and his wife came up to me. 'We owe you thanks. I am Geoffrey.' He extended his hand. 'I have a pottery stall in Tours. This is my wife, Isabel. My son, Thomas.'

'I'm Hugh.' I took his hand. 'A jester. Could you tell?'

'Hugh,' his wife enquired, 'where do you head?'

'I head to Tours as well.'

'Then we can go the rest of the way together,' Geoffrey offered. 'We don't have much food left, but what there is, you're welcome to share.'

'Why not?' I agreed. 'But I think we'd better put some distance between us and the night crawlers. My pack's just over here.'

Geoffrey's son asked, 'Are you going to Tours to be a jester at the court?'

I smiled at the boy. 'I hope to, Thomas. I've heard the one there now has grown a bit dull.'

'Maybe he has, 'Geoffrey shrugged, 'but you'll have a hard job in front of you. How long has it been since you have been to our town?'

'Three years,' I answered.

He lifted up his cart. 'These days, I'm afraid you will find Tours a hard place in which to raise a laugh.'

Chapter Forty

We had barely cleared the forest, two mornings later, when Geoffrey pointed ahead. 'There it is.'

The town of Tours, glistening through the sun, perched atop a high hill. Was Sophie truly here? There was a cluster of ochre-coloured buildings knotted to the rise, then, at its peak, the large grey castle, two towers thrust towards the sky.

I had been to Tours twice before. Once, to settle a claim against a knight who would not pay his bill, and the other, with Sophie, to go to market.

Geoffrey was right. As we approached the outlying village I could tell that Tours had changed.

'Look how the fields lie fallow,' Geoffrey pointed, 'while over there, the lord's demesne is trussed neatly for the winter.'

Indeed, I could see how the smaller plots of land sat with rotted crops, while the duchy's fields, bordered by solid stone fences, lay furrowed in neat, even rows.

Closer to town, serious signs of decline were everywhere. A wooden bridge over a stream had so many holes in the boards we could barely pass. Fences were broken and run down. I was dumbstruck. I remembered Tours as thriving and prosperous, the largest market in the province, a place of celebration on Midsummer's Eve.

We climbed the steep, windy hill that rose towards the castle. The streets stank of waste, the run-off from the castle lining the edges of the road.

The pigs were out. Each morning people got rid of their garbage by tossing it out on the streets. Then pigs were let loose to feed on the waste. Their morning meal was enough to turn my stomach.

At a crowded corner, Geoffrey announced, 'Our stall is down the street. You are welcome to stay with us, Hugh, if you have no place.'

I declined. I had to get started on my quest – *which lay inside the castle.*

The merchant embraced me. 'You'll always have a friend here. And by the way, my wife's cousin Nellie works in the castle. I will tell her what you did for us. She'll be sure to save you the best scraps of meat.'

'Thanks,' I waved. I winked at Thomas, and hopped around a bit like an ape until I got a laugh. 'Come to visit me, if I get the job.'

I left them behind and walked through the town, making my way up the tall hill. People stared, and I hopped and grinned and juggled my way in my new role. A new jester was like the arrival of a troop of players, festive and gay.

A crowd of raggedy children followed, dancing around me with shouts and laughs. Yet inside, my heart pounded with the worrisome task that lay ahead. *Sophie was here* – I could feel it. Somewhere in all this stone and decay, she clung on.

It took me nearly an hour to wind through the streets and finally make my way to the castle gates. A squad of uniformed soldiers in milk-pail helmets and Baldwin's green and gold colours stood, manning the lowered drawbridge, checking people going in.

A queue had formed. Some passed through. Others, arguing their case, were rudely pushed away.

This was it, my new pretext – my first test. My stomach churned. *Please, let me be up to this . . .*

Taking a deep breath, I stepped up to the front gate.

And once again, I could feel Sophie's presence.

Chapter Forty-One

'What's this, jester? You have business here?' a brusque-looking captain of the guard eyed me up and down.

'I have, sir.' I bowed in the guard's face and smiled. 'It is business I have come for, and business I will do. *Important* business . . . Not as important as yours, sir, but the stuff of lords, I mean *laughs* . . .'

'Shut your trap, fool,' the guard glowered. 'Who awaits you inside?'

'The lord awaits me.' I bowed. *And my Sophie.*

The guard scrunched his brow. 'The *lord* awaits *you*?'

'The Lord awaits us *all*.' I grinned and winked.

Some people queuing began to chuckle.

'Lord Baldwin then,' I went on. 'It is *he* who awaits me. He just does not know it yet.'

'Lord Baldwin?' The guard screwed up his eye. 'What do you take me for? *A fool?*' He roared out laughing.

I bowed humbly. 'You're right, sir, I am *not* needed, if such a wit as you is already here. You must truly keep the barracks up all night in stitches.'

'We already have a fool, jester. His name is Palimpost.

Not your lucky day, eh? It seems we're all fooled up.'

'Well, now we're *two*-fooled, aren't we?' I exclaimed. I had to say something that would gain me support. Even this mould-worm must be able to be charmed or swayed.

I kneeled down to a farmer's boy. I poked at his chin, his nose, then snapped my fingers and a small dried plum appeared in my hand. The child squealed with delight. 'It is a sad day, boy, is it not, when a laugh is barred with a sword. Don't tell me the great liege Baldwin has something to fear from a laugh?'

There was a trickle of applause from the by-standers. 'C'mon, captain,' a pretty, fat woman called. 'Let the fool in. What harm can he cause?'

Even his fellow guards seemed to give in. 'Let him through, Albert. The man's right. Things could use some lightening up around here.'

'Yes, Albert,' I quipped. 'I mean, sir. Things *could* use some lightening. Here, hold this . . .' I gave him my sack. 'That's much *lighter*. Thank you very much . . .' I folded my arms.

'Get your arse through,' the guard growled at me, 'before it ends up on the point of my lance.' He thrust my sack back into my ribs.

I bowed a last time, winking thanks to the woman and the farmer, as I hurried through.

A tremor of relief passed through me. I was in . . .

My steps groaned over the drawbridge; the walls of the castle loomed high above. Across the bridge, I entered a large courtyard, busy people scurrying to and fro.

I didn't know where to go. I didn't know if Sophie was

here, or even alive. A knot ground in my chest.

I stepped up to the castle entrance. It was before noon. Court would still be in session.

I had work to do. I was a jester.

Chapter Forty-Two

Baldwin's court was held in the Great Hall, down the main corridor that rose through tall stone arches.

I followed the official traffic: knights – dressed in hose and tunics; pages holding their masters' helmets and arms, scurrying at their sides; courtiers, in colourful robes and cloaks with plumed feathers; petitioners of the court, both noble and common. And everywhere I walked I searched for Sophie.

People caught my eye and smiled. I, in turn, responded with a wink or a juggle, or a quick sleight of hand. My role was working so far. I quickly realized, a man in a patchwork skirt and tunic, juggling a set of balls – who would believe such a man could be up to any harm?

The din of a large crowd ushered me towards the Great Hall. Two tall oak doors, engraved with panels depicting the seasons, stood open at either side of the entrance. Soldiers holding halberds stood at attention, blocking the way.

My blood was pounding. *I was here*. Baldwin sat on the other side. All I had to do was talk my way inside.

A herald wearing the eagle emblem of Baldwin seemed

to be keeping track of appointments. Some people were told to sit and wait; others, brimming with self-importance, were passed through.

When it was my turn I stepped up and announced, boldly, 'I am Hugh, from Blois, cousin to Palimpost the Droll. I was told I could find him here.'

At the herald's quizzical gaze, I whispered to him, '*Family enterprise.*'

'I pray, from the funny side of the family,' the herald sniffed. He gave me a quick once-over. 'You'll no doubt find him snoozing with the dogs. Just keep away while business is in session.'

To my shock, he waved me in.

I stepped into the Great Hall. The room was enormous – at least three storeys: tall, rectangular and long. It was filled with a throng of people, both queuing for the duke's attention or lying about idly at long tables. A huge hearth near the duke was ablaze with fire.

A voice rang out above the din. From behind a huddle of merchants and moneylenders arguing ledgers, I pushed to a vantage point where I could see.

It was Baldwin!

He was sitting, more like slouching, on a large, high-backed oak chair elevated above the room. A completely disinterested look was on his face, as if these boring proceedings were all that held him from a preferred day of hunting and hawking.

Beneath him, a petitioning commoner knelt upon one knee.

The sight of Baldwin sent a chill racing down my spine. For weeks I had thought of little more than driving my knife through the base of his neck. His jet-black hair fell to his shoulders and his chin was sharp with a short black beard. He was wrapped against the chill in a purple and gold robe over a loose-fitting shirt and hose.

I spotted my rival, Palimpost, in a similar garb to myself, reclined on a step to his side, throwing dice.

Some formal matter was under discussion. A yellow-clad bailiff, pointing towards the kneeling serf, said, 'The petitioner seeks to deny the right of patrimony, lord.'

'The right of patrimony . . .?' Baldwin turned to an advisor. 'Is the right of the first-born not the foundation of all property law?'

'It is, my lord,' the advisor agreed.

'For nobles, for men of property, yes,' the petitioner rose, 'but we are humble farmers. This flock of sheep is all we have. My older brother is a drunkard. He hasn't done a day's work at the farm in years. My wife and I . . . this farm is everything to us. It is how we pay our fief to you.'

'You, farmer,' Baldwin peered, 'you are a working man at all costs? You do not drink yourself?'

'On holidays, perhaps . . .' The farmer hesitated, not knowing how to answer. 'At feasts . . . when we celebrated our vows.'

'So, it seems, I am forced to decide how to divide these sheep between *two* drunkards,' Baldwin grinned. A wave of laughter echoed through the cavernous room.

'But, my lord—' the farmer rose.

'Be still,' the duke motioned. 'The law must be obeyed. And to do so, the flock must be transferred to a first-born. Is that not right? Yet, your reserve is warranted, I think, farmer. Should the flock be wasted, we will not be enriched in any way. It occurs to me, there is an option.' He beamed around the room. '*I* am a first-born.'

'*You*, my lord?' the petitioner gasped.

'Yes.' Baldwin smiled, broadly. 'The *first* of the first-born, wouldn't you say so, Chamberlain?'

'You are the lord, my liege.' The chamberlain bowed.

'Therefore, it seems the law would be upheld nicely should these precious sheep revert to me,' Baldwin declared.

The horrified farmer looked around for some support.

'So, I take them,' Baldwin announced, 'in the name of patrimony.'

'But, my lord,' the farmer pressed forward, 'these sheep are all we have.'

An anger swept through my veins. I wanted to lunge at Baldwin, plunge my dagger into his throat. This was the man who had stolen everything from me, with the same ease and indifference with which he now ruined this poor man. But I had to restrain myself. It was Sophie I came for, not revenge for the ills this farmer suffered.

A page leaned over to Baldwin. 'Your hawks await, my lord.'

'Good . . . Is there any more business before the Court?' Baldwin asked, implying he wanted none.

I swallowed nervously. This was my chance, the reason why I had come. I pushed my way to the front.

'I have business, my lord!'

Chapter Forty-Three

'There is the matter of your western lands,' I called out from the throng of petitioners.

'Who speaks?' Baldwin asked, startled. A surprised buzz worked through the crowd of petitioners.

'A *knight*, my lord,' I shouted. 'I have taken a raiding party and sacked and burned all the villages of your enemies in the west.'

Baldwin stood up. He leaned over to his seneschal. 'But we don't have any enemies in the west.'

I took a breath and edged myself out from the crowd. 'I am sorry, my lord, but I fear that you do *now*.'

Slowly, steadily, a trail of laughter trickled through the room. As the joke became clear, it grew heartier.

'It is a *fool*,' I heard someone say. 'A performance.'

Baldwin glared and stepped towards me. His icy stare made my blood run cold. 'Who are you, fool? What has prompted you to speak?'

'I am Hugh. From Blois.' I bowed. 'I have studied under Norbert, the famous jester there. I am informed that your court is greatly in need of a laugh.'

'A laugh? My court hungers for *a laugh*?' Baldwin

squinted, uncomprehendingly. 'You are certainly fool-born, man, I grant you that. And you have come all this way from the big city to amuse us.'

'That is so, my lord.' I bowed again, nerves flashing through me.

'Well, your journey is wasted,' the noble said. 'We already have a fool, here. Don't we, Palimpost, my droll pet?'

The jester sprang up, an old, club-footed man with white hair and thick lips, who looked as if he had just been jolted awake.

'With all due respect,' I said, stepping into the middle of the room and addressing the court, 'I have heard that Palimpost couldn't get a laugh from a drunken sot. That he has lost his touch. I say, hear me out. If you are not happy, I will be on my way.'

'The boy sports a challenge to you,' Baldwin grinned at his jester.

'Restrain him, my lord.' Palimpost pointed at me. 'Do not listen. He means to create unrest in your dukedom.'

'Our only unrest, my dizzy-eyed fool, is from the dullness of your wit. Perhaps the lad is right. Let us see what he brings from Blois.'

Baldwin stepped down from his platform. He made his way across the room towards me. 'Make us laugh, and we will see about your future. Fail, and you'll be practising jokes to the rats in our keep.'

'It's fair, my lord.' I vowed, 'I will make you laugh.'

Chapter Forty-Four

I strolled to the centre of the huge room. A hundred pairs of eyes followed me.

In a group of lounging knights, I spotted Norcross, the duke's military strategist and his chatelain. I eyed him tremulously, though he did not look my way. Every sense told me this was the man who had killed my son.

'You have all no doubt heard the tale of the cow from Amiens,' I crowed.

People looked at each other and shook their heads. 'We have not,' someone yelled out. 'Tell us, jester.'

'These two peasants had a single dinar between them. So to enlarge their fortune, they decided to buy a cow, and every day they would sell its milk. Now as everyone knows, the best cows in the land come from Amiens. So they went there, and they traded the dinar for the best cow they could find, who yielded lots of milk. And they sold the milk each morning. Then one of them said, "If we can mate this fine cow, we'll have two. We can double our milk and our money." So they searched their village and found the finest bull. Soon, they were going to be rich.'

I scanned the room. Everyone seemed to hang on my

words. A hundred smiles . . . knights, ladies-in-waiting, even the duke himself. I had them. I had their ears . . .

'The day of the mating, they brought in the bull. First, he tried to mount the cow from behind, but the cow wiggled away. Then, the bull came at her from the left, but the cow wiggled her rump to the right. If it came from the right, the cow wiggled left.'

I spotted an attractive lady and went up to her. I wiggled my own rump with a smile. Just enough to be considered charmingly amusing. The crowd *oooed* with delight.

'Finally,' I said, 'the peasants threw up their hands in frustration. There was no way this cow from Amiens would mate. But instead of giving up, they decided to consult the smartest person in the duchy, a knight of such rare wisdom, such vision, he knew why all things were as they were.'

I noticed Norcross reclining on his elbow, following the tale. I strode up to him. 'Someone like *you*, knight,' I snapped.

The crowd cackled. 'Your story errs there,' said Baldwin, laughing, 'if it's brains you want.'

'So I've heard,' I bowed to the duke, 'but for the purpose of the tale, he'll do.'

Norcross's amusement began to sour and he glared at me, red-faced.

'So the peasants came to this *very* wise knight and they told him of their problem with the cow. They moaned, "What must we do?"

'The wise knight replied, "You say, if you try to mount it this way, it wiggles left? And from this direction, it wiggles right?"

' "Yes," they cried.

'The knight thought it over. "I do not know if I can solve your dilemma," he said, "but I know one thing. Your cow is from Amiens, is it not?"

' "Yes, yes," the peasants shouted. "It is indeed from Amiens. How could you possibly know?" '

I turned back to Norcross. I perched on the table next to him. ' "Because my wife," the knight muttered, "*she* is from Amiens as well." '

The hall burst into laughter – the knights, the duke, the ladies – all except Norcross. Then the vast room echoed with applause.

Baldwin came up and slapped me on the back. 'You are indeed funny, fool. You have other jokes like this?'

'Many,' I replied. To punctuate the point, I sprang into a forwards flip, then one backwards. The crowd *oooed*.

'They must laugh well in Blois. You may stay, my new companion. You are hired.'

I raised my arms in triumph. The large room echoed with applause. But inside, I knew I stood inches from the very men I had sworn to kill.

'Palimpost, as of this day, you are retired,' Baldwin declared. 'Show the new fool your spot.'

'Retired? But I have no desire for that, my liege. Haven't I served you with all my wit?'

'With what little you have. So you are *un*retired then. I grant you a new job. In the graveyard. See if you can cheer up the audience there.'

Chapter Forty-Five

Two days after my arrival, Baldwin announced a great feast at court, with counts, knights and noble-born invited from all over the province. The duke knew how to waste what had been earned by his poor serfs.

I was instructed by the lord's chamberlain that I would be a main act at the festivities. Baldwin's wife, the Lady Héloïse, had heard of my audition and was eager to hear more.

This would be my first real test!

The day of the gathering, the entire castle bustled with activity. An endless army of servants wearing their finest uniforms, tunics of green and gold, marched elaborate silverware and candelabras into the Great Hall. Minstrels practised on the lawn. Cooks chopped giant logs, which were loaded in the hearths. The luscious aroma of roasting goose, pigs and sheep permeated the castle.

I spent the day polishing my routine. This was my coming-out, my first real performance. I had to shine, to remain in Baldwin's good graces. I juggled, twirled my staff, practised my flips back and forth, went over my tales and jokes.

Finally, the evening of the feast was at hand. Nervous as a groom, I made my way to the banquet hall. Four long tables filled the room, each covered in the finest linen cloth and set with silverware and candelabras engraved with the duke's eagle.

Arriving guests were greeted with a flourish of trumpets. I sauntered up to each, announcing them with playful epithets. 'His bawdiness, the Duke of Loire, and his lovely niece, er . . . *wife*, the Lady Kate.' It was all meant to trump the husband and praise his wife, no matter how plain she might be. Everyone played along.

Only when the room filled, did Baldwin and his lady, Héloïse, make their entrance. One glance made it obvious to me that Baldwin had not married for looks. The couple waded through the room, Baldwin hugging and joking with the men, Héloïse curtsying and receiving lavish praise. They took seats at the head of the largest table.

When their guests were seated, Baldwin stood and raised a goblet. 'Welcome, everyone. Tonight we have much to cheer. The court has been enriched by a new flock. And the arrival of a fool from Blois. Hugh will make us laugh, or else.'

'I have heard my husband's new pet is quite the rage,' Lady Héloïse announced. 'Perhaps he will set the tone with a few jests.'

I took a deep breath, then I hopped around to the head table. 'I'll do my best, my lady . . .'

I scampered towards her, but then threw myself into the lap of a fat old man seated down the row. I grinned, stroking his beard. 'I would be honoured to perform for you, your grace. I—'

'*Here*, fool,' Lady Héloïse called. 'I am over *here* . . .'

'Gads.' I shot out of the man's lap. 'Of course, my lady. I must've been blinded by your beauty. So much so, I could not see.'

There was a trickle of laughter.

'Surely, fool,' Lady Héloïse called, 'you did not have the crowd shouting your name the other day with such mild flattery. Perhaps it is I who am blinded. Is that Hugh I see there, or Palimpost?'

The room chuckled at their hostess's wit. Even I bowed, warming to the challenge.

At the end of the table, a pot-bellied priest was sucking down a mug of ale. I hopped on the table in front of him, plates and mugs clattering. 'There's *this one*, then. A man went to a priest to confess his many sins. He said he had much to share.'

The priest looked up. 'To me?'

'We'll see, Father, how you feel about it at the end. First, the man confessed he had stolen from a friend, but added that this friend had stolen something back of equal value. "One thing cancels out another," the priest replied. "You are absolved." '

'It is true,' the priest nodded.

'Next,' I went on, 'the fellow said he had beaten the man with a stick, but had received equal blows in return. "Again, these both cancel each other out," the priest replied. "You owe God nothing."

'Now this penitent sensed he could get away with anything. He said there was something else to confess, one more sin, but he was too ashamed. When the priest encouraged him, he said. "Once, Father, I had your sister."

' "*My sister* . . . *!*" the priest bellowed. The man was sure he was about to feel a holy wrath. "And I have had your mother, on several occasions," the priest said. "Again, they cancel each other out. So we are *both* absolved." '

The guests clapped with laughter. The embarrassed priest looked around the room and clapped as well.

'More, fool,' Lady Héloïse shouted, 'in the same temper.' She turned to Baldwin. 'Where have you been hiding this treasure?'

The room bubbled with good cheer. More food was served – swan and geese and pig. Goblets were filled by servants scurrying about.

I leaped up to a server carrying a roast goose on a tray. I took a whiff of the meat. 'Superb,' I sighed. 'Who knows the difference between medium and rare?'

Diners at the tables looked around and shrugged.

I went up to a blushing lady. 'This is medium, my lady.' I indicated a hand-span. Then extended my whole arm. 'But this is rare.'

Again, they roared, I had it going. I spotted Baldwin taking congratulations, seeming delighted with the performance.

To much fanfare, a train of servers marched in from the kitchen, carrying prepared plates. Baldwin stood. 'Lamb, guests, from our new flock. Made with a new spice from the east, called cinnamon, brought back from the Crusade.'

Baldwin stuck in a knife and chewed off a piece in front of his server. 'Delicious, server, wouldn't you say?'

'It is, my lord,' the server bowed stiffly.

To my horror, I realized that the dejected servant was the same farmer from whom Baldwin had chiselled the flock just two days before. Suddenly, my blood stirred in rage.

'Please, jester, do continue,' Baldwin said through a mouthful of meat.

'I will, my lord,' I bowed.

I spotted Norcross at the end of Baldwin's table amongst a row of knights, stabbing his meat. 'Is that my Lord Norcross I see stuffing his face over there?'

Norcross looked up, his eyes narrowed on me.

'Tell me,' I asked the crowd, 'who is a greater hero to Our Lord than the brave Norcross? Who, amongst us, could be more forgiven for conceit? In fact, I have heard this good knight is so *conceited*, that during copulation he calls out his *own* name.'

Norcross put his knife down. He stared at me, juice running through his beard. Laughter ensued, but as the knight's face tightened, it trickled away.

The knight shot up, drawing his sword. He lunged around the crowded table towards me.

I pretended to flee. 'Help me, help me, my lord. I have no sword, yet I fear I have struck too deep.'

I did a flip and ran around the table towards Baldwin. Norcross pursued, slightly drunk.

I easily avoided him, circling the table to the merriment of the crowd, who almost seemed to be taking bets whether the knight would catch me and cut my throat. Finally, I threw myself in the protection of Baldwin's lap. 'He will kill me, my lord.'

'He will not,' Baldwin replied. 'Relax, Norcross. Our new fool has managed to get under your skin. A good laugh, not a killing, should soothe the wound.'

'He insults me, my lord. I stand for that from no man.'

'This is no man,' Baldwin cackled, 'he is but a fool. And he provides us much entertainment.'

'I have served you well,' the red-faced knight seethed. 'I demand to fight the fool.'

'You will not.' Lady Héloïse rose. 'The fool has acted on my bidding. If anything untimely happens to him, I will know the author. You may feel safe, Hugh.'

Norcross exhaled a deep, frustrated breath, the object of all eyes in the room. Slowly, he let his massive sword slip back into its sheath.

'Next time, fool,' he said, 'the laugh will be mine.' He went back to his seat, never once removing his stare from me.

'You have picked an adversary who is not one to anger,' Baldwin chuckled as he ate his lamb. He tossed some bits of fat off his plate to the floor. 'Here. Help yourself.'

I looked across the room at Norcross. I knew I had made an enemy for life.

But so had he.

Chapter Forty-Six

I had no time to waste. I set out to find Sophie. She was alive. *I knew it.*

My confrontation with Norcross had given me instant status among the castle staff. I was given a name, Hugh the Brave, or, I was told, with respect to Norcross's wrath, Hugh *the Brief*. People whom I sensed served the duke only out of fear or obligation came and whispered their support. I was able to make a few useful friends.

There was Nellie, the cook, a roly-poly, red-faced woman with a sharp tongue who kept the kitchen running like a spotless ship. And Marcel, the upstairs *valet du chambre*, who took meals in the kitchen next to me. Even a cheerful sergeant-at-arms, Auguste, whom I noticed chuckling at my jokes.

I probed all of them, asking if they had heard of a beautiful, golden-haired woman held captive in the castle, keeping my reasons close to my chest. No one had.

'Checked the brothels?' Auguste winked. 'Once the nobles have no use for'm, they'd be sent there.'

So I did. I made the rounds, pretending to be a choosy

customer. But thank God no one fitting Sophie's description was among the poor whores at Tours.

'You look a little drawn in the face, for a jester,' Nellie observed one morning, as she pounded out her morning dough. 'Your lost sweetheart, again?'

I wished I could take her into my confidence. 'Not mine, Nellie, but a friend's,' I lied. 'Someone asked me to enquire.'

'A *friend's*, you say.' The cook eyed me sceptically. She seemed to play with me. 'Is she highborn or common?'

I looked up from my bowl. 'How would a rogue like me know anyone highborn?' I grinned, 'except *you*, perhaps . . .'

'Oh yes, me,' Nellie cackled. 'I'm the duke's own blood. That's why I slave in this hearth until dark every day.'

She laughed and went about her chores. But when she returned, lugging a pot, she crept behind me and said, almost seditiously, 'Perhaps it's The Tavern you want, love . . .'

I looked up. 'The Tavern?'

She reached on her tiptoes for a bowl of garlic heads high on a shelf. 'The dungeons,' she said under her breath, 'they're always filled with mouths to feed. At least, for a short while. We call them The Tavern. Everyone goes in on their own two feet, but usually it takes a team of four to carry them out.'

I looked to thank her, but Nellie quickly breezed to the other side of the kitchen, peeling the garlic for her soup.

For days afterwards, I spied upon the dungeons in the courtyard while taking my daily stroll, the heavy iron door always guarded by at least two soldiers from Baldwin's reserve. Once or twice I sauntered over, trying to warm up the guards. I did a little magic trick, tossed some balls in the air, twirled my staff. I never got as much as a snigger.

'Bugger off, fool,' one guard barked at me. 'No one here even remembers how to laugh.'

'You want a peek?' another barked. 'I'm sure Norcross'll find you a room.'

I hurried away, pretending his very name had sent me trembling. But I continued plotting. How to get in? Who could help me? I tried the chamberlain. I even tried to play my liege, Baldwin. One day, after court, I sidled up to him.

'Time for a drink, my liege. How about I buy you one . . . in The Tavern?'

Baldwin laughed to his coterie. 'Fool wants a drink so bad, he's willing to risk the pox to get it.'

One night, as I took my meal in the kitchen, Nellie sat down with me. 'You are a strange sort, Hugh. All day, you're smiles and tricks. But at night you sulk and brood like a lost lover. Why do I think this loss you feel is not a friend's?'

I could no longer hide my sadness. I had to trust someone. 'You are right, Nellie. It's my wife I seek. She was taken from my village by raiding knights. I know she is here. I can feel it in my blood.'

Nellie did not show surprise. She only smiled. 'I knew you were no fool,' she said. 'And I can be a friend,' she added, 'if you need one.'

'I need one more than you can know,' I said, desperately. 'But *why*?'

'Be sure, not for your silly tricks, Hugh, or your flattery.' Nellie's expression changed, grew warmer. 'Geoffrey and Isabel, Hugh – they are my cousins. Why do you think I always saved you the best scraps of meat? You don't think you're that funny, do you? I owe you their lives, Hugh.'

I grasped her hands. 'The Tavern, Nellie. I have to get in. I've tried everything, but there's no way.'

The cook stared at me a long time, searching my intentions. 'For a fool, maybe. Only a fool would want to get *in* to The Tavern. But there's a saying here: the best way to end up in the soup is to ask the cook!'

Chapter Forty-Seven

It was chilly in Blois. A wind blew stiff and cold over the gardens. The Lady Emilie huddled in her cloak against the night's chill. At her side was the jester, Norbert.

Emilie had tried to work on her needlepoint that night, but her mind kept drifting into space like wisps of smoke. Her heart ached with a confusion she had never known before. It always came back to one thing. One face.

What is happening to me? she wondered. I feel I am going mad.

Norbert had noticed her preoccupation. The jester had knocked on her door earlier that evening. 'I know laughter, my lady, and to know that, I must know melancholy too.'

'So you are a jester and now a physician too?' she pretended to scold him.

'It takes no physician to see what ails you, lady. You miss the lad, don't you?'

With anyone else, she would have bitten her tongue. 'I do miss him, jester. I cannot lie.'

Norbert sat across from her. 'You're not alone. I miss him too.'

This was something new for Emilie. She was used to

feeling that men were like flies, nuisances, always buzzing around her, too concerned with their boasting and their deeds for her to take them seriously. But this was different. How had it happened? She had only known Hugh for a few weeks. His life was a world apart from hers, yet she knew everything about him. Most likely, she would never see him again.

'I feel I have sent him on this quest,' she told Norbert, 'and now I wish I could bring him back.'

'You did not send him, lady. And, with all respect, he is not yours to bring back.'

No, Norbert was right. Hugh was not hers. She had only stumbled upon him.

So she huddled in the garden that night. She needed to feel the cold around her shoulders. Somehow, out here, knowing he was under the same moon, she felt closer to him. *I don't know if I will ever see you again, Hugh DeLuc. But I pray I will. Somehow, some way.*

'You risk a lot to have such feelings,' Norbert said.

'They are not planned. They just . . . *are.*'

He took her hand. There was a moment between them, not as lady and servant, but as friends. Emilie blushed, then smiled. 'It seems my heart is owned by jesters from all around.'

'Do not worry, my lady. Our Red is canny and resourceful. I taught him, you know. A chip off the old block. I'm sure he's fine. He'll find his wife.'

'A jester and a physician and now a seer too?' She hugged the jester. 'Thank you, Norbert.' Then she watched him go back inside.

Now the night air bit into her bones. It was late. The

garden was still. She had promised the priest she would wake early for morning prayers. 'Be safe, Hugh DeLuc,' she whispered, then turned back towards the castle.

She headed along the loggia above the gardens to the living quarters. Then, out of the night, voices came to her from below.

Who could be out here at this hour in the bitter cold? Emilie hid behind a column and peered into the deep shadows.

A man and a woman. Voices raised.

She strained to hear. 'This is not it, knight,' the woman said. 'This is not the treasure.'

It was Anne. Out there in the dark with a man. Not a knight – more like a monk. In robes. But with a sword.

Emilie thought she had stumbled across something she should not have seen. Anne was angry. She'd never heard her mistress's tone this hard.

'You know what my husband wants,' she said. '*Find it!*'

Chapter Forty-Eight

A few days later, as I took my evening meal, Nellie the cook winked and drew me aside. 'There's a way,' she said. 'If you still want to see The Tavern.'

'How?' I asked, leaning in close. 'And how soon?'

'It's not exactly a state secret, jester. People have to eat, don't they? Guards, soldiers . . . even prisoners. Every day my kitchen brings the evening meal. Who would mind if it was brought by the fool?'

My eyes lit up. The fool doing errands for the cook. It could work.

'I will give it a try,' Nellie said, 'the rest is up to you. If your wife is there, Hugh, it will take more than luck to get her out. Just don't bring the duke's awful wrath down on me.'

I took her hand and squeezed it. 'I would bring nothing down upon you except my gratitude. I owe you much, Nellie.'

'I told you, I owe you my cousin's life.'

'But somehow, I think it is more than what I've done for Geoffrey, Isabel and Thomas on the road here.'

She smiled and tossed a turnip in the pot. 'Baldwin is our

liege,' she sniffed, 'but he can never rule our hearts. I see why you have come. I can see you are in love. These hands may be rough and ugly, but I am not so removed from matters of the heart.'

I began to blush. 'Am I so transparent?'

'Don't worry, love, no one else would notice. They're too busy grabbing their sides and laughing at your silly jokes.'

I raised an onion, the way one would raise a mug to make a toast. 'We will keep each other's trust, Nellie.'

She lifted a turnip. We tapped them together.

'I feel a headache coming on,' she frowned, '*tomorrow eve*. Be here at dusk. And something else, Hugh. You asked if a woman was being held in the cells. I checked. There *is* a lady staying in The Tavern, one who might fit your wife's description. Fair-haired.'

These words were like the most exquisite magic for my soul. What was only a hope for so long now sprang free. *Sophie was here!* I knew it now. I would see her, tomorrow night. At last!

I hugged Nellie, almost knocking the poor woman into her pot of soup.

Chapter Forty-Nine

All the next day I waited for dusk to fall. Time passed with agonizing slowness. To make things worse, Baldwin called for me to entertain him while he got new boots measured by a shoemaker. What scum he was. I had to keep him amused while I thought of plunging a dagger in his heart.

Yet all the while, I could barely count the time. I kept repeating Nellie's words. I went over in my mind what I would do, how I would pull this off. I dreamed of Sophie's face – the face I had known since I was a child. I imagined us back at our old inn. Rebuilding it from scratch, starting our life again. Having another child . . .

I sat on my bare mat as the afternoon wound down, watching the sun decline. Finally, the light from the slats above my space grew dim. It was dusk, time to see Sophie.

I made my way down to the kitchen. Nellie was bustling about, complaining to the staff, a damp cloth pressed to her head for effect. 'I've got to lie down. I've got the duke's meals still to prepare. Who will carry the soup to The Tavern? Hugh, what luck,' she said, spotting me. 'Will you be a dear?'

'I am but two hands,' I joked to the staff, 'and *one*...' I wiggled a finger and sniffed with a turned up face, 'I use for scratching.'

'That's all I need.' Nellie led me away. 'Just make sure the other stays out of the soup.'

She lowered a covered pot from the hearth and announced. 'Give it to Armand, the gaoler. And give him that jug of wine. You've done me a good turn, fool.' Then she gripped me conspiratorially on the arm. 'I wish you luck, Hugh. Be careful. It's a bad place you go to now. It is Hell.'

I carried the load down the kitchen steps and across the dark courtyard. My arms trembled a bit. Two guards stood at the door of the keep, different ones from those who had booted me away the other day.

'*Ding, ding, ding*... it's the dinner bell,' I announced ceremoniously.

'Who the hell are they putting to work in the kitchen now?' one of them smirked.

'I do it all, jokes to dessert. The duke's expenses must be trimmed.'

'The duke must be bankrupt if he sent you,' the other guard said.

To my relief, they didn't question me. One opened the heavy door. 'If you had nicer tits, I'd carry it down for you,' he sniffed.

The door slammed shut behind me. I felt a tremor of relief. *I was in!*

I stood in a narrow stone corridor, lit only by dim candles, a stairway leading down.

A draught hit me, then noises – the *clang* of iron,

someone calling out, a high-pitched wail. I made my way down cautiously, my heart nearly bounding out of my chest, my neck beaded in a cold sweat.

I descended, one step at a time, the pot clanging against the narrow walls, the wine jug pressed to my chest.

The fearsome noises intensified. The smell grew horrible, like burned flesh. It made me think of Civetot.

Poor Sophie . . . I winced. If she was here, I had to get her out tonight.

Finally, the passageway levelled off into a low, dungeon-like setting. The foul stink of excrement was here, and also vomit and piss. There was shouting from within, like mad people, terrifying moans and shrieks. I saw a hearth, and in it, iron instruments, their tips white with heat.

My stomach grew hollow. Suddenly I did not know what to do if I found her.

Two soldiers sat straddling a wooden tabletop, dressed down to sleeveless tunics and skirts. A swarthy one, with hulking, imposing shoulders, sniggered at the sight of me. 'We must be fucked. Look who brings our dinner.'

'You're Armand?' I lugged the pot over.

He shrugged. 'And if you're the new chef, the duke's really got it in for these poor bastards. Where's Nellie?'

'Down with an illness. She sent me instead.'

'Just set it here. There's a pot from this afternoon you can take back up.'

I placed the pot on the table by a stack of wooden bowls. 'How many guests tonight in The Tavern?'

'What's it to you?' the other asked.

'Never been down here before.' I looked around, ignoring him. 'Cheery. You mind if I take a look?'

'This isn't a playpen, fool. You've done your chore. Now bugger off.'

My chance was slipping away. I felt I only had a moment more to make my case. 'C'mon, let me take in their food. I spend my day making silly jokes and spinning around like a top. Let me take a look. I'll bring them their bowls.'

I placed the wine jug on the table in front of him. 'Anyway, do you fellows really want to touch that slop?'

Armand slowly pulled the jug towards him. He took a swig of wine, then passed it along.

'What the hell?' He winked to his partner. 'Why not give the jester's dick its rise. Take what you want in there. It's free for the asking.'

Chapter Fifty

I turned a corner in the dungeon and then I could make out the cells. The odour here was beyond belief, nearly unbearable. *My God, Sophie . . .*

I set down the soup pot and started to work. These people had to be fed, and while I did the task, I would search for Sophie in every dark corner.

I began sloshing thin, murky gruel into bowls. Inside, my heart beat like a warning bell swung furiously back and forth.

I carried two bowls to the first cell. My hands were trembling. Soup splattered all over the floor.

At first glance, the cell seemed to be empty. It was like a cave opening, dug out from solid rock, just a few feet deep – no light or sound, just the reek of human filth. A wet rat slithered out in front of my eyes.

Then, in the back, I saw the glow of eyes. They flickered, tremulous and afraid. From out of the shadows – a head. Hairless, gaunt, a sunken face covered with sores oozing pus.

The prisoner crawled towards me, wild-eyed. 'I mus' be dead, if it's a fool come for me.'

'Better a fool than St Peter.' I kneeled and shoved a bowl through the bars.

His thin, palsied hand darted out and scooped up the wooden bowl. A momentary sadness ran through me. I had no idea what he had done to put him here. In Tours, there was no reason to assume he was guilty of anything.

But I was not here for *him*.

In the next cell was curled a Moor. He was naked and filthy; rats nibbled at sores on his legs. He muttered in a tongue I did not understand. He barely looked up at me, glassy-eyed. 'Take heart, old man.' I passed the bowl under the bars. 'Your time is almost up.'

I passed on to the next cells, not even going back for more soup. As with the first, the captives looked more like hunted animals than men. They groaned, peered out at me with beaten, yellow eyes. I took a breath against the urge to retch violently.

Then from further along came a wail. *A woman!* My body tensed. *Sophie?* I did not know if I could go on.

'There's your date, fool.' Armand brayed from his post. 'Feel free to slip inside if she suits you. She has a magical tongue.'

I clenched my fists and made my way towards the woman's cries. Inside my belt, I grasped the hilt of my knife. If this was Sophie, I would surely kill the guards. Norcross too.

The woman's wail echoed again. 'Go to her, fool. The bitch doesn't like to be stood up,' yelled Armand.

I held my breath and stepped in front of the woman's cell. The stench was worse here. Unbearable. Why was that?

She was crouched in a tight ball deep in the cell. A beam

of light slanted across her hair, which was long and straggly. She seemed to clutch on to a doll or toy, whimpering like an abandoned child herself. 'My baby,' she called, no more than a whisper. 'Please . . . my baby needs milk . . .'

I could barely see her. I could not make out her age or face. I gathered myself and said, 'Is that you, Sophie?' A fear shot through me. My breath froze. To be kept like this – it would be better if she were dead.

The woman sputtered out nearly incoherent phrases. 'Poor baby . . .' she muttered. 'Baby needs milk . . .' Then something that sounded like . . . *Philippe*.

Oh God. I froze. I stepped closer to the bars. What had they done to her? 'Sophie,' I called. It seemed her shape, her hair. *Please, turn towards me. Let me see.* My tongue grew dry on her name.

'Little one needs milk . . .' she mumbled again. 'What can I do? Breasts are dry.'

Tears welled in my eyes. I still could not see. 'Sophie . . .' I said again.

I rammed myself up against the bars. 'Baby needs milk,' I heard her say, then suddenly she emitted an ear-splitting, wrenching howl. It was like a blade running through me.

I reached out and her eyes finally caught sight of me. The breath froze in my chest. Her straw-like hair was falling over her face. But her eyes locked on mine. Yellow. Veins running through them. The nose flat and pocked.

Oh God! It was not her.

My legs buckled. *It was not her.* Part of me was giddy with joy; another, crestfallen and disappointed.

'My baby . . .' the woman called, pleading. She held out the doll for me to see.

Oh God, I cringed. My body recoiled. It was no doll. *It was real.* A tiny, nascent child, bound in a placenta, clearly dead, unborn.

'How can I help you?' I whispered. 'How?'

'Can't you see?' She pushed the placenta out to me. 'The child needs milk.'

'Let me help.'

'Milk!' the mad woman shrieked. 'Feed him!'

There was nothing I could do. The poor woman was raving mad.

I stared for a moment more, then flung myself back down the corridor towards the stairs.

The gaolers laughed as I went by. 'Leaving so soon, fool?' cried Armand. 'What, no jokes?'

I bolted out of the dungeon and up the stairs.

177

Chapter Fifty-One

I ran in a cold sweat back to the castle and my alcove under the stairs. There, I threw myself on my mat. My breath raced, panicked and wild.

It was not her . . .

My beloved Sophie must be dead after all.

For the first time, I knew what had been understood all along by the people in my town, Sophie's brother, even Norbert, my mentor. There was no hope. She had been ripped from her child, raped, and left to die on the road. I knew it now, the darkest lesson in my life.

I buried my head in my hands. This silly charade was over. I had clung to a hope and now that hope was dashed. I must go. I ripped off my jester's hat and threw it on to the floor. I was no jester. Just a fool! A bigger fool had never lived.

I sat there for a long time, letting the truth sink in.

I heard footsteps shuffling near my bed, then a voice. 'Is that you, Hugh?'

I raised my head to see Estella, the chamberlain's wife.

She had winked at me in court many times. She'd grabbed at me and teased. Tonight, she had a loose shawl covering her shoulders; thick, auburn hair, that I had only seen braided and pinned, fell all about her neck. Her eyes were round and mischievous. And her timing couldn't have been worse!

'The hour is late, my lady. I am not at work.'

'Perhaps I did not come for work,' Estella said, stepping into my bed-space. She let her shawl drop, revealing a loosely fitting bodice.

'What striking red hair,' she whispered. 'Now how is it such a fiery fool can look so sad?'

'Please, my lady, I am not one for jokes this night. I'll be funny again in the morning.'

'I don't need to laugh right now, Hugh. Let me feel you in another way.'

She sat down beside me. Close. Her body was scented with fresh lavender and lilies. She reached out and stroked my face. I moved back from her touch.

'I have never seen such hair.' She seemed fixed on it. 'It is the colour of a flame. What are you really like, Hugh, when you are free of all those jokes?'

She pushed herself even closer. I felt the fullness of her breasts press against my chest. One of her legs straddled mine.

'Please, my lady.'

But Estella pressed on. She wiggled her shoulders, letting her blouse fall to her waist. Her breasts tumbled forward. Then I felt the hot tip of her tongue dance on my neck.

'I bet other parts of you contain the same fire as your hair. Touch me, Hugh. If you do not, I'll tell the duchess you tried to grope under my dress. A commoner touching a noble's wife . . . Not a role you'd want to play.'

I was in a trap. If I denied her molestations, I would be charged with molesting her. She nibbled at me. Then her hand entered my tunic, probing for my cock.

At that moment I felt the tip of a blade digging into my neck. I held very still. A male voice boomed, 'What mischief have I stumbled on to?'

Chapter Fifty-Two

The knife slowly drew back my head and I turned into the face of Norcross. The monster was grinning down on me.

Norcross dug the blade in deeper and I felt the warmth from blood trickling down my neck.

'A nasty situation, fool. The Lady Estella is the wife of the duke's chamberlain, a member of the court. You must be mad to wag your dick at such a lady.'

Panic pumped through my chest as I realized I had been caught in a trap. 'I did nothing, my lord.' My heart pounded wildly.

'The little dick had no urge,' Estella sighed. 'It appears our fool's only ardour is in his hair.'

Norcross grabbed me by the tunic and raised me, blade under my chin. Suddenly the bastard's eyes lit up with recognition.

'His *hair* . . . I do know you from somewhere. Where, fool, tell me?'

I saw that I was doomed. I stiffened a glare back in his face. 'My wife . . . What did you do to Sophie?'

'Your wife?' the knight sniffed. 'What would I do with the

wife of a lowly fool? Except fuck her.'

I lunged towards him, but he gripped me by the hair, and with the leverage of his arms and the blade stuck firmly under my chin, forced me slowly down to my knees. 'Listen carefully, fool. I *have* seen you. But *where*? Where have I seen your face before?'

'Veille du Père,' I spat out the words.

'That little shithole.' Norcross snorted.

'You burned our inn. You killed my wife and child, Philippe.'

He was thinking back. The tiniest smile cracked his lips. 'I *do* remember now. You were the little red squirrel who tried to stop me from dunking the miller's son.' Norcross's smile widened. 'And what of the vaunted Hugh? The jester of jesters, who studied under Norbert at Blois?' His grin deepened into a roaring laugh. '*You?* You are an innkeeper! A fraud.'

I pressed towards him again, but his blade made a sharp stab into my neck. I felt it cut skin. 'You took my wife. You hurled my son into flames.'

'If I did, all the merrier, you lowly worm,' Norcross shrugged. Then he winked towards Estella. 'I can see you are greatly offended, my lady. Go now and report the affront.'

She righted her blouse and scurried away. 'I will, my lord. Thank you for coming when you did.' She ran out of the room. 'Guards!' I heard her shout echo. 'Help me! Guards!'

Norcross turned back to me. His eyes were hard-set and victorious. 'What do you say, fool? It seems the laugh is mine after all.'

Chapter Fifty-Three

I was hurled, hands bound, into a dark, empty room in the keep. There I nervously passed the night.

I knew my fate was sealed. Lady Estella would play the offended role, just as she had played me last night; Norcross, the vindicated hero. It would be my word . . . against that of nobles. All the laughter in the world couldn't save me now.

I was jolted by a loud rattling at the door. A sliver of light appeared through an aperture in the roof. It was day. Three brawny guards in Baldwin's uniform came into the room. The captain yanked me up. 'If you know any good jokes, Carrot-top, now would be the time.'

I was pushed roughly towards the Great Hall. The court was buzzing with knights and courtiers just as on the day I had arrived. A messenger was informing the court about some renowned knight who had been slaughtered by outlaws in a neighbouring duchy.

Baldwin slouched on his elevated chair, chin in hand, and beckoned the man forward. 'The vaunted Adhemar . . . killed in his own home?'

'Not just killed, my lord,' the messenger was clearly

uncomfortable, forced to deliver such news,' . . . impaled to the wall of his chapel, his wife next to him. The lord was *crucified*.'

'Crucified?' Baldwin rose slowly. 'You say he was roused from his own bed by bandits?'

'Marauders, more like. They rode in, armed and dressed for battle, their faces hidden behind their headpieces. They bore no markings on their armour, except for one, a black cross.'

'A black cross?' Baldwin stretched his eyes. I could not tell if his shock was sincere or pretended. 'Nor*cross*, do you know of such a band?'

From the crowd, Norcross stepped forward. He had on a long red surcoat and his war sword hung at his belt. 'I do not, my liege.'

'Poor Adhemar,' Baldwin swallowed. 'Tell me, messenger, what treasure did these cowards seek?'

'I know not,' the messenger shook his head. 'Adhemar had just returned from the Holy Land, where he had been wounded. He was said to have come back bearing valuable spoils. I had heard, the very ashes of St Matthew.'

'Such a prize would be worth the price of a kingdom itself,' Baldwin gasped.

'Only one is holier,' Norcross said.

'The lance of Longius,' Baldwin's eyes flashed, 'whose blade was dipped in the Saviour's own blood.'

Hidden riders, burning and slaughtering. I did not doubt Norcross was behind these murders too. How I wanted to cut his throat.

'My lord,' Norcross continued, 'Adhemar's fate is sealed, but there is other business to be done.'

'Ah, yes, the fate of our little fool.' Baldwin waved the messenger away, then sat back down and, with his finger, motioned me forward.

'I am told, fool, your little dick was wagging itself around where it did not belong. You seem to have offended a great many people in your short stay with us.'

I pushed myself to my feet and glared at Norcross. 'It is *I* who has suffered the greatest offence.'

'You? How so?' Baldwin chuckled. 'Was Briesmont's wife so unpleasant?' He picked a fistful of nuts out of a bowl and began to munch.

'I never touched the lady.'

'And yet, the evidence says otherwise. You contradict the testimony of a member of my own court. Of the offended party as well. Their word against the word of a fool – from what I am now told, not even a *true* fool.'

I wrestled in my binds towards Norcross. 'This noble member of your court has killed my wife, my lord. My wife and child . . .'

There was a hush in the crowd.

Norcross shook his head. 'The fool has it in his mind that I have ruined him as punishment for abandoning his obligation to you when he ran off to the Crusade.'

'And did you, knight?' asked Baldwin.

The knight merely shrugged. 'Truly, my lord, I do not recall.'

A trickle of the cruellest laughter sprinkled through the room. 'The knight does not recall, ex-fool. Do you contradict again?'

'It was him, your lordship. His face was hidden, just like it was to this poor knight spoken of today.'

Norcross stepped towards me, reaching for his sword.

'Again, you incite me, fool. I will split you in two—'

'Be still.' The duke stopped him with his hand. 'You will have your chance. You make a grave charge, fool. Yet, I am informed this Crusade continues, that the armies of Raymond and Bohemond are now in sight of the Holy City. Yet *you*, somehow, are *here*. Tell me, how was your service there discharged so soon?'

I was about to stammer back a reply, but to this charge I had none. I dropped my head.

A condemning silence filled the room.

Baldwin curled a smile. 'You claim injury, fool, yet it seems it is *your* offences that begin to add up. To the crimes of adultery and fraud I must add desertion.'

A rising anger swelled in my chest. I lunged, in my binds, towards Norcross, but before I had gone a step, the duke's men kicked me to the floor.

'The fool wants at you, Norcross,' Baldwin grinned.

'And I *him*, my lord.'

'And you shall have him. But it belittles you, knight, to take him in contest. I think I have let you suffer ill from this squirrel once too often. Take him away.' He waved. 'At noon tomorrow, you may chop off his head.'

'You honour me,' the knight bowed.

Baldwin shook his head sadly. 'Fool, innkeeper, spy ... whatever I should call you, it is a great shame. We will have to deal with Palimpost once more. For your stay here, you certainly provided a good laugh.' He stood, wrapped his cloak around him, and prepared to leave. Then he turned. 'And Norcross ...'

'Yes, my liege?'

'No need to waste a sharp blade on the fool's neck.'

Chapter Fifty-Four

I was hurled down the stairs to the dungeon, my knees and ribs scraping against the hard, rock floor.

My nostrils clawed for air, forced to suck in that repulsive stench from the night before.

I heard laughter, the clang of a heavy door, as two burly guards grabbed my arms and tossed me into an open cell.

When my eyes cleared, I saw Armand, the gaoler, this time with a mocking grin. 'Back so soon, jester? You must have liked the accommodation after all.'

I was about to tell him to go to Hell, but he kicked me in the stomach and the air rushed out of my lungs. 'This time I'm afraid we'll be supplying the stew.'

The other guards laughed. Armand, with the strength of a beast, yanked me up to a sitting position. He kneeled next to me and shook his head. 'Always the scum they bring me. Never a noble accused of a fancy crime. Just the whores and the outlaws, church thieves, beggars, a few Jews . . . But a jester – that's a new one.'

Armand's partner came in, lugging an armful of heavy chains. 'So we must bind you, jester, and for such a short stay. But the duke has paid for the deluxe room, so chains it is.'

Armand held me up, pinning my hands behind my back. 'You're a lucky fool. The blade's painless. Just a little pinprick . . . *here.*' He pinched my neck. 'If you stayed here a while, I could show you some real fun. Ball-crackers, nostril-rippers, eye screws . . . red-hot pokers, right up the old arse. Sure cleans out the sinuses.'

He nodded towards his partner, who slowly wound the first ring of chain around my chest.

My mind flashed to attention. 'Please . . .' I put up a hand. 'Wait a moment.' I took a deep breath and sucked in a chest full of air.

'I know,' Armand sighed, 'it's a little confining at first. But when you get used to them, you'll be sleeping like a log.'

I put my hand up for another moment, then I flashed him a smile of thanks. I took in three heavy breaths, forcing as much air as I could into my lungs. I felt my whole chest expand.

'Ready?' the gaoler arched his brows. 'Or should I bring you a feather bed?'

Yes, I nodded. 'Ready.'

Chapter Fifty-Five

Inside the tiny cell, I twisted and squirmed on my back, and I ground my arms against the tight binds.

There was no light. I had no idea what time it was, how long I had been here. I only knew if I was here when they came tomorrow, I was a dead man.

I let out all my breath. And the slightest space opened to move my arms.

Hours passed away. A hair's breadth of freedom came. Then another. I felt the chains loosen, but not far enough.

I narrowed my shoulders and tucked my chin inside the chain. For the first time in hours, I took a breath with ease. I snaked one arm through the binds. Then the other, and a loop scraped over my head.

Then I heard the echo of voices down the walkway: someone delivering dinner. Time for soup. The guards were taking their meal, laughing as they ate.

Other prisoners were grumbling, calling out. Then footsteps . . . a last meal arriving for me.

'So,' a familiar voice sighed, 'it seems I am back in business.'

I raised my eyes. It was Palimpost, the deposed jester, standing in front of my cell. He carried my staff.

'Come to gloat?' I muttered, swallowing the bitterest taste of defeat.

'Not at all.' He dangled a set of keys. 'In truth, I have come to set you free.'

I widened my eyes in surprise. I was sure this had to be some kind of cruel joke. *Payback* . . . I waited for the guards to come and laugh. But they did not.

'Nellie and I have drugged the guards with the soup. Quick now, let's get you out of here.'

'*Nellie and you?*' I could not believe what he was saying. This was the man I had had sacked. Now he was dangling my freedom before my eyes. 'Is this true?'

'It is true, if you can get up off your arse.' He inserted a key in the lock and turned it, the door creaking open.

I still could not believe it. But it did not matter. Even if this was just a cruel joke, even if Norcross hid a few feet away, set to cut me in two, I was dead tomorrow anyway.

'Somehow we have to get you out of those chains,' Palimpost sighed.

'Not a problem!' I exclaimed. I wiggled my shoulders and arms, and before his eyes, slithered through the top coils. To the jester's astonishment, I began to unwrap the binds until they fell to my ankles. I kicked them free.

The jester looked amazed. 'Damn, you *are* good!' he muttered. He handed me my rod. 'Quick . . . c'mon.'

I held him back. '*Why* . . . why are you doing this for me?'

'Professional courtesy,' the jester shrugged.

'Please, do not joke.' I put my hand on his shoulder. 'Tell me why.'

He looked at me with pained eyes. 'You saved the loved ones of a friend of mine. You think you are the only one who would risk everything for love?'

I stared at him in disbelief. 'You . . . and *Nellie?*'

'What's so hard to believe, man? Besides, it would've have been a shame to waste you. You really weren't half bad.'

I grabbed my staff and headed for the stairs.

'Not that way,' Palimpost cautioned and took my arm. 'Come, follow me.'

He led me deeper into the dungeon. The jagged cavern opened up, then narrowed into an opening no bigger than a small cave. At a spot he knew, Palimpost kneeled and pulled a stone up from the floor. A passageway appeared.

'There's a fork halfway through. When you reach it, head *left*. It empties into the moat. Head towards the forest. In the darkness you'll be safe. Go *right*, and you'll end up back at the castle. Remember – left.'

I crouched down to the level of the passage. 'You are a good man. I am sorry that I caused you any harm.'

'Oh, what's a little risk of one's life when there's love in the air?' He grinned. 'Tell Norbert, he should not sleep easy. Next time, it will be I who presses the attack.'

He pushed me forward and I steadied myself with my staff. The passage was low, narrow and jagged. My feet struck cold water up to my shins. It smelled grimy and foul. I bumped into floating objects. I was sure they were dead rats.

I waved goodbye and, levelling my rod, hustled through. Left, Palimpost had said, beyond the castle walls. To the forest. And freedom . . .

But when I got to the fork, I didn't hesitate. I turned right. I headed along the dark, murky walls back to the castle.

There was one last thing I had to do.

Chapter Fifty-Six

The dark tunnel let out, of all places, in the hearth of the great meeting room deep inside the castle.

I pushed a stone slab out of the way of the opening, and wormed my way through. Sleeping knights lay all around. If they woke, I was as good as dead.

I crept silently about the room, lifting a sword from one, who snored, dead to the world. I snatched a piece of cheese off the floor and ate the morsel guiltily. Then I hurried out of the room.

I knew not what hour it was, but the castle halls were dark and completely quiet. Declining candles guttered on the walls.

I rushed down a staircase towards the main entrance, cautious not to encounter anyone.

Outside the entryway, my heart relaxed; I had not been seen. Soldiers milled about the dark courtyard. Guards paced on the ramparts. A horse neighed as a rider galloped in from outside. I quickly crossed the courtyard, huddled in my cloak.

I knew the room where Norcross slept, one near the barracks. It lay up a narrow stone staircase, torches lighting the walls on either side.

I made my way to the door. Then I took several deep breaths. A flash of nerves slithered down my spine. From inside came curious noises. Giggling and squeals. The bastard was *in* all right.

I removed the sword from under my cloak. *This was for my wife and child* . . .

Chapter Fifty-Seven

I unlatched and pushed open the heavy door to Norcross's room. It was dimly lit. A mound of clothes lay on the floor. *Norcross's . . . and a lady's . . .*

Suddenly there was the sound of heavy panting and grunts.

On the heavy-posted bed, I saw a partially clad woman bracing her arms against the bedboard with her legs akimbo. Norcross, wearing only his undertunic, hammered her from behind.

It took me a moment to recognize the Lady Estella. Her and Norcross's ardour was so great I wasn't spotted until I was well into the room.

The knight turned first. 'Who goes?'

I stepped forward into the light and winked at Estella. 'My lady,' I bowed, 'it seems you are once again offended. As often as possible, it appears.'

'*You . . .*' Norcross grunted. His eyes lit up as if he was staring at a roasted side of beef.

'Me,' I replied, a smile curled on my lips.

Norcross pulled himself off Estella, who covered herself with bed sheets. He stood up, his prick still quivering, and crudely wiped himself with his own shirt. 'However you got yourself free, you have great balls to come here.'

'Good. Then at least one of us has,' I said, glancing down.

Norcross curled a smile. In no hurry, he reached about for his sword. 'I might as well take your head tonight. Then I can sleep late tomorrow.'

Estella grabbed her garments and ran, half naked, towards the door.

'Do not go, Estella,' Norcross said. 'Nothing perks my prick like spilling a man's guts in front of him. I'll be back inside you before you're dry.'

He chuckled. He seemed in no great haste as he circled away from the bed, flexing his chest muscles, looking at me contemptuously as if I were an insect he was about to squash. 'Here, fool, have your justice . . .' Then he let out a fierce cry and swung his sword at my neck in a mighty arc.

I stood my ground and his blade clashed against mine with a loud clang. At the impact, I swung underneath, but Norcross parried the low blow as if his sword had no weight.

He was a skilled fighter, I could see that from the first blows. I had learned well on the Crusade – I was certainly scared of no one – but it flashed through my head that he was far more experienced than I: a knight! And a killer of women and children!

Norcross grunted and swung his blade fiercely, as if to cut me in two. I leaped backwards, the blade slicing by with a loud *whoosh*.

Norcross swung the blade in a continuous motion and charged at me again. I raised my sword to take the blow, and forced his to the floor. We stood there, eye to eye, our swords pinned. 'You fight like a woman,' he grinned.

Then he butted me in the forehead and sent me reeling.

I caught myself on the bed, Estella scampering out of my way. He charged again, this time hammering his sword twice at my shoulders. Somehow I blocked both blows.

Sparks flew from the clash of steel on steel. The chilling clang of death reverberated in my ears.

I swung back. Norcross blocked my effort with ease. He stood up my sword almost effortlessly. Then flashing it downwards, he grazed it across my arm, taking a slice of flesh. I let out a howl. Singing pain sliced through me. The raw wound ran red on my forearm.

'Know the feeling,' Norcross grinned assuredly. 'That will be your head a moment from now.'

He came at me, swinging his mighty sword back and forth. I blocked it two, three times, but the weight was overpowering.

I felt my arms growing weary. Each blow, I found myself parrying late, a mere instant from having his sword plunge through my chest. I wanted to kill him. I wanted him to die with everything I had. But I was losing. Any moment might be my last.

Finally, he forced me back into a corner. Frantically, I swung one last time and he blocked me with ease. He was laughing, knowing he had me. His stale breath was in my face. The smell of his sweat tormented me. The awful sneer on his face could be the last thing I ever saw.

'Go to your grave knowing that I fucked your wife. I shot my seed in her, and when I finished, she asked for more.'

My blade was crumbling in my grip. His was closing on my neck, so near to slicing through the bone. With my free hand, I reached into my belt. *My knife there . . .* My last chance.

Norcross's eyes were fiery, his look single-minded. 'Listen closely, fool. That is the last thing you will ever hear . . .'

'For Sophie . . . for Philippe!' I yelled in his face.

In that instant, I shoved the knife upwards into his chest. I felt muscle tear, bone crack, *but he did not move a muscle in his face.*

I pushed the blade, harder and harder, but his gaze bore down on me. Incredible! He continued to press his sword down on my neck.

Then Norcross opened his mouth as if to add one last thought. This time a stream of blood rushed out. His grip weakened, his legs gave way. I saw his hands loosen on the sword. Then he took a step backwards. A stagger.

I pushed him away, my knife buried deep in his chest.

Estella screamed as if the knife were sticking in her.

Norcross was trying, like a drunken man, to regain his balance. He wobbled, then he fell to his knees. He looked up at me, disbelief in his eyes, cupping his own vitals in his hands. Then he keeled over dead.

I felt overcome, at first with relief and then with sadness. I had avenged Sophie and Philippe, but I realized, there was nothing for me now.

I picked up my sword. I had to get out of there. I took Estella by the hair. She had tricked me. She'd nearly cost me my life. I held her pretty head back, and ran the tip of my sword across her neck. 'Do not shout or call out. Do you understand?'

She nodded, terror blinking in her round eyes.

'You are most lucky,' I said, forcing a smile, 'that I am a *gentle*-fool.'

Chapter Fifty-Eight

Exhausted, and afraid that Estella would sound the alarm, I staggered from the fallen knight's bedroom. I was now a murderer.

I took my staff and sword and was able to climb down the ramparts from an undetected spot near Norcross's chamber. The moat was shallow and I crossed it on foot.

From there, I ran. Ran in the shadows through the surrounding village. Ran, until I found the woods.

My arm hung like a roast sliced open. The wound was bleeding profusely. I came upon a stream and cleaned it as best I could and tied it with the cloth from my shirt. I was an outcast again, a criminal now, not just a deserter from a far-off war, but a murderer – a killer of a noble. No doubt Baldwin would come after me. I needed to put as much distance as I could between me and Tours. *But . . . where would I go?*

I hid in the woods, keeping off the main roads. I was hungry and cold, but the knowledge that I had avenged Sophie and Philippe warmed me inside. I felt vindicated, restored. I hoped God forgave me too.

Just after first light, I heard a loud rumble. I hid in the brush as a posse of armed riders, dressed in Baldwin's colours, galloped by. I didn't know where they were heading. *East, west?* Veille du Père? Sweeping the roads and villages?

I headed east, tracking the main road, through the deepest part of the forest. I avoided any travellers I saw. I didn't know where I was heading. My bleeding arm ached and throbbed.

A day later, I came to a fork in the road that I now knew well. I had passed here, when I'd run like a madman after returning home. I had passed here again on my recent journey to Tours.

To the east lay my old village, Veille du Père. A day's trek away. My old inn was there; Mathieu, my brother-in-law; whatever family I still had. My friends, Odo, Georges ... Memories of Sophie and my poor, baby son ...

They would welcome me there. I was Hugh, spinner of tales. I made everybody laugh. Surely, they would welcome back a lost son.

Then a sharp sadness came over me.

I couldn't go back there. My village lay in Baldwin's terrain. They would look for me. And it was not my home, not any more. Just a place where memories would haunt my dreams.

Like a good song, life has verses, the goliards had taught me. Each verse has to be sung. It takes the whole of them to make a song. It is the entire *chanson* you name, but when you think of it, when you smile, it is a favourite *verse* that delights your ears ...

Sophie . . . for me, you will always be that verse. But now I must go . . . I must leave you.

I grabbed my staff. I took a deep breath.

I chose the trail north, towards whatever new life lay ahead. Towards Blois . . .

PART THREE

AMONG FRIENDS

Chapter Fifty-Nine

The door opened and the jester Norbert stood there, bent over a bowl, picking his teeth with a hazel twig. His jaw dropped as if he had seen a ghost.

'Gads . . . *Hugh*! You've come back after all.' He grinned broadly, then shuffled up to me with that side-stepping gait of his. 'What a joy to see you, lad.'

'And you, Norbert,' I replied, embracing him with my good arm.

'Wounded *again*? You're like a human archery target, son,' he cried. 'But come in, I'm glad to see you back. I want to hear it all.'

The jester yanked out a low stool for me to sit on. Then he poured a cup of wine and sat facing me. 'I can see in your eyes you've not come here with much cheer. So tell me, did you find her? What is the fate of your Sophie?'

I lowered my eyes from those of my friend. 'You were right, Norbert. It was just a dream to think she had somehow survived. I am sure she is dead.'

He nodded, then leaned across and squeezed me in a fatherly way. 'A man's allowed to dream every once in a while. We little people live on it. I'm sorry for your loss, Hugh.'

Then suddenly Norbert shuddered, letting out a gravelly cough.

'You're ill?' I asked with concern.

'Just under the weather.' He waved me off. 'Too many years of crawling around with the beetles down here.' He cleared his throat again. 'Tell me this – how did it go at court with Baldwin? Did you get the job?'

Finally I could smile at something. 'I *did*, just as we planned. In fact, I think I was a success.'

'I knew it!' The jester leaped up. 'I knew you would. I taught you well, boy, didn't I? Tell me. I have to know it all.'

Suddenly the weariness in my body seemed to recede; my face blushed brightly with the memories of entertaining the court. I told him everything. How I had managed my way into the castle, how I had seized upon the moment to go before the court. The jokes I had used . . . How the duke had sent away poor Palimpost.

'That old fart. I knew the old sod had lost all inspiration.' Norbert hopped around, cackling with delight. 'It served him well to be sacked.'

'No,' I protested, 'he turned out to be a friend. A true one.' I continued my tale, through my run-in with Norcross, how I'd been tricked, and how Palimpost, the very fool I'd shamed, had saved my life.

'So the goon still has some virtue in him. Good . . . There's a brotherhood of us, Hugh. I guess you're part of it now.' He patted my shoulder warmly, then once more doubled over in the throes of a most horrible cough.

'You *are* sick,' I said, supporting him with my arm.

'The physician says it's just the croup; tells me I'm a miserable excuse for a man of mirth. But still, Hugh, maybe your return is well-timed. Why not stand in for me, until I'm well? It's a plum job.'

I dragged my stool closer. 'Stand in for *you* . . . here in Blois?'

'And why not? You're in the trade now. A professional. Just try not to do it *too* well.'

I thought about the offer. I did need a place to be. Where else would I go? Or what else would I do? I did have friends here. Their trust was strong. And another aspect of the offer appealed to me, undeniably.

I had liked it. The crowds, the applause, the acclamation . . . This new *pretext* . . . I had liked it very much.

'I will stand in for you, Norbert,' I said, holding his shoulder, 'but only until you recover.'

'That's a promise then.' We shook hands warmly. 'I see you are still lugging that big stick around with you. And you wear the garb.'

'My normal tailor was unable to dress me at such short notice.'

'Not a problem,' Norbert laughed. He shuffled over to his chest and tossed me a felt cap. 'Bells, I know. But, as they say, beggars can't be choosy.'

I placed the cap upon my head. I felt a strange sensation, my blood warm with pride.

'You'll knock 'em dead, lad. That I know for sure,' the jester grinned. 'And I know for sure there is another here who will be *most* pleased to see you back.'

Chapter Sixty

I watched Emilie from outside the hall before she had the chance to spy me. She was amid the other ladies-in-waiting, attending to their embroidery. Her golden braids spilled out from under a white hood. Her little nose seemed as soft as a button. I saw what I had known that first day, but looked beyond, due to the nature of our friendship: *Emilie was beautiful. She was beyond compare.*

I winked at her from the doorway, flashed her a familiar smile. Her eyes stretched as wide as wildflowers bursting in July.

Emilie rose, placing the embroidery neatly down on the table, and with perfect politeness, excused herself and hurried towards me. Her pace quickened as she did.

Only when she rushed up to me and grasped my hands, did she show her true delight. 'Hugh DeLuc . . . *It's true* . . . Someone said they had seen you. You have come back to us.'

'I hope I don't wear out my welcome, my lady. And that you are not displeased.'

She grinned widely. 'I am most pleased. And look at you . . . Still in your jester's garb. You look good, Hugh.'

'The same you made for me, just a bit more frayed. Norbert has taken ill. I promised I would stand in for him.'

Her eyes, vibrant and green, seemed to illuminate the darkened hall. 'I have no doubt we will all be the merrier for it. But tell me, Hugh, your quest? How did it go?'

I bowed my head, not for a second hiding my disappointment or true feelings.

Emilie led me down the hall, where no guards were posted and we were able to sit upon a bench. 'Please . . . I can see you are sorely troubled, but I have to hear.'

'Your plan was excellent. On the subject of my *pretext*, everything went well. I dispatched the fool in Tours, gained access as we had spoken, and was able to snoop around.'

'I did not mean our pretext, Hugh. I meant, your quest. Your dear Sophie. What did you find? Tell me.'

'As to my wife,' I swallowed drily, 'I am now sure that she is dead.'

The light in Emilie's hopeful eyes began to dim. She reached out for my hand. 'I am most sorry, Hugh. I can see in your eyes how it saddens you.' We sat there silently for a while. Then she noticed my arm. 'You are injured again.'

'Just a bit. It's nothing. It's healing. I found the person who was responsible for the deaths of Sophie and my son. I ended up having to face him off.'

'Face him off . . .' A look of concern flashed in her eyes. 'And the outcome?'

I bowed my head again, then raised it with a slight smile. 'I am *here*. He . . . is not.'

Her eyes lit up again. 'And I am glad. And most glad to hear that you will stay a while too.' She rolled up my sleeve and studied the sword marks on my arm. 'This needs treatment, Hugh.'

'You are always nursing me back to health,' I said. I was surprised at how easily I fell back into her trust – almost without trying. It felt good to be here. A calm spread over my face.

'But there is more I have to tell you, I'm afraid. This man I fought . . . he was a knight. More than a knight, in fact . . . He was Baldwin's chatelain. It ended up in battle . . . I killed him.'

Emilie gazed intently into my eyes. 'I have no doubt that what you did was right.'

'It *was*, Lady Emilie, I swear it. He murdered my wife and son. Yet the man was a noble. And I—'

'Is it not regarded as justice when one takes recompense for the loss of his property?' Emilie cut in. 'Or defends the reputation of his wife?'

'For nobles, yes,' I bowed my head again, 'but I fear there is no justice in this world that shines on a low-born man who kills a knight. Even if it is deserved.'

'That may be,' Emilie nodded, 'but it will not *always* be.'

Her eyes met mine. 'You are always welcome here, Hugh. I will talk to Lady Anne.'

Instantly I felt as if the heaviest weight had been lifted from my shoulders. How did I deserve such a friend? How in this one pure soul had all the boundaries and laws by which I had lived been set aside? I felt so glad to have come here.

'There's no way for me to thank you.' I clasped her hand, then realized my mistake, my forwardness, my stupidity.

Her eyes drifted to my hand, but she made no move to bring hers back. 'The duke's chatelain, you say ...' She smiled, finally. 'You may be lowborn, as you say, Hugh DeLuc, yet somehow your aim is remarkably high.'

Chapter Sixty-One

'You are thoroughly misplaced, child,' Anne scolded her later, in her antechamber, 'to stick your nose where you do. For such a pretty one, it always seems to end up where it is most unwelcome.'

Emilie brushed her lady's long brown hair in front of the mirror. Anne seemed noticeably out of sorts. In the past, Emilie had always been able to soften her with a few well-placed assurances and affable cheer. Her freethinking was always a source of discussion between them, and, though her lady hid it, a bond.

But not so now. Not since word had arrived that her husband would soon be back from the Crusade.

'I am no child, madame,' Emilie said back.

'Yet you act like one sometimes. You urge me to look the other way at this fool who admits to killing the chatelain of a duke, and who seeks refuge here.'

'He does not come to hide from justice, my lady, but because he feels among friends who understand what justice is.'

'And what is this friendship worth to you, Emilie? This friendship with a common scut who always finds his way back home when he is injured? Is it worth the loss of our laws and custom?'

'The knight was killed in a fair duel, ma'am. The man's beloved wife was abducted by him.'

'What *proof* is there? Who pledges for this man? The baker? The smith?'

'Who pledges for Baldwin, ma'am? Armed thugs? His cruelty and greed need no witness.'

Anne met Emilie's bright eyes sharply in the mirror. 'A *lord* needs no pledge, child.' There was an awkward silence between them, then Anne seemed to soften. 'Look, Emilie, you know that Baldwin is no friend to this court. But do not make me choose between your heart and what we know as the law. A lord manages his own vassals as he sees fit.

'Men have always shown greed,' Anne continued. 'They spread your legs and plant their seed, then pick their nose on the pillow and fart. Your common fool will prove no different.' Anne turned and seemed to sense that she had hurt the younger woman. She held the brush and clasped Emilie's hand. 'You must know, it would be my joy to shame Baldwin in my husband's absence. But your price is too high. Given the choice between *cads*, high- and lowborn, don't ask me to choose.'

'Showing justice on this, my lady, is how you will choose.'

Anne's eyes hardened. 'Don't flaunt your fancy concepts at me, Emilie. You have never had to govern. You are not *subject to a man*. You are still a guest at our court. Perhaps it is time we sent you back.'

'*Back...?*' Emilie was startled. Fear shot through her. Anne had never threatened her before.

'This is an education, Emilie, not your life. Your life is *written*. You cannot change it, no matter how strong your passions.'

'My heart is not the issue, madame. He is just, I assure you.'

'You do not know just,' Anne snapped. 'You know only a dream. You are blind, child. And stubborn. So far you have not found a husband here, despite the best efforts of some of our bravest knights.'

'They are trumped-up oxen, and smell like them too. Their exploits mean nothing to me. Less than nothing!'

'And yet this low-bred pup does. What makes you think you can expect more from him? You must stop this dalliance. *Now*.'

Emilie stepped back, knowing she had gone too far. She had offended her.

Gradually, Anne seemed to soften. She reached for her hand. 'Yet,' she went on, 'you've never lacked the courage to stand up to *me*.'

'Because I have always trusted you, my lady. Because you have always taught me to do what's right.'

'You trust too much, I fear.' Anne got up.

'I have given him my promise, ma'am.' Emilie bowed her head. 'Keep him here. I will not go further in the heart. If I did not press this to you, you would not be the wiser. Please, let him stay.'

Anne gazed at her, searching her eyes. She reached a tender hand to her face. 'What has life done to you, my poor child, to have so hardened you against your own kind?'

'I am not hardened,' Emilie replied, kneeling and placing

her head upon Anne's arm. 'I only see that there is a world beyond.'

'Get up,' Anne raised her gently. 'Your fool can stay. At least, until Baldwin enquires of him. Hopefully, with Norbert not well, and gone from court, we will find him a boon.'

'He has learned well, my lady,' Emilie promised, cheered.

'It is what he learns from you that troubles me. This other world you speak of, it may seem real, it may stir your curiosity, and your heart. But hear me, Emilie, *it will never be your home.*'

A tremor ran through Emilie. She rubbed her cheek against her mistress's hand. 'I know, my lady.'

Chapter Sixty-Two

The next morning, I made my debut in front of the Lady Anne's court.

I had only seen the Great Hall at Blois from behind Norbert's back on my first visit, studying his skills, watching him perform. Now, with its buttressed arches rising thirty feet and more above me and jammed to its hilt with colourfully dressed knights and courtiers, the hall looked even more enormous and imposing than I could ever imagine.

My chest was pounding. Not only for the gigantic room and the simple fact that Tours was like a cow town compared to this; nor for my new liege and the favour that must be won. But also because of whom I was replacing. Norbert was a jester of the highest rank. To sit in for him here, in front of the court, was an honour that touched me deeply.

The arrival of the court did nothing to abate my nerves. A blast of trumpets announced the Lady Anne with her long silk train and a steady line of ladies, Emilie among them, bringing cushions and refreshments, attending her needs.

Pages in green and gold surcoats and overtunics

announced the business of the day. Advisors flitted around, vying for Anne's ear. Scores of knights did not languish in their casual tunics as at Tours, but sat at formal tables, finely dressed in the duchy's colours of blue and white.

That day, there was a minor dispute before the court, a bailiff and a poor miller arguing over the levy of the fief. As was the custom in towns everywhere, the bailiff felt the miller was holding out on him. I had seen this a hundred times in my village. And it was always the bailiff who won.

Anne listened distractedly, but soon seemed to grow weary. In her husband's absence, she was forced to rule on such tiresome matters and this was as mundane as business got.

Anne's gaze began to wander.

'This bickering is the stuff of comedy, my lords. Jester, this is your domain. What say you? Come out and rule.'

I stepped out from the crowd behind her chair. She seemed to regard me unexpectedly, as if surprised at the new face in the clothes. 'You say it is *my* rule, my lady,' I bowed.

'Unless you are as dull as them,' she replied. Mild laughter trickled through the room.

'I will not be,' I said, calling back on all the times I saw my own friends cheated, 'but I must answer with my own riddle. What is the boldest thing in all the world?'

'It is your stage, fool. Tell us, what is the boldest thing?'

'A bailiff's shirt, my lady. For it clasps a thief by the throat most every day.'

A hushed silence spread over the court, replacing the amused buzz. All eyes looked to the bailiff for his response.

Anne fixed on me. 'Norbert informed me he was leaving

his position at court, but he didn't inform me he was leaving his duties to such a rash wit. Come forward. I know you, do I not?'

I kneeled in front of her and doffed my cap. 'I am Hugh, good lady. We met once before. On the road from Tours.'

'Monsieur Rouge!' she exclaimed, her expression indicating she knew exactly to whom she spoke. 'You seem a little better patched together than when I saw you last. And you have found a trade. When last seen you had donned your armour and ridden off on some quest.'

'My armour was merely this,' I motioned towards my checked tunic, 'and my sword, this staff. I hope I was not too greatly missed.'

'You are *hard* to miss, monsieur,' Anne pinched a smile, 'since you do not go away.'

Many of the ladies began to giggle. I bowed ceremoniously at her demonstration of wit.

'Norbert said I would find you a fitting replacement. And there is another at court who defends you well. And look how you perform. Here, before our court, with your first step you have already soiled your boots. You take the miller's side on this?'

'I side with justice, lady.' I could feel the heat rising in the room.

'*Justice?* What would a fool know of justice? This is a matter of what is law and right.'

I bowed respectfully. 'You are the law here, my lady, and the judge of what is right. Was it not Augustine who said, "Remove justice, and all that a kingdom remains is a gang of criminals on a larger scale." '

'You know about kingdoms as well, I see . . . in your full and varied life.'

I motioned to the bailiff. 'Actually, it is *criminals* I know. The rest was just a guess.'

Some laughter snaked around the court. Even Anne consented to smile. 'A jester who quotes Augustine? What sort of fool are you?'

'A fool who does not know Latin, ma'am, is just a greater fool.' Again, a trickle of applause, some nods. And another smile from Anne.

'I was raised by goliards, my lady. I know a lot of useless things.' I sprang on to my hands, balanced myself into a handstand, then slowly released on to one arm. From upside down I chuckled, 'And some useful enough, I hope.'

Anne gave a smile of approval. 'Useful enough,' she applauded. 'So much so, bailiff, that I am forced to side with the fool here. If not by right, then surely by wit. Please, forgive me. I am sure next time, the scale will tilt to you.'

The bailiff shot me an angry glance, then backed off and bowed. 'I accept, my lady.'

I pushed off and landed on my feet.

'So, boar-slayer,' Anne turned back, 'your friends are right. Norbert has taught you well. You are welcome here.'

'Thank you, ma'am. I won't disappoint.'

I felt expanded. I had performed in front of the hardest audience in the kingdom, and succeeded. For the first time in a long while, I felt out of harm's way. I shot a wink towards Emilie. My body tingled with pride as she smiled back.

'. . . At least, until my husband returns,' Anne added sharply. 'And I must warn you, his views of custom are quite different from my own. He is known to be much less charmed by a fool's knowledge of Latin than I.'

Chapter Sixty-Three

The following days, I worked freely at the court, entertaining Lady Anne, reciting tales and *chansons* from my goliard days, providing a mock council when she called on me and needed a laugh.

My trouble at Tours grew distant in my mind. I even found myself craving my new role and the power that came with it. *The power of my lady's ear.*

A few times, I was able to poke fun at a situation and gently twist her into a certain mind, always in favour of the aggrieved party. I felt she listened to me, sought my views, however couched in jest they were, amid the clutter of her advisors. I felt I was doing some good.

And Emilie seemed pleased. I caught her approving eye amid the other ladies-in-waiting, though I did not see her alone after that first day.

One day, as the court was being dismissed, Anne summoned me. 'Do you ride, jester?'

'I do,' I answered. I told her I had served in the war.

'Then I will set a mount. I want your presence on an outing. Be ready at dawn.'

An outing . . . with the duchess.

This was an unusual honour, even Norbert said. All night, I tossed on my straw mat. What would she want with me? Amid his fits of coughing up phlegm, Norbert chided me. 'Don't get too cosy in my hat. I will be back shortly.'

The following dawn, I was ready at the stables, expecting a coterie of fancily dressed ladies and courtiers.

But it was clear from the start this was not some idle jaunt in the country. Anne was dressed in a heavy woollen riding cloak, accompanied by two knights I recognized: her political advisor, Bernard Devas, and the captain of her guard, a fair-haired knight named Gilles. With her also was the Moor who had propped me up on a harness that first day in the woods, and who never left her side. The party was guarded by a detachment of a dozen additional soldiers.

I had no idea where we were headed.

The gates opened and we rode out from Blois in the chill of first light. A finger of orange sky peeked over the hills to the east. Immediately, we took the road south.

I rode behind the formation of nobles, just ahead of the rear guard. Anne was a steady rider, trotting capably atop her white charger. Occasionally, she exchanged a few terse words with her advisors, but mostly we rode, at a quick and steady pace. We did not rest until we reached a stream an hour south.

I was a little nervous. We were heading straight for the province of Tours – Baldwin's territory. I was not guarded or watched, but a flicker of concern tremored through me:

Why had she asked me on this journey? What if I was being returned to Tours?

At a fork in the road, the party cut south-west. We were

on roads I had never been on before, occasionally passing hilltops clustered with tiny villages. By midday we had entered a vast forest, trees so dense and tall, they blocked out the sun. Gilles led the expedition. At one point he announced, 'Our border ends here, my lady. We are now in the province of Baldwin of Tours.'

Yet still we rode on. My blood quickened. I wasn't sure what was going on. I had an urge to run. But where? I would not get far if they wanted me caught.

Anne trotted up ahead. I had to trust this woman. I dared not show my fear. Yet every time I placed my trust in a noble, I had been far the worse for it. Could they be betraying me now?

Finally, I kicked my steed and caught up to Anne on her charger. I rode alongside her for a while, nervous, until she could see the question on my face.

'You want to know why I asked you along?'

Yes, I nodded.

She did not answer me, but trotted on.

I knew these roads now. Tours was a day's ride straight ahead. On the side, I could make out farms and dwellings. There was a sign scratched on to a tree: 'St Cecile'.

Our party slowed to a trot.

Finally, Anne motioned for me.

I rode up, fearing that any minute Baldwin's soldiers might come out of the woods to murder me.

'Here is your answer, fool,' she said with a taut face. 'If we encounter what I am told is in this village, I think on the way back we will all be in great need of mirth.'

Chapter Sixty-Four

I relaxed, but only for an instant. The first thing that hit me was the smell. The stench of human putrefaction, the rot of death.

Then ahead, wisps of white smoke rose above the trees. The leaves themselves were singed with the stomach-turning char of roasted flesh.

My mind brought me back instantly . . . Civetot.

Anne rode ahead, seemingly unaffected by the repugnant stench. I felt no danger to myself now, only that this was something awful we were nearing.

The road widened. A clearing. Then a stone bridge. We were at the outskirts of a town. But there was no town. Only what were once huts and dwellings, thatched roofs caved in from fire, the smoke from cinders still rising in the air.

And people, sitting around numbly, with their faces blank and charred, as if mimicking the still silence of the dead.

We rode into the village. Every single dwelling seemed to have been burned to the ground. Each had a tall stake driven through the ground in front of it. On them, like a spit, was a charred mound, unrecognizable. The strange mix of smells turned my stomach – burned hair, flesh, blood. The totems looked like pagan warnings, gutted animals to ward off demons from the homes that were no more.

'What are they?' Anne enquired, as she trotted by.

Gilles, the captain of the guard, sucked in a breath. 'They are children, m'lady.'

The colour drained from her face, and Anne pulled her mount to a stop. She stared at the mounds, and for a moment, I thought she would teeter. But then she righted herself. Her face became composed.

She called out, firmly, to the villagers, 'What has happened here?'

No one answered. The people just stared. I actually feared someone might have taken out all of their tongues.

The captain called again, 'The Lady Anne of Blois speaks to you. *What has happened here?'*

At that, the fiercest howl rang out from behind. All heads turned to see a large man clothed in a tattered hide, hurtling towards us with an axe.

When he was no more than a few feet away, a soldier tripped him with a lance and the assailant crashed to the earth. Two other soldiers pounced on him immediately, one thrusting a sword to the neck of the fallen man and looking up at Anne for the word.

A woman screamed and ran to him, but was held back. The man did not turn to her, just glared at Anne with grief-filled eyes.

'He has lost his son,' a voice called out. 'His home . . .' It came from a gaunt, white-haired man in charred and tattered clothes.

The soldier was about to kill him, but Anne shook her head. 'Let him be.'

The man was yanked to his feet. Anne's guards pushed him forcefully to his grateful wife, where he stayed, breathing heavily, without thanks.

'What has happened here? Tell me,' Anne said to the white-haired man.

'They came in the night. Faceless cowards with black crosses. They hid under their masks. They said it was to purify the village for God. That we had stolen from Him.'

'Stolen? Stolen what?' Anne asked.

'Something sacred, a treasure. Something that they could not find. They tore every child from its mother. Put them on spits in front of our eyes. Set them aflame . . . Their cries still ring in our ears.'

I looked around. This was the work of Baldwin, I knew it. The same savage cruelty that had taken my wife, tossed my son in the flames. Yet this carnage seemed even greater than Baldwin could be responsible for. Norcross was dead. Yet this hell still continued.

'And what did they find, these killers?' Anne asked.

The man replied, ashen-faced, 'I do not know. They torched us and left. I am the mayor of this village. The mayor of nothing, now. Maybe you should ask Arnaud. Yes, ask Arnaud.'

Anne dismounted. She walked directly up to the mayor and looked in his eyes. 'Who is this Arnaud?'

The mayor snorted a disdainful blast of air. Without replying, he began to walk. Anne set off behind, followed by her own guard, who ran to clear the way.

We wound through the streets of the devastated village:

the stables, levelled, smoking, reeking of mutilated horses; a mill, more ash than stone. A wooden church, slashed with blood, the only structure left standing.

At a low stone hut the mayor stopped. The entrance was smeared with blood, not randomly, but in large red crosses. A butcher-house smell came from inside.

Holding our breath, we stepped in. Anne gasped.

The place was ravaged. What scant furniture there was was split like firewood, the ground beneath it ripped up. Two bodies still hung by the arms, a man and a woman, their torsos flayed of flesh. Beneath their dangling legs lay their own severed heads.

My body recoiled in horror. I could not breathe. I had seen these horrible things before. Heads severed and roasted, bodies stripped of skin. My mind hurtled backwards, *Nico, Robert* . . . the bloodbath of Antioch. I turned away.

'Go ahead, *ask* Arnaud,' the mayor cried. 'Maybe he will answer your questions, Duchess.'

We stood in horror.

'Arnaud was born here and always called it his home. He was the bravest man any of us knew. Yet, they carved him up like a pig. They cut out his wife's womb, looking for some treasure. "Stolen from God," they said. He had just returned from fighting abroad . . .'

'From fighting where?' Gilles, the captain, asked.

I knew. I had seen such horror before. I knew, but I could not answer.

'The Crusade,' the mayor spat.

Chapter Sixty-Five

I walked from the hut, and tried to clear the repulsive sights out of my mind. I had seen it all before. Men and women hung and flayed, body parts scattered as if the murders meant nothing at all.

Civetot. Antioch. The Crusade . . .

These riders in the dead of night, who wore no colours and who would not show themselves. The towns burned, savagery. Were these acts Baldwin's? Norcross was dead. Could his men still be running free, terrorizing villages? What precious treasures did they seek?

Put it together, I told myself. What does the puzzle signify? Why can't I solve it?

The Crusade . . . Suddenly it resonated everywhere. The knight Arnaud had just returned from there. Adhemar too, whose horrible death I had heard of at Baldwin's court. Their villages were ransacked and destroyed – *just like my own.*

Dread shot down my spine. These faceless riders who killed with the savagery of Turks – were they the same who murdered my own wife and child?

Cold, clamming sweat clung to my back. It all began to fit.

The killers wore no crest or markings, only a black cross. No one knew where they came from, or what they sought. Then I remembered something. Mathieu had said it was as if it was my home, only our inn that the bastards attacked.

What did they want with me?

During the long ride back, I kept to myself. I racked my brain. What did I have that could connect me with these killings? I had tucked a few worthless baubles into my pouch. The old scabbard with the writing I'd found in the mountains? The cross I'd pilfered from the church in Antioch? It didn't make sense!

I watched Anne riding up ahead. Her face was tight and sombre, as if she wrestled with some inner turmoil. Something wasn't right.

Why did we come out here? What had she needed to see?

Then a chill ran through me. Anne's husband, the duke, was returning any day. From the Crusade . . .

Anne knew . . .

Anne knew these atrocities were going on.

My stomach went cold. All along, I was sure it was Norcross who had done these things to me as punishment for going on the Crusade. Was it possible it was Anne? Could it be that the answers that I sought were not at Tours, but at Blois?

I should not stay there any longer, I thought. There was a danger that I could not place.

'Fool, ride up here,' Anne called from up ahead. 'Lift my spirits. Tell me a joke or two.'

'I cannot,' I replied. I pretended that the horrible sight

had made me too sick. It wasn't far from the truth.

'I understand,' Anne nodded, and continued on.

No, you do not, I said to myself.

We rode the rest of the way back in silence.

Chapter Sixty-Six

For the next few days I kept my eye on Anne, trying to determine what connection she might have to the murdered knights. And the killing of Sophie and Philippe.

Her husband's return was only a matter of days away; all of Blois was in a state of anxiety and preparation. Flags were hung from the ramparts; merchants put out their best wares; the chatelain led his troops in their welcoming formations. Who could I trust?

I waited for Emilie on Sunday morning as she filed out of chapel amid the other ladies-in-waiting. I caught her eye and we lingered until the others had filed away.

'My lady,' I took her aside, 'I have no right to ask. I shouldn't ask. But I need your help.'

'Here,' she motioned, leading me to a prayer bench in a side chapel. She sat next to me and lowered her hooded shawl. 'What's wrong, Hugh?'

This was very hard. I sought the right words to begin. 'Be certain, I would never speak to you of this unless it was of the highest need. I know you serve your mistress with all your heart.'

She wrinkled her face. 'Please do not hesitate with me.

Haven't I proven my trust for you enough?'

'You have. Many times,' I said.

I took a breath and recounted the horror of my trip to St Cecile. I told it in detail: the charred mounds, the eviscerated knight, the most graphic images sticking in my throat like memories that did not want to come out.

I told her of Adhemar, whose similar fate I had heard of at Baldwin's court. Both knights were slaughtered, their villages razed. Both had recently returned from the Crusade. Just as I had.

'Why do you tell this to me?' she finally asked.

'You have not heard of such deeds? At court? Around the castle?'

'No. They are vile. Why should I?'

'Knights who disappear and return? Or talk of sacred relics from the Holy Land? Things more valuable than a simple fool like me would know.'

'You are my only relic from the Holy Land,' she smiled, trying to shift the mood.

I could see she was trying to put the puzzle together. Why these horrible murders? Why now?

She took a wary breath. 'I did not know of any such violence. Only that word has spread that Stephen has sent an advance guard to conduct his affairs before he returns.'

My blood was up. 'This guard? They are here at the castle?'

'I overheard the chatelain speaking of them with some contempt. He has served the duke loyally for years, yet these men are charged with some horrid mission. He feels they are ill-trained for knights.'

'Ill-trained . . .?'

'*Beyond honour*, he said. Owing no allegiance. He says it is fitting that they sleep with the pigs, since they have the hearts of them. Why do you ask me this, Hugh?' Emilie looked into my eyes. I could see fear and I felt awful for causing it.

'These men are hunting for something, Emilie. I do not know what. But your mistress . . . she is not innocent in this herself. These might be Stephen's men, but Anne knows what they do.'

'I cannot believe that.' Emilie shot upright. 'You say this is a matter more important than any in the world to you. I hear it in your voice. These things you describe . . . they are most vile, and if they are Stephen's work or Anne's, they will have to answer to God for what has been done. But why is this so urgent for you? Why do you put yourself at risk?'

'It is not for them,' I said, swallowing. 'It is for my wife and child. I am sure, Emilie, their killers are the same.'

I leaned back, trying to let the pieces fit in. This guard, doing the duke's bidding – they had come from the Crusade. As had Adhemar. And Arnaud. *And I.*

'I must confront her,' Emilie said. 'If Anne is behind such acts, I cannot serve here any longer.'

'You must not say a word! These men are vicious. They kill without a thought to God's judgement.'

'It is too late for me not to be involved.' Emilie stared at me glassily. Her look was not anxious, but perplexed. 'The truth is, when you were away, Hugh, I may have seen something too.'

Chapter Sixty-Seven

Anne flinched from the cold morning air in the maze of hedges under the balcony. She heard footsteps creeping up on her. A stealth-like presence, most foul, like a shift in the wind. She turned and he was there.

His frame was large, his face ruined with scars from battle. But it was not these things that made her cold. It was his eyes. Their remoteness – rigid, dark pools. His face was buried deep in his dark hood. On the hood – a small black cross.

'Not in church, knight?' she scowled, her words stabbing with irony.

'Do not worry for me.' His cold voice crept out from the drawn hood. 'I make peace with God in my own way.'

He came before her as a supplicant, yet he was possessed of the harshest cruelty. He wore the tunic of a knight, but a disgraced one, now in rags. Still, she was forced to deal with him.

'I do worry for you, Morgaine,' Anne scorned him to his face, 'for I think you will burn in Hell. Your methods are evil. They pervert the goal you aim to achieve.'

'I may burn, lady, but I will light the way for others to rest next to God. Perhaps, even *you*.'

'Do not flatter yourself that you are God's agent,' Anne sneered. 'You make my skin crawl that you do my husband's work.'

He bowed, unoffended. 'You need not bother with my work, madame. Just know that it goes well.'

'I saw how well it goes, knight. I was *there*.'

'*There*, madame?' The knight's eyes narrowed.

'St Cecile . . . I saw what you did. Such cruelty even beasts from Hell would find shame in. I saw how you left that village.'

'It was left a better place than when we arrived. Closer to God.'

'Closer to God?' She stepped up to him, looked into his depthless eyes. 'The knight, Arnaud. I saw him flayed apart.'

'He would not bend, my lady.'

'And the children . . . They would not bend as well. Tell me, Morgaine? For what precious prize did these innocents roast like cattle?'

'Just *this*,' the hooded knight said plainly. He reached under his cloak. His hand emerged with a small wooden cross in it, the size of his palm. He cradled it gently in Anne's hand.

Though she wanted to spit on it and hurl it far into the bushes, her breath froze.

'It has journeyed far, my lady, this simple trinket. From Rome to Byzantium. A thousand years. And now, you hold it here. For three hundred years it slept in a coffin, the coffin of St Paul himself, Word of our Lord, until it was unearthed by the Emperor Constantius. This cross has changed the tide of history.' A smile crept out of the hood. 'That's why your prayers for me are not needed, good lady.'

Anne's hands trembled with the relic in her palm. Her mouth went dry. 'My husband will no doubt be honoured,' she said, 'yet you know this is just the start of what he hungers for. How does the real quest go?'

'We are working,' the dark knight nodded.

'You'd better work faster, knight. All the rest is just decoration. Even this piece is a bauble compared to the real prize. He is in Nîmes, only days away. If Stephen finds you have failed him, it will be your head we'll be looking at on a stake.'

'Then I will be smiling, lady, knowing that I will have everlasting life.'

'The smile will be mine, Morgaine, most assuredly.' Anne wrapped herself in the cloak and turned back to the castle. 'Thinking of *you* rotting in Hell.'

Chapter Sixty-Eight

I found no trace of the unholy soldiers I was seeking, or anyone who knew of mysterious knights in dark robes. Nor was I able to gain access into the barracks. Time was growing short. Stephen was due back at the castle in days now. Once he returned, it would be too dangerous to press my case.

Two days later, Emilie took me aside as I was playing jacks with Anne's son, William. She saw my demeanour was glum.

'Do not be so sad, jester,' she said with a smile. 'I have a job for you. And a new pretext.'

There was a celebration that evening in the chatelain's hall, she explained. A bachelor's party. Gilles, the captain of the guard, was to be married in the next few days. There would be knights, soldiers, members of the guard. Lots of speeches and drink. Their guard would be down, so to speak.

'I have arranged for you to be the entertainment,' Emilie announced.

'You seem to have a skill at this sort of thing, my lady. Once again I am in your debt.'

'Thank me by finding what you seek,' she said, and touched my hand. 'And, Hugh, be careful. Please.'

That night, there was lots of wine and awful singing. Gilles's friends stood and made bold and mocking speeches, until they slurred their words and fell back on their benches. I was to be the last act before they dragged Gilles down to a brothel in town.

I had to make them laugh, and yet my eyes kept searching for the rogue knights. I did sleight-of-hand tricks with eggs to warm them up, simple stuff Norbert had shown me, pulling them out of tunics and from behind ears to the drunken awe of the assembly.

Then it was on to the jokes. 'I know this man,' I announced, sliding to a stop on the table top in front of the groom-to-be, 'whose cock was permanently engorged—'

'You flatter me,' Gilles pretended to blush, 'but, joker, must you betray my secret to *all*?'

Everyone roared with laughter.

'Try as he could,' I went on, 'he could not get the damn thing to go down. Finally he sought out his local apothecary. There, he encountered a stunning young woman. "I'd like to speak to your father," the man with the problem said.

' "My father is dead," she answered. "I run this apothecary with my sister. Anything you can tell a man, you can tell us." "Very well," he agreed, in dire need. He pulled down his hose. "Look, I have a permanent erection. Like a fucking horse. What can you give me for it?"

' "Hmm," the lady apothecary replied. "Let me go and confer with my sister." After a minute she returned with a small pouch and said, "How about a hundred livres and half the business?" '

The room roared. 'Tell us more . . .'

I began again – the one about the priest and the talking crow – when from outside the walls, a terrible shout pierced the celebration. There was the clop of horses being drawn to a stop, voices raised. Then once again a man's scream. 'Please, God help me. I am being killed!'

The drunken laughter ceased. Several of the party rushed to the window overlooking the courtyard. I followed close behind. Through a narrow opening I saw two men dragging a third by the arms across the courtyard.

I recognized them instantly! They wore slitted helmets over their heads and carried war swords strapped to their belts. It was just as Emilie had described. They wore no armour, but robes. Their feet were covered with threadbare sandals.

The prisoner hollered defiantly, but his shouts for help echoed off the stone walls.

Then I caught sight of his face. My own twisted in horror.

It was the mayor of St Cecile – who had stood up to Anne only a few days before. They dragged the poor mayor over towards the keep.

'Who are these men?' I asked one of the soldiers at my side.

'These dogs . . . the duke's new business partners. The Returnees . . .'

'Returnees?' I muttered.

My eyes followed the soldiers and the poor mayor until they dragged him through a heavy wooden door and into the keep. The dying shouts of the prisoner faded in the night.

'Not our worry,' Bertrand, the chatelain, sighed. He

peeled back from the window. 'C'mon, Gilles, beauties await in the town. How 'bout we get that blade of yours wiped one last time?'

Meanwhile, my heart was beating at a gallop. I had to talk to the mayor of St Cecile. He might know why knights were being murdered and villages burned. And these awful killers . . . the Returnees . . . I thought that I had seen them before.

But where?

Chapter Sixty-Nine

The following night I waited until long after vespers. Norbert lay snoring on his bed. I crept off my own mat and tucked a knife under my tunic.

I sneaked out of Norbert's chamber, hurrying up the back stairs behind the kitchen to the main floor. I had to traverse the entire castle, from the large rooms of the court to the military end, and talk my way past anyone who would stop me. Well, I was the jester after all.

The halls were dark and draughty; shadows danced on the walls from waning flames. I hurried past the huge oak doors of the Great Hall. A few knights still lounged at tables there, drinking and conversing, while others, too far gone, snored curled up on their cloaks. Occasionally, there was a guard. But no one stopped me. I was their lady's fool.

The castle was a squared-off U shape, a loggia of stone arches circumventing the courtyard, and across it, the duke's garrison, the officers' quarters, the barracks, the keep. I successfully wound my way around the entire main floor. As I passed outside, I saw the tower above me where the mysterious knights had dragged their prisoner, lit up by the moon. I hurried that way, then slipped inside.

I was in the tower, all right, but I didn't know where to go, or who might try to stop me. My stomach churned with nerves; the breath clung tight in my chest.

A cold draught followed me up the stairs. At each floor, the odour grew more foul. The smell of death I knew all too well.

On the third landing, two guards slouched around an open archway. One was tall and lazy-looking; the other short and squat with a mean eye. Not exactly the duke's crack troops, I thought, just babysitting a few cursed souls in the middle of the night.

'You're a long way from the kitchen, aren't you, strawberry?' the mean-looking one growled at me.

'Never been up here before,' I said. 'Mind if I take a quick peek?'

'Tour's over.' He stood up as if to send me away. 'Go back the way you came.'

I went up to him, my eyes stretched wide as if I had seen a fright. As if yanking something out of his ear through my closed fist, I produced a long, silk scarf. 'C'mon . . . even a *damned* soul could use a last laugh.'

To my delight, the oaf reached out and felt the scarf. Then he took it, my bribe for him. He looked down the hall and finding the coast clear, stuffed it into his uniform. 'One look,' he said. 'There's nothin' in there anyway, but the pox. Then juggle your arse back to the pantry, where you belong.'

'Thank you, sire,' I clucked. 'A lifetime of stiff manhood to you.'

I darted up the stairs behind him and through the

archway. A row of narrow stone cells stretched out before me. The putrid stench made me hold my breath. I hoped the man I was seeking was in here.

I hoped the mayor of St Cecile was still alive.

Chapter Seventy

I crept inside the hellhole. The prison was dank and cold. A flickering torch spat its dim light on a row of narrow cells. They were barely four feet high, enclosed by rusted iron bars, tight as coffins. Prisoners curled on the floor like dogs.

Between the awful smell and my worry that the guards would come, I hurried down the line, searching for the man I had seen dragged in the night before. I prayed he was still here.

In the first cell, a man with a long, dark beard, naked, barely more than a skeleton, lay on his back amid his own waste. In the next, a large, dark-skinned man – swarthy as a Turk – curled under a tattered white robe. Neither raised an eye. The cells reeked. A rat licked the inside of an eating bowl right in front of me.

The third cell contained the person I was seeking. The mayor of St Cecile. The poor man lay crumpled in a ball, with blotches of blood and bruises on his face and arms. To my alarm, I could not tell if he was alive or dead.

'Sir . . .' I crept close. I had to know. What did these dark knights want? What had they razed his entire village to find? What treasure was worth so many lives?

I crept up close to his cell. 'Please . . .' I whispered again, almost begging. Would he recognize me? Would he speak or call out?

Suddenly a whimpering moan caught my attention from the next cell. I stepped over and saw a pathetic creature – a woman, her skin as white as a ghost, her hair dry as rotted hemp, muttering under her breath like a deranged witch. Her skin was blotted with oozing sores.

I cringed . . . What a sight! What heresy had she done to be left to rot away like this?

I turned back to the mayor. Time was short. 'Do you remember me, sir? I saw you in St Cecile,' I whispered.

But the witch's muttering grew louder. I shushed her to stop. Then a jolt froze my body.

The words she moaned – at first softly, almost inaudibly, into her bony hands. Then, louder. My God! I could not believe what I was hearing:

' "A maiden met a wandering man/In the light of the moon's pure cheer." '

Chapter Seventy-One

M y heart slammed against my ribs. *This could not be! Could not, could not.*

I ran to her cell, eyes flattened against the bars, straining to distinguish her face amid the shadows of the gloomy interior.

Nothing could ever prepare me for what I saw . . . Not the sight of Nico plunging from my grasp. Nor poor Robert gazing at his own body as it was hacked in two. Not even the Turk looming over me, his blade raised in the air.

I was staring at my wife.

'Sophie . . .?' I muttered, the word catching in my throat.

She did not move. Or speak a word to me.

'Sophie!' I called again. I felt my heart start to crumble. Part of me prayed she would not turn.

Then she tilted her face towards me.

'Sophie, is that you?'

She lay huddled in shadow and I could not tell for certain if it was her. The scant light from a nearby torch traced her bony face. Her hair, that once had smelled like honey, hung wildly from her head, pulled out in spots, and white. Her sunken eyes, glazed and distant, were runny with yellow pus. Yet the nose . . . the soft line of her chin as it met her delicate neck . . . They were the same, unmistakably, though she cowered before me as a fevered wretch, pocked with sores.

It was her! I was sure of it.

'Sophie . . .?' I cried, my hands reaching desperately through the bars.

She finally turned towards the sound, sallow light spreading across her face. I simply could not believe what I was seeing! How could she be here? How could she be alive, after all this time?

Grateful tears welled in my eyes. I reached towards her, her emaciated bones covered with a filthy rag. I tried to speak, but I was too overcome. *It was Sophie. She was not dead.* At last, I knew that much for sure.

'Sophie . . . *look* . . . it's me, Hugh . . .'

Slowly, she lifted her face into the light. She was like an artist's disfigured recreation of the beautiful image I held in my mind: gaunt, ghostly, covered in sores. Her eyes perked at my voice. I could see that she was sick, that she barely clung to this rotting existence. I wasn't sure she knew who I was.

'We have to give it back to them,' she finally spoke. 'Please, I beg you. Give them back what's theirs . . .'

'*Sophie!*' I was shouting now. '*Look.* I am here . . . Hugh!' What had they done to her? A burst of anger surged through me. I could see her suffering, and I felt it too. I forced my hand through the bars. 'You are alive. Sweet God, you're *alive* . . .' Tears streamed down my face.

'*Hugh* . . .?' She blinked. Then she almost seemed to smile. 'Hugh'll be back. He's in the East, fighting . . . But I'll see him again, my baby. He promised.'

'No, I am here, Sophie.' My fingers grasped at air, trying to reach her face. 'Please. Come close. Let me hold you . . .' Oh God, let me hold you, Sophie.

'He'll be sad about the inn,' she continued to mutter. 'But he'll forgive me, you'll see. You'll see.'

'I'm going to get you out of here. I know about Philippe, about the inn.' My body was bursting with heartache. 'Please, come here. Let me hold you.'

Sophie pulled herself towards the sound of my voice. Her cheeks were slick with fever, her eyes glassy. Her neck had swollen to twice its size. I could see she was terribly sick. I just wanted to hold her. God, I wanted to hold her.

She blinked both eyes, hugging the walls like a frightened doe. 'Hugh . . .?' she whispered.

'Sophie, it's me . . . It's me, darling . . .' I whispered the words to our song: ' "A maiden met a wandering man . . ." '

'You must give it back now,' she muttered again. 'They say it is theirs. I tried to tell them, "Hugh will be back. He'll find me." They said they'll give Philippe back to us, our little son. All we have to do is give them what is theirs . . .'

I finally wrapped my hands around her, my dear wife. I touched her face, brushed the sweat off her hollow cheeks. She was so precious to me, even more so in this misery. Tears streamed down my cheeks.

'They want what belongs to God,' she said, and her body rattled. 'Please. Give it to them.'

'Give them *what*?' I cried. What did she think I had? I did not know if it was the fever, or a deeper madness talking. Or even if Sophie still recognized she was talking to me.

Suddenly she jerked out of my grasp and scampered back

into shadow, which broke my heart. Her eyes bolted past me, wide with fear.

I felt as if everything I loved had slipped through my fingers one last time.

Then, I saw what had driven her away. My heart nearly came to a stop.

One of the duke's rogue knights was standing over me.

Chapter Seventy-Two

I recognized the disguise worn by the bullies who had dragged away the mayor the other night.

His head was covered in a dark hood, and the eyes peering through were dark and depthless, like sunken caves. He wore his sword belted over a threadbare robe and stood, hands on hips, grinning down on the two of us.

'Go ahead, have a poke,' he shrugged. 'The whore won't mind, fool. Anyway, she'll be dead in a week. Just be careful you don't get the pox all over your dick.'

I stared at his mocking face, and the greatest rage I had ever known tightened up in my blood, a boiling, uncontrollable force.

I reached for an iron poker lying next to me on the floor. In my mind, this grinning lizard represented every cruelty that had been heaped on my wife and child, every suffering and loss I had witnessed since I first went away. My world had been hurled upside down.

With a cry, I rushed at him, a wild exhalation escaping from my lungs. I swung the weapon towards his head before he could draw his sword. The startled knight threw up his arm to defend himself and the rod smacked against it with a sickening crack.

He yelped, and staggered back in pain, the arm hanging at his side. I did not stop. I battered him again and again, like some mad beast myself, every sinew of my body concentrated on driving this piece of metal into his skull.

I shoved him against the bars of the cell. I drove my knee into his groin and felt him groan and buckle. I jammed the poker under his neck.

'Why?' I hissed into his face. The soldier gagged, his eyes bulging, darting around. *'Why is she here?'*

A garbled cry emerged from his throat, but in my rage I was not waiting for his answer. I forced the rod deeper into the soft flesh of his neck. A force rose inside me that I could not stop. I wanted to kill this man.

'Who are you?' I screamed in his face, uncontrollably. 'Where have you come from? Why did you bring her here? Why did you kill my son?'

As I shouted these things, my thumbs pressed sharply under his hood. I dug at his throat, squeezing the breath out of him. Bit by bit, the hood fell away from his neck.

My eyes were pinned to the frightful mark I saw there. *The black Byzantine cross.*

It shot me back a thousand miles. Suddenly I was in the Holy Land, re-envisioning the horrors I had seen there.

These bastards were Tafurs.

Chapter Seventy-Three

I staggered back in shock. Our eyes met, and it was as if some terrible knowledge had been passed between us.

The Tafur took my surprise as an opening, and dug his hands into my face. I pressed the rod into his neck even tighter. Then I heard a bone crack in his neck. His eyes darted and bulged, a final, desperate resistance. A trickle of blood seeped from his mouth. A moment later, his legs began to sink. When at last I let go, the Tafur crumpled to the prison floor.

I stood over him, breathing furiously myself. My mind hurtled back again. *Tafurs* . . . I saw them ravaging their captives in their filthy tents. I saw them butchering the Turk who had saved me, then darting like beetles to the crypt, scavenging for spoils. *What were they doing here in Blois? What did they want with me? With Sophie?*

Suddenly, my ears rang with shouts and commotion. The prisoners were clanging the bars in their cells.

Now, with what little time we had left, I had to get Sophie out of here. I rummaged over the Tafur's body, frantically searching for a key.

I ran my eyes about the prison. Keys must be here somewhere.

I turned towards Sophie, eager to let her know that I would help her escape.

But the sight left me rigid as stone.

She was slumped against the bars, her face icy white. Her eyes, a moment ago mad with terror, seemed calm, their focus far-off. I did not see her breathe.

Oh God, no!

I crawled to her, cupped her face in my hands. 'Sophie, stay with me. You can't die. Not now.'

She blinked, barely more than a tremor. A glimmer of life flickered in her eyes.

'Hugh?' She blinked a smile.

'Yes, Sophie. It's me.' I brushed the sweat off her face. It was icy cold.

'I knew you would come back,' she said, and finally seemed to know who I was.

'I'm so sorry, Sophie. I'm going to get you out of here. I promise.'

'We had a son,' she said, and started to cry.

'I know. I know it all.' I wiped her cheek. 'He was a beautiful boy. Philippe.'

I looked around, desperately searching for something to help her. 'The guards will be back,' I said. 'I'm going to find a way out. Hold on. Please, Sophie.'

Please!

I kneeled and held her hands in mine. I whispered, 'I'll take you home. I'll pick sunflowers for you. I'll sing you a song . . .'

Her mouth twitched, and she took a long time to breathe

again. But when she did, I also saw her smile – a faint one, unafraid. 'I've never forgotten, Hugh . . .' The words fell off her lips, one at a time, so softly I could almost kiss them there:' "A maiden met a wandering man . . ." '

'Yes,' I said, 'and I've been true to you ever since we were children.'

'I love you, Hugh,' Sophie whispered.

Suddenly, she lurched in my arms. I felt her heart starting to beat out of control. Her eyes bolted wide.

I didn't know what to do to help her. She shook terribly up and down. All I could do was hold her tight. 'I love you, Sophie . . . I've never loved anyone else. I knew I would find you again. I'm so sorry I left you alone.'

Her hand gripped me by the tunic. 'Hugh . . . then don't . . .'

'Don't what, Sophie?'

A final sigh escaped her lips. '*Don't give them what they want.*'

Chapter Seventy-Four

And then my sweet Sophie died in the prison cell.

She passed with a calm, far-off quiet in her eyes. Her mouth hung in the slightest smile. Perhaps because I had finally come back, as I had promised.

Tears streamed down my cheeks. I wanted to scream, 'Why did Sophie have to die? Why her?'

I grabbed the Tafur by the collar of his robe and hurled his dead body against her bars. 'Why, you bastard? Tell me, what did she mean? Why did you kill my son? Why are innocent people dying?'

Then I sank down with my head in my hands.

I wanted to take Sophie home. That's all I could think of, to bury her with her son. I owed her that. But how? The dead Tafur was slumped before me. Any moment, the guards would come. I couldn't even open her cell.

The truth hit me: Sophie was gone. There was nothing I could do for her now. Except maybe one thing – *don't give them what they want*. Whatever that could be.

I ran and found a ragged cloth, and came back and laid it under Sophie's head. I covered her body, as if she were in our bed at home, though I knew nothing could disturb her now. I took one last, loving look at Sophie. The person who had been my everything since we were ten. *I'll come back for you*, I promised. *I'll take you home.*

Then I staggered out of the prison, hurtling down the stone stairs. I ran out of the military wing, through the maze of darkened halls.

My body shook with incomprehension and shock. What had she been doing here? It wasn't a dream – my wife was dead. Rotted like some diseased dog. *Here in Blois* . . . The shock tore at my brain. I shouldn't have left her. Part of me wanted to go back, to wrap her up, take her home. But there was nothing I could do.

Then a new thought crawled through the haze in my brain . . . something I had to do. I had to right this wrong. I finally knew who was behind it. The blame wasn't at Tours, but here. *Anne* . . .

In a rage, I raced back towards the living quarters. No alarm had been sounded. Guards smirked at me along the way, a laughable fool who had perhaps tipped the jug once too often, staggering home to sleep it off.

Yet all the while, madness reigned in my mind: *Anne knew.*

I bounded up the stairs towards her living quarters. Two guards stood watch on the landing. They looked at each other. What harm could I do? I was the lady's fool. They let me pass. Just as they always had before. Then a new guard stepped in my way. A Tafur. 'Whoa, fool, you are not permitted,' he barked.

I didn't stop to reason. I spotted a gleaming halberd hanging on the wall, crossed over a coat of arms. I grabbed the axe from its anchor and ran at the startled guard, taking him by surprise.

I swung with all my might, the blade catching him on the base of his neck. He let out a garbled groan, his side nearly splitting away from his body like a side of beef. He toppled to the floor, dead.

Now I had killed one of Anne's guards.

One of her Tafurs.

Chapter Seventy-Five

Shouts rang out from behind me, deep male voices echoing in alarm.

I stormed ahead like some madman. *Where is she? Anne!* I had one single-minded desire: to hear the truth from her lips, even if I had to die for it.

Two guards from the stairs ran my way, their swords raised. I forced myself through a set of doors and bolted them shut with a lance. I ran deeper into the ducal chambers. I had never been in here before. There was furious pounding on the door behind me.

I knew I would die here. At any moment I expected a blade to tear into my back, to see my own blood spilling out on the floor. No matter. All that was important to me was to ask my lady, *why*?

I stormed deeper into her quarters. The bedroom. An engraved wooden table with a basin and ewer, tapestries hung on the walls. A vast, draped oak bed, larger than any I had ever seen.

But empty. No one was there.

'Goddamn you,' I shouted in frustration. 'Why my family? Why us? Someone tell me!'

I stood there, not knowing what to do next. I saw myself in my fool's costume, blood spattered on my face. Why, why, why?

Suddenly a door opened behind me. I tensed my knife, expecting to face Anne, or one of her Tafur guards.

But it was not.

For a moment, I felt as if I were back on the road to Tours, blinking out of the haze, and everything that had happened since – Norcross, St Cecile, Sophie's death – were just figments of a dream, terrors that could be washed away with a soft word.

I stared at Emilie's face.

She gasped, her eyes fastened on my blood-spattered clothes. 'My God, what has happened to you?'

Chapter Seventy-Six

'**S**ophie's dead,' I whispered.

She stared at me, transfixed. Then she moved forward to support me. 'What has happened? Tell me.'

'The duke's men have had her all along, Emilie. Sophie has been *here*, not in Tours, with my enemies. But *here*, in the tower, among *my friends*.'

'This cannot be . . .'

'It *can*, Emilie. It is the truth.' I leaned back. 'There are no more games to play. No more pretexts. It ends now.'

Shouts and pounding rang at the door. What a wretched sight I must have made, my clothes torn, slick with blood, the look of madness in my eyes.

'Anne,' I muttered, 'I told you . . . She is behind it all. I have to find out why she allowed these men to destroy my family. Stephen's *guard*. . .' I chortled, almost a laugh, 'these are not knights, Emilie. They are scavengers from the Holy Land. The lowest form of butcher. Even the Turks ran in fear of them. They hunt for relics, spoils. That is why the two knights have been murdered. But my family – *we had nothing*.'

The commotion behind us grew louder. Anne's men were

trying to smash the door in. Emilie gripped my arm. 'It doesn't matter now. Anne is not in the castle. She has gone to meet her husband at La Thanay. Come with me.'

'It is too late. The time for kindness is finished. There is nothing left for me now but to face her men.'

She put her face inches from my own. I could feel Emilie's breath on my cheek. 'Whatever you've done, if Anne is behind this, I will do everything to see justice is given to you. But you must come. I can't help you if you're dead.'

Emilie hurried me out of the room, down a narrow corridor in the ducal quarters. She pushed me into a small chamber and quickly barred the door. I could see she was scared, how her heart was jumping, and it touched me deeply.

Emilie searched through her linen chest and came out with a heavy brown cloak, which, upon closer inspection, proved to be the robe of a monk. 'Here . . . I thought at some point you might need this. Put it on.'

I stared at it, confused, amazed that Emilie did this for me.

'Go, now . . . They will search every room. Send me word through Norbert. You have friends here, you must believe that.'

A moment later, I was no longer a jester, but a monk, the hood pulled over my head.

'Your new pretext,' Emilie smiled bravely.

I took a deep breath. 'I fear this one will be an even greater trick than before.'

'Then let me add to it,' Emilie said. She pulled me close by the collar, and to my surprise, pressed a quick, hard kiss upon my lips.

My blood came to a halt with the softness of her lips, the boldness of her touch. I felt my knees lock, the breath massed inside my chest. In truth, I didn't know what to feel at that moment. My head spun.

She looked into my eyes. 'I know your pain is deep. I know every part of you cries out for vengeance for your wife and child. But, common or noble, there is something special within you. I saw it the first time I looked into your eyes. And I have never seen it waver. We will find a way to right these wrongs. Now *go*.'

There was a small window above her bed. From there, it was only a short jump to the courtyard and then to the gardens.

I hoisted myself up and pushed through a leg. I looked out and saw the darkened shadows of roofs in the distance. I looked back into Emilie's face. 'By what luck, lady, have I earned you as a friend?'

'By *leaving*, right now. This instant.'

I smiled and lifted myself through the narrow window. I turned. 'I hope, in all the world, to see you again.'

There was a battering at her door. I waved at Emilie, then dropped from the window.

'You will, Hugh DeLuc,' I heard her voice from above. 'If you hope that . . . *you will*.'

Chapter Seventy-Seven

The afternoon sun splintered the day's late chill. Anne stood outside her tent on a field near La Thanay.

At her sides two formations of Blois's infantry clad in the duke's crest stood in even rows. Banners of blue and white flapped in the stiff breeze.

A shiver of dread rippled through Anne's blood. She had brooded over this moment for weeks now, her husband's return. There were times when she had actually prayed he would be lost in the war.

She had been married to him since she was sixteen, more than half her life. She was betrothed as a sign of union between her family's duchy in Normandy and Stephen's father, a cousin to the King. But if this union had fostered trust and commerce between their two cities, it created only isolation for her.

Once she bore him his son, Stephen forgot her, coming to her only when he tired of his whores from town. When she resisted, she felt the stab of his powerful fingers on her neck or the scrape of the back of his hand.

She felt those same tremors now, shooting through her blood. Though she kept up the appearances of state and family that were her duty, she felt only contempt for her husband, trapped as she was in the prison women were confined to – even duchesses and queens. She felt old, so much older than her years. The time when he was away had almost freed her. But now, knowing he was near, the old fears returned.

Up ahead, a formation of about twenty knights appeared over a knoll, travelling slowly, their war-worn helmets barely glinting in the sun.

'Look, my lady,' Gaston Morais, the duke's chatelain, pointed. 'There they are. The duke returns.'

A cheer rose up from the men.

So he is back. Anne sighed, pretending to smile, fattened, she was sure, on the meat of greed and glory he had feasted on on the Crusade.

Anne nodded, and the trumpeters broke into a flourish, announcing the arrival of the duke. A rider broke away from the pack and galloped towards them. Anne felt her stomach stiffen in disgust.

'God's grace to Stephen,' the chatelain shouted, 'Duke of Blois. He has returned.'

Chapter Seventy-Eight

The soldiers stood at stiff attention, swords and lances raised in salute. The duke galloped into their camp. He raised his arm to salute them, then grinned triumphantly at Gaston, and Jean Dueux, his seneschal, the overlord of his affairs.

Almost as an afterthought, he turned his eyes to Anne.

Stephen then jumped off his mount. His hair had grown long and wild since she had last seen him, like a Goth's. His cheeks were hard-edged and gaunt. Yet he still carried that narrow glint in his eye. As was his duty, he went up to her. It had been almost two years.

'Welcome, my husband,' Anne stepped forward. 'To God's grace that He has brought you home safely.'

'To God's grace,' Stephen smiled, 'that you have shined like such a beacon as to guide me back.'

He kissed her on both cheeks, but the embrace was empty and cold. 'I have missed you, Anne,' he said, in the way a man might exult in seeing the health of his favourite steed.

'I have counted the days as well,' she replied coldly.

'Welcome, my lord.' Stephen's counsels rushed forth.

'Gaston, Jean,' he held out his arms, 'I trust the reason you have come all this way to greet me is not that we have misplaced our beautiful city.'

'I assure you your beautiful city still stands,' the chatelain grinned, 'stronger than ever.'

'And the treasury even more filled than when you left,' promised the seneschal.

'All this later.' Stephen waved them aside. 'We've been riding for twenty days since we docked. My rump feels as though it's been kicked all the way from Toulon. Tend to my men. We are all as hungry as beggars. And I . . .' he mooned his eyes towards Anne, 'I must attend to my lovely wife.'

'Come, husband,' Anne said, trying to seem teasing to his men, 'I will try to kick it towards Le Puy, so as to even it out.'

All around them laughed. Anne led Stephen back to their large tent draped in blue and white silk. Once inside, Stephen's loving look disappeared. 'You perform well, my wife.'

'It was no performance. I am glad for your return. For your son's sake. And if it has brought you back a gentler man.'

'War rarely has that effect,' Stephen answered. He sat on a stool and removed his purple cloak. 'Come here. Help with these boots. I will show you just what a petting pup I've become.'

His hair fell over his tunic, greasy and greyed. His face was sharp and filthy from the road. He smelled like a boar.

'You look as if the wars have done you no worse for wear,' she said tartly.

'And you, Anne,' Stephen reached out to pull her down to

him, 'you look like a dream from which I am not yet willing to wake.'

'Then awaken now,' she pulled herself away. It was her duty to tend to him, remove his boots, rinse out a damp cloth for around his neck. But there was no way in Hell she would let him touch her. 'I have not sat alone for two years to be mounted by a pig.'

'So hand me the bowl and I will wash, then,' Stephen grinned. 'I will make myself fresh as a doe.'

'I did not mean your stench,' she said.

Stephen still smiled at her. He slowly removed his gloves.

A servant stepped in, carrying a bowl of fruit. He placed it on the bench and then, feeling the stiffness in the air, hurried out.

'I have seen your new interests,' Anne said derisively, 'the dark troops you have sent from the Holy Land. Your *noble* men of the Black Cross, who kill and slaughter women and children like curs, innocents and nobles alike. Your governing has reached a new low, Stephen.'

He got up, slowly sauntered up to her. Her skin felt as though an insect were crawling up her back. He walked around her as if he were inspecting a steed. She did not face him.

Then Anne felt his hands caress her neck. Icy and loveless . . . She felt his lips close to hers.

'I may be your wife,' she turned away, 'and for that, Stephen, I will tend to your health and welfare, for the sake of my son. I will stand for you, as is my duty, in our court. But *know*, husband, you will not touch me, ever again. Not in my weakest moment, or in your most urgent need. Your hands shall never soil me again.'

Stephen grinned and nodded, as if impressed. He stroked her cheek and she pulled away trembling. 'How long, lovely Anne, have you been working on that little speech?'

Before she even knew it was happening, he tightened his caressing grip on the nape of her neck. A pain flashed through her. Slowly, he increased the pressure, all the while smiling fondly at her.

The strength shot out of her lungs. She tried to cry out, but to no avail. No one would come. Her cries would be misunderstood as pleasure. Her heart echoed like a loud drum.

Stephen pushed her down to the ground. He followed, all the while pinning his thumb and forefinger into her neck and forcing her thighs apart with just the power of his legs.

He tried to kiss her, but Anne twisted her head in the other direction, leaving his vile slobber all over her neck.

Then he pressed himself against her rump. She felt him erect and hideous, the detestable hardness she had grown to loathe.

'Come,' he whispered, 'my bold, headstrong, Anne . . . After all this time, would you deny me what I want?'

She tried to pull herself away, but his grip was too strong. He slithered up the length of her spine, and yanked her underdress down, about to force himself in.

Anne swallowed back an urge to vomit. *No, this cannot be happening;* her heart beat in panic. *I swore, not again . . .*

But just as quickly, he pulled off her, grunting back a

laugh, leaving her trembling. He pushed his greasy mouth close to her face.

'Do not misunderstand me, wife,' he hissed in her ear. 'I did not mean I desire your cunt. *I meant the relic.*'

PART FOUR

TREASURE

Chapter Seventy-Nine

The hulking man in the large sheepskin jerkin pounded in the fence post with well-timed strokes of his heavy mallet.

I crept from the woods, still in the torn remnants of my jester's garb. I had clung to the forest for a week now, hungry, avoiding the pursuit. I had nothing. No money or possessions.

'You'll never mend a fence by lazing away like a fat cow,' I said boldly.

The burly man put down his mallet and arched his thick, bushy eyebrows. He stepped forward to the challenge. 'Look what's crawled out of the woods . . . some scrawny weasel in a fairy's costume. You look as though you wouldn't know a day's work if it jumped up and strummed your dick.'

'I could say the same for you, Odo, if it wasn't always in your hand.'

The big smith eyed me closely. 'Do I know you, malt-worm?'

'Aye,' I doffed my cap, 'unless, since I've seen you last, your brains have grown as soft as your gut.'

'Hugh!' the smith exclaimed, his eyes wide with wonderment.

We embraced, Odo lifting me high off the ground. He shook his head in astonishment.

'We heard you were dead, Hugh. Then in Tours, wearing the costume of a fool. Then word that you were in Blois. That you killed that prick, Norcross. Which of these are true?'

'All true, Odo. Except for rumours of my demise.'

'Look at me, old friend. You killed the duke's chatelain?'

I took a breath and smiled, like a little brother embarrassed by praise. 'I did.'

'Ha, I knew you'd outfox them,' the smith laughed.

'I have much to tell, Odo. And much to regret, I fear.'

'We too, Hugh. Come, sit down. All I can offer you is this rickety fence. Not as fine as Baldwin's cushions . . .' We leaned against it. Odo shook his head. 'Last we saw you, you ran into the woods like a devil, chasing the ghost of your wife.'

'She was no ghost, Odo. I knew that she lived, and she did.'

Odo's eyes widened. 'Sophie *lives*?'

'I found her. In a cell in Blois.'

'Good God!' the smith grunted. His eyes lit up, delighted. Then he searched mine, serious. 'Yet I see you've crawled back out of the woods alone.'

I bowed my head. 'I found her, Odo, but only long enough for her to die in my arms. They held her as hostage, thinking that we held something of theirs, something of great value. I've come back to tell her brother, Mathieu, of her fate.'

Odo shook his head. 'I'm sorry, Hugh. That won't be possible, though.'

'Why? What's happened, Odo?'

'Baldwin's men were here again. For you ... They said you were a murderer and a coward. They said you ran from the Crusade and killed the lord's chatelain. Then they ransacked the village. They said any who harboured you would be tried on pain of death. A few of us stood up ...'

A grim ugly stench sent a panic through my stomach. 'What is this stench, Odo?'

'Mathieu was one who stood up for you,' the smith went on. 'He said you had been wronged. That the chatelain had burned your house and child, and taken your wife, and if Norcross was dead, it was justly deserved for what he had done. He showed them the inn, which he was starting to rebuild. These men were horrible, Hugh. They hung Mathieu up. Then they stretched him, his neck in a noose and his legs tied to their mounts. They whipped the horses ... until his body split in two.'

'No!' A pain shot through my chest. Another weight seemed to crush my heart. Poor Mathieu. Why him? Now another was dead, because of me. This nightmare had to end!

I raised my head. A terrible fear pulsed up in my gut. 'You did not answer me. What is that smell?'

Odo shook his head. 'They burned the village, Hugh.'

Chapter Eighty

I walked with Odo into the desolate village, the place that only two years before I had called my home.

All around, farms, cottages, grain holds were no more than mounds of cinder and stone. Dwellings were either caved in to rubble, or in some beginning stage of being rebuilt. We passed the mill, once the finest structure in the village, its majestic wheel now a heap of ruin in the stream.

People put down their hammers, stopped chopping wood.

A group of children shouted and pointed. 'Look, it's Hugh. He's come back. It's Hugh!'

Everyone looked up in a state of disbelief. People I knew rushed up to me. 'Is it you, Hugh? Have you truly come back?'

A kind of procession picked up around me. What a sight I must've been, in my ragged, checkered tunic, my torn, red hose. I marched through the cluttered street, directly to the square. My last time here, I had been in such a daze, having found out what had happened to my wife and son. Now, everything was new, unreal, and so very sad.

A clamour built up, some crying, 'Glory to God, it's Hugh.

He's back,' while others spat in my path. 'Go away, Hugh. You're the devil. Look what you've done.'

By the time I reached the square, maybe seventy people, most everyone in the village, had formed a ring behind me.

I gazed at our inn. Two new walls of rough logs had been erected, supported by columns of quarry stone. Mathieu had been rebuilding it, better and sturdier than it was before. A flood of anger rushed through me. God damn them! *I* was the one who had killed Norcross. *I* was the one who had infiltrated the court. What right did they have to take vengeance on this village?

A rush of tears welled in my eyes. They streamed down my cheeks. I began to weep – weep in a way I hadn't done since I was a small child.

God damn you, Baldwin. And God damn me, for my stupid pride.

I fell to my knees. My wife, my son... Mathieu... Everything was ruined. So many had died.

A ring of villagers stood there and let me weep. Then I felt a hand upon my shoulder. I choked back tears and looked up. It was Father Leo. I had never paid much heed to him, with his little, domed head, his sermons. Now, I prayed he would not remove his hand, for it was all that kept me from keeling over in a ball of shame and grief.

The priest lovingly squeezed my shoulder. 'This is Baldwin's doing, Hugh, not yours.'

'Aye, it *is* Baldwin's work,' someone shouted from the crowd. 'Hugh's meant us no harm. It is not his fault.'

'We pay our shares, and this is how the bastard repays us,' a woman wailed.

'Hugh must go,' another said. 'He killed Norcross. He will cause us all to burn.'

'Yes, he *did* kill Norcross,' echoed another. 'God's praise to him! Who among us has stood up like that?'

Voices rose. The shouting built into a vicious clamour – some for me, some against. A few, including Odo and the priest, begged for reason while others started throwing pebbles and stones, which stung me as they fell.

'Have pity on us, Hugh,' someone wailed. 'Please, go, before the knights return!'

In the midst of the clamour, a woman's voice shouted above the din. Everyone turned and grew quiet.

It was Winnie, the miller's wife. I remembered her kind face and the familiar floral bonnet she always wore. She and Sophie had been best friends; they had been to the well together that day her son was drowned.

'We've lost so much.' She scanned the crowd. 'Two sons. One to Baldwin. One to the war. Plus our mill . . . But Hugh has suffered more than any! You point your scorn at him because we are all too scared to point it towards the one who deserves it. It is *Baldwin* who deserves our rage, not Hugh.'

'Winnie's right,' said her husband. 'It is Hugh who killed Norcross, and avenged my son.' He helped me to my feet and put out his hand. 'I'm grateful you're back, Hugh.'

'And I,' said Odo, his voice booming. 'I'm sick of quaking every time I hear horsemen come near the village.'

'You're right.' Martin the tailor hung his head. 'It is our own liege who is responsible, not Hugh. But what can we do? We are pledged to him.'

It hit me there, in that moment, as I observed my

neighbours' helplessness and fear. I knew what I must do.

'Then break the pledge,' I said.

There was a moment of stunned silence.

'Break the pledge?' the tailor gasped.

People turned to each other and shook their heads, as if my words were a sign that I was mad. 'If we break the pledge, Baldwin will come back. This time it won't be just our houses that he burns.'

'Then next time, friends, we'll be ready for him,' I said, turning to catch every eye.

A wary silence filled the square. These villagers looked at me as if the words I uttered were heresy that damned us all.

I knew that these words, and this idea, could set us free.

I stared out at them, and shouted, *'Break the pledge!'*

Chapter Eighty-One

E milie stormed past the guards to Anne's bed chambers and pushed her way through. 'Please, ma'am,' one guard went to restrain her, 'the lady is resting.'

Emilie's blood was surging. The duke had returned the night before, yet it was not Stephen who was on her mind, but Anne, her mistress, the person she served, *who had lost touch with what was right.*

All morning, Emilie had prayed about what to do. She knew she had crossed a line with Hugh. My God, she had given aid to someone who'd killed a member of the duke's guard. For that she could be imprisoned. She asked herself over and over: if I cross this line, am I prepared to lose everything? My family's blessing, my position in the court? My name . . .? And each time the answer came back clear and strong. *How can I not?*

She pushed open the large, wooden door to Anne's chamber.

William, Anne's nine-year-old son, was about to leave, dressed in his hawking attire. Anne waved him off. 'Go. Your father awaits you, son. Catch a prize for me.'

'I will, Mother,' the boy said, running off.

Anne was in bed at this late hour, still wrapped in bedclothes.

'You are ill, madame?' Emilie asked.

'You storm into my chambers,' Anne turned her face away, 'as if concern was not the issue at all.'

'On the contrary, I have much to take issue with you,' Emilie said.

'Take issue, child? No doubt this, as all things, concerns your protégé, the fool.'

'You are right, madame, he is a fool. But only to have trusted you. As am I.'

'So, this is no longer about him, I see. But you and me . . .'

'You have wronged him in a great way, my lady, and, by doing so, wronged me.'

'Wronged you?' Anne laughed coldly. 'Your Hugh is a wanted man now. A murderer, a deserter as well. He is sought in two provinces and will be caught. And once he is, he'll be hanged in the square.'

'I hear your voice, my lady,' Emilie stared, aghast, 'but the words do not seem as if they could come from you. What has become of the woman who was like a mother to me? Where is the Anne who stood up against her husband? Who ruled in his absence with even temper and grace?'

'Go away, child. Please go. Do not lecture me on things you do not know.'

'I know *this*. Your men raided his village. They killed his son, stole and imprisoned his wife. She is dead now. In your prison. You knew.'

'How would I know?' Anne shot back. 'How would I know some worthless harlot thrown in our prison was in fact this man's wife. I do not govern these Tafurs. They are my husband's. I do not know who they rouse and what insane deeds they do.'

'These deeds, my lady,' Emilie met her eyes, 'they are now imprinted on you.'

'Go,' Anne waved her away. 'Do you not think that if I knew the person we sought was here, at Blois, in our court, he would still be running around, pained and aggrieved, but *alive*? He'd be dead as his wife.'

'You sought Hugh?' Emilie blinked back. 'For God's sake – why?'

'Because the fool holds the key to the greatest prize in Christendom, and he does not know it.'

'What prize? He has nothing. You have taken everything from him.'

'Just go.' Anne sank back in bed. 'And take with you your mighty sense of what is right and just. All that propelled you to run away from your father and your destiny. Go, Emilie!' In her anger, Anne turned her face, exposing for the first time what she had kept concealed.

There was a large, red welt. And much worse.

'What is that?' Emilie moved forward.

'Stay away,' Anne snapped, shrinking into her pillows.

'Please, my lady, do not turn from me. What is the bruise on your face?'

Anne took a sharp breath. She dropped her head and let her hand fall. 'It is my *own* prison, child. You want to see it – well, look!'

Emilie let out a gasp. She rushed over and, against Anne's efforts, gently stroked the wound. 'Stephen did that? To you?'

'You should know it, child, for it is the very *truth* that you claim to know so well. A woman's truth.'

Emilie recoiled in horror. The side of Anne's face was swollen to twice its normal size.

Chapter Eighty-Two

The first thing I did was go up to the hill overlooking the village where my infant son, Philippe, lay buried.

I kneeled by his grave and crossed myself. 'Your mother spoke of you in her last breath . . .' There I sat on the frozen earth. 'Dear, sweet Philippe.'

I still did not know what these sons of bitches wanted with me – what they thought I possessed, which clearly, I didn't; why my wife and son had to die.

I dug up the pouch I had brought back from the Crusade and spilled the contents on to the frozen grass.

The painted perfume box I had bought for Sophie in Constantinople . . . How sure I had been that I would bring it back to her with pride. Just thinking of all that had happened since – Nico, Robert, Sophie – I felt my eyes fill up.

Then I scattered the rest of my treasure upon the ground.

I picked up the inlaid scabbard with the writing I had found crossing the mountains. Then the inlaid Byzantine cross I had taken from the church. Were these the treasures? The things that cursed me? If I gave them back, would they leave me, and the village, alone?

An angry wave swept over me, a mixture of grief and tears. 'Which are you?' I screamed at the pieces. 'Which is the thing that caused my wife and son to die?'

I picked up the gold cross and went to hurl it into the trees. Trinkets! Baubles! None of it worth the lives of my wife and son!

Then I held back, remembering Sophie's last words: 'Don't give them what they want, Hugh.'

Don't give them what, Sophie? Don't give them what?

I sat by my Philippe's grave and cried, my fingers digging into my scalp. *'Don't give them what?'* I whispered over and over again.

Finally, I pulled myself up, spent and exhausted. I gathered the things back into the pouch and laid it in the hole, replacing the earth. I took a deep breath and said goodbye.

Don't give them what they want.

All right, Sophie. I won't.

Because I don't know what in God's name it can be.

Chapter Eighty-Three

Winter gave way to spring, and bit by bit, I fell back into the life of the village: rebuilding.

I picked up the work Mathieu had begun, bringing our inn back to life. All day, I lugged heavy stones and logs, hoisted them into place, and notched them together in joints to form a wall. At night, I slept at Odo's hut, his wife and two children and I curled up by the hearth in a single room.

Piece by piece, the town came back to life. Farmers brought out their ploughs and prepared their fields for seed. Crumbled homes were patched together with mortar and stone. Spring would bring travellers: travellers meant money. Money brought food and clothes. People began to laugh once more, and to look forward.

And I was a bit of a hero with my neighbours. In no time at all, my stories of how I had dazzled the court at Tours and fought the knight Norcross became part of the local lore. Children clung to my side. 'Show us a flip, Hugh. And how you got out of the chains . . .' I amused them with my tricks, removed hidden beads or stones from their ears, told stories of the war. I felt my soul being restored in the sound of their laughter. Yes, laughter truly heals. This was the great lesson I'd learned as a jester.

And I mourned my sweet Sophie. Each day before the sunset, I climbed the knoll and sat at my son's grave. I spoke to her, as if she rested there too. I told her of the progress of the inn. How the village had banded together around me.

And sometimes, I spoke to her of Emilie: what a gift it had been to have her as a friend; how she saw something special in me like no other noble had, from that very first day. I recounted the times she had saved me. How I would have been a lifeless mound had she not come upon me after my fight with the boar.

Each time I talked of Emilie, I could not fail to notice the flame that stirred within my blood. I found myself thinking of our kiss. I did not know if it was meant to bring back my wits in a frantic moment. Or just the last goodbye of a true friend. What did she see in me to risk so much? *A special something . . . A special something Sophie . . .!* Sometimes, I even felt myself blush.

One such afternoon, as I was heading back to the village from the grave, Odo ran up the path towards me. 'Quick, Hugh, you can't go back there now. You have to hide!'

I gazed beyond him. Four riders were approaching over the stone bridge. One, an official, was colourfully robed, with a plumed hat. The others, soldiers, were wearing the green and gold of Tours.

My blood stood still.

'It's Baldwin's bailiff,' Odo said. 'If he sees you here, we will all be dead.'

I ducked behind a copse of trees, my mind flashing

through options. Odo was right, I could not go back. But what if someone gave me up? It would not be enough just to run. The village would be held accountable.

'Bring me a sword,' I said to Odo.

'A sword? Do you see those soldiers, Hugh? You must *go*. Run as if a beggar had your purse.'

I crouched, hidden from sight, and headed towards the eastern woods. A few people saw me scurry away. I crossed the stream at a low point and thrashed my way into the brush.

I found a spot near the square and watched the bailiff clip-clop his way forward like Caesar on a stallion.

An anxious crowd formed around him, buzzing. A bailiff never brought good news: only higher taxes and harsh decrees.

He took out two official-looking documents. 'Good people of Veille du Père,' he cleared his throat, 'your lord Baldwin sends his greetings.

' "In compliance," ' he began, ' "with the laws of the state, in the reign of Philippe Capet, King of France, Baldwin, Duke of Tours decrees any subject known to give aid or shelter to the fugitive known as Hugh DeLuc, a cowardly murderer, shall be treated as an accomplice to the above-mentioned high crimes and receive the full and swift measure of the law," which, to you sow-addled farmers who may not fully understand, means hanged by the neck until dead.

' "Additionally," ' he went on, ' "all lands, property, and belongings, owned or leased from the Duchy by such person, shall be immediately forfeited, confiscated, and returned to the demesne, and all spouses, siblings, and descendants, free or indentured, shall be sworn into lifelong service to his liege." '

My blood almost burst through my veins. The village was being punished for my crimes: all property handed over, worked lands returned, families ripped apart. I waited, holding my breath, for a voice to cry out against me. A wife, at her wits' end, afraid to lose any more. An unknowing child . . .

The bailiff took a long, measuring look around. He was an obscenity. 'Villagers . . . do I hear a sudden change of heart?' There was a tense, drawn-out silence. But no one spoke up. Not one of them.

Then Father Leo stepped forward. 'Once again, bailiff, our Lord Baldwin shows he is a wise and charitable liege.'

The bailiff replied, 'Appropriate measures, priest. Word has it, the scut is back in these parts.'

'So what *good* news have you brought in your other decree?' someone called out.

'I almost forgot . . .' he smiled and rapped his head. He unfurled the seal, and, without reading, nailed the document on to the church wall. 'General increase in taxes. All tithes, allotments and fiefs raised by a tenth.'

'*What!*' A gasp escaped from the crowd. 'That's not fair. It cannot be.'

'Sorry.' The bailiff shrugged. 'You know the reasons: harsh winter, stocks are down . . .'

Then, all at once, the bailiff stopped talking. Something had caught his eye. He stood there motionless. It was the inn. My heart clenched in my throat.

'Is this not the inn that only months ago was burned to the ground? The one belonging to the person we seek?' No one answered. 'Who is rebuilding it? If my memory serves me, the last of its proprietors was, shall we say . . . torn apart by grief.'

A few eyes travelled about, unsure of what to do.

'Who rebuilds it, I say?' The bailiff picked up one of the stones.

My blood began to tremble. This was surely it! The end of me.

Then a voice rang out of the crowd. 'The village rebuilds it, bailiff.' It was Father Leo. 'The village needs an inn.'

The bailiff's eyes lit up. 'Most charitable, priest . . . And most assuring to hear this from you, a man whose word is above refute. So tell me, who will run this establishment?'

Another silence.

'I will,' shouted a voice: Winnie, the miller's wife. 'I will tend to the inn while my husband mans the mill.'

'You are most enterprising, madame. A good choice, I think, since you seem to have no heirs to run your mill.'

The bailiff held her gaze. I could see he was unsure whether to believe a word. Then he tossed the stone aside and made his way to his mount.

'I hope this is all true,' he sniffed, and pulled the reins. 'Perhaps on my next visit I will stay longer, madame. I look forward to the chance to test your hospitality for myself.'

Chapter Eighty-Four

As soon as the hated bailiff was out of sight, panic spread through the village. I marched back out of the woods, grateful that no one had spoken against me. But I saw the mood had changed.

'What do we do now?' A frightened Martin the tailor shook his head. 'You heard him; the prick suspects. How long can we keep up this ruse?'

Henri, a farmer, looked ashen. 'Our land returned to the demesne? We'd be ruined. Our entire lives lie in this land.'

A ring of people crowded around us, shouting and afraid. I was the cause of their misery. 'If you want me to leave, I will.' I bowed my head.

'It's not you,' the tailor said, looking around for support. 'Everyone's scared. We've only just picked ourselves up from the ruins. If Baldwin's men come back . . .'

'They *will* come back, Martin,' I said to his worried face. 'They will come back again and again. Whether I stay or go.'

'We took you in,' Marie, the baker's wife, shouted. 'What is it you now expect us to do?'

I went over to the inn, and I felt my wife's soul stirring

in the rubble. 'Do you think I drag these rocks every day and sweat on these walls, so that this inn I promised my dead wife I would rebuild can be brought down once again?'

'We all feel that way, Hugh,' the tailor groaned. 'We've all rebuilt. But what can we do to stop it?'

'We can defend ourselves,' I shouted.

'Defend?' The word whispered through the crowd.

'Yes, *defend*. Draw the line. Fight them. Show them they can never take away our lives again.'

'Fight? Our liege?' People looked stunned. 'But we are all pledged to him, Hugh.'

'I told you before, *break the pledge*.'

The gravity of these words silenced the buzzing crowd. '*Break it*,' I said again.

'If we did, that would be treason,' the tailor stammered.

I turned to the miller. 'Any more *treason*, Georges, than the murder of your son? Or you, Marte – your husband lies not far from my son – was it any less treason when he was struck down defending your home? Or my own boy, who did not even know the word, when he was tossed into the flames?'

'Baldwin's a ruddy prick,' the miller replied. 'But these obligations you want to cast aside, they are the law. Baldwin would come at us with everything he has. He would crush us like moths.'

'It can be done, Georges. I've seen how a small, able detachment can defend themselves for months against a greater force. I'm not trying to stoke up fire like the little hermit, then have you follow me to ruin. But we can beat Baldwin, if we stand up to him.'

'The duke has trained men,' Odo stepped forward, 'weapons. We are just farmers and smiths. One village. Fifty men.'

'Yes, and in each village between here and Tours there are another fifty men who hate Baldwin just as you do. Thousands who have suffered the same misery and oppression. We beat them back just once, these men will join us. What can Baldwin do – fight us all?'

Some were nodding in agreement; for others, the thought of standing up against the liege was almost impossible to conceive.

'Hugh's right.' Winnie, the miller's wife spoke. 'We have all lost husbands and children. Had our homes ruined. I'm tired of quaking in my bed every time we hear the sound of riders.'

'I too,' Odo shouted out. 'We've pandered to that bastard our whole lives. What good comes out of it? Just a load of shit, and death.' He stepped over to me and shrugged. 'I'm a smith. I know metal work, not soldiering. But if you need me, I can wield a hell of a fucking hammer. Count me in!'

One by one, other voices rose up in agreement: farmers, carters, shoemakers . . . people who had simply reached the end of their tether.

'What say *you*, priest?' the tailor begged, hoping for an ally. 'Even if we beat Baldwin back, will we survive one hell only to be damned in another?'

'I cannot say,' Father Leo shrugged. 'What I can say, though, is that the next time Baldwin's riders come here, you can count on me to throw a stone or two.'

There were shouts of acquiescence all around. But the

village was still divided. The tailor, the tanner, some farmers were petrified to lose their lands.

I went up to the tailor. 'One thing I *can* promise: Baldwin's men will come. You'll rebuild your homes and pay to the bone every year until your hands blister or your will dies. But they will always come. Until we tell them *they cannot.'*

Martin shook his head. 'You wear a patchwork skirt and a bell upon your cap, and *you're* going to show us how to fight?'

'I will.' I looked him in the eye.

The tailor seemed to measure me up and down. He fitted the tunic back upon my shoulders. 'Whoever did this, it's a nice job.' Then he took my hand and clasped it wearily. 'God help us,' he declared.

Chapter Eighty-Five

'**M**ove it here!' I called to Martin, at his perch atop the tree. 'A little to the right. Where the road narrows.'

High above the road, Martin hoisted a heavy wheat sack bulging with rocks and gravel. He tied off the sack with a long rope and double-knotted the other end to a sturdy branch.

'I'll send the horse,' I said to him. 'When it reaches my position, let the rocks go.'

Since the bailiff's visit, we'd begun the task of fitting the village for its defences. Woodsmen sheared off wooden barriers, to be placed in rows along the village's western edge. Stakes were sharpened, and driven into the ground at jutting angles that even the bravest warhorse would not advance upon. Large stones were inserted, half-buried, in the road.

And we began to make weapons. A few old-timers brought out their swords, rusty old things. Odo polished and sharpened them on his lathe. The rest of our arsenal consisted of clubs and mallets, a few spears and billhooks, iron tools. From these we sharpened arrows that could pierce armour and spears. We were a village of Davids preparing for Goliath.

I backed off and signalled down the road. Apples, the baker's son, slapped the horse and sent him coming. Martin braced himself on his perch, tipping the weighted sack to the edge. When the horse passed my spot, I shouted, 'Release!'

Martin let it go. In a sweeping arc, it hurtled out of the sky like a boulder picking up speed. As the horse passed, the sack swung across the road with a loud *whoosh*, at exactly the height of a man atop his mount. It might as well have been hurled by a catapult. Even the staunchest rider would not withstand its force.

Martin and Apples cheered.

'Now it's your turn, Alphonse.' I turned to the tanner's oldest boy, who had a slight stutter. He was a strapping fifteen, muscles beginning to bulge. I placed the club in his hands. 'The fallen knight will be stunned. For a few moments, he'll be pinned to the earth by his armour. You cannot hesitate.' I looked him in the eye and swung the club hard into an imaginary shape in the ground. 'You have to be prepared to do the deed.'

'I w-will,' the boy nodded. He was big and strong, but had never been in as much as a tussle. Yet he had seen his brother sliced in half by Baldwin's men. He took the club and sent it crashing down. 'D-don't worry about m-me,' he said.

I nodded approvingly.

It felt so good to see the village come together. Everyone could do something useful. Woodsmen could shoot; children could throw stones; the elderly could sew leather armour and sharpen arrows.

But when it came down to it, it would take more than high spirits and eagerness to ward off Baldwin's raiders. We would have to fight. I prayed to God we were up to this – that I was not, like the hermit Peter, leading them into a murderous rout.

'Hugh . . .' I heard an urgent voice call from the direction of the village. Pipo was running towards me, Odo's little son. His face was ruddy with importance. I felt a shudder of alarm.

'Someone's here,' he gasped, out of breath.

'Who?' For a moment, my heart clenched. *Who knew I was here?*

'A visitor,' the boy said. 'And a pretty one. She says she came all the way from Blois.'

Chapter Eighty-Six

E *milie!*
I ran the dusty road back to the village, my heart bounding with excitement and surprise. I had thought of her so much, yet I always felt it was just another stupid dream to believe she would find me, that I would ever see Emilie again!

I took a short cut through the stables and blacksmith's stalls, and saw her in the square – with her maid. She wore a simple linen dress, her hair pinned up under a cap, and a plain, brown riding cloak about her shoulders. And yet she was lovely, so beautiful. I had to tell myself this was no dream. She was here!

I came out from behind the barn and let her see me. I did not know whether to run and sweep Emilie up into the air, or just stand there. 'In all the world, my lady,' I said, 'you have no idea what joy this brings me.'

' "In all the world" is *right*, Hugh DeLuc,' she smiled, her eyes twinkling, 'for it feels like I have travelled it to find you.'

How I ached to wrap her in my arms. I did not know what feelings had brought her here – or even what feelings were my own. Yet I held back. She was still a noble, and I was there in torn rags and a patched skirt.

'I'm sorry for your trouble,' I told her, 'but you are a sight for dreaming eyes no matter how far you've come. But *how*? How did you find me here?'

'You said you were from the south,' Emilie picked up her satchel and walked up to me, 'so I merely went to the spot where we found you on the road, and continued south. And south. And *south*, even more. Every village we passed, I asked, "Is there a very strange person here who has come from Blois, who wears a jester's suit?" I had gone so far south I thought I would hear Spanish, when this nice boy answered, "Yes, ma'am. You must mean Hugh." I thanked God to hear that word since we could not drag ourselves on one more mile. This is Elena.' She waved her attendant forward. 'She accompanied me on the trip.'

'Elena,' I bowed, 'I have seen you at Blois.'

The servant curtsied wearily, clearly delighted their journey had come to an end.

I turned back to Emilie. 'So tell me, how have you come here? And why?'

'Because I promised I would come. Because I told you I would do what I could do to find you the answers you sought. I will explain later.'

'And you came all this way alone? The two of you? Do you not know the risk you took?'

'I told Anne that I had arranged a visit to my Aunt Juliette in Toulon. There was such commotion in Blois, with Stephen's return, I am sure she was happy to be rid of me. We were escorted on our way by a party of priests heading south on a pilgrimage.'

'But your aunt? When the party arrives in Toulon, you will be missed.'

Emilie bit her lip, guiltily. 'My Aunt Juliette does not know. There never was any visit. I made it up.'

I broke into a wide grin. 'You have taken on the world to visit me. But you and Elena must be tired and hungry. I'm afraid we have no castles in these parts,' I smiled, 'but there is no shortage of hospitality. Come, I know just the place.'

I threw her leather satchel over my back. Everyone had come out and was staring. It must have seemed an incredible sight: Hugh, who had come back from his travels with empty pockets, in torn and preposterous clothes, with this very special visitor. A woman of high-born status. *A noble* . . . And a most beautiful one.

I stopped before my inn. 'This was our inn. I have taken up the work to rebuild it.'

I noticed a twinkle of approval light up Emilie's eyes. 'It is good work, Hugh.'

'It's no castle, I know, but you'll be warm and comfortable. It's got a good roof and a hearth.'

'I am honoured. Don't you think, Elena? I have heard the fare in such country places is quite good. And they say the innkeeper's charming.'

I beamed. 'Then welcome, ladies. To the Château DeLuc. You will be my first guests!'

Chapter Eighty-Seven

There was a big celebration in the village that night.

We ate at Odo's table, which filled most of his hut. His wife, Lissette, cooked, helped by Winnie, the miller's wife. There were Odo and Georges, my closest friends, and Father Leo. And, of course, Emilie.

A special meal was prepared, a goose roasted in the hearth. With carrots and turnips and peas, a soup of vegetables in a garlicky broth, and fresh bread that we dipped in the soup. There was no wine, but the priest brought along a cask of Belgian ale he'd been saving for the bishop's visit. By our standards, it was a rare feast.

Odo played the flute and we all pitched in with *chansons*. And I performed a few tricks, a flip or two. Everyone laughed and danced – Emilie too. For a few hours, everyone forgot the past. For the first time in years, I felt a smile etched on my face.

All the while I could not keep my gaze far from the brightness of Emilie's eyes. They were as light as the moon, and just as natural. She clapped and laughed as Odo's children tried to reproduce my flips, as if this were the most natural role for her in the world. She told them of life in the castle. It was a golden moment, free from all barriers and stations in life.

Afterwards, I walked with her back to the inn. There was still a chill in the air and Emilie huddled tightly in her cloak. Part of me wanted to put my arm around her; another part quivered with nerves.

We walked amid the noises of the spring night – crickets chirping, owls hooting, birds fluttering in the trees. A bright, round moon peeked through the clouds.

I asked her, 'How is Norbert? His health?'

'He is fine again,' Emilie said, 'except he is still unable to do that trick with the chains. But things have changed since Stephen's return. The Tafurs are everywhere, and the duke is behind them.'

'Stephen and *Anne*,' I replied.

'Anne . . .' Emilie hesitated. 'I believe with all my heart she did not act on her own accord.'

'You mean the raids she directed in her husband's absence, the slaughter and mayhem, these were not hers.'

'I only meant that she behaved from fear. I do not justify it. She said something to me, Hugh, that I did not understand. I pressed her on why she allowed these things to occur, and she laughed and said, "You don't know how lucky your Red is. If it was known the person we sought all along was amongst us, your jester would be dead, beside his wife, not running free."'

I narrowed my eyes. 'They sought *me*?'

'She called you the *innkeeper*, from the Crusade. It was why they took your wife. But she claimed she did not know this was you.'

'Why? Why in God's name would they want me?'

' "Because you hold the greatest prize in Christendom," ' Emilie tilted her head to me, ' "and do not know." That is what Anne says.'

'The greatest prize in Christendom . . .' I started to laugh. 'Are they mad? Look around you. I have nothing. All that I had they've already taken.'

'I told her the same. But you were there, Hugh, on the Crusade. Perhaps they confuse you with someone else.'

I stood there, dumbfounded. I had nothing in my pockets, no loot overflowing my vault, and no *vault*, only the very clothes on my back. What had I taken from them? My God – what could it be?

We had arrived at the inn. Emilie shivered in the cold night air, and I ached to hold her, just for a moment. I would have given anything to have her in my arms. Even 'the greatest prize in Christendom'.

'I brought something for you, Hugh. I have it here.' We ducked inside the door. By the fiery hearth, Elena was already asleep on her mat. Emilie went over to her satchel.

. She came back with a calfskin pouch fastened at the top, and from it removed a wooden box the size of my two palms. It was finely engraved, the mark of a craftsman, with an ornate letter 'C' inlaid on its lid.

She placed the box in my hands and stepped back. 'I called it a gift, but it's not. This always belonged to you, Hugh. It's why I came.'

I stood there, examining the box a moment, then lifted the tiny latch and opened the lid.

Burning tears welled in my eyes. Immediately, I knew what the box contained.

Ashes.

Sophie's ashes.

'Her body was burned the following day,' Emilie said softly. 'I went and gathered these. The priests say her soul will not reach Heaven unless she is buried. I promised you I would bring her back.'

A knot rose in my throat and chest. I took the deepest breath, sucking air through every fibre in my body. 'You cannot know how much I treasure this gift, Emilie.'

'As I said, Hugh, it always belonged to you.'

I wrapped my arms around her and drew her close. I felt her heart beating against mine.

I whispered beneath my breath, so only I could hear. 'I meant you.'

Chapter Eighty-Eight

The following morning, I rose before the sun. I took the calfskin pouch that was next to my bed and slipped out of the inn.

Next to the woodshed, I found a few scattered tools. I took a carpenter's pick and a stake sharpened for the town's defences. The cocks had not yet crowed.

A few early risers fluttered about their chores. A carter was heading out with his mule. By the baker's hut, the smell of dough baking perfumed the air.

I climbed the hill to the knoll overlooking our village.

I had dreamed of this so many times since Sophie had died in my arms – bringing her home. The thought that her soul was not at rest, that no rites or blessings had been performed, tormented me. Now, her life would be complete. She would rest here for ever.

By the ford in the stream I began to climb a second steep hill. Now the morning was alive with birds chirping in the softening light. The sun tried to burn through the mist. I climbed for a few minutes; soon, I was above the village. I looked back over the waking valley. The little huts had begun to show life. I saw the square, and the inn. Emilie was sleeping there.

On top of the hill, I went to a spot near a spreading elm where my son's grave lay.

I kneeled and placed the calfskin pouch down. Then I began to dig. I made a space in the ground next to him. Tears glistened in my eyes as a heavy drum pounded inside my chest.

'At last you're home, Sophie,' I whispered. 'You and Philippe.'

I opened the pouch and held the box with the C. Then I scattered her ashes into the earth. I took out the half of Sophie's comb I had found in the ashes of the inn. I placed it in the earth. I stood there at her grave and looked back over the awakening village.

You are finally home, Sophie. Your soul can rest.

Chapter Eighty-Nine

S tephen of Blois sat stolidly on the high-backed chair in his court. A crowd of toadying favour-seekers stood in line as his bailiff brought him up to date on a new tax. Behind him, the seneschal readied a report on the status of his demesne. His mind was a thousand miles away.

An incompleteness jabbed at Stephen. Since he had been back, the business of his estates, his holdings, things that had once meant everything to him, now seemed trivial, worthless. These functionaries droned on and on, but he could not concentrate. His mind was a brooding pit that focused on a single, far-off point of light.

The prize. The treasure.

It haunted him, invaded his dreams. This holy relic miraculously preserved for centuries in the tombs of the Holy Land. He longed for it with an avarice he had reserved for no woman. Something that had touched Him. He woke in the night dreaming about it, his body consumed in sweat. His lips grew dry, just thinking of its touch.

With such a prize in hand, Blois would be among the most powerful cities in Europe. What a cathedral he would build to house its glory. What was the worth of the meagre bones of St Laumer, his own patron saint, resting in his reliquary? It was nothing compared to this prize. People would come from all over the world to make pilgrimages to Blois. No cleric would be greater than he, nor closer to God.

And it was *here*. He knew who had it.

A fury built in Stephen's chest. His lords were blathering on, blabbering about his holdings, his wealth. It was all rubbish – insignificant. He felt as if he were about to explode.

He stood up and screamed, '*Get out!*' The bailiff and the seneschal looked at him surprised. 'Get out! Leave me be! You go on about this new tax, or a new flock of pigs. Your eyes are fixed on the ground. I am dreaming of everlasting life.'

He swept his hand across the table and a tray of wine goblets clattered to the floor. Everybody scurried, fleeing their places as if the whole building were about to collapse.

Only Norbert remained, his jester, who clung to the base of his chair, shaking like a man in seizure, trying to make him laugh.

'It is no use, Norbert. Do not waste your jest. Let it be.'

'It is no jest,' Norbert shook, lips trembling. 'Your chair is on my hand.'

Finally, Stephen grunted back a smile and the loyal jester rolled away, shaking his swollen hand.

A servant nervously approached to clear the mess. Stephen waved him away. He followed the trail of spilled wine, until his eyes came to rest upon someone's boot.

Who is so presumptuous as to approach? Stephen thought. He looked up, his eyes coming to rest on the face of Morgaine, the leader of his Tafur guard. *Black Cross.*

'Have you come to taunt me, Morgaine, with news of another village laid waste, without my prize?'

'No, I have come to cheer you, my lord, with news that I know where the treasure is.'

Stephen's eyes widened. 'Where?'

'Your cousin, the Lady Emilie, has led me right to it,' Black Cross said with a pinched smile.

'Emilie?' Stephen's face twitched. 'What has Emilie to do with this prize? She is in Toulon.'

'She is not in Toulon,' Black Cross said. He whispered close. 'But in a little pisshole in the province of Tours, Veille du Père.'

'Veille du Père . . .? I know that name. I thought you had already sacked—'

'Yes,' Morgaine nodded, seeing Stephen come to the understanding. 'She is with the innkeeper as we speak. And so is the treasure that we seek.'

Chapter Ninety

To my amazement and delight, Emilie did not leave as soon as she had delivered her gift. She stayed on for the next few days. I was in Heaven.

I showed her the work I was doing to fortify the village: the perimeter defences of sharpened stakes, strong enough to repel a sudden charge; the battle stations high in the trees from where we could rain arrows and stones on any attackers. She saw the passion with which I urged my friends and the villagers to resist. And she heartily approved!

In between, I treated her to the best sights of our village. The lily pond in the woods where I liked to swim. A field high in the hills where the early sunflowers ran wild. And she helped me at the inn. I showed her how to fit logs into a support column with pegs and joints. She helped me hoist up a log as a support beam. Then we carved her initials into the wood: *Em. C.*

I knew this fantasy would have to come to an end. Soon, she would leave. Yet she seemed comfortable. So I allowed myself to pretend. That Emilie would not be missed and looked for. That it was safe here, free from attack. That something unthinkable was happening between us.

It was on a warm spring afternoon a few days later that I tossed down my tools before noon. 'Come,' I took Emilie by the hand, 'it's not a day to be working. I want to show you a beautiful place. Please, my lady.'

I took her up in the hills, past the knoll where Sophie and Philippe lay. The sun beat deliciously against our skin. High above the village, an open meadow stretched out, filled with sunflowers about to bloom. The scent of wild lavender was in the air.

'It's gorgeous!' Emilie exclaimed, her eyes soaking in every burst of blue and flash of yellow.

She flung herself down in the field and fanned her arms and legs into the shape of a star. 'Come here, Hugh, this is Heaven.' She patted the grass next to her for me to join her.

I lay down beside her. Her soft golden hair fell off her shoulders and I could see the hint of her breasts peeking under the neckline of her dress. My blood was running wild and it terrified me for obvious reasons.

'Tell me,' I propped myself up on my elbow, 'what does the C stand for?'

'The C . . .?'

'Your family name . . . It was on the box you gave me, and the initials we carved into the wood at the inn. I know nothing about you. Who you are? Where you are from? Your family?'

'Are you concerned,' she laughed, 'that I may not be a high enough match for you?'

'Of course not, I just—'

'I was born in Paris, if you must know. I am the fourth sister, with two brothers, all older. My father is remarkable, as you say, but not for the reasons you suspect.'

'He is a noble, that much I know. A member of the royal court?'

'He is important, leave it at that. And educated. But sometimes his vision is as narrow as a fly's.'

'You are the baby,' I winked, 'and yet you have wandered away from the nest.'

'The nest is not always a welcome place.' Emilie looked away. 'At least not for a woman down the pecking order. What is there for me, except to be educated in lofty arts and concepts I will never use? Or to be married off for gain to some old sod twice my age? Can you see me, entertaining and receiving gifts from gassy old coots?'

'I have met only two duchesses,' I said, beaming, 'and you outshine them in both beauty and heart.'

She put her palm against mine, and we held it there, for a moment, in silence. Then Emilie pushed me away. 'Make me laugh, will you?'

'Make you laugh?'

'Yes, you were a jester. Quite a decent one.' Her eyes shone. 'Come on. It shouldn't be hard for you.'

'It's not so easy,' I stammered. 'I mean, you just don't blurt out a joke, in a place like this, and have it succeed.'

'Are you embarrassed then? By *me*? Come,' she pinched my arm, 'it is only us. I will close my eyes. In all the world, it should not be so hard to know what will make me smile.'

Emilie closed her eyes with her chin raised. I stared at her face, the delicate yellow hair falling off her shoulder.

I felt my breath come to a halt.

She was incredibly lovely . . . and kind, generous and smart as a whip.

All of a sudden, there was nothing between us, no words, no barriers, just our two beating hearts. I placed my hand on her hip. Nervously – I prayed she would not take offence – I moved it up her side, over the curve of her hip and waist, the thrill of feeling skin I had never touched before.

She made no move to resist. I felt the strangest urge come over me. My breath tight, my spine tingling. Had I felt this from the start? From the first moment I opened my eyes and saw her face?

I moved my hand over her shoulder, and let it fall, gently, against the round of her breast. I felt her heart quiver. I had felt this only once before. Yet here it was again.

Slowly, I placed my mouth upon her lips.

Emilie did not resist, only leaned closer, her mouth softly parting. Our tongues seemed to merge and dance, as softly as clouds meeting in the sky.

She put her hand on my cheek and moved over me, her breath as heavy as my own. Her skin smelled of lavender and balsam. In the warm rush of our kiss, I felt a new world open to me.

In a breath, we pulled away. She put her chin on my chest and smiled. 'You take advantage of me. I was warned of such country boys.'

'Tell me to wake up,' I said. 'I know I am in a dream.'

'Wake up, then,' she placed my hand upon her heart, 'and know that this is real.'

My own heart almost exploded with joy and I could not believe what was happening.

Then I heard the loud peal of church bells coming from the village.

Chapter Ninety-One

I knew such a sound was a call of *warning*.

My heart jolted back to the present. I frantically rose to my knees and peered down towards the village. I saw no riders, no sign of panic yet. We were not under attack.

But a crowd was forming in the square. *Something had happened.*

'Come,' I pulled Emilie up, 'we have to get back.'

We ran down the hill as fast as we could. As soon as I came within earshot of the village I heard my name shouted.

Georges the miller ran up to me. 'Hugh, they're coming. Men from Blois are on their way.'

I looked at Emilie, then back at Georges. 'How do you know this?'

'Someone is here to warn us. Come, quick, in the church. He looks for you.'

Georges ran with me into the main square. The village had assembled, and voices rang out, panicked and afraid.

I pushed through the crowd around the church and came upon a young man resting on the steps, no more than sixteen, panting, clearly out of breath. When he saw me, he stood up and eyed me.

'You are Hugh,' the boy said. 'I can tell by your red hair.'

'I am,' I answered. He looked vaguely familiar. 'You come from Blois?'

'Yes,' the boy nodded. 'I have run for two days. I am sent by your friend Norbert the jester.'

'Norbert sent you?' I went up to him and stood close. 'What news do you bring?'

'He said to tell you – they are coming. For everyone to prepare.'

'I must try to go back,' Emilie said, clutching my arm. 'I must tell them it's a mistake.'

'You cannot.' The boy shook his head, alarmed. 'Norbert said you *must not return*. That Stephen knows you are here. You were followed. The duke's guards are on their way. They will be here, tonight perhaps. Latest, tomorrow.'

Frantic cries rose in the crowd. A woman fainted. Martin the tailor pointed at me. 'Now what? This is your work, Hugh. What are we to do?'

'Fight!' I shouted back. 'This is what we expected.'

There were whimperings and worried faces. Wives sought out their husbands and clutched children to their bosoms.

'We are prepared,' I said again. 'These men come to take away what is ours. We will not bow down to them.'

Dread hung over the crowd. Then Odo stepped forward. He looked around, tapped the head of his hammer on the ground. 'I'm with you. So is my hammer!'

'I'm with you too,' said Alphonse. 'And my sharpened axe.'

'And I,' cried Apples.

They ran towards their positions as the rest of the crowd stood still. Then others followed, one by one.

I turned back to the messenger. 'How do I know you are who you say? That you've come from Norbert? You say the Lady Emilie was followed. This could be your trick.'

'You know my face, Hugh. I am Lucien, the baker's boy. I sought an apprenticeship with Norbert.'

'Apprentices can be bought,' I challenged him further.

'Norbert said you would press me. So he sent proof. Something of value to you, that could come from no one other than him.'

He reached behind him on the church steps and unwound a woollen blanket.

A smile curled on my face. Norbert was right. What the boy had brought was of great value to me. I had not seen it since I left Blois in the middle of the night.

Lucien was holding my staff.

Chapter Ninety-Two

In the next few hours, the village bustled with a purpose I had not seen before.

Bales of sharpened stakes were dragged to positions just inside the stone bridge and driven into the ground. Heavy sacks filled with sand were readied in the trees. Those who could shoot sharpened their arrows and stocked their quivers; those who could not sat with hoes and mallets in their hands.

By the time night had started to fall, everyone was nervous, but prepared.

The plan was for old folk and some of the women and very young children to flee to the woods before the first sign of trouble. I told Emilie she had to go too. But when the time came, no one would leave.

'I'm staying with you.' Emilie shook her head. She had torn her dress at the hem, and her sleeves, to move about more easily. 'I can stack arrows. I can distribute arms.'

'These men are killers,' I tried to reason with her. 'They'll make no distinction between noble or common. This is not your fight.'

'You are wrong. The distinction between noble and common is clear here today,' she replied, with that same unbending resolve she'd shown when she'd rescued me at Blois. 'And it has become my fight.'

I left her stacking rocks and ran to the first defences under the bridge. Alphonse and Apples were tightening the rope.

'How many will come?' Alphonse asked.

'I do not know,' I said. 'Twelve, twenty, maybe more. Enough to do what it takes.'

'M-maybe when they see the fire they will run away,' he said.

'They won't run away,' I told the boy.

I took my station upstairs in the tailor's house, near the entrance to the village. From there, I could oversee the attack. I had a sword, an old clunker sharpened to a point.

My stomach ground in knots. Now, all that was left to do was wait.

Emilie met me in the evening light. We sat with our backs to the wall, her head resting on my shoulder. I felt the steady beating of her heart against my chest. I knew what I had always known about her. *She gave me strength.*

'Whatever happens,' she tightened against my arm, 'I am glad to be here with you. I don't know how to explain, but I feel you have a destiny in front of you.'

'When the Turk spared me, I thought it was just to make people laugh,' I chuckled.

'And you became a jester.'

'Yes. Thanks to you.'

'Not me,' Emilie raised herself and looked at me. '*You.* It is you who had the court at Blois eating out of your hand. But now I think God has found you a higher purpose. I think this is it.'

I pressed her tightly to my body, feeling her breasts against my ribs, the cadence of her heart. In my loins, I felt desire spark. We looked at each other, and something told me, unspoken, that this was right. She was where she belonged. And so was I.

'I do not want to die,' Emilie said, 'and never know what it is like to be with you.'

'I won't let you die.' I cupped her fist.

She lowered herself on to me and we kissed. Not as before, but with the thrill of friendship deepening into something more forceful, more profound. The tempo of Emilie's breath began to quicken.

I put my hands under her dress and felt the smoothness of her stomach. My skin jumped alive all over.

She raised herself on my lap. We looked in each other's eyes and there was no hesitation. 'I love you,' I told her. 'From the first. There was no doubt.'

'There was doubt,' she whispered, 'that I loved you too.'

She lowered herself on top of me and gasped as I entered her. Soon, she was calm and at ease. I held her by the hips and we rocked. Her eyes lit with pleasure and my skin grew heated and damp and we increased the pace. We were eye to eye, rocking against time, a smile and a sheen of ardour on her face. 'Oh, Hugh,' she squeezed her pelvis into me, 'I do love you.'

At last she cried out, a body-tremoring moan. I held her close to me and squeezed her shoulders as though I would never let go. She trembled once more in my arms.

'Do not wake me,' she sighed, 'for I am in the midst of the most marvellous dream.'

She buried her face in my chest and I could have stayed like that for ever. I looked out at the moon and thought: what a miracle it is that I have found this woman. I wanted to hold her and protect her with all my heart, as she had risked everything to protect me.

Was this why I had been saved? I could ask no better purpose.

Then I heard a shout, and an alarmed cry. A chilling, far-off rumble came from the earth. My body clenched.

I ran to the window. A fiery arrow arced towards us across the sky. The lookout's signal.

I looked at Emilie, the calm of a moment ago replaced by a stabbing dread. *They are here!'*

Chapter Ninety-Three

B lack Cross's men stood just outside the sleeping village. The moonless night covered their approach. They had ridden for the better part of two days, barrelling at full speed, knocking people and carts out of their way, as they charged through tiny forest villages. Black Cross knew that the hard journey only heightened his men's eagerness for blood.

Up ahead, a scout crept back from the woods. 'The village sleeps, my lord. It is ripe for attack.'

'And their defences?' Morgaine enquired.

'Only one,' the scout smirked. 'They have piled their shit in the road so high, our horses may not see.'

Morgaine chuckled as well. This would be child's play. Babes slaughtered in their sleep. He had sought this beetle all the way from Antioch. Now, he was only minutes from holding his prize, the greatest of all of them. This insect would not slither away again.

Morgaine said to his men, 'Whoever finds the prize will have a castle on his return. Kill who you have to, fuck who you like, just find the redhead. Run a blade up his arse and bring the worm to me.'

His men's eyes lit up. Senses eager for battle, one by one they applied their breastplates and shoulder pieces over their riding leathers. They chose their arms – maces and pikes and heavy swords. They strapped them over their steel-beaded gloves. In a few moments they would turn this sleepy mound of dung into a slop of blood. They fitted on their helmets. Bright eyes glinted through the slits.

Morgaine's lieutenant signalled to him. 'What orders, sir?'

'Level it,' Morgaine said evenly. 'Every home, every child. Other than the innkeeper, nothing lives. I want nothing left, and that includes the Lady Emilie.'

The Tafur nodded. At Morgaine's nod, he gave the signal to charge.

Chapter Ninety-Four

The ground shook beneath my feet. The rumble of hoofs grew louder and louder, intensifying like an avalanche approaching fast.

I ran into the street. People stuck out their heads from their positions, looks of anxiety and terror building in their eyes.

'Do not panic,' I urged them. 'They think this will be child's play. Everyone, remember the plan.'

Inside, I felt the grinding fist of fear that must now be intensifying in everybody's gut. I hurried towards Alphonse and Apples, bracing the rope on either side of the bridge. I told them, 'Remember what they did to your friends and the village children the last time they were here. Remember what you swore in your heart you would do to them if you ever had the chance. Now is that chance!'

The thundering noise had risen to a terrifying pitch. It was hard to stand; the ground was shaking beneath my feet. I could not tell if the noise crashing through me was the drum of approaching hoofs or my heart beating out of control.

Finally we saw them – a black cloud bearing down on us

from out of the woods, torches in hand. Twelve to fourteen, howling cries of death.

A spark of hope flared in me. The village was dark. I knew they could not see our defences.

'Hold tight,' I hollered, as the horses neared, but then my words were drowned in the advancing roar.

The first line of horsemen galloped over the bridge, then straight into the tautness of the tightened rope. In a tangle of groans and shouts, the horses came down. The bodies of the two lead riders were pitched in the air. With a terrifying scream, one was hurled headlong on to the sharpened stakes and impaled through the chest, his limbs out-stretched and twitching. The other catapulted off his mount, landing on his neck, his body tossed and trampled under the advancing hoofs.

Seeing the ambush, the next line of marauders attempted to stop, but their speed was too great. A third rider fell, screaming. Then another.

I saw Odo leaping out from under the bridge and as one struggled to right himself, swing his heavy club downwards, smashing it into the man's head. His helmet caved in like tin. Buoyed by the sight, Apples dashed out as well, thrusting his sword through the other raider's neck.

The torches carried by the fallen riders sent the wooden defences up in flames. Horses whined and bucked. Arrows shot out from the trees and two more riders hit the ground, pierced through the neck and head. The other marauders, seeing what had happened, regrouped on the bridge. One by one, they darted single-file through the burning defences, into the village.

Now guards on horseback were in the streets, flinging

torches into our homes. I waved my sword up to the trees. 'Now, Martin, *now*!'

Suddenly a dark shape fell out of the sky, hurtling across the road and crashing into one of the riders, knocking him off his mount with a loud groan. He remained there, stunned, pinned to the ground by the weight of his armour. I raised my sword and screamed into the slits of his helmet, 'This is for Sophie, you bastard. See what it's like to be killed by a fool.' I crashed the sword down, penetrating cleanly through the seam above the chest plate. There it remained embedded. I couldn't pull the sword free.

For a moment, and even without a weapon, I felt exultant. This was working. People were fighting. Seven of the invaders were down, perhaps slain. One or two more were off their horses, surrounded by village men, pelting them with clubs and stones. The Tafurs tried to fight in all directions, overwhelmed, thrashing at air.

I watched as Alphonse climbed up the back of one of the attackers and pushed a knife through the eye slit in his helmet. The Tafur pitched forward. He thrashed back and forth, jabbing his mace, trying to twist the boy off. Another boy swatted a beam at the man's knees and sent him to the ground, where Alphonse jerked the blade across the bastard's neck and soon he rolled over, dead.

All around, people were screaming, running back and forth. A few riders made their way through the village, hurling torches on to the thatched roofs, which shot into yellow flame. I counted only six invaders left, but six armed and deadly, still on their mounts. If we backed down now, they were enough to take the village.

I started to run – weaponless – towards the square.

'Here!' Emilie yelled, and tossed me my staff.

Across the road, I saw poor Jackie, the ruddy-faced milk woman, hurling stones at one attacker while another galloped up from behind and knocked her to the ground with a mace. Arrows shot out of the trees and the attacker staggered. He was immediately consumed by villagers, kicking and bashing him with clubs and farm tools.

Suddenly the square lit up in flames.

Amiée, the miller's daughter, and Father Leo had set fire to the line of brush ringing the square. The horses of the circling invaders reared in the air. One was immediately thrown, landing in the flames. The others dashed and circled, unable to break through.

The fallen rider stood up, engulfed in flames. He thrashed about hysterically, smoke pouring through the slits in his armour. Fire had seeped inside; his skin was boiling like a pot over a flame.

Two other attackers remained trapped inside the ring of flame. One tried to force his mount through, but Martin the tailor ran up and whacked at the horse's legs. The rider clubbed at him, but was thrown from his mount. He flailed on the ground, struggling to right himself, his weapon out of arm's reach. Then from behind out of the darkness Amiée ran out. She raised an axe and crashed it solidly into the man's head.

We were winning! The town continued to battle, as only people clinging to their last hope can do. Still, three or four invaders remained.

Then, to my horror, the last Tafur who'd been contained within the ring of fire burst free. He reared his steed, and made his way, axe whirling, towards Amiée, who still stood staring at her victim's mangled corpse.

'Look out, Amiée!' I yelled. I started towards her, help-lessly screaming at the top of my lungs. I couldn't bear to see the miller lose his last child. The girl did not move, oblivious to death descending upon her. I was running as fast as my feet would fly, not thinking. The rider crouched and reared his axe.

I shrieked, 'No . . .!'

I reached her at a cross angle, just as the Tafur swung his axe. I swept Amiée to the ground and covered her, expect-ing at any moment to feel the blade of the axe buried in my back. But no blow came.

The Tafur galloped by, then reversed. He stood for a moment, tightening his reins, surveying the rout of his fellow men.

I knew his mind; I had seen it many times on the Crusade. It was the time of the battle when one knows all is lost; the only thing left is to fight whatever comes in your path and cause as much death and mayhem until you too are taken down.

I pushed Amiée out of the square and raised myself to my feet. I stood there, facing the attacker, nothing to defend myself with but my wooden staff.

I didn't want to die here. But I would not run.

The raider reared his giant warhorse and galloped into a charge. I stood my ground, as the thundering iron shape barrelled towards me.

I braced myself and raised the staff.

Chapter Ninety-Five

As the charging horseman raised his axe, I darted to the side opposite his weapon. I swung my staff as hard as I could at his mount's legs. The animal neighed in pain, buckled, then threw his rider. The Tafur hit the earth with a mighty crash and rolled over several times until he came to a stop ten feet from where I stood.

His giant war axe had fallen to the side. I ran to grab the weapon. The Tafur was wearing an armour of ringed mail and in the time I took to arm myself, he had managed to right himself and draw his sword.

'*Deo iuvante*,' he sneered at me. 'With God's help, I will send this little rat-tail back to his maker.'

'By all means, God, look on,' I replied in kind.

He charged at me with a ferocious roar.

I could see him go high with his blade and met his blow, our weapons crashing with a loud clang. We stood there, eye to eye, each trying to drive his blade into the other's neck, muscles straining to the edge. All of a sudden the Tafur jerked his knee into my groin. The air rushed out of me. I gasped and bent in two. In the same instant, he swept his weapon towards my knees and I summoned every sliver of strength to counter with the axe.

Again we faced each other, pupils blazing. He tried to head butt me with the crown of his helmet, but I threw myself back. I stumbled and the Tafur leaped at me, swinging his blade back and forth with a maniacal fury.

The Tafur saw that I was slowed. He laughed, 'Come here, fairy. You look as if you might want to feel a set of real balls.'

I crouched back warily. His sword was too quick. In this form of fighting, I was no match for him. The axe was clumsy and heavy in my weakened grasp.

'Come . . .' He blew me a kiss.

I looked him in the eye, panting heavily. I knew I would not be able to ward off the blows much longer. I felt my legs wobble; I was out of strength. I searched my mind for any form of skill or trickery I had seen in the wars. Then one clicked in. It was crazy, desperate, not a soldier's, but a jester's trick.

'Why wait?' I said, lowering the axe-blade, pretending to be beaten, exhausted. 'What's wrong with now?'

I turned my back to him. I hoped I wasn't crazy.

I bent into a deep crouch, flipped up my doublet, and let him see my rear. 'C'mon . . .' I winked, 'I'd wait for a real man, but you're the only one here.' I tossed the axe about four feet ahead.

In my crouch, I saw him raise his sword and come. Just as he was set to run me through I sprang into a forward flip. The Tafur whooshed at the air, where suddenly there was no person. His sword stuck in the soggy earth.

I landed on my feet and in the same movement, pivoted and grabbed the handle of the axe. I sprang back round as the surprised Tafur struggled to free his sword.

A look of panic spread over his face. This time it was I who smiled, and blew *him* a kiss.

I swung with all my might and sent the Tafur's head hurtling like a kicked ball.

I sank to my knees, out of breath. Every muscle in my body felt as though it were about to explode. I dropped the axe, sucking precious air into my lungs.

Then I rose and picked up my staff. Further up, there was still a battle raging. I headed back towards the fight, but a sniggering voice intoned, 'Well done, *innkeeper*. But you must conserve your kisses. You may need one or two over here.'

I turned. There was another Tafur. He had a black cross painted on his helmet, but his visor was up, revealing a cold, scarred face that I thought I had seen before.

But it was not the face I focused on.

The bastard was holding Emilie.

Chapter Ninety-Six

'**L**et her go,' I told him. 'This isn't her fight.'

The Tafur was large and strong, and twisted Emilie roughly by the hair with his sword edged into her neck. His dark hair was long and greasy and fell over his scarred face. A black cross was burned into his neck.

'*Let her go?*' he laughed. The Tafur twisted her harder and Emilie sank to her knees. 'But she is so pretty and sweet. What a treat she'll make for me.' He inhaled her hair. 'Like you, I am not used to sifting my pole through such high-born trash.'

I took a step towards him. 'What is it you want from me?'

'I think you know, *innkeeper* . . . I think you know where we have met once before too.'

I focused on his hard, laughing eyes. Suddenly the past rocketed through me. The church in Antioch. *He was the bastard who had killed the Turk.*

'*You* are Black Cross? You are the one doing these terrible deeds?'

The Tafur grinned in recognition. ' "*You are free . . .*" innkeeper, do you not remember? When I saw you last you had an infidel about to plough your arse. But enough of old times.' He forced Emilie to her knees. 'I would be happy to let her go. You only have to hand over what is mine.'

'Tell me what you want,' I shouted. 'You've already taken everything I have.'

'Not all, innkeeper.' He forced up Emilie's chin and edged his silvery blade along her neck. She sucked in a gasp. 'Where is it? Her future awaits.'

'*Where is what?*' I screamed. I looked at Emilie, so helpless there. Anger and panic flared in my blood.

'Do not toy with me, Red,' the Tafur glared. 'You were there in Antioch, the church. I saw you. You were no more sightseeing than I. Quick, now, or I will ram my blade through her pretty skull.'

I was there . . . Suddenly, it came clear to me. The cross. The gold cross I had stolen from the church. That is what this was all about; why so many people had died. 'It is buried on the hill,' I said. 'Let her go. It is yours.'

'I will not barter with you.' The Tafur's face began to twitch with rage. 'Hand me what I want, or she will be pig-slop, and you next.'

'Then take it. I stole it from the church. It was just a trinket to me. I don't even know what it is, what it signifies. Just let her go and I will bring the gold cross to you. Just let her go.'

'*Cross?*' I could not tell if it was confusion or rage that shook his lips. He dug the blade into Emilie and spat, 'I do not want your fucking cross, not if you took it from St Peter's arse. You know very well what prize you hold.'

'I *don't* know . . .' My head was spinning. Panic shot up in my veins. 'I do not have anything else.'

'You must.' He jerked Emilie's head back.

'No!' I cried. *What else could it be?* I looked at this monster, Black Cross. He had killed Sophie. He had tossed my son into the flames. He had taken from me everything I loved. And now he would do it again. For what . . .? *For a thing I did not have!*

'Whatever it is, is it worth following me all the way back from the Holy Land? Slaughtering innocent villagers and children? My wife and child?'

'It is!' His eyes lit up. 'Those souls are meaningless compared to it, and a thousand more like your wife and seed. *Now*, innkeeper!' he yelled. 'Or I will rid the world of yet another you claim to love.'

'No.' I shook my head, at first numbly, then with rage in my eyes. 'You will not take anything else from me.'

I looked at Emilie. Her eyes bravely glistened back.

I knew, if I charged him, he would *not* kill her. It was me the Tafur needed. I was the path to his precious prize, not her. He would not risk leaving himself unguarded. I gripped my staff firmly in my palms. It was all I had, this stick against his sword. And my hands. And my will.

In the next breath, I screamed and charged the bastard.

Chapter Ninety-Seven

I swung my staff at him with everything I had.

In the same instant, Black Cross flung Emilie to the ground and readied himself for my blow. He was huge and agile, and blocked it easily with his sword.

'What is this prize!' I screamed, smashing and flailing my staff at all angles, 'that you would murder people who had never even heard of it? Was it worth my wife, my little son? Or even the most worthless soul you stamped out in your way?' I swung at him again and again – for Sophie, for Philippe, each blow crashing harmlessly against his sword. I thought my staff would surely split, or that at any moment I would feel it run through my gut.

'Is this pretence, jester? Do you mock me again to explain the meaning of the prize you stole?' He forced me backwards and began advancing, swinging his sword with half strength and forcing me to block the blows with the staff, the wood rattling in my grasp.

'*I do not have it,*' I shouted. 'I never have. You are mistaken.'

He swung at my legs and I darted back. Slivers of wood chipped away with the weight of his sword. 'You were there, jester. The church in Antioch. We all sought it out. Do you think these nobles were fighting for the souls of a few nuns? You try to tell me you don't know that the relic you fought the infidel for, that lay for centuries in that vault, was the same used to sacrifice Our Lord, and stained with his Holy Blood?'

I had no idea what he was talking about. He cut at my torso. I blocked the swipe again, the blade slicing against my hand, but it was only a matter of time before he landed the blow that would do me in.

'Did you sell it? Have you profited to some Jew? If you have, your death will only be more warranted.' He swung again, this time knocking me backwards to the ground, shattering a piece from my staff that I barely held up in defence.

My knuckles bled. My mind ricocheted back and forth. 'I do not have it. I swear!'

He swung again, the brute force of his blows almost shattering the staff in two. I knew it could sustain only a few more hits.

I heard shouts behind me. Emilie was screaming. She tried to leap on him and ward him off, but he flung her across the ground as if she were a toy.

The Tafur's eyes flashed. 'Give it to me, thief, *now*. For in another minute you will surely be in Hell.'

'If I am,' I whacked my stick at him, 'it will only be to welcome you.'

I was done. Out of breath and strength. I blocked the blows, but each one hacked a little further into the staff. I wanted to kill this man with all my heart – for Sophie, for Philippe – but I didn't have the strength.

He kicked me into a ditch off the road. I looked about for a weapon, anything to fight him. He raised his sword above my head. 'I give you this final chance,' he grunted. 'Produce it. You can still go free.'

'I have nothing!' I yelled at him. 'Can't you see that?'

He came down with his sword. I think I closed my eyes, for I knew this last, desperate defence would not hold. A chunk of my staff shattered. To my astonishment, a shaft of something shiny gleamed underneath.

Black Cross slashed at me again and again, yet each time, the staff miraculously held. The wooden rod split open, like a casing, revealing something underneath.

Iron.

My eyes clung to it. I was staring at the long, rusted shaft of an ancient spear.

The Tafur stopped, his gaze transfixed. The spear shaft led to a moulding in the shape of an eagle, a *Roman* eagle. The blade that came from it – dark, blunt, rusted – was encrusted with a dried, blood-like stain.

Good Lord in Heaven, I heard myself gasp. I blinked, twice, to make sure I wasn't in Heaven already.

My staff . . . the wooden staff I had taken from the church in Antioch, from the dying priest's hands . . . it wasn't a staff at all.

It was a lance.

Chapter Ninety-Eight

I do not know how to describe what happened next. Time seemed to stand still. Neither of us moved, transfixed by the incredible sight. Whatever this was, I could tell by the Tafur's stupefied amazement that the lance was what he sought all along. Now, miraculously, it was in front of him. His eyes were as large as moons. Though it was rusted and dulled, just a common thing, a phosphorescent aura seemed to burst from it.

Suddenly he lunged for it! He was still above me, with all the advantage. He reared back his sword. I had no defences. He would surely split my chest this time.

I thrust with the only thing I had – the lance. The blade split his mail and pierced into his ribs. Black Cross cried out, his huge, dark eyes gleaming wide, but even with the lance in him, he did not stop. He went to raise his sword again. I pushed the lance in deeper. This time his eyes rolled back in his head. He tried to lift the sword once more, his arms reaching the height of his head, hands squeezing on the hilt.

But his arms suddenly dropped. He gasped, opened his mouth as if to speak, and blood leaked out.

I pushed hard on the lance again and he froze, upright, disbelieving, as if he could not lose now, not with his prize in sight, so close. Then with a final grunt, Black Cross crumpled over and fell on to his back.

I lay there for a second, stunned that I was alive. I forced myself to my knees, and crawled to the dying man, his hands still wrapped around the shaft. 'What is it?' I asked.

He did not answer. Only coughed: blood and bile.

'*What is it?*' I cried. 'What is this thing? My wife and son died for it.'

I dug the spear out of his body and held it close to the dying man's face. He coughed again, but this time, it wasn't blood – he was laughing. 'Do you not know?' His chest wheezed – and then his face took on a thin smile. 'All along . . . you were blind?'

'Tell me,' I pulled him by the mail, 'before you die.'

'You *are* a fool,' he coughed again and smiled. 'You are the richest man in Christendom and do not know it. Do you not understand what lay in those tombs for a thousand years? Do you not recognize your own Saviour's blood.'

I stared at the ancient, blood-stained spear, my eyes almost bulging out of my head. The Spear of Longinus, the centurion who had stabbed Christ while He was dying on the Cross.

A numbness was in my chest. My hands began to tremble.

I was holding the Holy Lance.

Chapter Ninety-Nine

I staggered to my feet, cradling the precious relic in my hands. Emilie rushed up first, and threw her arms around my neck. The battle had ended and we had won. Georges, Odo, Father Leo came running towards me.

People approached, cheering, dancing with joy, but I could not take my eyes from the Lance. 'My staff . . .' I was barely able to speak. 'All along, it was the Holy Lance.'

Everyone stopped, converged. A hush fell over the crowd. *'The Holy Lance?'* someone gasped. A ring formed around us; murmurs of exclamation and joy. All eyes fell on the rusted blade, the tip slightly broken.

'Mother of God,' Georges the miller stepped forward, his tunic splattered with blood. 'Hugh has the Holy Lance.'

Finally, everyone kneeled, myself included.

Father Leo pushed through us. He examined the blade without touching it, fixing on the hardened blood upon the blade. 'God's grace,' he shook his head with a look of wonderment sparkling in his eyes. He recited scripture from memory,' "But one of the soldiers with a spear pierced His side, and forthwith came there out blood and water." '

'It's a miracle,' someone shouted.

'It's a sign,' I said.

Odo spoke, his coarse voice laughing, 'Jesus, Hugh, were you trying to save this thing until we really needed it?'

I could not speak. People were shouting my name. Stephen's henchmen were dead. I did not know whether it was our will or the Lance that was responsible, but either way, we had beaten them back.

I looked at Emilie. What a knowing smile she had, as if to say, *I knew, I knew* . . . I reached for her hand.

Everyone whooped and shouted, 'Hugh! Lance of God!'

I had been saved. Not once, but many times. Who could understand it? What had been entrusted to me? What did God want with a serf? With a jester?

'The Holy Lance!' everyone shouted, and I threw my fist in the air.

But inside I was thinking, *Good Lord, Hugh, what is next?*

Chapter One Hundred

What was next was bolder and more amazing than anything I could imagine.

Our victory was complete, but it came at a great cost. Thirteen of Stephen's mercenaries lay on the ground, but we had lost four of our own: Apples, the baker's son; Jackie, the stout and cheery milk woman; a farmer, Henri; and Martin, the tailor. Many others, like Georges and Alphonse, nursed messy wounds.

One strange thing happened to puzzle us: when the smoke cleared, the body of the Tafur I had fought with the Lance was nowhere to be found. He had not died after all.

In the ensuing days, we extinguished the fires and bid goodbye to our brave fallen friends. For the first time in anyone's memory, vassals and bondsmen had stood up to a noble. And to the fear that we could not defend our fiefs and tracts simply because they were rightly born and we weren't.

Word spread fast. Of the fight *and* the Lance. People from neighbouring towns came to see. No one could believe it at first. Farmers and tradesmen had stood up against a noble and his bullies.

Yet I did not join much in the celebration. I spent the next several days in a troubled state atop the hill. I couldn't work on the inn. I had to make sense of what had happened. That I had picked up the Lance from the dying priest's hands in Antioch. That, penniless, I now held a prize worth kingdoms. *Why had I been picked? What did God want of me?*

And a deeper dread hung over me. What would happen next – when news of the battle reached Stephen's ears? That we possessed the prize he so desperately coveted? Or when word reached Baldwin in Tours?

Had the poor tailor been right? Had I saved them from one slaughter, only to lead them to another?

Emilie stayed with me the whole while. I looked at the Lance and did not know what to do, but to her, the answer was clear. She understood what I resisted. 'You have to lead them, Hugh.'

'Lead them? Lead them *where*?' I asked.

'I think you know where. When Stephen hears of this he will send men. And Baldwin . . . your village is pledged to him. He will not permit such rebellion in his domain. The stone has been pushed, Hugh. You've sought a higher destiny. Here it is. It's in your hands.'

'I'm just a lucky fool,' I said, 'who picked up a silly antique, a souvenir. I'll end up the biggest fool of all time.'

'I saw you in that costume many times, Hugh DeLuc,' Emilie's eyes shone brightly, 'and never once thought you a fool. A while back, you left this village on a quest to make yourself free. Now, leave it again, and free them all.'

I picked up the Lance, weighed it like a measure in my hands.

Lead them, against Baldwin? Would anyone follow? Emilie

was right about one thing. We could not remain here. Baldwin would burst a vein when he heard the news. Stephen would send more troops, this time hundreds. Something had been started from which we could not draw back.

'You will be by me?' I took her hand, searched her eyes. 'You will not change your mind when we are standing against Baldwin's army and it is just us two?'

'It will not be just us two,' she said, crouching beside me. 'I think you know that, Hugh.'

Chapter One Hundred and One

That day, I called the villagers together in the church. I stood at the front, in the same bloody rags I had worn in the fight, holding the Lance. I took a sweeping look around the room. The place was full – Georges the miller, Odo, even people who never went to church.

'Where have you been, Hugh?' The miller stood up in his place. 'We've all been celebrating.'

'Yes, that lance *must* be holy,' Odo rose too. 'Since it found you, it's been hard even to buy you a beer.'

Everyone laughed.

'Don't blame Hugh,' Father Leo stepped in. 'If such a pretty maiden were visiting me, I wouldn't waste my time drinking with you clowns, either.'

'If you had such a pretty maiden, we'd all be in church a lot more often,' Odo roared.

Everyone laughed again. Even Emilie smiled from the back.

'I do owe you a beer,' I said, acknowledging Odo. 'I owe you all a beer, for your courage. We did a great thing the other day. But the beers must wait. We are not done.'

'Damn right, we are not done,' Winnie, the miller's wife,

stood up. 'I have an inn to run, and when that fat bailiff comes back, I intend to stuff him so full of squirrel droppings he pukes himself dead.'

'And I'll be happy to serve it to him,' I smiled to Winnie, 'but the inn . . . it has to wait too.'

Suddenly everyone saw my face. The laughter settled into a hush.

'I pray I have not drawn you in against your wills, but we cannot stay here. Life will not return to what it was. Baldwin has made a promise to all of you, and he will keep it. We have to march.'

'March?' voices rang out, sceptical. 'To where?'

'To Tours,' I answered. 'Baldwin will come at us with everything now. We must march against *him*.'

The church went silent. Then, one by one, people shouted up to the front.

'But this is our home,' Luc, a farmer, stood up. 'All we want is for things to go back to the way they were.'

'Things will never go back, Luc,' I said. 'When Baldwin hears of this, he'll send his henchmen to ride down upon us with the full fury of his will. He will raze the village.'

'You talk of marching against Tours,' Jocelyn, the tanner's wife, declared. 'Do you see any warhorses or artillery? We're just farmers and widows.'

'No, you are not,' I shook my head, 'you're fighters now. And in every town and village there are others, who have farmed and toiled their entire lives, only to hand over what their liege demands.'

'And they will join us,' Jocelyn sniffed, 'these others? Or will they just cheer and cross themselves as we march by?'

'Hugh is right.' Odo's deep voice cut in. 'Baldwin will

make us pay, just like the bailiff promised. It's too late to back down.'

'He will surely take my lands anyway,' Luc the farmer moaned, 'after what's happened here.'

Alphonse rose. 'H-Hugh has the Lance. It is a greater weapon than all the arrows in Tours.'

Shouts and murmurs rose around the church. Some stood in agreement, but most were afraid. I could see it in their looks. Am I a soldier? Am I fit to fight? If we march, will others follow?

Suddenly from outside, a pounding was heard on the church steps. People froze. Everyone in the village was already inside.

Then three men stepped into the doorway. They were dressed in working hides and tunics. They kneeled, gave the sign of the Cross. 'We seek Hugh.' One of them, a large man, took off his hat. 'The one with the Lance.'

'I am Hugh,' I said from the front.

The man grinned to his companions, seemingly from relief. 'I am glad you truly exist. You sounded more like a fable. I'm Alois, a woodsman. We've come from Morrisaey.'

Morrisaey? Morrisaey was a good three days away – halfway between here and Tours.

'We heard about your fight,' one of the others said. 'Farmers, bondsmen fighting like devils against our liege. We wanted to know if it was true.'

'Look around. *These* are your devils,' I grinned. Then I showed him the Lance. 'Here is their horn.'

Alois's eyes grew wide. 'The Holy Lance. Word is that it changes things for us. That it's a sign. No way we could just sit by and twiddle our thumbs if there was going to be a fight.'

My chest expanded. 'This is good news, Alois. How many men do you have?' I was hoping it was more than these three.

'Sixty-two,' the woodsman shouted proudly. 'Sixty-six if the fucking masons don't back down.'

I looked around the church. 'Go back, and tell your townsmen you are now one hundred and ten. A hundred and fourteen, if the fucking masons take part.'

The man from Morrisaey grinned to his companions. Then he turned back, 'Too late for that,' he said.

He swung open the church doors wide. I saw a crowd huddled in the square. Everyone rushed out of their seats to look and saw woodsmen carrying axes; farmers with hoes and spades; ragged-looking peasants carting hens and geese. Alois smiled. 'Already brought 'em.'

Chapter One Hundred and Two

That was how it began, that first day.

Little more than a hundred of us, farmers, tailors and shepherds, makeshift weapons in hand, what we could eat carted behind. We started on the road towards Tours.

But by the next town we were two hundred, people kneeling before the Lance, grabbing their belongings. By Sur le Gavre, we were *three* hundred, and at the crossroads between north and south, a hundred more were waiting, clubs and hoes and wooden shields in hand.

I marched at the front, carrying the Lance. I could not believe these folk had come to follow me, in a fool's suit, yet at every corner, more joined in.

They kneeled – husbands, wives – kissing the Lance, and Christ's blood, singing praise and vowing the nobles would not crush them any longer. Banners were hoisted, with the green and gold eagles of Tours upside down or with the crest slashed and tattered.

It was like the hermit's march all over again – the hope and promise that had swept up in my own soul three years before. Simple men – farmers and serfs and bondsmen – banded together to raise up their lives. Believing that the time had finally come; that if we stood up in the might of numbers, no matter how long the odds, we could be free.

'Are you tired of being shat on?' went the refrain as we wound past a watching goatherd.

'Aye,' came the nod. 'I've been tired my whole life.'

'And what would you risk,' another would shout, 'to gain your freedom?'

'All I have. Which is nothing. Why do you think I'm here?'

The ranks swelled, from all corners of the forest. *'Follow the Lance,'* was the *crie de coeur. 'The Lance led by the Fool.'*

By St Felix, we had grown to seven hundred strong. By Montres, we had lost count. We could no longer feed them; we had no stocks or provisions. I knew we could not stand a drawn-out siege, yet people continually joined in.

Near Moulin Vieux, Odo edged his way up to the front. Behind us was a column of peasants at least a thousand strong.

The big smith grinned, walking alongside me. 'You have a plan, don't you, Hugh?' he eyed me warily.

'Of course I have a plan. You think I brought all these folk along for a picnic in the woods?'

'Good,' he sighed, then dropped back in the ranks. 'Never doubted . . .

'Of course Hugh has a plan,' I heard him whisper to Georges the miller, a row behind.

From Moulin Vieux, Tours was two days' march away. That night, I curled up at our fire with Emilie. Behind us, the glow from hundreds of others lit up the night. I stroked her hair. She nestled close. 'I told you this was no accident,' she said. 'I told you if you stood up to lead they would follow.'

'You did.' I held her. 'Yet the real miracle is not them, but you. That you have followed.'

'For me there was no choice.' She rolled her tongue and toyed with my jester's tassel. 'I always had a thing for a man in uniform.'

I laughed. 'But now comes the real miracle. Tours is two days' march away. I have a thousand men and only fifty swords.'

'I overheard you had a plan,' Emilie said.

'The outline of one,' I admitted. 'Father Leo says we should draw up our demands: that taxes must be reduced immediately; that all fiefs should apply towards purchase of a parcel of land; that any nobles who take part in raids must be brought before the court.'

'Look at the numbers.' Emilie nodded optimistically. 'Baldwin will have to sue for peace. He cannot fight us all.'

'He won't fight us,' I shook my head. 'At least, not right away. He knows we cannot provision such an army for a long siege. He will wait us out. He'll stall, and let the songs subside, until the food runs out and people lose patience and start to go home. Then he will open the gates and send out his dogs to slaughter us. He will chase us down, and burn our towns so thoroughly, even the scavengers will not think anything was once alive there. I've seen Baldwin's diplomacy. He will never submit.'

'You have known this from the start, haven't you? That the duke would never comply. It was what was troubling you back at Veille du Père?'

I nodded.

'So if you know this, Hugh, what then? All these people, they've given you their hope, their very lives.'

'What it means . . .' I tucked my head on to her lap, begging to drift off to sleep' . . . is that we must *take* him.'

Emilie raised herself up. 'Take him? In order to take Baldwin you must seize his castle too.'

'Yes,' I yawned, 'that is usually the case.'

Emilie shook me. 'Do not jest with me, Hugh. This requires weapons and provisions. For this you have a plan?'

'The outline of one, I told you. But it lacks but one thing.' I curled myself into her warmth. 'Fortunately, it is the thing you are best at.'

'And what is that, Hugh?' She pounded my shoulder.

'A *pretext*, my lady.' I glanced up and winked.

Chapter One Hundred and Three

Daniel Gui's armour clattered as he rushed into the duke's private chamber. He was Baldwin's new chatelain, having taken over from Norcross.

'You can't go in there,' said a page, flashing a cynical wink. 'The duke's in council.'

'The duke will find this news more urgent than any meeting,' Daniel said, and pushed by the page.

His lord was upright against a wall, his hose down, fucking a young chambermaid.

'Liege.' Daniel cleared his throat.

The maid gasped and fixed her skirt, running out through another exit.

'I am so sorry to interrupt,' the chatelain said, 'but I have news you must hear.'

Baldwin pulled up his hose as if it were the most natural thing in the world and tied his tunic. 'I hope this news is crucial, chatelain, for it has taken me months to back that little sow up against a wall.' He wiped his hand across his mouth.

Baldwin disgusted the young chatelain. Daniel looked at his service as a chance to rise through the ranks and serve his native town, not plunder and slaughter defenceless subjects. He had to remind himself that being in the duke's pen was not tantamount to being a pig.

'It is news of the redhead you seek, the jester who escaped after killing Norcross.'

'Hugh. That little canker.' Baldwin showed sudden interest. 'What of him? Speak!'

'He has turned up. In his own town, after all. It seems he has led an uprising there against a raiding party from Blois.'

'Uprising? What do you mean, *uprising*? There's nothing but fieldmice and manure out there.'

'Apparently, these fieldmice defended their nest quite well. Our messengers report all of Stephen's men were killed. The whole section's up in revolt.'

Baldwin shot up out of his seat. 'You tell me this little maw-worm has led a bunch of farmers and hayseeds against Stephen's crack troops?'

'It is so, but it is only the tip of it, my lord.' A tremor of enjoyment rippled through Daniel as he knew the next piece of news would send Baldwin into a rage. 'The thing they sought – this will amuse you – was apparently a relic stolen from the Crusade. Some kind of lance . . .'

'The Holy Lance?' The duke pursed his lips sceptically. 'The Holy Lance belongs to a jester? You must be mistaken, chatelain. The Holy Lance, if it even exists, exceeds in value everything I own. It is a child's fancy to conceive it could be in the hands of that kitchen-rot.'

'Then, apparently, it is a tale children from all over seem to believe. And grown men too, for they flock to him like to a crusade. The whole region is up in revolt.'

'*Revolt!*' Baldwin's eyes were ablaze. 'There is no revolt in my domain. Rouse the men, chatelain. We'll ride tonight and nail the little bastard to a cross if he's so holy.'

'I do not think that is wise, sir.'

'Not wise?' Baldwin stepped up, eyes twitching. 'And why is it not *wise*?'

'Because,' said the chatelain, 'this little maw-worm, as you call him, commands an army of these worms over a thousand strong.'

The colour drained from Baldwin's face. '*A thousand* . . . That cannot be. That is all the towns and villages in the forest. That is three times the size of our own garrison.'

'Perhaps more,' Daniel said. 'This news is days old. Every peasant in the province seems to have joined him.'

Baldwin sat back on a bench. His face grew taut, and was the colour of spoiled fruit. 'Ready the men anyway, chatelain. I will call to my cousin, in Nîmes, for additional troops. Together, we will cut them down in the forest like cucumbers.'

'Then I think you must hurry,' Daniel said, 'for these cowherders are in Moulin Vieux as we speak. It appears they are coming *to you*.'

Chapter One Hundred and Four

We came out of the forest only a half-day's march from Tours.

There it was, in the distance – many-towered, seemingly hung in the clouds – the sun glinting off its ochre walls. The mood of our march dimmed, replaced by a troubled silence. There would be no deceiving them now. All of Tours – Baldwin – now knew we were here.

I called the people closest to me together: Odo, Georges, Emilie, Father Leo, Alois, the woodsman from Morrisaey. I had constructed a plan, but it all depended on help from within. 'I have to go into Tours,' I told them.

'I do too,' Odo chortled. 'And Georges. And Alois here. I want to open Baldwin's eyes. With an eye-wrench.'

'No,' I smiled at his joke, 'I meant alone. In Tours, I have friends who will help.'

'Just how do you intend to get in there?' Georges asked. 'Sneak past the guards while Odo here juggles balls? They'll never let you through the gates.'

'Listen, if we are to take this castle it can only be through trickery, not force of arms. Baldwin has few friends, even within his own walls. I have to gauge the mood inside.'

'So be it, but it's a huge risk,' Alois agreed. 'What's your big plan?'

I pointed towards the town. 'Father, your eyes are best. Are those riders coming from there now?'

Everyone spun round to see.

'Where?' Father Leo said. 'I don't see anyone.'

When the priest turned back, I handed him his prayer beads that I had lifted out of his robe. His eyes widened with surprise. Emilie smiled. Everyone started to laugh.

'I'm a jester. You don't think I would go in there without a trick or two?'

'Your tricks may be artful enough here,' Odo grunted sceptically, 'but if you're killed in there, the rest of us are left ploughing the north hectare with our God-given hoe, if you catch my drift. Send someone else.'

'I don't see another way,' I shrugged, 'except to surround the castle with our shovels and picks and storm Baldwin's army in one massive charge.'

Odo and Georges swallowed uneasily at each other, weighing that unseemly prospect.

The smith glanced around, weighing up my suggestion, then slapped me on the back. 'So, Hugh, when do you go?'

Chapter One Hundred and Five

That night, I lay with Emilie, curled up by a fire. I felt her nervousness as I wrapped my arms tightly around her.

'Don't be worried for me,' I said.

'How could I not? You are walking into a lion's den . . . and there are other things on my mind.'

'What things? The stars are out. We are here. I can feel the beating of your heart . . .'

'Please, do not mock me, Hugh.' Emilie turned in my arms. 'I cannot help myself. My mind has been returning to Blois.'

'Blois?'

'Anne.' Emilie rose up on an elbow. 'Stephen's wrath will be great now that his men have failed. He'll want this Lance more than ever. I am worried for her.'

'I don't share your concern.'

'I know you have no love for her,' she stroked my face, 'but Anne is a prisoner too, just as surely as if she were behind bars. You must understand that. I am pledged to her, Hugh. It is a bond I simply cannot run away from and break.'

'You are pledged to me, now,' I tickled Emilie's ribs. 'Can you break that one?'

'No,' she sighed and kissed me on the forehead. 'That I will never break.'

I leaned down to her and kissed her. She opened her mouth to me, but showed a little hesitation. A thousand people were about. Her breasts came to life at the feel of my touch, hard, willing, through her robe. I felt my cock spring alive too.

'Come with me,' I said.

'Come, *where*? We are in the forest, dummy.'

'A country boy knows,' I winked, a bit mischievously. 'I have a spot. Just for us.'

I pulled her up and, in the dark of night, with the glimmer of campfires and sleeping soldiers huddled around, we sneaked off.

'You can be so impressively aroused,' Emilie pretended to pull against me, 'with what lies before you in the morning.'

In a small clearing, we threw ourselves beneath a tree, into each other's arms, cushioned by a small tuft of leaves. Without speaking, we lifted our robes and felt our bodies warm to the touch of each other, still new, a gift I could not believe was mine.

There was a deeper, knowing look in Emilie's eyes. She put my hand on her breast and took a breath. I felt her heart beating like a doe's. Her nipple grew tight and firm in my touch.

'Is my spot to your satisfaction?' I asked.

'That depends,' she grinned. 'Just which spot is that?'

She kissed me, her tongue searching mine with an

ardour I had not felt from her before. She climbed on my lap and I buried my head in the softness of her breasts. I was aching for her and I could see in her eyes that she felt the same for me.

I moved inside Emilie. Her breath became heated and purposeful. Her eyes did not leave mine. I *loved* that. I felt as if every thrill and instance of her passion, each tremor and jolt shooting through me, narrowed into one enormous burst.

At the moment of climax, we cried out. Then we muffled each other and laughed.

Emilie rested with her head on my chest, crickets and fireflies lighting up the night. She sighed, so I knew she was happy, but then a shiver rippled across her shoulders.

'What happens,' she said warily, 'once Baldwin is defeated? Things just cannot go back. These lands have been in his family since France began.'

'I have been thinking that too,' I held her and said. 'I have no wish to govern, only to right this wrong. I was thinking I would write to the King. I have heard he is a fair man.'

'I have heard he is fair,' Emilie took a breath, 'but he is also a noble.'

I turned her face to mine. 'You said you know the King. You said your father was a member of the royal court.'

'Well, yes . . . I have met him, but—'

'Then you could intercede,' I said. 'You could tell him we are only humble men who want to return to their lives and work in peace. We have no thought to stealing anyone's title or territory. He will have to see.'

I felt Emilie nod, her chin upon my chest, but distantly, as if she were not convinced.

'Do not be so worried for me.' I held her tightly. 'You have made me strong.'

'I do not worry just for you, but for all that will follow. For you, I have a secret charm.'

'And what is this charm that will protect me?' I laughed, stroking her hair.

'I'm coming along.'

'What?' I raised her up. 'That is not possible, Emilie. I cannot allow it.'

'But it is,' she said, her eyes unwavering. 'I am in this as deeply as you, Hugh DeLuc. I told you, we are together, our fates entwined. I am going with you. That is all.'

I moved to argue, but she stopped me with a finger to my lips. Then she put her head back on my chest, and held me as if she would never let go.

Chapter One Hundred and Six

D aniel Gui bolted into Baldwin's private hall.

'My lord, your jester's army has been sighted. It lies a half-day from the city, at the edge of the Loire.'

'You mean their rabble,' Baldwin sniffed. His advisors, the bailiff and chamberlain, seemed delighted with the news.

'You must attack, then,' the bailiff wheezed. 'I know these peasants. Their courage will crumble at the first sign of a fight. Their resolve is only as strong as their last beer.'

'That must be why your rump is so sore, bailiff,' Daniel smirked, 'and why you galloped back here at full speed, not even looking behind until you ducked through the gates. It appears their resolve has stiffened. This jester has given them hope. They outnumber us three to one.'

'But we have horses and crossbows,' Baldwin said. 'They have only tools and wooden shields.'

'If we go after them in the woods,' Daniel said, 'all our horses and crossbows would be reduced to nothing. Your men would be slaughtered just like Stephen's. The jester has this Lance. It emboldens them.'

'The chatelain is right, my lord,' said the chamberlain. 'Even if you won, you would bury each carcass in a hero's grave. You must hear their demands. Consider them, even disingenuously. Promise them the slightest gain if they return to their fields.'

'You are wise, chamberlain,' Baldwin grinned. 'These peasants have no means for a long siege. They will grow bored and tired as soon as their bellies start to ache.'

The bailiff and the chamberlain puffed back their agreement.

'Do not forget, my lord,' Daniel insisted, 'the jester has this Lance. They believe it makes them right.'

Baldwin sneered. 'This Lance will rest in Tours before the negotiation is done. They will give it up for a bag of wheat. And they will give *him* up too. I will have the fool's head upon his precious Lance and place it before my bath.'

'I merely meant,' Daniel pressed on, 'that you take a risk by inviting this siege.'

Baldwin slowly rose. He walked round the table and put his arm round Daniel's shoulder. 'Come,' Baldwin motioned him towards the fire, 'a word with you, by the light.'

A lump grew in Daniel's throat. Had he gone too far? Had he angered his liege whom he was pledged to serve?

The duke wrapped his arm around him tighter, drew him close to the flame, then smiled. 'Do you for a moment think I have any intention of handing over even a cup of grain to this traitorous puke? I would be the laughing stock of France. I have contacted my cousin. He sends a thousand troops. Let the idiots begin their siege. We will eat meat while they boil roots and radishes. When the reinforcements arrive, we will open the gates and crush them. You and I, Daniel, we will make sure not a single grey-haired grandmother among this rabble leaves Tours alive.'

He brought Daniel's hand so close to the flames that he had to restrain himself from crying out.

'No one threatens my rule, least of all these miserable spawn. So how does that plan sound, *chatelain*?'

Daniel's chest pounded furiously. His mouth was dry as dust. He looked into his liege's eyes and saw nothing but dark holes. 'Most wise, my lord.'

Chapter One Hundred and Seven

The following night, outside the gates of Tours, a Hebrew merchant, carrying his sack of wares across his back, approached the gates as they began to close.

He wore the dark, wool robe and the fringed shawl of the Sephardi; had a skullcap upon his head, and held a rusted staff. With him was his young wife, dressed in modest clothes, her hair pinned under a black scarf.

'Move along, Jews,' growled the guard. The checkpoint was manned by a team of pail-helmeted soldiers, hurrying the travellers along like oxen into a pen. 'Where do you come from?' the guard stopped them.

'From the south.' I peeked from under my hood. 'Aix. Roussillon.'

'And what is in the sack?' He poked around.

'Wares for the kitchen. Olive oil, pans, a new utensil called a fork. You stab your meat with it. Want to see?'

'What if we stab *you* with it, you little pests? You say you came from Roussillon? What have you seen? We've heard the forests are teeming with rebels.'

'In the west, perhaps, but in the south there are only squirrels. And Italians. Anyway, it's no concern to us.'

'No, nothing's a concern to your lot, except a fee. C'mon,' he pushed us, roughly, 'get your tick-bitten arses in.'

Emilie and I hurried through the gates. Within the thick limestone walls, heavy beams were braced against the ground to bolster the gates against assault. I glanced around. The towers and ramparts were manned by dozens of troops. They were heavily armed with crossbows and lances, gazing westward.

Horses and carts clattered past us. From under my hood, I flashed Emilie a wink. 'Come.'

We climbed the hill leading to the centre of town and Baldwin's castle. Soldiers on horseback shot about, clattering on the rough stone. Carts dragged rocks and shields down to the outer walls. The defences were being readied. The air was sharp with the sulphurous smell of vats of burning pitch.

'Here . . . this way,' I said. It was the market street. Stalls of bakers and butchers were still open for business, and swarming with flies. Others, that sold tin and tools and cloth, were closed for the night.

Emilie and I hurried through a neighbourhood that seemed to be home to these merchants. There were not only huts, but stone houses, some with iron gates guarding small courtyards. The smell of lard burning was everywhere.

I stopped before a two-storey dwelling, a tin scroll-like ornament hammered next to the archway. 'Emilie, we're here.'

I knocked on the door. A voice called out from inside, some shuffling, then the door cracked open. A familiar face looked out from under a skullcap.

'We've travelled a long way,' I said. 'We were told we would find friends here.'

'If you are in need, we are friends,' the man replied, 'but who told you this?'

'Two men in the forest,' I said.

The man arched his brow, confused.

'One was named Shorty. I asked him what species makes the ugliest children. When he could not say, I told him: "Ask your mother!" '

The man's eyes grew wide, then his beard parted into a smile.

'So, Geoffrey,' I grinned, removing my hood, 'can it be you do not remember your jester?'

Chapter One Hundred and Eight

The merchant whose life I had saved on the road to Tours broke into a hearty smile. He held me by the shoulders, then hugged me, and hustled Emilie and me through the door. I took off my skullcap and shook out my red hair.

Geoffrey laughed, 'I said to myself, you look like no Jew I had ever seen before.'

'We are pork-eating Jews,' I grinned.

We hugged each other again, like old friends. I laid down my staff and unfastened my robe. 'This is Emilie. She's a close friend. This is Geoffrey, who once helped save my life.'

'And I was only able to,' Geoffrey said, 'because Hugh had once saved mine – *ours* . . .'

Isabel and Thomas came in from another room. 'As I live and breathe,' she gasped, 'it is the jester, with the lives of a cat.'

We were led to a room lined with weavings, and with documents on a shelf. Geoffrey offered us his bench.

'What is the mood of the city?' I asked.

He frowned. 'Foul. What used to be a thriving place is now just a pigpen that feeds the duke. And it will only get worse. There is talk of an uprising somewhere, an army of peasants in the forest, who took up arms, headed here. Farmers, shepherds, woodsmen, led by a fool, with some kind of relic acquired from the Crusade – a lance with their Saviour's blood on it.'

'You mean *this*?' I took out my staff and let his eyes wander over it. I smiled. 'I have heard of such an uprising.'

The merchant's mouth fell open. 'This is *you* . . . You are the jester . . . *Hugh*.'

I nodded. Then I told Geoffrey my plan.

Chapter One Hundred and Nine

The following morning, my work was done and it was time to head back to the forest.

Emilie agreed to stay behind in Tours. It was safer for her there, with the terrible battle that was to come. She fought me gamely, but this time I would not back down. When it was time to leave, I hugged her close and promised I would see her in a couple of days.

I lifted her face and smiled at her. 'My beautiful Emilie, when we first met I was afraid even to talk to you. Now I am afraid to let you go. Remember how you laughed at me and said, "That may be, but it will not *always* be . . ."?'

'In a day or two, I suppose we will find out,' she said, trying to look brave.

She leaned up and kissed me. 'God bless you, Hugh.' Tears welled in her eyes. 'In all the world, I hope to see you again.'

I hoisted my sack and headed down the street, waving a final farewell at the corner. I buried my head in my hood and hunched under my shawl, avoiding any eyes in uniform. As I wound back down the hill, I turned, watching Tours recede. Pain tore at my heart. All that I now loved remained in this place. A tremor of panic tore through me that I might never see Emilie again.

When I got back to the forest, I found the men waiting and ready for a fight. We marched at the break of day – farmers, woodsmen, tanners and smiths, in every form of clothing imaginable, carrying homemade bows and wooden shields, stretched out as far as I could see.

At the head of the procession, I felt my blood surge with pride. Whatever the outcome, these men and women had stood tall. They were people of courage and character. To me, they were all highborn.

Every settlement we came to, a crowd formed, cheering us on. 'Look, it is the Jester.' They would point. They would bring out their children too. 'See, child, you will always say you saw the Lance.'

Word spread like a brush fire. More joined the march all the time.

All the while, Tours grew closer, the colour of an amber sunset. Its formidable towers reached high into the sky. The closer we got, the more the mood stiffened; the ranks grew worried and quiet.

As the sun started to wane, we reached the outskirts of town. No force had charged out to confront us yet.

Instead, downtrodden townspeople stood aside, exhorting us on. 'It is the Jester. *See*, he exists! *He is real!*'

The massive limestone walls of the outer city rose above us with their battlements. At each opening, I could see teams of soldiers, their helmets gleaming.

They did not attack, though. They let us come. They allowed us to march within a hundred yards of the outer walls.

Just out of arrow shot, I signalled the column to a halt.

I ordered the ranks to fan out around the perimeter, forming a massing ring, twenty men deep. No one knew what to do, whether to shout or to charge.

'Go on, Hugh,' Georges the miller nodded with a smile. 'Go on and tell 'em why we're here.'

I stepped out, trying to calm the thumping in my chest. I shouted to the defenders above the gate.

'We are from Veille du Père, and Morrisaey, and St Felix, and every town in the province. We have business before the Lord Baldwin.'

Chapter One Hundred and Ten

For a moment there was no answer. I thought: *what do I do now? Say the same words again?*

Then a brightly clad figure, whom I recognized from my stay here as Baldwin's chamberlain, leaned out. 'The lord is napping,' he yelled back. 'He knows no business before him today. Go back to your wives and farms.'

Curses and taunts began to rise out from the crowd. 'The pig is napping?' someone growled. 'Let us be careful not to wake him up, friends.'

A thunderous jeer rose. Weapons rattled, shouts rang out.

Someone rushed forward and pulled down his hose. 'Come on, Baldwin. Here's my arse. Try to fuck me now.'

A few brave ones charged up to the walls, spitting curses and insults. 'Stay back,' I yelled. But it was too late.

From the ramparts, the blood-chilling whine of arrows shrieked down in reply. One man gagged, an arrow piercing through his neck. Another clutched his head. A young boy sprinted up and hurled a stone, which fell harmlessly halfway up the wall.

A wave of burning black pitch rained down on him. The

boy fell, thrashing the ground with his limbs, his skin sizzling with flame.

'Go home, you stinking filth,' spat a soldier from the top.

Some of us shot off bows, fire arrows streaking across the sky, but they died harmlessly against the massive walls.

Volleys of heavy arrows whooshed down on us, so taut and strong they tore through flimsy shields and could still pierce a man in two. The volley sounded like a thunderstorm.

Images from the Crusade burned in my brain.

I waved frantically for everyone to move back. Some were angry and wanted to charge. They had followed me for days, with little food. All they had thought of was striking their picks and hammers against the walls of Tours, tearing it down, chunk by chunk. Others, seeing blood and death for the first time, swarmed back, afraid.

This is what Baldwin wanted. To show that our make-shift weapons were useless. Anger was setting in, and we hadn't even begun the siege. My blood was racing. I had brought a thousand men here. We had the town surrounded. We had the will to fight, but not the weapons to break through. All Baldwin had to do was open the gates and, I knew, all but the most hardened fighters would turn and flee.

But the gates did not open. No warhorses thundered out. He was probably amused at our spineless lack of resolve.

The commitment of this entire army hung in the balance. All eyes looked towards me.

A farmer carrying a broken hoe came up to me. 'You have brought us here, jester. How will we take this castle?

With *this*?' He threw the hoe down as if it were a useless twig.

'No.' I tapped my chest where my heart was. 'We will take their castle with *this*.

'Get the raiding party together,' I told Odo. My blood stiffened with resolve. 'We go tonight.'

Chapter One Hundred and Eleven

That night, as most of our ranks dozed, I got together the twenty brave men who would sneak into the castle.

There was Odo and Alphonse from our town; Alois, and four of his best from Morrisaey. From the rest, we chose strong-hearted men we could trust, who would not back down from killing with their bare hands.

One by one, they arrived before my fire, wondering why they were there.

'How do you intend to take this castle with *us*,' Alois shrugged, 'when you can't make a dent in it with a thousand men?'

'Then we'll have to take it without a dent,' I said. 'I know a way inside. Come with me now, or go back to sleep.'

We armed ourselves only with swords and knives. Father Leo blessed us with a prayer. I handed him the Lance – 'On the chance that I don't return.'

'Are you ready, then?' I looked around at the men. I clasped each of their hands. 'Say goodbye to your friends. Pray we see them on the other side.

'I was speaking of the wall,' I said, and faked a laugh.

Under the cover of night, we crept away from the camp-sites and waded out behind the hutted settlements and narrow streets that clung to the city walls. Torches lit up the defences above us, lookouts peering for signs of life. We crouched in the ruts of the wall below, in shadows.

Odo tapped my shoulder. 'So, Hugh, this ever been done before?'

'What?'

'People like us, bondsmen, rising against their liege.'

'A group of farmers rose against the Duke of Bourges,' I said.

The smith seemed satisfied. We crept a little further. He tapped me again. 'So, how'd it turn out for them?'

I pressed my back against the wall. 'I think they were slaughtered to a man.'

'Oh,' the big smith grunted. His face turned white.

I mussed his shaggy hair. 'They were discovered, talking under the walls. Now shush!'

We continued, creeping along the east edge of town. In the crook of a ravine, we came across a shallow moat. It reeked, stagnant with putrid water and sewage. It was more of a large ditch; we could cross it with a jump.

Frequently, I scanned the base of the wall for a sign of the tunnel once shown to me by Palimpost. *None.* As we moved along, the terrain grew tougher to traverse and the walls arched high above, too tall for any kind of assault. That was good: no lookouts would be manning the walls.

But where was the blasted passageway?

I began to get worried. Soon it would be light. Another day. There was the chance Baldwin would unleash his warriors to break our will.

'You're sure you know what you're doing, Hugh?' Odo muttered.

'Hell of a time to ask,' I snapped.

Then I spotted it, a formation of piled rocks, concealed behind some brush on the bank of the moat. I sighed with relief. 'There!'

We scurried down the embankment and straddled the moat. Then I pulled my way up the other side. I ripped through the dense brush and began to tear apart the rocks.

The declining pile revealed the entrance to the tunnel.

'Never doubted you for a second,' Odo laughed.

Chapter One Hundred and Twelve

The crawl-space was as I remembered – dark, narrow, barely enough room for a man to pass. And shin-deep with murky, foul-smelling water trickling down to the moat.

There were no torches to light our way. I had to trust my instincts against the dark, feeling along the cold, rocky walls. I knew each one in my party had his heart in his throat too. It was like crawling into Hell – cold, pitch-black, odorous. Floating refuse and shit lapped against our feet. Moments stretched along like hours. With every step, I grew less sure of the way. After countless prayers, I came upon a fork in the tunnel. One path continued up, the other left. I looked for something familiar.

'We are all right,' I whispered. But I wasn't really sure. The word rippled down the line. We climbed higher and higher, cutting through the mound on which Baldwin's castle was built. Above us, Tours slept.

Suddenly, a blast of air hit me from up ahead. I noticed light slanting on to the wall. I quickened my pace and came to a spot I vaguely remembered: *the* dungeon where Palimpost had sneaked me into the tunnel.

I passed the word: 'Ready your weapons.' Then, with a deep breath, I pressed at the stone in the cave ceiling where the light trickled in.

It moved. I pushed it up a little more. The slab gave way.

Soon, all twenty men had pulled themselves up out of the tunnel. By my reckoning, it was still before dawn. The relief detail had not come.

Two guards were asleep, their feet up on the table. One was that pig, Armand, who had delighted in torturing me when I was captive here. Another guard snoozed against the wall on the stairs.

I signalled Odo and Alois, and each silently crept behind one of the guards. We had to take them quickly. A sound would be as good as an alarm.

At my nod, we were on them. Odo took the one on the stairs, and as he gagged on a loud snore, wrapped his thick, muscular arms around the man's throat.

Alois cupped his hand over the mouth of the one sleeping at the table. His eyes bolted awake. As he strained to scream, the woodsman slid a sharp blade across his neck. The guard's legs stiffened and shook, more of a spasm than a fight.

Armand was mine. At the sound of commotion, he blinked himself awake, befuddled. Clearing his eyes, he bolted up to see his partners slumped to the ground, and a familiar face grinning down at him.

'Remember me,' I winked.

Then I bashed him in the face with the hilt of my sword. He toppled backwards, kicking the table aside, and landed, mouth bloody, on his back.

He reached behind him for an iron stake leaning on the

wall. François, one of the Morrisaey woodsmen, stepped up.

'No need to be so civilized,' the woodsman shrugged, and hammered Armand to the floor with his club, stepping on his throat and pinning the struggling guard's airway with his huge, muscular legs. The guard gagged and choked, flailing his arms from side to side, but the woodsman's step was like a vice. Soon, Armand's arms relaxed.

'Quick,' I said to Odo and Alois, 'into their uniforms.'

We stripped the guards, donning their green and gold tunics and helmets, arming ourselves with their swords. We dragged the bodies back down the corridor.

Suddenly there was the creaking of a door opening from above. New voices coming down the stairs.

'Time to wake up, sleepy-heads,' someone called ahead. 'It's almost light. Hey, what's going on?'

Chapter One Hundred and Thirteen

Nellie, the duke's cook, had risen early that morning. She hurried down to the kitchen and, by dawn, was busying herself with her usual task of preparing the morning meal.

She stirred the porridge pot until it was the perfect consistency. She took down a jar of cinnamon, the sweet new spice brought back from the East, and sprinkled it over the simmering grain. There was cured pork that she fried over the flame and gave off a delicious, fatty smell. She dressed the porridge with the sweetest blueberries she could find.

Two guards stood watch outside the pantry, who, she knew were about to end their overnight shift. Pierre and Imo, lazy slobs. This wasn't exactly crack duty, guarding the royal kitchen when an army threatened at the gates.

Nellie knew they would be dead tired, ready for a snooze, and that their bellies would be aching for something to eat. The early-morning cooking smells would lure them like a whore's scent.

As the sun broke through the early mist, Nellie tied up the burlap sack filled with last night's mess. Then she poked her head out of the kitchen.

'What are you cooking? Smells like Heaven,' said Pierre, the plumper of the guards, his eyes wide.

'Whatever it is, the duke seems to prize it,' Nellie winked, 'and there's some extra this morning, if I can get a chore done for me.'

'Show us, Cooky,' Pierre said.

Nellie led them back through the kitchen. She showed them the two heavy sacks of garbage.

'Toss them in the back,' Nellie instructed. 'Just make sure you captains of war don't spill them all over the pen.'

'Pile on those berries,' Imo grinned, hoisting his sack. 'We'll be right back.'

'Yes,' Nellie nodded.

She looked out of the window. An anxious tremor fluttered in her heart. This was a dangerous line she had crossed, but she had crossed it long ago. When the duke unceremoniously hanged her friend Millie as a thief for stealing a bit of salve from the physician's chambers; and when her second cousin Teddy had his flock confiscated and was forced to tend them in the duke's own pen. She would have gladly poisoned the prick herself, if Hugh had asked.

The two soldiers went in the back and flung the sacks slipshod on to the garbage pile, drooling over their forthcoming meal.

From behind two other soldiers dressed in green and gold stood up and grabbed them by their necks. Pierre and Imo's eyes bulged as they were dragged to the ground.

Nellie wiped her hands on a rag. Yes, it was a dangerous line she had crossed . . . but what choice was there?

It was a crazy time, she sighed, when you had to choose between a madman and a fool.

Chapter One Hundred and Fourteen

Within an hour, fourteen of our men stood about the courtyard, dressed as Baldwin's own brigade.

The rest kept from sight, concealed behind the dungeon door. Besides Nellie, three of Geoffrey's friends had helped lure soldiers into our trap. Geoffrey had arranged it all.

Odo and I stood guard at the dungeon door, looking for a sign that the duke was conducting business. Across the courtyard, two guards stood with halberds on either side of the castle entrance. Others crossed back and forth at a crisp pace, wheeling weapons and armaments down to the ramparts.

From down the road, we could hear our own men massing at the city walls – shouting and taunting, just as I had ordered them.

Finally, I spotted Geoffrey emerging from the steps. He scratched his head, then flashed me a purposeful nod.

'It's time,' I said, rapping at the dungeon door.

Odo slid it open. The balance of our party, some still in their own garb, headed out. In the hubbub, no one noticed. We made our way across the courtyard and were joined by the rest of our ranks in Baldwin's uniforms, loitering about.

As we approached the guards, one of them lowered his halberd in our path. 'Only military personnel in the castle today.'

'These men have business before the duke,' I said, holding my breath. 'They have come from the woods and know of the jester.'

The guards hesitated. They eyed us up and down. My heart beat wildly. 'We've come from the wall,' I said in a firmer voice. 'Do you have the time to conduct an investigation when there's important news to deliver to the duke?' Finally, eyeing our uniforms, the guard raised the halberd and let us by.

We were inside the castle. I boldly led the group down the main vestibule towards the Great Hall.

To my surprise, the halls were not as busy as I had expected. Most of the duke's manpower was manning the walls. The times I had been here before, these same halls were crowded with petitioners and favour-seekers.

Outside the Great Hall, two more guards stood to attention. The duke's voice bellowed from inside. My stomach churned.

'We are wanted within.' I snapped a nod to the guards. We wore the green and gold. We'd made it this far. No one tried to block us.

Our ranks sifted into the duke's large meeting room. It was just as I remembered when I had been a jester here. Then it had been packed with people conducting business; today, mostly with Baldwin's retinue and knights.

Baldwin was slouched in his chair. He wore a military tunic with his crest, and high leather boots. His sword was sheathed in an ornate scabbard.

The pig!

A high-ranking officer was in the midst of a report on the scene outside the walls. Two of my men remained behind, in positions near the guards at the doorway.

'My lord,' the chamberlain was saying, 'the rabble has made a petition for you to consider.'

'A petition?' Baldwin shrugged.

'A list of demands,' the new chatelain, who had presumably taken over from Norcross, replied.

My men circulated around the room. Odo and Alphonse took positions behind the duke. Alois and two others from Morrisaey edged near the chamberlain and chatelain.

'Who brings these demands?' Baldwin perked up. *'Our fucking jester?'*

'No, my lord,' the chamberlain replied. 'Your jester is nowhere in sight. Perhaps he is afraid to get out of bed. But it is as we spoke. Let them deliver their complaints. And you, give them the impression that you will seriously take them into account.'

'Into account.' Baldwin stroked his beard. He turned to the chatelain. 'Chatelain, choose your lowest, most unfit foot soldier, prop him up on a mule and send him out to receive these grievances. Have him convey to the filth that their petition will receive our most urgent review.'

A few of the knights snickered back a laugh.

The chatelain stepped up. 'I beg you, sir, not to mock these men.'

'Your protest is heard, Chatelain. Now, hurry off and find this latrine-cleaner. And, Chatelain, when your man is safely back, kill a few of them, just to assure them we are placing their petition under our most urgent review.'

'But, my lord, they will be protected, under truce,' the chatelain hesitated.

'Are you whining again? *Chamberlain*, do you think *you* could head to the walls and carry out this decree? My military man seems to have come down with a case of cold dick.'

'I can, my lord.' The fat weasel scrambled away.

About the room, everyone stood aghast at the chatelain's rebuke.

'Now,' Baldwin stood, staring around the room, 'is there anyone else in here who has a similar plan?'

'Yes,' I shouted from the back. 'I think we should *attack*. Attack your enemies in the west.'

Chapter One Hundred and Fifteen

Baldwin pounded his fist on the table before him. 'We don't *have* any fucking enemies in the . . .' Then he sat perfectly still. His eyes bulged like dark plums. 'Who said that? Who is that man? Come forward.'

I stepped out from the crowd, and let the military tunic fall off my shoulders. I stood in my checked tunic and hose. I removed my helmet. I watched his eyes home in on my face.

'You do *now*.' I winked at him.

Baldwin's face drained of colour. Then he pointed, stammering, 'It's him. The jester!'

Soldiers went for their arms, but were immediately intercepted by men in their own uniform, *my men*, pressing swords to their throats.

The chatelain made a move towards me, but Alois subdued him before he drew his sword.

'Seize him. Do you hear?' Baldwin spat, ordering the guards behind his throne.

They made a move towards me, but in almost the same motion, took hold of the duke. Odo was one of them. He placed a knife against his throat; Alphonse dug his lance into the square of Baldwin's back.

The duke's eyes grew wide in disbelief. He looked towards his knights, many of whom had scrambled for their arms.

'If they charge, you're a dead bastard,' I said to him. 'It would give me much pleasure.'

Baldwin looked about, his neck muscles twitching. A look of outrage smouldered in his eyes. All around, men loyal to the duke were held at knifepoint. Some knights drew their swords, looking to Baldwin for the word.

'Tell them, arms *down*,' I said. Odo pressed his knife, and finally drew a trickle of noble blood.

Baldwin's eyes flitted desperately from side to side, estimating the probable outcome of any resistance.

'Trust me, liege, these men who hold you hate you more than I,' I said. 'I do not know if they will heed even me, they want to spill your guts so badly. But on the assumption that they want their children to live in peace more than they want your steaming entrails on the floor, I beg you, tell the knights to put down their arms. Otherwise, when I drop my hand, *you are dead*.'

Baldwin did not answer, but looked about. Then he nodded, almost imperceptibly. One by one, the knights' blades clattered to the floor.

My chest heaved a sigh of relief. 'Now, we go outside, my liege. You'll tell your men on the walls to do the same.'

The duke swallowed, a lump slowly travelling down his throat. 'You are insane,' he spat.

'And you seem to be a little *foolstruck* as well, my lord, if you don't mind me saying.'

An amused snigger travelled across the room.

'You will be dead by nightfall.' Baldwin burned his gaze into my face. 'Towns will come to my defence. To rise against a lord this way, you could only be the biggest fool in history.'

My gaze slowly drifted around the room. Odo curled back a smile, then Alphonse, then Alois.

'Perhaps the second biggest,' I replied.

Chapter One Hundred and Sixteen

We dragged the Lord Baldwin outside, forcing him at sword point to the castle gates.

Each soldier we passed looked on with dumbfounded shock. Some, no doubt eager to resist, looked to their liege for a sign, but at the sight of Baldwin's beaten eyes, and the bailiff and chamberlain trailing submissively behind, held their weapons at their sides.

As we marched, stunned townspeople rushed to line the streets. They must have thought themselves hung-over.

A few began to jeer: 'Look at Baldwin.' 'It's what you deserve, you greedy hog . . .' There was laughing, and scraps of food and debris were thrown.

As we approached the walls, I saw that word must have travelled ahead. Soldiers were just staring at us, lances and bows held at their sides.

'Tell them the battle is over.' I pushed Baldwin ahead. 'Tell them to lay down their arms and open the gate.'

'You can't expect them to stand by and let in that mob,' Baldwin sniffed. 'They will be ripped to shreds.'

'Not a soul will be harmed, you have my word on it. Except, of course, *you*,' I pressed the sword in deeper, 'if you fail to comply. My guess is, not one of them would mind the sight of that very much.'

Baldwin swallowed. 'Put down your arms,' he said through gritted teeth.

'Louder,' I prodded him. 'Tell them you have reviewed our demands in full.'

'Put down your arms,' Baldwin shouted. 'The castle is lost. Open the gates.'

Everyone remained still, in disbelief. Then two of my men ran and threw off the heavy beams that secured the gates. They flung the doors open, and a band of our men, Georges the miller at the lead, burst into Tours.

The miller came up to me. 'What took you so long?'

'Our liege was so thoroughly set on hearing each last grievance, we lost track of time,' I grinned.

Georges ran his eyes over the captured duke. No doubt he had been thinking of this moment for a long time. 'My apologies, lord. You raised our allotments. I think I owe you my last instalment.'

With that, he spat a thick, yellow wad all over the duke's face. His eyes remained on him while the spit slowly trickled its way down Baldwin's chin. 'Now here's *my grievance.*' He put his face close to the duke. 'I am Georges, miller of Veille du Père. I want my son back.'

All around us, farmers and peasants spilled into the streets and climbed up the ramparts. Hesitant soldiers climbed out of the towers and ran, terrified, off the walls.

A few people started to shout my name, 'Hugh, Hugh, Hugh . . .' I looked with pride at the miller and Odo, and we thrust our arms victoriously into the air.

Chapter One Hundred and Seventeen

We tossed Baldwin into his own dungeon – into the dark, cramped cell where I was once held myself.

There was much in those first hours that needed my attention. With the duke under lock and key, his reserve had to be disarmed, as well as the plotting chamberlain and bailiff. The chatelain too, though strangely, I did not feel him an enemy. Order had to be maintained in our ranks as well, if we intended to press our case in a peaceful way before the King.

My mind ran to Emilie.

Where was she? I needed to share this with her. Our victory was as much hers as mine. A flash of worry went through me.

I hurried out of the castle and down the narrow streets in the direction of Geoffrey's home. People tried to stop and cheer me, but I pushed through, keeping up a brave face, but inwardly beseeching them to let me pass. *Something was wrong!*

My pace quickened as I neared the market. Some of the merchants shouted my name, but I ignored them and finally turned down the street to Geoffrey's home.

I pounded on the door. Something now terrified me. I slammed my fist against the door, my heart galloping with each desperate knock.

Finally, the door creaked open. Isabel was there! She had a look on her face that was first pleased to find me well, then all at once serious and alarmed. Now I knew that something was wrong.

'She's gone, Hugh,' she muttered.

'Gone.' *Gone where? How?* All the strength in my body seemed to drain away.

'At first, I thought she went to find you, but just a while ago I saw *this*.' Isabel handed me a note, scribbled in a hurried hand.

My brave Hugh,

Do not fear as you read this, for my heart is yours – always. But I must go.

By now, your victory is complete. I was not wrong, was I? 'What once was will not always be.' You have climbed a rung to your own destiny. To see you do this confirms the special quality I saw in you from the first; nothing in the world could make me more proud.

But now, I must return to Blois. Don't be angry. Anne is like a mother to me. I cannot abandon her and be joyous in the glow of your triumph.

Please, do not worry. There are some things I have not shared with you, and even Stephen would not dare to do me any harm. Write to the King, Hugh. Make your triumph true. I will do my part.

This was so cruel. My eyes welled with sharp, stinging tears.

I could not lose her. Not now, after so much had passed. I swallowed hard, struggling to read the end:

> You have been my true love since I saw you that very first day . . . I know I shall say that to you when we see each other again. I hold up my palm. Remember the words: In all the world . . .
>
> Emilie

A sharp pain lanced through me, bleeding out the joy and triumph of all that had taken place. I had won the day. But I had lost the woman I loved.

Chapter One Hundred and Eighteen

'**W**ho is there?' a cranky voice barked from behind the door. 'Speak to me!'

Emilie hunched inside her dark hood. The familiar testiness was like an old friend, and made her smile. 'Have your wits become as dull as your jokes, Norbert?' she called back.

Slowly, the door to the jester's chamber cracked open. Norbert peeked out, his tunic unbuttoned to his chest and his hair tousled and awry.

At first, he ran an eye over the huddled shape suspiciously. Then, as she removed the hood, his eyes opened wide. 'Lady Emilie . . .!'

Norbert glanced down the corridor to make sure she was alone, then spread his arms and embraced her. 'It's a beautiful sight to see you.'

Emilie squeezed him back. 'It's good to see you too, jester.'

Norbert hurried her inside his room. He shut the door, then frowned. 'It's a beautiful sight, my lady, but not necessarily to see you *here*. You've taken a great risk to come back. But tell me quick, you've been with Hugh?'

Emilie brought him up to date – first, on the raid on Veille du Père, and the existence of the Lance. *'The very staff you sent to Hugh.'* Then, of the incredible events that followed: the townspeople who rose up with him; Tours. With each piece of news, the jester's eyes grew more incredulous, his cackles of delight more unrestrained.

When she told him of Baldwin's capture, he almost fell out of his seat. He danced around and fell back on his mat, kicking his legs with glee. 'I knew that boy was a gift from God, but *this* . . .'

He lifted himself back up, his laughter subsiding. He studied her face, the rosy cast upon her cheeks. 'But tell me, my lady, why are you here now?'

Emilie lowered her eyes. 'For my mistress. It is my duty.'

'Your mistress! Then you have travelled a long way and at much risk for no end. Things are much changed here. The duke dreams of killing Hugh with the zeal of a dog slobbering over a cooking roast. Does anyone know you have arrived?'

'I mingled with a party of monks returning from pilgrimage. I came to you first.'

'That is wise. If Stephen knew you were here, you would be bound already. Your last running-off is exposed. It is assumed you were with Hugh. If not for Lady Anne's protest, you'd have a poster with *your* face on it.'

Emilie's face lit up. 'I *knew* she would be true. I was right about Anne.'

Chapter One Hundred and Nineteen

It took a few days to secure Tours completely. There were a few stubborn knights still loyal to Baldwin. And word of a purported reprisal from one of the duke's 'supposed' allies. But no reprisal came.

Tours was ours.

Now, there was the matter of what to do with it.

There was the issue of the duke's treasury, which had been fattened on the backs of those who now occupied his city. And vast stores of grain and livestock had to be redistributed fairly.

A debate raged between those who had been with us from the start, and those who joined later, on what to do. Georges the miller said, give out the keys to the grain holds. Let each man leave with a sack and a hen. Alois said, why stop there? Raid the treasury. Redistribute all the taxes. Put a noose to the bastard!

I wished Emilie were there. I had no skill to govern, nor the urge. I did not know exactly what to do, or what was right.

It was only a matter of time before I would lose my army. The ranks were growing impatient. They wanted to go back to their homes. 'It's growing time,' they said. 'When do we get what we were promised?'

And not just food and money. They needed laws to protect them. The right to choose: where to live, who they could serve. If a man was pledged to his lord, need his children and their children be bound by the same pledge? Someone had to rule on such things.

One night, I found a sheath of paper with Baldwin's seal and a vial of viscous, red-tinged ink. I sat down and started to write the most important letter of my life.

To His Majesty, Philippe Capet, Ruler of France,

I pray God grants me the words by which to write this, for I am a humble villager. A bondsman, in fact, thrust into a larger role.

I am said to be the leader of a group of brave men. Some call it a rabble; I call it an outpouring. An outpouring of farmers, tanners, woodsmen – all your servants – who have risen up against our liege lord after repeated, cruel and unnecessary attacks.

I write from Tours, Your Majesty, where I sit at the Duke Baldwin's own table, his lordship held prisoner, while I await word from you as to what to do next.

We are not traitors, far from it. We bound together to fight cruel injustice, and only when it threatened our safety and well-being. We bound together to demand laws, so that rape and murder could not be committed on us freely, and property confiscated without cause. We bound together to free ourselves from an indenture beyond what even the most prosperous could afford to pay.

Is it such an incredible dream, sire, that all God's men, common and noble alike, should be governed by just laws?

Many who marched with us have served Your Majesty in wars, or taken up the Cross of His Holiness in the ongoing struggle against the Turk. We ask only what we have been promised for such service: the right to a fair tax and a fair fief; the right to grievance and recompense for harsh penalties forced upon us; the right to face an assailant at trial, noble or not; the right to own land, fairly paid to our Lord, for years of labour and toil.

We have done all this with little bloodshed. We have acted in peace and respect. But our ranks grow weary. Please send us word, Your Majesty, of your conviction on such matters.

In return for your judgement, I offer you the only tribute I have – but, I think, a worthy one: the most holy treasure in all of Christendom, thrust into my possession in Antioch.

The very Lance that pierced the Lord Jesus Christ upon the Cross.

It is a treasure worth having, yet amazing as it is, it is not nearly as great as the hearts of these men who serve you.

We await your answer.

In faith, Your humble servant,

Hugh DeLuc, Innkeeper, Veille du Père.

I waited for the ink to dry.

A tightness pulled at my chest. So many had died.

Sophie, Mathieu, my newborn son. Nico, Robert, the Turk. *All to get me here?*

The Lance was leaned against the table. What if I had died in that church at the hands of the Turk? I thought. What if none of this had taken place?

Finally, I folded the parchment and bound it with the duke's own seal. I saw that my hands trembled.

The most miraculous thing had just taken place. I, a bondsman, a jester by trade. A man without a home. Without anything to his name. I had just addressed a letter to the King of France.

PART FIVE

SIEGE

Chapter One Hundred and Twenty

Stephen, Duke of Blois, winced as the physician applied another repulsive leech to his back. 'If you bleed me any more, physician, there will be more of me in these *suckers* than left in *me*.'

The physician went about his work. 'You complain of ill humour, my lord, yet you complain of the cure as well.'

Stephen sniffed. 'All the leeches in the world couldn't bleed me enough to raise my mood.'

Ever since the failure of Morgaine's raid, he had been hurled into a biting melancholy. His most trusted and ruthless men had been routed. Worse, he had lost his best chance to grab the Lance. Then, to make matters worse, the arrogant little pest had had the gall to march on Tours. It made his choler boil to a fever pitch.

Then, only yesterday, he received the incredible news that the fool had taken Tours; that Baldwin, idiot of idiots, had actually surrendered his own castle.

Stephen grimaced, feeling his humours sucked out of him by these slimy little slugs.

So the Lance was still to be had! He thought of calling a crusade to liberate Tours, to return the prize that had been pilfered by the deserter, and restore it to its rightful place. Blois, of course. But who knew where it would end up then? Paris or Rome or even back in Antioch.

At that moment, things got even worse – Anne walked in. She looked at him, prone, covered with welts, and held back a smile of amusement. 'You asked for me, my lord?'

'I did. Physician, give me a word with my wife.'

'But the leeching, my lord, it is not over . . .'

Stephen jumped up, swatting the slimy little creatures off his back. 'You have the hand of an executioner, sir, not a healer. Get these creatures out of here. From now I'll handle my ill temper my own way.'

Anne regarded him with a slight smile. 'I'm surprised these slimy things offend you so, since you are akin in so many ways.'

She came over and ran her hand along his back, mottled with fiery red welts. 'From the look of this, your ill temper must have been most severe. Shall I apply the salve?'

'If you are not too offended to touch me.' Stephen kept her eye.

'Of course not, husband.' She dipped her hands in the thick white ointment, applying it liberally to the welts on his back. 'I am quite used to offence. What was it you needed of me?'

'I hoped to enquire into the well-being of your cousin Emilie; that her visit to her aunt went well.'

'I suspect so.' Anne spread the salve. 'She seems quite rosy.'

Rosy . . . Both of them knew the bitch never went within fifty miles of the old hen, her aunt. He would just as soon have strung Emilie up by her tits while he fucked her eyes out from behind if he weren't so grateful for the heartening news she brought back.

'I would like to talk with her,' he said, 'and hear the details of her visit.'

'These leeches seem to have dug particularly deep,' Anne said, applying pressure to one sore. Stephen jumped. His head spun. 'All this leisure here does not seem to suit you, husband. Perhaps you should return to the Holy Land for some more amusement. Regarding Emilie, I'm afraid she is too weary to provide many details. *Weary* . . .' she squeezed again, 'yet rosy, as I say.'

'Enough.' Stephen seized her arm. 'You know I do not need to ask for your permission.'

'You do not,' Anne glared, 'but you also know she remains under my protection. Even you, my scheming husband, must know what price you will have to pay if any harm comes to her.'

She dug the edge of her nail into a particularly swollen welt, Stephen almost jumping off the table.

He raised his arm as if to strike. Anne did not flinch. Instead, she merely looked at him, detestation firing in her eyes. Then she slowly eased into a smile. 'I am *here*, husband, if you wish to strike. Or I can call one of the housemaids, if you find my face too rough.'

'I shall not be mocked,' Stephen brushed her away, 'within my own house.'

'Then, perhaps, it would be wise to move,' Anne smiled sharply.

'Get out,' he shouted, passing his hand within an inch of her face. 'Do not pretend, Anne, that your little vow of protection gives me even a moment of hesitation. In the end you will regret such mockery. *You*, and the pink-cheeked *whore* that waits on you, and the lowborn *fool* she is so wont to fuck.'

Chapter One Hundred and Twenty-One

'**Y**our Grace!' Stephen rose, and kneeled to kiss the ruby ring of Barthelme, Bishop of Blois, even though he thought him the most air-filled, well-fed functionary in France. 'So good of you to join me at such short notice. Please, sit here, by me.'

Bishop Barthelme was a corpulent, owl-eyed man with a sagging jowl that seemed to sink almost undetectably into his massive purple robe. Stephen wondered how such a man could take a step, or climb a stair, or even perform his sacraments. He knew the bishop did not like being summoned. He thought he was too good for this diocese, and longed for a more distinguished position in Paris, or even Rome.

'You have taken me from my sext for this?' the bishop wheezed.

At Stephen's nod, a young page poured out two silver cups of ale.

'It's called Lambic,' Stephen raised his goblet. 'It is brewed by Trappists, near Flanders.'

The bishop managed a smile. 'If it's God's work, then I feel I have not strayed too far.'

They both took a deep draught. 'Aaah,' the cleric licked his lips. 'It is most sweet. Tastes of apples and mead. Yet I feel you did not call me to hear my opinion of your ale.'

'I have asked you here today,' Stephen said, 'because there is a hole torn in my soul that you can help mend.'

Barthelme nodded, and listened.

Stephen leaned close. 'You have heard of this uprising in the south, where a jester has led a rabble of peasants?'

Barthelme smirked. 'I know a stupider man does not exist than Baldwin, so it is not so far-fetched that he was outfoxed by a fool. Yet reports say this man was *your* fool once, your lordship?'

Stephen put down his goblet and glared through the bishop's haughty smile. 'Let me get to the point, Your Grace. Do you know what this jester carries with him, that is the source of his appeal?'

'The message of a better life. The freedom from material bonds,' the bishop said.

'It is not his *message* that I speak of, but his *staff*.'

The cleric nodded. 'I have heard that he parades around with a spear purported to be the Holy Lance. But these petty prophets are always claiming this or that – holy water from the baptism of St John, burial shrouds of the Virgin Mary . . .'

'So this does not concern you?' Stephen asked. 'That a trumped-up country boy uses the name of Our Lord to incite rebellion?'

'These local prophets,' the bishop sighed, 'they come and go like the frost, every year.'

Stephen leaned forward. 'And it does not concern you that this peasant marches around with the word of Christ, inciting the rabble to overflow their lieges?'

'It sounds as if you are the one that is worried, Stephen. Besides, I have heard it is not grace this lad is seeking, but grain.'

A smile etched on to the cleric's face, the smile of a man on a certain bet. 'What do you want, Stephen, for the Church to fight your battles? Shall we contact Rome, and declare a holy crusade against a fool?'

'What I want, Your Grace, is to strike these ignorant puppets where they most ache. More than their bellies or their desires, or their silly dreams of this precious freedom they long to taste.'

Barthelme waited for him quizzically.

'Their *souls*, Your Grace. I want to *crush their souls*. And you are the man who can do it for me.'

The bishop put down his drink. His expression shifted from amusement to concern. 'Just what is it you want me to do?'

Chapter One Hundred and Twenty-Two

No reply came from the King, and day by day, the ranks grew more tired and impatient. These were not soldiers, prepared to occupy a city like Tours. They were farmers, tradesmen, husbands and fathers. They longed to go home.

Lookouts were scattered along the road to the north, but each day, no answer came.

Why? If Emilie had contacted him? If she was able. And what if she was not?

Then one day the lookouts did spot a party travelling south towards the castle. I was in the Great Hall. Alphonse burst in. 'H-Hugh, a party of riders is approaching. It looks like it could be from the King!'

We rushed to the city walls as fast as our legs would carry us. I climbed the rampart and watched the party approach, my heart racing. From the north, six riders, at full gallop. Knights, carrying a banner, but not in the purple and gold of the royal flag.

But with a cross upon it. Knights pledged to the Church.

They escorted a rider in the centre of their group, in the dark robes of a cleric.

We drew open the outer gates and the party rode into the courtyard. A full crowd gathered in the square – all of us, Odo, Georges, the Morrisaey men included. Many grinned optimistically.

'Is this good or bad?' Alphonse asked.

'I think it's good,' Father Leo said. 'The King wouldn't send a priest to rebuke us. You'll see.'

The gaunt, clear-eyed priest slowly dismounted. He wasted no time and faced the crowd. 'I am Father Julien, emissary to His Grace, Barthelme, Bishop of Blois. I bear an urgent decree.'

'I am Hugh,' I called, jumping down from the ramparts. I bowed and made the sign of the Cross to show respect.

'My message is for all to hear,' the priest said, passing his eyes right through me. He removed a folded document from his robe and held it aloft.

'Occupiers of Tours,' the cleric began in a loud, clear voice. 'Farmers, woodsmen, tradesmen, bondsmen and free, all followers of the man known as Hugh DeLuc . . . a *deserter* from the Army of the Cross, which still valiantly fights to free the Holy Land . . .'

A flash of worry chilled my blood. The ranks grew still.

'His Grace, the Bishop Barthelme Abreau, rebukes you for your false rebellion and urges you, this day, the seventh of May ten ninety-nine, to disband at once, to renounce all claims and territory seized from the Duke, Baldwin of Tours, and return to your villages at once; or face the full consequence of its actions: immediate and total excommunication from the Church of Rome and the separation from Grace, *for ever, for your eternal souls*.'

A hush came over the crowd. The priest paused to

observe the look of shock that was on every face, including mine.

'His Grace insists,' he continued, 'that you repudiate all teachings and promises of the heretic, Hugh DeLuc; deny the legitimacy of and confiscate any relics or symbols claimed to be of holy origin in his possession; and discredit all claims made that present him as an agent of Our Lord Jesus Christ.'

'No,' people shook their heads, 'this cannot be . . .' looking about, to each other, to me, with terror and alarm.

The young priest shouted over them, 'In the hopes that you will adhere to this decree immediately and that your souls may be made available to receive once again the Holy Sacrament, a two-day period of enforcement is declared, citing me as the final overseer. This edict is signed, His Grace, Barthelme Abreau, Bishop of Blois, representative of the Holy See.'

Blois! I thought. Stephen has done this!

A terrified hush continued over the crowd.

'This is madness.' Father Leo spoke. 'These people are not heretics. They only fought for food in their mouths.'

'Then I suggest they chew quickly,' the young priest said, 'and return to their farms, before their souls remain hungry for ever. And you as well, country priest.' He tacked the edict on the church wall.

'This is Stephen's blackmail,' I shouted to all around. 'It is the Lance he wants.'

'Then give it to him,' someone yelled, 'if it buys back our immortal souls.'

'I'm sorry, Hugh. I came for a fight,' another shook his head, 'but I'm not prepared to be damned for eternity.'

All around, our army, looking terrified and overwhelmed. Some climbed down from the walls and meandered slowly towards the city gates.

'That's right,' the priest nodded, 'the Church welcomes you, but only if you act now. Go back to your farms and wives.'

How could I fight against this poisonous assault? These brave men and women thought they were doing something good when they followed me. Something that God would shine on.

I watched as a steady stream of friends and fighters passed dejectedly by me and towards the city gates. A tightening anger burrowed deep into my chest.

We had just lost the war.

Chapter One Hundred and Twenty-Three

That night, Odo found me huddled by myself in the chapel.

I was actually praying. Praying for what to do. If there was indeed a God, I did not believe He would let a bunch of scheming, well-fed pawns like Father Julien, who didn't give a thought to whether my men lived or died, crush their resolve.

'I know we're deep in shit,' Odo said with a snort, 'if we've got *you* praying.'

'How many of our men are still left?' I asked.

'Half, maybe less. By tomorrow, who knows? Perhaps not even enough to hold the city. We still have some good ones: Georges, Alphonse, the Morrisaey boys . . . even Father Leo. Most of who've been with us from the start.'

I sniffed back a weak smile. 'Still trusting me?'

'No, I wouldn't say that. Let's just say, if they're making their bet with God, they trust the Holy Lance more than they trust that slimy church mouse.'

I smiled. I pulled the Lance up from the bench next to me and cradled it in my palms.

'So . . .?' Odo sniffed. 'That thing providing any answers? What is next?'

'What is next,' I smiled, 'is that it's me Stephen wants, or, at least, *this* ... Not your souls. This edict is a challenge. Come face me if you have the will. I've no choice but to go.'

'Go?' Odo laughed, 'You're going to march on Blois, with what we've got left?'

'No, my friend,' I shook my head. '*I'm* going to march on Blois *alone*.'

It seemed to take Odo a second to decide whether to object or roll his eyes. 'You're going to Blois? Just you. And that spear?'

'You see what he's telling me, Odo? He has burned villages to get this Lance. He killed my wife and child. He has Emilie now. What else can I do?'

'We can wait. Keep Baldwin under guard, until word comes. The King will surely stop this lunacy.'

'This *is* the King's word.' I shook my head. 'The King is noble. He will side with Baldwin and Stephen without even hearing our claims. These men are pledged to him. They raise armies to fight his wars. *We* ... what do we raise – hens?'

'Even a king can be swayed by a good omelette,' the big smith chuckled. Then he looked at me plainly. 'I am with you, Hugh, until the end.'

I grabbed his wrist. 'No more, Odo. You've been a loyal friend. You've trusted me more than any fool could ever ask for.' I shot him a smile. 'But now I have to face this. This *thing* ... it has brought me mostly pain. But some things – seeing the town stand up, feeling the pride as we marched on Tours, Baldwin's face – they've been a joy.'

'You've become quite a bad philosopher since you put on that skirt,' Odo sniffed.

'Maybe . . . but I go alone.'

Odo didn't answer, just took a deep breath and smiled. Then he looked around. 'So this is what it's like on the inside of a church. The seats are hard and there's nothing to eat. I don't see the attraction.'

'That makes two of us,' I grinned in reply. We sat a moment, draped in silence.

'So where would we be,' I mused, 'if I hadn't wandered off that day and followed the hermit? If I had never left, and Sophie and Philippe were still alive? And Father Leo was preaching dull sermons? And you still put in an honest day's work?'

Odo checked the window for the angle of the sun. 'I would say, hoisting a beer. Listening to your stupid jokes.'

I stood up, patted him on the back. 'Then let's do that, friend. I'm sure there's a cellar here. And I still know a few you haven't heard.'

Chapter One Hundred and Twenty-Four

At dawn the next morning, I pulled on my tattered jester's tunic, said goodbye to my old friends who had been with me from the start, put the sacred Lance under my arm, and left.

Georges, Odo, Father Leo and Alphonse met me by the city gates. I urged them not to buckle, but to remain, and hold the city. That what we had done was right, and would one day be honoured.

But that what *I* had to do now was right too. And I must face it, alone, whatever the cost.

As I prepared to mount my horse, I gave Georges and Odo heartfelt hugs. 'God bless you both,' I said. I thanked them for following me, for believing. For taking the chance! In their strong, silent embrace and held-back tears, I felt the grip of a sadness that we might never see one another again.

Then, glancing back a final time, with a wink and a smile I headed down the hill. I vowed not to look back again.

At the foot, with the gates closed and Tours rising behind me, I broke the promise to myself. I stared back at the tall, foreboding walls, the high, unscalable towers. The town that could not be taken. I couldn't help but utter a laugh. A spark of pride warmed my blood. Serfs and bondsmen had seized their liege's castle with the very minimum of force. Baldwin's apoplectic face rose up in my mind – and for that single moment, it had all been worth it.

But now, Baldwin was behind me. One final challenge lay ahead. It was with the person who had burned our village, who killed my wife and child. Who now held the one I loved. I knew this battle was no longer simply about rights and freedom. It had narrowed to something deeper, personal.

I turned my back on Tours a final time, and kicked my mount upon its way.

My sights set on Blois.

Chapter One Hundred and Twenty-Five

Stephen's boot heels sounded loudly as he pushed into a small, squalid room near the rear of the barracks. Hunched silently in a dark corner, its occupant turned, a man who was filthy and covered with sores.

'Come, Morgaine.' Stephen threw the door wide open. 'Your moment is here again. I need to make use of your talents. You are still a knight, are you not?'

The dishonoured knight slowly lifted his muscular frame off the floor. Tattered, soiled cloth still hid the spot where the Lance had pierced his side, and the tiny cubicle reeked of putrefaction.

'I am here to serve you, my liege.'

'Good,' Stephen said. 'You must air this place out. Your hygiene is odious anyway, Morgaine, but these days a latrine would smell less foul.'

'It is unavoidable, my liege. The stench keeps the memory of my wound awake in my mind, and the lowly bastard who gave it to me.'

'I'm glad your memory is fresh,' Stephen told him, casting a look at his hand, 'for if God grants it, you will have a chance for vengeance.'

The Tafur's eyes lit up. 'Each breath I force myself to take is in hope of such a moment. How?'

'Events, larger than you can contemplate, bring the fool back to me.'

'The fool! He comes to Blois? You know this?'

'Do you think I would soil these boots in this pit of infection for any other reason? Now, get up. I will have the physician mask that stench.'

The Tafur pulled his war tunic off the floor, still torn and bloodstained at the spot where the jester's lance had ripped through. He moistened his lips, the way a famished man would await, impatiently, a fresh roast.

'The thought of vengeance has made you alive again, warrior,' Stephen grinned. His instincts had been good. He'd been right to save this drooling beast and not lop off his head when he crawled back without the Lance.

'I will gut him,' the Tafur ground his teeth, 'and run my sores through his wound so that he may die knowing the contagion that he inflicted on me.'

'That's the spirit.' Stephen slapped him on the shoulder. He leaned close to the wounded warrior as if they were drinking mates, then dug the hilt of the knight's own sword sharply into his side. Morgaine gasped.

'This time make sure you come away with the Lance,' Stephen sniffed. 'But first, there is other work to be done.' He returned to his earlier tone. 'In your absence, all sorts of scum have come to Blois. That is why I come to you. Whom else am I to trust?'

'Just tell me what you need done.'

'Good.' Stephen's look brightened. 'That's what I hoped to hear. You seem like a man who lacks entertainment,

Morgaine. Let us call upon the jester, Norbert. You know Norbert, don't you, Morgaine? Why don't we see if we can prod him to make us laugh?'

Morgaine nodded, and Stephen knew he understood perfectly. It wouldn't matter whose blood was on his blade, as long as it led to the fool.

'And, Morgaine . . .' Stephen said as he departed the filthy room, 'as it's a party, why don't we ask along the Lady Emilie?'

Chapter One Hundred and Twenty-Six

I had travelled in the forest for two days, riding during light until my back ached, then, once it was dark, curling up in the brush, my mind racing, as I drifted off to a troubled sleep. I dwelled on many things: the friends I left behind, Emilie's safety. What I would do when I got to Blois, still four days' ride away.

I had just finished a few bites of bread and cheese one morning, and was preparing to go on my way, when I became aware of the slow advance of a rider approaching from behind.

I ducked behind a tree, and took out my knife.

Gradually, a single rider clip-clopped into view. A churchman, a friar perhaps, covered with his burlap hood, riding by himself in the midst of dangerous woods.

I relaxed and stepped out from my cover. 'You must be either foolishly brave to chance these woods alone, priest,' I called to the advancing shape, 'or just as foolishly drunk.'

The churchman stopped. 'That's an unusual warning,' he replied from under his hood, 'coming from a man in a checked skirt.'

To my shock, the voice was familiar!

He lifted his hood and I saw it was Father Leo, with a smile the width of his face. 'What are you doing here?' I gaped.

'I thought a man on a mission like yours might need his soul tended to,' he sighed, struggling to get off his mount. 'I hope you don't mind.'

'Mind? I'm delighted to have the company, old friend.'

'I knew it was a risk,' the priest sighed, brushing dust off his robe. 'Truth is, it's taken me so long to find a true sign from God, I couldn't bear being separated from the Lance.'

I laughed again, and helped him brush off the road dirt. 'You look tired, Father. Drink.'

I handed Father Leo my calfskin and he tilted it back. 'We will make quite an army when we get to Blois,' I smiled, 'the fool and the priest.'

'Yes,' Father Leo said, and wiped his mouth, 'very imposing. I knew we would frighten no one, so I hope you don't mind, I asked along a friend.'

'A friend . . .?'

From down the road, the trot of another rider could be heard, and as he came close I blinked twice and realized it was Alphonse. The lad trotted up to me dressed for battle. He flashed me his shy, awkward smile.

'You two are crazy!' I exclaimed.

'Dressed as you are, and marching to attack the castle at Blois alone, and you call us *crazy*?' challenged the priest.

'Well, now we are three fools,' I grinned, my heart warmed.

'No,' Alphonse sniffed, and shook his head. 'No, we are not.'

'Got anything good to eat?' another voice called from the

forest. 'Anything sounds good after these squirrels and lizards I've been chasing.'

Odo!

I looked at the smith, dressed in his leather armour, carrying his mallet, one of Baldwin's green and gold cloaks slung around him. 'I knew you must be behind this,' I said, attempting to look stern.

'Nah,' Odo grinned. He pointed with his head. 'It was *him* . . .'

Behind him, Georges thrashed his way out of the woods. 'I told you, this was *my* fight,' I protested, feigning anger.

'You also told us we were *free*,' Odo shot back. 'So I reckon this is *my* choice.'

I stammered. 'I put you in charge, Georges. I left you with Baldwin. And four hundred men.'

'So you did, didn't you?' the miller winked.

From down the road, the heavy rumble of footsteps rose in my ears: many people, marching. From around a bend, the first of them came into view. It was Alois, from Morrisaey, and a few of his townsmen, carrying their axes and shields.

The column grew. Alois's four turned into forty. Then forty more. Faces I recognized. From Morrisaey, Moulin Vieux, Sur le Gavre. Some on horses, others marching. Their faces rugged, silent, proud. A lump caught in my throat. I didn't speak. They kept coming, line after line, men who still believed in me. Who had nothing left but their souls.

Then, on a pale stallion, bound like a sack of wheat, *I saw Baldwin*. And, his chatelain, close behind.

I could not believe what I was seeing!

'They all came. All one thousand?' I said to Alois.

He shook his head. 'One thousand and *four*,' he grinned, 'if the Masons came along.'

Odo looked at me. 'We thought, if our souls are fucked anyway, what do we have to lose?'

My heart almost exploded with pride. I stood there watching the columns grow and grow. Feeling the common heart of these men. Some called out to say hello, 'Hey, General, good to see you again.' Others simply nodded, many whom I did not know by name. Until the end of the column came in sight, and it was trailed by four scruffy men hurrying to keep up, hoisting a white banner with an eye painted on it – the sign of the Masonic society.

I mouthed, 'Thank you,' to Odo and Georges, the words sticking in my throat. I wanted to tell them how proud I was of them. Of everyone.

I merely put my hand on the miller's shoulder.

'Suppose we're going to Blois,' Odo shrugged, and I nodded, watching the column as it stretched round a bend.

'You'd better have a real plan if you want to take *this* place,' he muttered.

Chapter One Hundred and Twenty-Seven

Just as it happened weeks before, when we marched on Tours, every village we came to, every crossroads on the route, people joined our ranks. Our fame had spread, and it was embarrassing. Certainly, it was humbling.

Farmers in their fields, carpenters, goatherds with their flocks, ran to their fences to see a lord like Baldwin bound behind a fool.

'How can you continue on?' people asked in wonder. 'Stephen has damned your very souls.'

'He might as well,' we called back, 'since that's all we have left.'

Once again I marched at the front in my tattered jester's suit, carrying the Holy Lance. But this time the army was properly outfitted. We had real swords and newly minted shields taken from Baldwin's men and painted in the green and red checks that had become our crest. We also had crossbows and catapults to mount a siege; oxen, and stores of food to sustain an entire army.

'You cannot take Blois,' some mocked us. 'Even so many could not take Blois.'

'We could not take *Tours* either,' Odo replied with a huff.

'We trust the Lance,' Alphonse would say. 'It is truer than any bishop's judgement.'

New recruits fell constantly in line. *I'll come. This is a new world if a lord is dragged by a fool!* Young and old kneeled before the Lance, and fell in.

Yet even as we marched, I knew this new battle would not be as easy as the last. Stephen would never let our ragtag army approach without a fight. He had a much larger and fiercer army than Baldwin, better trained. He himself was known to be a formidable fighter.

And to be sure, *I was no general.* The only military skills I had were those I had picked up on the Crusade. Nor did Georges, or Odo or any of my men. They were farmers and woodsmen. An old worry began to consume me: that I could be leading innocent men, who believed in my call, to slaughter.

I needed a leader, but where could I get one?

The third night out, I wandered over to where Baldwin and his men were being held. The duke glared at me belligerently. I merely shook my head and laughed.

I kneeled beside his chatelain, Daniel Gui. He was handsome, and held himself with a strong bearing. He'd never complained of being held captive, unlike Baldwin, who spat disparaging curses and threats to anyone who met his eye. I'd heard other good things about him.

'I have a dilemma.' I sat on the ground next to him. I looked Daniel Gui in the eye, man to man.

'*You* have a dilemma?' the chatelain laughed, showing me his binds.

'Mine first,' I smiled. 'I am at the head of an army, but I know little of how to fight a great battle.'

'Is this a riddle, jester? If it is, let me play. I *know* how to fight, yet my army is disarmed and scattered.'

I offered him a sip of ale. 'It seems we are aligned, yet opposite. But you command the duke's forces.'

'I command Tours's forces,' he responded firmly. 'My job was to lead them in defence of my city, not slaughter innocent subjects that our lordship did not trust.'

'Tours *is* Baldwin, though. You try to separate them, but you cannot.'

'My *dilemma*,' the chatelain smiled. He showed his wrists. 'By which I am now unfortunately bound.'

'I need a general, chatelain. If we march on Blois, we will not overcome it with sleight of hand.'

He took another sip of ale, seemed to think this over. 'What do I get if I help you take this city?'

I smiled. 'Mostly, a lot of trouble with your old lord.'

The chatelain grinned. 'I'm not exactly sure I can return to that job now anyway.'

Indeed, Baldwin would already be savouring the taste of someone to blame. 'Only a chance,' I answered. 'The same chance any of us has. To sue for peace, and go back and live our lives as free men.'

'There's an irony here somewhere,' the chatelain chuckled. 'So far, you have taken my castle and put my liege in chains. You don't seem too bad a soldier for a man in a checked skirt.'

'I was at Antioch and Civetot,' I said, 'on the Crusade . . .'

The chatelain nodded, in a deep and acknowledging way.

'So, will you help us? I know it will mean breaking your pledge to Baldwin, which will not raise your fortune in that quarter. Yet we are not such a bad bunch, for heretics and rebels and fools.'

Daniel took in a deep breath and smiled. 'I think I will fit in just fine.'

Chapter One Hundred and Twenty-Eight

We came out of the forest the next day facing the River Loire. A truly terrifying sight stood before us.

On the high ground, directly in our path, waited an ominous horde of warriors. Maybe three hundred of them.

They wore no colours, just rough skins and high boots, swords and shields gleaming in the noonday sun. They were long-haired and filthy, and regarded us with no particular alarm. They looked ready for a fight.

Panic shot through our troops, and through me as well. The ferocious-looking horde just stood there, watching us assemble out of the trees, as though battle were an ordinary thing for them.

Horns blew. Horses brayed. A few carts toppled over. At any moment, I expected them to charge.

I ordered our column to a halt, our backs to the river. The rabble ahead of us looked restless. *Shit, had I led us into a trap?*

Odo and Daniel ran up to me. I had never seen Odo this scared.

'They growl like Saxons,' Odo muttered. 'These ugly bastards are meaner than shit. I heard they live in caves and when food is scarce, they eat their young.'

'They are not Saxon.' Daniel shook his head. 'They are Languedociens. From the south. Mountain men. But they are known to eat their young even when the harvest is good.'

His words chilled me. 'Are they from Stephen?' I asked.

'Could be,' he shrugged. We watched them watching us, showing no concern about our larger ranks. 'Mercenaries. He has used them before.'

'Have the men fan along the ravine,' I said. I hoped to make a show of strength. This threat had come upon us so suddenly. 'Lances to the front in case they charge.'

'Keep the horses in reserve,' Daniel said. 'If these bastards come at us, they'll do so on foot. To a Languedocien, it's a sign of cowardice not to.'

Everyone rushed into formation. Then we stood there, hearts tense, holding our shields. The field was silent.

'Seems a good enough day to meet my Maker,' Odo strapped on his mallet, 'if you're still *listening*, God.'

All of a sudden, there was movement in the Languedoc camp. *Get ready.* I gripped the Lance.

Then two riders rode out from the pack and galloped towards us.

'They wish to talk,' Daniel said.

'I'll go,' I said. 'Here,' I turned to Odo, 'hold the Lance.'

'I'll go with you,' Daniel said.

Daniel and I rode out between the armies. The two Languedociens sat there indifferently, eyeing us as we came up to them. One was large and stout, built like an ox. The other leaner, bald and just as mean-looking. For a moment, no one spoke. We just regarded each other, circling.

Finally, the ox grunted a few words in a French I could barely make out. 'You are the jester *Hugh*? The one with the Lance?'

'I am,' I replied.

'*You're* the little fart who has led the peasants and bondsmen against their lords?' the other growled.

'We've risen up, in the face of murder and oppression,' I replied.

Ox sniggered. 'You don't look so big. We were told you were eight fucking feet tall.'

'If we have to fight, it will seem that,' I said.

The Languedociens looked me up and down in a way I could not read. Then they looked at each other and started to laugh. '*Fight* you?' the bald one chortled. 'We've come to *join* you, fool. Word reached us you intend to march on Tours. We are sworn enemies of that prick Baldwin. For two hundred years.'

I looked at Daniel and we broke into grins. 'This is good news . . . but you're too late. Tours is already taken. We are marching on Blois.'

'*Blois* . . . ?' the thinner one said. 'You mean against that prick Stephen?'

I nodded. 'The same.'

For a moment, the two Languedociens drew their horses close and huddled together. I could hardly understand the tongue that they were speaking in. Then Ox looked back to me and shrugged, 'Right, we march on Blois.'

He raised his sword to his ranks, and they erupted – lifting their swords and spears in a riotous cheer.

'You're lucky,' Ox grinned through his beard. 'We've been enemies of Blois for *three* hundred years.'

Chapter One Hundred and Twenty-Nine

Stephen was inside his antechamber when Anne stormed in and found him, in a chair, peeling an apple. Annabella, a lady of the court, was bent over his waist, sucking his cock.

At the sight of her, Annabella gagged. She jumped, frantically replacing Stephen's hose as if to hide the evidence. Stephen looked on, seeming not to care.

'Oh, do not bother, Annabella,' Anne sighed. 'When the lord hears what news I bear, we shall all be amused to see to what size his manhood shrinks.'

The lady smoothed her ruffled tresses, bowing, then scurried out of the room.

'These are my private quarters, not your hall,' Stephen said, hitching himself up. 'And do not feign offence, dear wife, since you obviously knew what business you would find here.'

'I do not feign offence,' Anne eyed him sharply, 'only regret, to have interrupted you from such pressing work.'

'So,' Stephen rose. 'By all means let me know. What's the big surprise?'

'A runner has arrived from Sardoney. He's brought with

him word that your little jester is on the way. Two days away. With his Lance.'

'*This* is the news you thought would disarm me?' Stephen seemed to yawn, taking another deep bite from his apple. 'That this poor scut marches on us. Why should this mean any more to me than a bite of this fruit? But come,' he said, eyeing the bulge in his hose, 'as long as the table is set, why not put the little weasel to some work?'

Anne crept behind him and smoothed her hands across his chest, even though the pretence of such affection was as repulsive to her as kissing a snake. She bent down to his ear and whispered, 'It is not the fool that I thought would concern you, my husband.' She rubbed her hand near his cock. 'But the thousand men and more who march along with him.'

'*What?*' Stephen twisted around. He screwed up his face in disbelief.

'Oh, has the weasel crept back in his little cave?' Anne laughed. 'Yes, my liege, apparently an army follows him that is even greater than before. An army of lost souls, *heretics*, thanks to you. And, thanks to Baldwin, fully armed.'

Stephen jumped out of his seat, hot with rage. 'Impossible! They damn their souls to follow him.'

'No, husband, it is *your* soul that is damned.'

'Get out of my way.' Stephen shot out his hand. It slashed across Anne's face, knocking her to the floor. 'If you have any hope for that little brat you call your cousin you will mock me no more.'

'If you harm her, Stephen . . .' Anne forced herself up to her palms.

Stephen burned his gaze right through her. He came over

as if to strike again. She did not flinch. Then the colour came back into his face, and he softened, and kneeled, and cupped her quivering face in the palm of his hand.

'Why would I want to hurt her, my precious wife? She is a part of you.' He raised himself, smoothing his tunic, the veins in his forehead now calm. 'I have merely detained her, for her own protection. There are dangerous conspirators about who plan us harm, even within these very walls. *Haven't you heard?*'

Chapter One Hundred and Thirty

L *ook.* Men began to point. *Up on the hill. There it is. Blois!* Above the rolling hills of vineyards and farms, the city's limestone towers rose with roofs of blue, like jewelled lazuli etched into the sky. There was the façade of the famous cathedral, gleaming white; and the castle that I had stayed in, its donjons reaching to the sky – where Emilie was.

As we neared, the exhilaration spread: 'I'm going to take Stephen in one arm and his largest hen in the other, and squeeze them till they both lay fucking eggs,' a boastful farmer yelled.

Behind me, the procession of my new army stretched out nearly a mile long. In each row, men marched in different uniforms: tailors, woodsmen, farmers in their own garb, but with thrown-together mail and helmets they had swiped from Baldwin. They carried pennants from their towns; pikes and clubs and bows on their backs. Some even spoke different dialects.

The vast line included men and horses, carts drawn by heavy oxen, catapults, mangonels and trebuchets with their ammunition of heavy stone; the cloud of dust that arose from them all seemed to smother the sky.

But as we got closer, the giddy boasts and dares began to fade. Blois was no ants' nest in the middle of nowhere with a pompous duke who did not want to dirty his hands with combat. This was a city, the largest many of us had ever seen. We had to take this place! It was protected by rings of walls, each manned with archers and artillery. Its reserve of knights was twice our number and emboldened by bloody victories in the Crusade. The closer we got, the higher the walls loomed over us. I knew the same reality drummed through every soul: *many of us would die here.*

All around, farms near to the city were shuttered and abandoned, livestock nowhere to be seen. Plumes of smoke trickled into the sky, from bales of hay and grain carts set afire. Stephen was giving us no sustenance or quarter. He was preparing for a siege.

People we passed did not cheer us as at Tours. They spat at us, or averted their eyes. 'Go home, rebels, heretics. You're God's curse!'

'Look at what you've brought on us,' a woman wailed, scavenging for food. 'Go on, your welcoming party lies just ahead.'

Welcoming party . . . ? What did she mean by that?

As we neared the city, men at the front pointed to what seemed a row of crosses lining the road. A few ran ahead.

As they did, their faces lost some colour. A silence came over the ranks, who only moments before had boasted of what they would do when they reached Blois.

The welcoming party.

These were not crosses, but bodies, some still alive, muttering, moving their limbs feebly, impaled on long shafts that split their torsos.

Some through the anus. Others, even worse, upside down. Men, young and old, farmers, tradesmen in common garb. Women too, stripped naked like whores, moaning, choking for breath, eyes glazed over in agony. There was a row of thirty of them.

'Get them down,' I shouted. My heart sank as at Civetot, or riding into the damned village of St Cecile. What had these poor people done? I rode by, barely able to look.

Then I stopped at one of the bodies. My blood came to a halt. My eyes rolled back in my head.

It was Elena, Emilie's maidservant.

I jumped off my horse and with my sword, started to hack at the stake, until it sheared and I gently eased her down.

I lifted Elena's head in my hands and stared at her chafed, white face, peeking through tufts of bloodied hair. She was in torn, soiled rags, desecrated like some shameless murderess. All the poor soul had done was serve her lady.

Anger dug into my ribs, sharp as knives. If this was Elena, what had happened to Emilie?

What kind of warning was this monster giving to me?

My breath stuck in my chest. 'Georges,' I turned to the man behind me, 'bury her.'

Chapter One Hundred and Thirty-One

Further ahead, we came to a fieldstone bridge, which forded the river, along the outskirts of the city.

It was guarded by a stone tower. I drew the ranks to a halt within sight of it. Three or four of Stephen's knights were waiting there, mounted on horseback, draped in their lordship's blue and white colours.

The first sign of the enemy.

They began to taunt us. 'You call this rabble an army?' one yelled. He lifted his leg as a dog pees. 'It's a bunch of peasants who wouldn't know a fight from a good fart.'

'They are only trying to bait us into something stupid,' Daniel cautioned. 'Stay your ground. They will peel back as soon as we advance.'

A few of the men, fuelled by the horrific sight they had just seen, ignored him and ran towards the taunting soldiers, ready to do battle with their clubs and swords.

As the men neared, archers appeared in the tower, armed with crossbows. They sent a volley of arrows whooshing and thudding down. Four men dropped immediately, clutching their chests. The rest peeled back out of range.

Behind me, I heard Alphonse yell out, 'They want their fight, they'll get it!'

'No,' I called, 'we can't lose more.' But despite my futile shout, he took off. He and his group ran bravely towards the tower.

Arrows hissed down on them, thudding into their shields. Another man fell, struck in the thigh. Our own archers loaded and sent out a reply of fire arrows towards the tower.

Now our men were pinned, huddled under their wooden shields. I saw Alphonse race out and pull one wounded man out of range.

Then one of our arrows struck the wooden roof of the guard tower. Chaos broke out among the archers as the flames caught. Our ranks began to cheer. For a second the enemy archers disappeared, then we caught sight of them on the ground, scampering back with their heavy bows towards the city walls.

Once again, our men set after them, Alphonse leading.

At first, they were met by knights on horseback, who fought bravely. But soon there were too many of us to fight. Stephen's knights were pulled down from their mounts, their bodies bludgeoned with swords and clubs. Several of us took after the retreating archers, overtaking them in a gully by the river. One kneeled, ready to fire into the back of one of our men, as Alphonse leaped and clubbed him into a heap.

To a man, the archers were hacked to bits. A chorus of cheers rose in our ranks. Our party of rescuers returned, dragging the wounded and dead, raising aloft captured crossbows.

It was our first engagement, and we had shown Stephen we were here to fight.

Alphonse passed by me, tossing a captured crossbow into a supply cart. Though I was relieved to see him safe and held back reproaching him for his recklessness, he could see I was angry. Four of our men lay dead.

He shot me a contrite wink. 'W-wouldn't know a fight from a good fart, eh?'

Chapter One Hundred and Thirty-Two

E milie opened her eyes. She pulled up her covers to warm herself in the dark, draughty tower room that had been her cell over the past days. The narrow slit of a window high upon the wall barely let in an angle of outside light. She was not sure if it was day or night.

For the past few hours, she had heard the rumble outside of troops and heavy carts being dragged down to the walls. Something was happening. A flicker in her heart told her it had to do with Hugh.

A pitcher of drinking water and a plate of half-eaten food rested on a table by her side, next to a few of her embroideries. But she had no mind to eat or weave.

Stephen was a dog, foaming with the madness of greed. All honour and law had been set aside to detain her. All reason too.

But it was fear for Hugh that gnawed at her, that festered in her heart through the dark, isolated nights.

Hugh . . . Stephen would not dare harm her, but he would see Hugh dead with the relish of a cruel child picking the wings off a fly. Now he prepared his army, his awful Tafurs, his archers, and death-dealing machines of war.

Do not come, she prayed, whispering herself to sleep. *Please, Hugh . . . do not come . . .*

But something was different this day. There was a far-off rumble and a sharpness to the voices nearby. The tremor of large machines being wheeled in place.

Battle machines!

Emilie threw the covers from her bed. She had to know what was going on. The commotion outside grew louder. Horses, shouting, the constant hammering of wood. *Preparations for war.*

Emilie wrapped herself in her bedclothes and dragged a table over to a spot beneath the high, narrow window. Then she hoisted a sitting bench and placed it on top of the table. As a child she had played such games of 'king of the hill' with her brothers. High above the floor, she balanced herself on the bench and raised herself to her toes.

Emilie craned her neck to see over the lip of the narrow ledge.

Below, on the inner walls of Blois – soldiers in pail helmets and blue and white tunics were bustling along the ramparts.

Emilie pushed herself even higher.

What was beyond was a sight that stole away her breath.

A vast gathering of men, beyond the walls, as far as the eye could see. In peasant clothes, with weapons and oxen and mangonels.

She felt her heart glow.

An army of them. Stephen's edict be damned! She began to laugh. She could not help herself. It was as if everyone who had ever marched alongside Hugh was here. Every peasant in the forest!

Then something else caught her eye.

She raised herself on the bench, as high as she could. She stood on her toes.

Yes, standing out from the troops. A head of fiery red hair. Could it be?

Her heart almost exploded. She wanted to scream at the top of her lungs, but knew he was too far away and could not possibly hear. She waved and shouted and whooped. She *heard* herself giggling, uncontrollably.

Standing there – in the very tunic she had sewn for him herself, facing Blois as if he knew *precisely* where she was – she saw Hugh.

Chapter One Hundred and Thirty-Three

The following morning, we pushed our siege engines forward under the watchful eyes of Stephen's men. Mangonels, their tightened baskets stretched back, followed by wheel carts of giant stones; massive rams hewn from tree trunks; ladders stacked in piles.

We began the construction of wooden towers, tall as the outer walls; as well as smaller platforms called 'cats', covered in moist, bloody hides to protect our charging ranks from the rain of burning pitch.

I was in Daniel's tent, running through the siege plans, when shouting was heard outside. I rushed out – and saw that everyone was running for their weapons and pointing towards the city gates. The drawbridge was lowering. *This was it!*

At any moment, I was certain a formation of blue-and-white-clad knights would come swarming out.

As the portcullis opened, two priests clad in sacramental robes slowly rode out under the banner of the Church.

After a pause, Gaston Morais, Stephen's captain of the guard, followed. And behind him, as if his presence alone would cause the field to kneel, a noble clad in full battle gear on a white charger.

Stephen himself.

Chapter One Hundred and Thirty-Four

'**H**e wishes to talk,' Daniel said. 'He hides behind the priests as a flag of truce.'

'He wishes to trap you, more like it,' Odo said. 'You'd be a fool.'

I couldn't wait to put my vengeful eyes on the bastard. 'Don't forget,' I put on my cap, 'I *am* a fool.'

I rushed to the front, found my horse, and called for Father Leo. 'Come, here's your chance to be an equal to the highest priests in Blois,' We fetched him a horse. 'And, Daniel?' I slapped him. 'Want a chance to see a duke piss in his pants?'

We mounted our horses and rode halfway out into the rutted no-man's-land separating our camp from Blois.

Stephen waited for us to reach a spot, then, gauging his own distance from our archers, trotted his own entourage to meet me. My blood was racing just to see this reptile. His look sent chills through me. He wore no helmet; his greying hair hung long and greasy. Elaborate chain mail with his colourful dragon crest was displayed on the chest plate. His hands were covered in studded gauntlets, and a heavy sword, befitting a Crusader, was strapped to his side.

As he reached us, he did not stay his horse. He circled us, his glance darting from my face to the Lance.

Then Stephen drew his mount to a rest. He smiled, quite amiably. 'So, you are the deserting coward who rouses men against their lords in the name of heresy.'

'And you are the prick,' I spoke, unrelenting, 'who killed my wife and child. With all respect.' I bowed to the priests.

'What a shame, then,' Stephen sniffed, 'if a similar fate befell another whom you prize.'

A fury tightened in my chest. 'If any harm comes to her, it will take more than a delegation of priests to save you. Lady Emilie returned here of her own will, out of loyalty and concern for her mistress. She has no conflict with you.'

'And do you? Jester, rebel, heretic . . . How is it I should address you?'

'Hugh,' I said, fixing on his cold, superior eyes. 'I am Hugh DeLuc. My wife was Sophie. My son, who never saw his first year, was Philippe.'

'I'm sure all of us here are delighted to hear your family tree, but what is it you want here, Hugh?'

'What do I want?' Part of me wanted to pull him off his mount right there, and end this thing, just he and I. I directed my horse one step closer to him. 'I want your admission for the wrongs you have done. I want restitution paid for each man, woman and child killed in pursuit of this.' I put forward the Lance. 'I want the Lady Emilie sent to me at once.'

The duke looked to his emissaries, as if he was restraining a laugh. 'I heard he was entertaining. And now I think no less myself. You want a lord to be a mule keep. You parade behind a purported relic of the Church, and yet you put the souls of a thousand followers at risk.'

'These men are here of their own mind,' I said. 'I doubt they would go home even upon my demand.'

'Does the welfare of their immortal souls not matter to them?' one of the priests enquired.

'I don't know. Let's see.' I turned back towards my ranks. 'Go home. Lay down your arms. All of you. Fight's over. I have his word that the duke promises to spare your souls.'

My words echoed across the field, but not a single person moved. I turned back to the priest. Shrugged.

'And what if I said the Lady Emilie was here, of her own mind too?' Stephen snapped. 'That it is her choice to stay, even upon my demand?'

'Then I would call you a liar, Stephen. Or a hopeless fool.'

'Again, jester,' he yanked his horse, 'you waste precious time on jokes. Your new chatelain will tell you, you are on the verge of a blood bath.'

'We are ready, my lord. This battle has your handprint on it, if it occurs, not mine.'

Stephen curled a smile. 'Just know that I will not be as lenient with you as was that codswipe Baldwin. You have seen the fate of certain villages and people who I believed had something I wanted. Expect no less, jester. I will see your heart burned out of your traitorous body. You will be hanged, upside down, as heretics, all of you . . . your insides left to soil your face as they run to the ground. Even God will avert His eyes!'

'Then, what do you say, Daniel?' I glanced at him with a smile, 'We must make sure we fight this fight on a full stomach, so as not to disappoint.'

Stephen sniffed back a laugh. Then he ran his eyes over

the Lance. 'You know, should I return with that, all I described could be avoided. You could have the little slut and ride off to the far corners of the earth, for all I care. As for your men, I will see that we restore their souls.'

'Most tempting,' I replied, pretending to ponder his offer for a moment. 'The problem is, my men have not assembled here for Lady Emilie, but for the single purpose of seeing the offences of your rule brought to justice. They're here to demand recompense for your crimes. To see you bow down, lord, nothing less. Then I will give you the Lance. That is *my* offer. In the meantime, with all respect to the bishop, we'll take our chances on our souls.'

'I could simply take it, you know. My archers could cut you in half with just a nod.'

'And mine too, my lord. Then God would have to decide.'

A tiny twitch tremored on Stephen's nose. 'You think I would trade the dignity of my name even for a vault of such lances?'

'It should not be so hard,' I held it to his face, 'since you have traded most of it already, just to be *this* close.'

Stephen reared his horse and smiled. 'I can see why the court grew fond of you. Get prepared, jester. I will reply. Within an hour.' He yanked his horse away and started to head back towards the gate.

Chapter One Hundred and Thirty-Five

O ur army waited just a fraction of a league from the towering walls in a broad and teeming line.

Archers tensed their bows, fire-arrows tipped in oil. Foot soldiers, holding ladders like crosses, focused on the walls, on the line of silent, blue-and-white-clad defenders as we prepared to charge.

A thousand men, cradling their weapons, muttering last prayers, awaiting my sign.

'What are you thinking now?' Odo asked.

I took a breath. 'That Emilie is in there. And you . . . ?'

'That those are the biggest fucking walls I've ever seen,' the smith shrugged.

I fixed on the impressive main gate, waiting for Stephen's reply, Odo to my left, Georges, Daniel, Alphonse flanked to my right. The tension beat around like a drum of war.

Stephen's defenders crowded the walls, crossbows tilted down at us. There were no taunts or curses rattling back and forth, only a heavy silence hanging like a fog between the two armies. In the distance, the chirping of birds could be heard. Any second, the tense calm would be shattered like a club smashing through ice.

Odo leaned close, clutching his enormous pike. 'One of the Languedociens told me a good one. You have the time to hear it?'

I kept my eyes fixed on the gate. 'If I must.'

'What's hairy underneath, stands tall and erect in a bed, has reddish skin, and is guaranteed to make even a nun cry out in tears?'

I looked down the line. Everyone was ready. 'I don't know.'

The big smith shook his head. 'Don't know . . . What kind of a shit jester are you? It's a wonder I keep putting my life in your hands.'

'If you put it that way,' I cocked my head towards him, 'it's an onion.'

'Oh, you know that one,' Odo groaned. A trail of sniggering filtered down the line. Then he elbowed me and grinned. 'That's my boy.'

All at once, from behind the walls, the *ping* of a catapult releasing splintered the air and a black projectile shot high into the sky. Murmurs rippled through the ranks, men pointing, as the object descended towards our front line.

'Brace yourselves! Here it comes,' someone yelled.

The projectile struck the ground and rolled only a few yards from where I stood. My stomach fell.

The mound had features – hair, charred and singed like horsehair; startled, round eyes bulging out of their sockets.

I let out a sickened cry.

The face seemed to be staring at me. It had a grin that was both impish and impudent. The twisted eyes glared back in its moment of death, familiar, unmistakable.

Norbert!

His eyes looked at me as they did that first day, when Emilie brought me to his chamber. I almost expected him to wink: *had you fooled, didn't I, boy? This is the best you can do? Watch this!*

I rushed out of formation and kneeled over the remains. My ears were filled with a deafening ringing. Countless images that had transpired since I first set out from home flashed before me.

The ringing finally subsided. I raised the Holy Lance, and perhaps for the first time, I believed in it. I looked at my men, whose readiness reminded me of horses unwilling to be held back.

'Your freedom lies within those walls. Now,' I shouted. *'Now is the time!'*

Then the cry from my lungs became drowned by the stampede of more than a thousand men hurling themselves at the walls of Blois.

Chapter One Hundred and Thirty-Six

The first sound of battle was a belching groan from one of the mangonels, as a massive boulder of rock was launched high into the sky and came crashing with a thunderous blast into the wall above the main gate. Fragments of stone and sparks and dirt exploded everywhere. But when the dust cleared, the wall still held.

Then another boulder whistled into the sky. Followed by a third, both striking high on the wall, shattering guard posts, sending bodies and battlements flying like debris. Then a volley of flaming arrows. *Whoosh!* Some struck against the walls, sticking in wooden battlements, where small fires ignited; others clattered harmlessly to the ground.

Then the mangonels again, this time with a cargo of burning, molten pitch. Defenders ducked; some screamed in pain, slapping at body parts. Others ran around with buckets, dousing flames. The smell of tar and sizzling flesh singed the air.

I raised my arm. 'Now, men. What is yours is within those walls. *Charge . . . !*'

As a single line, our men raced towards the walls, a

mountainous wave of steel, spears and ladders. The closer we got, the larger the walls grew.

Then I could see faces of the defenders – ready for our charge, holding fast, waiting for us to come in range.

Then all of a sudden, the cry of, 'Fire!'

Arrows, whooshing down from above. Our warriors stopping in their tracks, arrowheads ripping viciously through their chests and necks. Hands clutched to the exposed tips.

Our roar became replaced by a thudding terror, followed by groans and death cries. 'Aagh . . . Aagh . . . Aagh . . .'

I tumbled over a Languedocien writhing on the ground, an arrow protruding from his knee. To my left, a man in the skins of a shepherd spun around, his eyes rolled back, holding both ends of an arrow through his jaw. Men fell to their knees, howling in pain, praying, or both.

'*Don't* stop,' I heard Daniel shouting. 'Get behind your shields. You *must* make the wall.'

The sweeping advance, narrowed to a crawl, continued still. I saw Odo and Daniel and Georges in the first charge.

Above us, soldiers stood and fired. Lances were flung in reply. Some defenders clutched at their chests with a yelp, and fell over, screaming as they dropped from the walls.

Dozens of ladders were thrown against the walls, the men climbing up. Defenders reached over to push them off.

'Bring in the cats,' I shouted, as waves of boiling tar splattered down on us, followed by squeals and the smell of sizzling flesh. Advancing ranks pressed into us from behind. Those in the front rank tried to climb the walls, but were met with burning pitch or lances. They toppled back into the arms of the men behind them, spitting blood or swatting at their blistering skin.

The tall cats were pushed up to the front. For a moment, they produced a refuge from the smouldering pitch, which sizzled on the moist, stretched skins. Under its protection, men with a ram backed up and battered the gate over and over. Crossbows were fired from directly above. A man next to me, not wearing a helmet, had an arrow pierce through the top of his skull. From behind, the mangonels continued; an enormous boulder crashed into a tower. A cloud of smoke rocketed up, and when it cleared, the top of the tower was caved in and a maze of mangled body parts fell away from it like branches.

Panic reigned everywhere. 'Where is the mead table?' someone gasped staggering, completely befuddled. 'God save me,' wailed another, holding in his palm his other arm. In the furore, I lost touch with anyone I knew.

The once-shiny walls of Blois were soaked with blood. I had no idea if we were winning, or in the midst of being routed.

Some distance away I spotted Odo, leading a charge up a ladder. He wrestled in a tug of war with the lance of a defender, then Odo won, pulling his opponent over the edge.

Then another defender reared up and ran the point of his lance into the smith's leg. I screamed. Odo arched back in pain. He wrenched the lance out of the defender's grasp and frantically tried to pull the blade out.

'Odo!' I yelled, but the roar of battle made any shout indistinguishable from another.

I watched him take two Blois soldiers by the tunics, then fall back against the wall, swarmed over among the wave of men. I tried vainly to fight my way along the wall to get to him, but the line would not bend.

Arrows whooshed down from above with terrifying force. Men were huddling under shields, starting to cry, realizing they were trapped. *Where was Odo?*

Those of our men who made it up the ladders were hurled backwards or run through as they tried to fight their way forward. I realized we were losing. I could see the will in the men begin to bend.

Then a voice cried, '*Look out!*' A huge wave of rocks crashed down on us from above. One of the cats collapsed under the weight, pinning down the men with the ram.

'The towers themselves are coming down,' someone yelled. 'Get back, or be crushed.'

But it was not the towers. Stephen's soldiers were toppling bins of heavy stone over the edge.

The wall of men began to push their own comrades back. I could not stop it. My eyes were singed by pitch; I was coughing amid the dust.

I tried to spot Odo, but he had disappeared.

'Go back, go back.' I heard panic rippling down our line.

'Stay!' I yelled at the top of my voice, and so did Daniel. 'Don't quit the fight now! Don't give up ground!'

But I realized we had lost. The rear of our line finally broke, men heading back from the walls at a run. Then the first ranks, suddenly exposed, drifted back. A shout of joy came from the defenders.

Nausea rose in my gut as the men peeled back, running for their lives. They were farmers and cobblers and serfs, not trained soldiers.

I trailed the field and scanned for Odo, arrow whizzing

by my head. But the smith was nowhere to be found. The ground was piled with bodies. I could not believe our losses. I staggered back, finally out of arrow range. A horrible moaning came from the field, wounded who would soon die. Grown men wept, and muttered desperate prayers.

I saw the miller limping back supported by Daniel, both men as white as ghosts.

'Have you seen Odo?' I asked them. They shook their heads and stumbled on.

I turned back towards Blois. Men on the walls were cheering. They were shooting arrows at anything that moved. My friend was still out there. What was once a blossoming field was now a swamp of blood.

Not a single man had made it over the walls alive.

Not one.

Not Odo.

Chapter One Hundred and Thirty-Seven

We had lost!

Alphonse hurled down his sword, unable to speak, as were so many others. Georges threw himself back against a wall, spent and drained. Father Leo did his best to comfort everyone, but his face was as desolate as any.

'You men must not let down your guard,' Daniel yelled. 'Stephen may send his horsemen to finish the job tonight.'

His warning, however real, seemed the least of our concerns. Darkness was falling. Mercifully, as if its black cloak offered some reprieve. Our soldiers sat down around fires, exhausted, placing salve on their burns and wounds. Some wept for their friends; others thanked God that they were still alive.

'Did anyone see him?' I looked around. I had known Odo since I was a youth. Alois and Georges merely shook their heads.

'He's a wily sort,' Georges finally said. 'If anyone could make it back, it's he.'

'Yes,' Alphonse pretended to be upbeat, 'he was so close

in, he probably just ducked behind the walls to steal a keg of Stephen's best mead.'

'Many died today,' Daniel sighed, spreading out a map of Blois. 'We can't spend time on one man.'

'The chatelain is right,' Ox nodded. 'Thirty of my men are dead, maybe more.'

I looked in the Languedocien's eye. 'Your men were brave to join us. But this is not your fight. I release you from your pledge. Go, take the rest home.'

Ox stared back, as if insulted. 'Who said anything about going home?' He cracked a toothy smile through his beard. 'In the south, we say a good fight doesn't even begin until some blood is on the floor. God gave us all two arms, but hell, one's just for scratching our balls, anyway.'

Around the fire, we all started to laugh. Then the din subsided. Georges shrugged. 'So, what do we do now?'

I looked at the men, face by face.

'Continue the fight,' Alphonse said. 'Stephen massacred our town. That's why we came here, no?'

'You've grown a lot of spunk, lad,' the miller sniffed, 'but tomorrow it could be you who's left moaning out there.'

'Keep pounding the walls,' Daniel insisted. 'By the river, they are not as fortified. We can hit them with our mangonels all day. Sooner or later, they'll cave in.'

Father Leo cut in, 'Maybe soon, word from the King will come?'

'It is June,' Daniel pressed on. 'It's warming up. You've been to Antioch, Hugh. You've seen, a siege is not determined in one day. Stephen has scorched his own earth. They couldn't have stockpiled food and water for the entire summer.'

I had to ask: 'Is anyone for meeting Stephen's terms?' I looked around, awaiting their reply. There was only silence.

Finally, the miller picked himself up off the ground. 'I was raised to grind grain, not to soldier. But we've all made our choice here. We've all lost loved ones. My boy Alo. Your friends, Ox . . . Odo. What would any of their deaths mean if we turned it in now?'

'*Whose* death are you speaking of?' a voice barked in the darkness.

We looked up. A huge, hulking shape rolled forward. At first, I thought it was an apparition.

'Dear God . . .' the miller shook his head.

The big smith limped stiffly towards our fire. Odo's skins were torn and smeared with blood, his bushy brown beard matted with who knows what.

I met Odo's eyes, which, for the first time, showed the horror that he had faced. I was so exhausted, I could not even get up to give him a hug. 'What the hell took you so long?'

'Fucking hard to claw your way out with all those blue-and-white shits buried on top,' he sighed, with an exhausted grin. 'So, anything to drink?'

I got up and wrapped my arms around his shoulders and slapped him with an adoring hug. I felt his broad shoulders wince. His arms were covered in burns and his leg was bloody and raw. Someone put a mug in front of him and he drained it in a single swallow. A nod from Odo said, *One more*.

Then he looked up at us, our incredulous smiles. 'It was a bad day today, huh?'

We stared back.

'Well . . .' Odo swung his wounded leg up, the gash in his leg causing even Ox to cringe. He took the second mug and doused it all over the wound, sucking back pain. 'No matter.' He shrugged at our blank stares. 'We'll kick their arses tomorrow.'

Chapter One Hundred and Thirty-Eight

We pummelled Blois again and again over the next few days. Our catapults battered the walls with their missiles of heavy rock. Our sturdiest rams pounded at the gates. Charge after charge, ladders were pitched against the walls, only to be thrown aside, and the men on them killed.

The bodies of our fallen comrades piled high outside the walls. I feared we could not take the city. It was too strong, too fortified. With each repelled charge, the hope of victory faded. Food and drinking water were growing scarce. No answer was received from the King. Our will began to crack.

This was what Stephen had relied on, I realized. All it would take was one mounted strike by his knights against our depleting ranks, and we would be finished.

I called our leaders to the dilapidated grain tower we used for strategy meetings. The mood inside was anxious. Many friends had been left on the field. A sombre look was etched on every face, even Daniel's.

I went up to the hearty Languedocien. 'Ox, how many men do you have left?'

'Two hundred,' he said grimly, 'from what were once three.'

'I want you to take them then . . . *tonight*, and leave camp. And the Morrisaeys . . . you, Alois, I want you to take your men too.'

Ox and Alois were stunned. 'Give up? Let that bastard win?'

I did not reply. I stood in the centre of our ranks, catching Odo and Alphonse's eyes, sucking in their looks of disappointment and anger.

The Languedocien shook his head. 'We came a long way to fight, Hugh, not to run.'

'We too, Hugh,' Alois protested. 'We've earned our place.'

'Yes, you have,' I nodded. 'All of you have.' I turned and faced each one as if to convey my thanks.

'And you shall have it,' I declared, my voice coming alive. 'You shall have the chance that each of your friends sought as they were cut down.'

They stared at me, lost between alarm and confusion. 'Oh shit,' Odo's jaw dropped, 'it's another of those fucking *pretexts*.' He came and looked in my eyes as if he were trying to gauge the weather inside. 'We have Emilie to blame for this. What is the plan, Hugh?'

My eyes gave away nothing.

'We're going to take this city,' I spoke again, 'but not as soldiers. I have tried to fight this as a military man, and as a general, but I'm really a fool . . . And as a fool . . . even the great Charlemagne would have no advantage over me.'

'I'm not sure this is a revelation I'm pleased to trust my life to,' Ox screwed a sceptical gaze my way, 'but I'm all ears. Tell us about this pretext of yours.'

Chapter One Hundred and Thirty-Nine

Stephen was in the midst of stabbing a piece of breakfast ham, the morning light tumbling into his quarters, when his page called out, 'Look, your lordship, to the window, quick. The rabble has fled.'

Just minutes before, the duke had woken in a sour mood. These rebels had proven more resistant than he'd imagined. Wave after wave, they came at him; he could not understand their zeal to die. Also, for the past two weeks, Anne had moved to her own quarters. He'd been sleeping alone.

At his page's call, he hurried to the window. His empty stomach filled with glee. The boy was right! The rebel ranks had thinned, cut by more than half.

Those fucking Languedociens had fled, with their arms as thick as ox-legs and their horsehair jerkins. All that remained was a measly little force, standing around like chickens waiting to lose their heads.

And there at the head of them, the green and red rooster himself, in full view. *With the Lance!* This decimated rabble of peasants and farmers was no more than mop-up work for his men.

From behind, his aides burst in: Gaston, the chatelain, followed by Morgaine.

'Look,' Stephen cackled, 'the gutless bastards have given up. Look at that stupid, prancing cock, standing about as if he still has something to command.'

'You said, when the opportunity arose, the little fool was mine,' Morgaine rasped.

'So I did.' Stephen beamed a gloating grin. 'I did promise you that. Tell me, Captain, what strength do you estimate they still have?'

The chatelain scanned the field. 'Barely three hundred, my liege. All foot soldiers, with limited weapons. It should be no great feat to round them up with our horsemen and achieve a quick surrender.'

'Surrender?' Stephen's eyes widened. 'I hadn't thought of that. Yes, it might be good to extend a hand and save these poor, misguided fools a bit more blood. How does that word sound to you, Morgaine? Surrender?'

'These men are soulless, my liege. We'd be doing God a service by removing their heads.'

'So, what are you waiting for?' Stephen jabbed him in the chest. 'The little bastard's Lance still makes an ache in your side, does it not? You heard the chatelain's advice. Let the knights ride with you.'

'My liege, those are my men,' Gaston insisted. 'They are our castle's reserve—'

'You know, Gaston,' Stephen interrupted. 'That surrender thing . . . I've never been particularly keen on it. Morgaine makes a case. These men have already forfeited their souls. No reason to keep them fluttering around in this world.'

The chatelain's stomach sank.

'The Holy Lance, or my dignity, that was the jester's choice, was it not?' Stephen's eyes lit up. 'Now it seems that I will have them both. Won't I, chatelain? And Morgaine . . . one more thing. I know how you enjoy your work, but do not forget your real purpose out there.'

'The Holy Lance, my lord. My thoughts have never strayed from the prize.'

Chapter One Hundred and Forty

'Look!' A cry of alarm spread among the troops. Several men pointed towards the castle.

The gates of Blois had suddenly opened. We watched, all eyes fixed on the sight, not knowing what would emerge. Then, a rumble of heavy hoofs could be heard clattering over the lowered bridge. Behind it, the sight of armoured men atop massive, crested chargers, trotting in rows of two.

Everyone's heart was still. Silently, we watched the deadly battle formation assemble.

No one moved. I knew even the strongest among us debated whether to fight or throw down our arms.

'Positions, men!' I called. The troops remained, eyeing the ever-growing enemy force massing on the ridge. '*Positions!*' I called again.

Then, slowly, Odo picked up his gigantic club. And Alphonse, taking a deep breath, strapped on his sword. Then Georges and Daniel too.

They took their places without saying much. One by one the rest began to fall in. We gathered into a tight formation, covered by shields. I prayed this final pretext would work.

'H-how many of them do you c-count?' Alphonse took a breath.

'Two hundred. All armed to the teeth.' Daniel shrugged. He continued to count as they steadily poured out of the gate and stood their place on the field. 'Make that three.'

'And how many are we?' the boy asked again.

'Never mind.' Daniel sniffed, raising his weapon. 'What are warhorses and pikes against a good hoe, anyway?'

A flurry of grim laughter trickled around the ranks.

'What is this city, just one big fucking garrison?' Odo shook his head.

On the walls, blue-and-white defenders of Blois stood silently, gaining confidence as the ranks of their horsemen grew. Chargers hissed and snorted, held back from the ensuing charge.

Knights glowered at us, adjusting their armour and weapons, as if we were crickets, about to be crushed.

When the force was finally set, a sole rider walked his horse out of the gate and took his place at the head of the formation. I expected Gaston, the chatelain, but it was not.

On his face-plate, I saw the outline of a dark Byzantine cross. My blood went still. Once again, I was facing the man who had killed my wife and baby son.

Odo swallowed drily. He leaned close to me. 'Hugh, I know I've said this before . . .'

'Yes, I think it'll work,' I told him. 'But if it doesn't – what's the cost? I always thought you made a better soldier than a smith.'

'And you were a better jester than a general,' he sniffed back.

I started to laugh, but suddenly my voice was drowned

out by a terrifying rumble from across the field.

'Here they come!' Daniel cried. 'Shields!'

There was a harried, desperate murmuring. Men could be heard muttering their last prayers. I slung the Holy Lance through a strap across my back and took hold of a heavy sword.

The ground had started to shake. Shouting and cheers erupted from the castle walls.

We linked together in tight formation, our perimeter protected by a wall of shields. The drum of heavy hoofs grew closer and closer like an advancing landslide.

'Hold together,' I yelled. Then they were on us!

Chapter One Hundred and Forty-One

The wave of horsemen crashed into our ranks with the impact of a tidal wave of water swallowing up a ship. Sparks and shields and armour flew into the air.

Our ranks staggered backwards from the force, recoiled, shields raised over our heads. Steel came crashing down on us. But the men did not break.

A knight barrelled into me, chopping furiously against my shield with an enormous pike. My legs buckled under the heavy blows. All around were the sounds of groans and terror; the chilling clang of iron; shields splitting against the weight of steel, horses braying, soldiers crying out.

Fighting back, I managed to pin the face of my attacker's pike against the dressings of an adjacent mount. Then I lashed upwards with my sword, praying it would strike anything. It pierced the armour just above the rider's knee plate. The knight howled, and his mount bucked. I was able to drag him from the saddle and throw him under the hoofs of his own horse.

Our ranks were already two-thirds encircled. Men groaned and dropped in their places; the ranks narrowed. We could not withstand much more of this onslaught.

'Back,' I shouted. 'Now!'

Slowly, we started to retreat, still fighting in formation, making our way towards the cover of the woods.

Across the way, I saw Black Cross, fighting with fury and rage, cutting down men with a single stroke, pushing his own knights out of the way. I knew he was trying to get to me.

We made our way back towards the trees. Stephen's horsemen followed, closing for the kill. We continued to resist in formation. Someone's blade slashed across my arm. All about, we were being encircled, a vice squeezing our ranks. I saw Black Cross steadily approaching, watching me as he came.

Suddenly, a roar rose behind us in the woods. In a trick of the eye, the trees seemed to come alive – hide-clad horsemen and club-wielding warriors springing forth out of the green. Stephen's knights spun round. All of a sudden they faced a charging enemy *from behind*. Their horses, caught in the squeeze, tripped and reared, tossing riders off. We began to strike at them, using our swords like battering rams, crumpling armour until it gave, and running the knights through.

Suddenly Stephen's horsemen were pinched, fighting a renewed foe from all sides. You could see in their darting eyes the terror of this unanticipated shift of fortune. More knights began to be stripped from their mounts, their heavy weapons useless in the closeness of battle. It was a massacre. A massacre – but not the one they had planned.

Soon, barely half of Stephen's knights were standing. Many were off their horses, fighting two or three of us at a time in their cumbersome suits. Shouts of exhortation were replaced by pleas for mercy. Some ceased fighting and put up their hands. Weapons dropped to the ground.

Relief rippled through me. I could not believe it. I was so tired I wanted to sink to my knees.

Then a fearsome voice pierced through me, sharp as any lance. 'You rejoice too soon, jester. Before we call it a day, let us see how much power that little stick of yours really has.'

Chapter One Hundred and Forty-Two

H is visor was up, his face cold and scarred. I fastened on the smirking, hard-set eyes of Black Cross, the man I hated more than any other in this world.

'*Twice*,' I spat at him.

'*Twice what*, innkeeper?'

'Twice I have to rid the world of the scum who killed my wife and child.'

I rushed towards him, wielding my sword at his neck.

The Tafur stood his ground, pinning back my strongest thrust with ease. I hacked at him again and again. Each time he pinned my blade.

'You have caused me *shame*,' Black Cross hissed, the pupils of his eyes darting through his visor's narrow slits.

With a ferocious howl, he leaped and swung his blade down on me with the force of a rock from a mangonel. I darted backwards, the wind from his blade only inches from my face.

The Tafur did not even stop to gain his breath. He swung again, backhanded, aiming to slice through my legs. The mighty force of his blow almost drove my own blade into my thigh.

Slowly, I forced his blade upwards, but it took every sinew of my strength. I felt like a boy straining against the power of a fully grown man.

'You are every bit the fool, as your reputation speaks,' Black Cross sneered. 'When I kill you, Stephen will take the Lance *and* the lives of your men. Your severed head will be at the foot of your whore's bed.'

He swung at me again, each blow harder to fend off. I darted to the left, trying to catch my breath. Only my speed prevented me from being cut in half. But my quickness was waning. I couldn't beat Black Cross, I realized.

He butted me, helmet into my head. I staggered back, the crash reverberating through my skull. The breath was heavy in my chest. A voice inside me, pleaded, *Please God, show me the way*.

The Tafur pressed closer and I stumbled, trying to scamper away. I crawled along the bank of the river, knowing my death was only seconds away. Stephen would end up with the Holy Lance after all.

Black Cross stood in front of me. There was no escaping him now. He rolled up his visor and let me see his awful, scarred face.

He sniffed, 'Your soul is already lost. I only do God's scut-work by delivering your corpse to Him.'

For a moment, I blinked, disoriented by the sun glinting off his armour. I felt I was in another place, Antioch, staring up at the Turk, sucking in the last, precious breaths of my life.

Once again, the craziest urge took hold of me.

I began to laugh. I did not know at what. That I had come full circle, back to the moment of my death? That despite all my hope, life in the duchy would remain as it was? That I would die in the patchwork clothing of a fool?

Something crazy came into my head. A line from a stupid joke. I don't know why it seemed funny to me, but I could not help myself. I was a fool, wasn't I?

'It certainly is deep,' I said. Then I started to laugh again, twisting up my legs and rolling on my side.

'You die witless, jester. Tell me what image is so funny that you will carry it to your grave?'

'Oldest joke in the book.' I caught my breath. I did not know if it was cunning or total lunacy that was in control. 'Two men pissing on a bridge. Each trying to prove to the other who's bigger. One rolls out his pecker. "*Bbrrr* . . . this water's cold," he shivers. "Yeah," goes the other, "and it certainly is *deep*".'

Black Cross looked blank, not understanding. He circled in front of the river, ready to dispatch me to Hell.

'It certainly is deep,' I said again, this time a renewed certainty upon my face.

It was only a flash, but I was sure I saw on his face the subtle recognition that *all was not what it seemed*, that he had misjudged something.

Before he could work it out I kicked my legs and struck him squarely in the mid-section. The blow sent him reeling backwards, stumbling to the edge of the water.

Black Cross struggled to keep his balance. And he did! He smiled, disdainfully, as if to say, *You little man. That's all you have?*

Then his boots could not hold the ground. He teetered, his armour dragging him backwards. And still, his look was not of peril, but merely annoyance. *Little man, little problems.*

But then he began to fall. A clang of iron, the armour dragging him, picking up speed like a boulder, until he rolled, grasping at rocks and weeds, all the way down the embankment and slid into the river.

He tumbled under the surface. I am certain that what flashed through his mind was that he would pick himself up and climb back and finish me off. Moments passed. I could not believe what was happening myself. The Tafur *did not* rise. A gloved hand thrashed into the air, struggling for something to grasp on to.

More moments passed. Air bubbles rose to the surface. His glove flailed back and forth. But the Tafur never rose again. Black Cross was done, drowned, *dead*.

I forced myself to crawl over to the edge of the embankment. The fighting had wound down. Stephen's men were kneeling, groaning, hands in the air. Our men were beginning to cheer, hoisting their swords above their heads.

Then everyone was cheering. Jubilant faces reflecting the same incredible thing. We had won! Stephen was defeated. *We had actually won!*

All around, people came rushing up to me. I didn't know whether to laugh or cry. Finally, tears bit at my eyes, tears of joy, and exhaustion. People shouted my name, as if I was a hero.

I reached behind me for the Holy Lance. With whatever strength was left in my body, I thrust it high into the air.

Towards Heaven.

Chapter One Hundred and Forty-Three

E milie did not hear cheering. Why . . . ?

She knew a fierce battle was underway. She'd heard the pounding gallop of horsemen leaving the castle, the walls shaking with their chargers' strides.

Oh God, she writhed, that could only mean Stephen had attacked. Hugh's army was now fighting for its life.

Emilie could not bring herself to look out of the window of her cell. *How could God let this ruthless bastard win? Fight, Hugh, fight.* But she knew the odds against him.

She waited for the roar, close-by, announcing victory. It would tell her Stephen's killers had done their job. That Hugh was dead.

But there was no roar.

After the first rumble of horsemen there was only the clash of metal, the gnashing din of battle, far-off cries. Then, in the distance, a trail of cheers. Why were the ranks on the wall so silent? She finally pulled herself up on her mat.

No cheering . . . *Could Hugh have won? Was it possible?*

Suddenly, the bolt jangled on the door and it was flung open.

Stephen was there, his eyes fierce. Two soldiers followed him into the cell.

She forced a smile. 'I hear no cheers coming from the walls, cousin. Why do I think the battle has not gone your way?'

'For *both* of us,' Stephen snorted and seized her arm. 'There's a noose in the courtyard that awaits your pretty neck. Tomorrow morning, you traitorous bitch!'

'You have no right to pass such judgment.' Emilie tried to twist away. 'You sentence me to death on what charge?'

'Sedition, abetting the rebels, fucking a heretic . . .' Stephen counted them with a shrug.

'Have you lost your mind? Is there no honour left in you? Have you bargained everything with the Devil for that Lance?'

'The Lance,' Stephen's eyes flashed, 'is worth more to me than you, *and* your fool, and all the pitiful *honourable* souls left in France.'

Emilie shouted, 'You will not beat him, Stephen, whether you hang me or not. He came for you as one man, now an army stands behind him. You cannot stop him, not with all your titles and mercenaries, no matter how many men.'

'Yes, yes, your ruddy little fool. Oh, now you've really got my knees knocking,' Stephen laughed.

'He *will* come for me.'

Stephen shook his head and sighed. 'Sometimes I think the two of you actually deserve each other. Of course the fool will come for you, my pathetic cousin. That's precisely what I'm counting on.'

Chapter One Hundred and Forty-Four

The realization settled over the men that the battle was finally over. No more fighting. No more blood.

They looked around – stunned and elated. Those who had lived sought out friends and embraced them. Georges and the Languedociens; Odo and Father Leo; farmers and Masons, jubilant, just to be alive.

I led our men back to the castle walls, exhausted, out of fight. But as *conquerors*!

The same defenders who had pushed aside our attacks now sullenly watched us, arms at bay. Stephen's captured knights were pushed to the front, stripped of their armour, and forced to kneel. A cry rose up. Not a chant of victory, but a single, steady voice that grew in power until all joined in.

'Submit, submit,' they chanted.

Finally, from a parapet above the front gate, Stephen appeared, dressed in a ceremonial purple cloak. He surveyed our ranks contemptuously, as if he could not believe this ragtag rabble had beaten back his troops. 'What happens now?' I asked Daniel.

'You must talk with him. Stephen has to comply or his

knights will lose their heads. He is bound by honour.'

'Go on,' Odo pushed me forward. 'Tell the bastard he can keep his fucking grain. See if there's any beer in there.'

I grabbed the Lance. Someone hitched up a mount for me.

'I'll go with you,' Daniel said.

'I'll come too,' the miller said.

I looked at Stephen. I didn't trust this bastard, no matter how deeply he was bound. 'I think not.' I shook my head. I had someone else in mind.

We brought up Baldwin, bound. He had long been stripped of his fancy clothes, and was dressed in a burlap tunic like any common man. His wrists were bound; his haggard face badly in need of a shave.

'It is your lucky day,' I said, plopping a plumed hat upon his head. 'If all goes well, you'll soon be back in silk.'

'You do not need to truss me up,' he threw off the hat. 'You can be sure Stephen will recognize one of his own.'

'Suit yourself,' I nodded solemnly.

We headed forward out of the ranks, Baldwin's mount tethered to my side. Soldiers on the walls watched us approach silently.

We stopped, just out of arrow shot from the wall. Stephen gazed down, barely acknowledging me, as if he had been called away from a meal.

'Black Cross is dead. The fate of your best knights, what's left of them, awaits your word. We have no more urge for blood. Submit!'

'I commend you, Carrot-top,' the duke replied. 'You have proven to be as worthy a fighter as you are a fool. I have taken you too lightly. Come, ride forth, where I can see your face. I will present my terms.'

'*Your* terms? It is our terms you are bound to hear.'

'What do I detect, jester. Do you not think me a man of honour? Ride forth, and claim your prize.'

'I think you bargain freely, lord, with something you are short of. Do not be offended if I send out my man, instead.'

A smile curled on Stephen's face. 'Your man, then, jester. And I will send mine.'

'Shall I go?' Daniel offered.

I shook my head, and glanced towards Baldwin. 'No . . . *him.*'

Baldwin's eyes bolted wide. A film of sweat broke out on his forehead.

'Here's your chance.' I pulled the hood over his head. 'Show us how your lord recognizes you.'

I gave a hard slap to the rump of his mount and the horse bolted forward. The duke, hands bound, tried to gather it under control. As he crossed over into no-man's-land, he began to shout, 'I am Baldwin, Duke of Tours!'

A few guards on the wall began to point and laugh.

The duke's voice became more agitated. 'I am Baldwin, you fools. Disregard these clothes. Look at me, Stephen. Do you not see?'

All that could be seen was a lowly clad figure galloping towards the gates on his mount.

'Here, jester,' Stephen called from the wall. 'Here are *my* terms.'

A chilling *whoosh* was heard and an arrow thudded into Baldwin's chest. The duke keeled back. Then another, and a third arrow cut into him. Baldwin's body slumped in the saddle. The mount, sensing something was wrong, reversed its course and drifted back towards our ranks.

'There are my terms, fool,' Stephen called from the wall. 'Enjoy your victory. You have *one day.*' Then he wrapped his purple cloak about his shoulders and left, without even waiting for a reply.

Daniel rode out to meet the returning mount. Baldwin's lifeless body crumpled to the ground.

A parchment was rolled around one of the arrows in his chest.

Daniel leaped off his horse, and without pulling out the arrow, unfastened the paper bound to its shaft. He read, then looked up. I saw the bitterness in his eyes.

'Lady Emilie is decreed a traitor. We have the day to lay down our arms. Unless *we* submit, and turn the Lance over to him, she will be hanged.'

Chapter One Hundred and Forty-Five

That night, I went out into the fields behind our camp, my chest exploding with rage.

I needed to be alone. I headed past the sentries manning our perimeter. What did I care if I was in danger? I wanted to hurl the blasted Lance against the castle walls. *Keep it, Stephen. My life has been sorrow and misery since I found it!*

Behind me, the flames of a hundred fires sparkled in the night, my men dozing or making bets on what tomorrow would bring: fight or surrender.

I began to feel heartened; my shoulders free of strain. Maybe I would see Emilie if I walked close to the walls, just for a moment, as I passed by the gates. The thought lifted me – that I might see her beautiful face one more time.

I let out a breath, cradling the Lance in my palms, staring at the massive walls.

Suddenly, I felt a muscular arm around my neck. I gulped for air; the grip tightening. The tip of a blade was pressed into my back.

'Most accommodating, jester,' hissed a voice in my ear.

'You've picked a daring place for a murder. If I shout out, you will be meat for our dogs.'

'And if you shout, you would be out of a very dear friend, boar-slayer.'

I slowly turned, and was face to face with the Moor who always guarded Anne.

'What are you doing here, Moor? Your mistress, Anne, is no friend of mine. You're not welcome either.'

'I come with a message,' he said. 'You must listen, just listen.'

'I have already seen your lady's message, but my wife died in her dungeon.'

'A message not from my lady,' the Moor smiled, 'but from *yours*. Emilie. She bids you come with me tonight. I told her no sane man would come back with me through these walls. She said to tell you, "That may be, but it will not always be." '

The sound of those words took my breath away. I could hear Emilie's voice, see her as I set off that day in the jester's suit to Tours. My blood lifted with the thought of the brave twinkle in her eyes.

'Do not smile yet,' warned the Moor. 'It will be a long shot to save her. Choose two men. Your best. Two whom you would be happy to die with. Then we must go. Inside. Now.'

Chapter One Hundred and Forty-Six

I chose Odo and Ox. Who else? They were the two bravest, and they had got me this far.

Around midnight, we left, snaking our way through the camp without attracting attention. We followed the river along the perimeter of the city walls. Then we headed west, away from the main gates.

Through the darkness, I saw the outline of the great cathedral, lit by the flames of sentry fires. We could even hear Stephen's men talking and manning their positions on the walls.

We kept close to the river, approaching a part of the city I did not know. We forded the river at a low point the Moor knew.

Creeping under the walls, we finally reached a spot where the wall seemed to be the exterior of a large stone building that rose many storeys high. Narrow window slits were carved in the wall. I had no idea where I was.

The Moor climbed up to one of the narrow slits. He scratched at the opening. A voice hissed back. 'Who is there, fool or king?'

In his broken accent, the Moor said, 'If fools were crowns,

we'd all be kings. Quick, let us in – or we'll all be hanging tomorrow.'

Suddenly, chunks of the wall began to shift. The slit grew larger, a block at a time, and I could see it was not a window, but a tunnel.

'What the hell is this?' I asked.

'*La porte d'idiot,*' the Moor said, hurrying us through. The Fool's Gate. 'It was dug during the wars with Anjou as an escape route, but the Anjous found out and they were waiting there. They slaughtered all who came out. Anyone who went through was said to be a fool. Thought you'd appreciate the touch.'

'Very reassuring,' Odo swallowed uneasily.

'My apologies,' the Moor said. 'I would have suggested the main gate, but all these men in blue-and-white surcoats with big swords were standing around guarding it.' He pushed Odo forward.

We crept through the narrow opening. A dim light appeared up ahead. 'Come, quick,' I heard a voice say at the other end. I did not know where I was or whom I was heading towards. I prayed this was not an ambush.

The tunnel was not long, only the length of the thickness of the castle's walls. We came out into a cell, arms assisting us as we jumped into a torch-lit room.

A man in a deep blue robe with a white beard helped us out. I immediately recognized him: Augustus, the physician who had healed me after my attack by the boar. This was his hospital. People in the throes of disease reclined on mats or leaned half-naked against stone walls.

Augustus led us down a hall into a large adjoining chamber. A study. The walls were lined with heavy manuscripts, scrolls all about.

I had barely enough time to thank Augustus for his help before the physician scurried off, shutting us in. My heart beat nervously.

'What is next?' I turned to the Moor.

'What's *next*,' a voice came out of the shadows, 'is to pray that Holy Lance of yours has a fraction of the powers it's said to – if you intend to save the life of the woman you love.'

I spun round, to see a huddled shape in a hood emerge from the corner. I did not know whether to raise my knife, or bow.

I was staring at Lady Anne.

PART SIX

LAST RITES

Chapter One Hundred and Forty-Seven

A drum beat slowly in the courtyard outside the castle. An anxious crowd had begun to form, eager to see what was happening.

Usually, before a thief or a murderer took the rope, people gathered around, laughing and gossiping as if they were going to a feast. Pedlars hawked cakes and candles; children played hide and seek through the crowd, hoping for a front-row vantage point to taunt or spit.

But today, the mood was different. Everyone knew they were going to see something they had never seen before.

A noble was going to be hanged.

A noble woman.

High above the courtyard, I hid on a castle ledge, crouched into a nook the Moor had found for me. In the square, I spotted Odo in the crowd near the gallows. And Ox, balancing two pails on his shoulders, making his way in the direction of the main gate.

On the walls, soldiers lined the ramparts, poised if the rebels should charge. A bonfire burned in the square, its flames fanned by a whipping wind. The fire was for Emilie's body, once she was hanged.

Suddenly, a flourish of horns shattered the restive calm. Murmurs buzzed through the crowd. It was time! The door to the donjon opened.

A detachment of blue-and-white dressed soldiers marched out, Emilie at their centre.

'There she is,' someone shrieked.

'I beg you, pray, lady,' a woman wailed. 'God's womb is great. If He finds room for us, He will for you.'

I crept closer to the ledge. My heart was pounding against my ribs, just to see her after such a time.

She wore a plain linen smock and a shawl wrapped tightly around her shoulders. Her golden hair was pinned and fell about her neck. She didn't look noble, just brave, as I had ever seen her.

Oh God, how I wanted to catch her eye, call out to her. Let her know that I was here.

A drumbeat began. The crowd grew hushed.

'Let her go,' someone yelled. 'We have no fight with her.'

Emilie stopped for a moment, a smile of kindness on her face, but a soldier pushed her towards the scaffold.

The crowd hollered to save her life, even as a masked hangman pulled her by the arms up the stairs and led her to the noose. I knew how scared she must be, I knew how her heart must be fluttering. I glanced at Odo: *Hold!* The same to Ox. How I wanted to rise and shout, 'I am here . . .'

Then the horns sounded again – this time, the duke's flourish. From the entrance to the castle Stephen appeared, flanked by his lackey bailiff and the chamberlain.

The bailiff pulled out a scroll and began to read: ' "In accordance with the laws of the Duchy of Blois and sanctioned, heretofore, by the Archbishop of the Diocese and the Holy See, it is willed that all known abettors and care-givers to the heretic rebels will be deemed agents of corruption to both Duchy and Church, and thereby be hanged by the neck until dead, and their body burned, as is the law." '

'Let her live,' a voice shouted from the crowd. 'It's Stephen's neck that fits the noose, not hers.'

Stephen's face reddened. 'Where is your jester, now, cousin?' He stepped up to the gallows, and said to all, 'I have given him a chance to spare her life, to spare the city more blood, and yet he does not appear. Cousin, you have only these weak-willed women to speak for you.'

'Your deeds speak for me,' Emilie said. 'I pray he does not come.'

Stephen narrowed his eyes. 'We will wait, but only a few moments more.'

Odo looked at me with readiness. *Now*, his eyes said. *We must strike now.* I gave him no signal.

Suddenly, a lookout called from the walls, 'My lord, it is the jester's army. Their arms are down. They *submit*.'

Stephen's face lit with joy. 'Be sure, Sergeant. Submit or attack? There must be no tricks.'

'No, the sergeant is right,' confirmed the chatelain, from the ramparts. 'They carry their banners down. They do submit. And the jester, he is at the head of them.'

From my perch, I could make out rows of my men approaching with their arms at bay. And Alphonse, in my checked skirt and cap, at the head.

'Your fool's stupidity amazes even me,' Stephen smirked, bounding up the steps and peering over the walls. 'He lays down everything for a woman. What chivalry! Come forth, jester,' Stephen called beyond the walls. 'We will open the gates. I have something you will want to see.'

He signalled to his gatekeeper to draw up the portcullis. Two men twisted the heavy metal gate skywards.

At the same time, Stephen ordered, 'Hangman, secure the noose.'

The crowd gasped with murmurs of protest. Something vile was about to occur. The masked executioner fitted the rope around Emilie's neck and positioned her body over the trap.

'Stay away,' Emilie shouted to the men approaching outside the gates. A black hood was placed over her head. 'Please, Hugh, go back. *Go back.*'

Stephen laughed out loud. 'Sorry to disappoint you, cousin. It seems he is every bit the fool he is supposed to be.'

I could no longer restrain myself. I signalled to Odo in the crowd, and to Ox hovering by the opening gate. Across the way, I spotted the Moor, on a balcony above the square.

I signalled to Odo. *Now!*

But suddenly Stephen shouted, 'It is not him!' He strained over the wall, his eyes bulging. 'It's a trick! The jester is not there! Close the gates!'

Chapter One Hundred and Forty-Eight

The Moor's arrow streaked across the square, striking the gatekeeper in the back, slumping him to his knees.

Ox threw off his pails and jammed a rod in the pulley, bringing the heavy portcullis to a stop. He ran his knife into the back of the other gatekeeper, who was struggling to reverse the gate.

A swarm of my men, Alphonse at the lead, rushed inside. They overwhelmed the soldiers at the gate, as arrows rained down on them. Soon they were battling Stephen's men hand to hand.

Stephen leaped down from the walls towards the scaffold and Emilie. 'Where is your fool, cousin? He lets you die? He does not come for you?'

He gave the nod to his hangman. Then Odo pushed his way past two guards. He plunged his knife into the hangman's gut, hurling him off the scaffold. He went to Emilie.

'He *does* come, Stephen.' I stood up. I held my lance. Our eyes locked in a hateful exchange. 'I am here, my lord. Norbert told me you were a jester short.'

The thrill of victory hardened into rage on Stephen's face. '*Get him!*' he screamed. 'A hundred livres for the man who brings me that lance. *Five* hundred livres!'

His guards moved towards me, but I raised my arm with the lance I held.

'You threw my son into the flames,' I said, fixed on Stephen. 'Here, fetch your lance.'

I hurled it with all my might into the centre of the bonfire. To everyone's horror, it stuck firmly amid the flames.

'No . . .!' Stephen hollered.

He ran like a madman to the fire, desperately pulling at branches and wood, flames biting at his flesh. He hurled sticks towards the lance, trying to break it free. Then he backed off, driven away by the raging heat. He stared at the lance fixed in the centre, *melting*.

Then he turned towards me, murderous hatred in his eyes. 'You!' he screamed. 'You incredible *fool*!'

Chapter One Hundred and Forty-Nine

Stephen bounded up the stone stairs two at a time and on to a parapet, climbing his way to my level with great speed and agility for such a large man. His eyes burned.

I took my sword and leaped from my ledge to the balcony of the castle on the second floor. One of his soldiers moved to stop me and I slashed him across the chest, sending him flying.

The duke hurdled another ledge, racing towards me in a frenzy. He came to face me on the same balcony – a few strides away.

'Your wit has never been in doubt, Carrot-head,' he sneered, leering into my eyes. 'Now we'll see if you can fight.'

He leaped upon me, bringing down his blade. A bone-chilling clang reverberated through my limbs. Stephen pivoted deftly, and swung his sword, two-handed, at my chest. The blade creased my side.

I buckled, stung with terrible pain.

'Come on, fool,' he seethed. 'I thought you had some passion for the fight. You will see, there is more to being noble than sticking your dick in a highborn cow. You wanted restitution for your shit-covered wife and son? Come on!'

He pressed his blade further, forcing mine back, inches from my neck. His eyes were ablaze; hot breath fumed in my face.

With the last of my strength, I kneed him. Stephen groaned and his legs buckled. I pushed him away and swung my blade, knocking the sword from his hand. His eyes widened as it toppled over the ledge. He stood there, defenceless, yet still glaring.

Then he jumped up on a ledge, overlooking the square. He laughed, 'Just know, if I get to her first, she is dead!'

He leaped across to the next balcony. Then he darted inside the castle.

I ran to the edge, scanning the courtyard, looking for Emilie. I couldn't see her anywhere. Odo neither. Blood was seeping from my side.

I ran into the castle, expecting Stephen and a fight to the death. I was in the living quarters. No sign of the bastard anywhere.

'Where are you?' I shouted down the halls. Only echoes answered.

I smashed through a door and into Stephen and Anne's private quarters. I looked around madly. I had been here that night when I hunted for Anne after finding Sophie in the dungeon.

I looked down at my side. A damp patch of blood clung to my tunic. 'Stephen!' I yelled. *God damn it, come fight with me.*

A voice came from the shadows behind me. 'You want me, I am here, jester. Tell me a joke.'

Stephen emerged from a corner, smirking, a loaded crossbow aimed at my chest. 'I may *be* a jester short, as you say,' his lip curled into a smile, 'but you, it seems, are the one who is out of tricks.'

A chill went down my spine. I backed up to the balcony. There was nowhere to run.

'What do you say? Our little fool is out of tricks? He dreams of being noble, but he has only fucked one. Shame about the Lance, though,' he said with a grin, 'don't you agree, wife?'

Wife . . . ? Anne?

Chapter One Hundred and Fifty

From behind him, Anne stepped into the light. My legs grew weak. A hollowness was in my gut.

In her hand she held the Lance. *My Lance* . . . not the plain one I had cast so theatrically into the fire. The Lance I had entrusted to her last night! Entrusted.

'I *am* a fool,' I said, seeking out her eyes. I had trusted her. How could Emilie have been so wrong? How could I?

I looked at the crossbow levelled at my chest, and Stephen's mocking grin. For the first time, I felt ready to die.

'One last word, jester,' Stephen smirked, stepping in front of his wife. 'Your death is trivial to me, serf. All that mattered was the Lance. But what would *you* do with such a thing, anyway? You could not possibly know the power it holds. I hunted the world for it. By all God's justice, it is mine.' He tensed his finger on the trigger of the crossbow.

'Then *have* it, Stephen,' Anne's voice rang from behind him.

Suddenly, Stephen lurched and his eyes wrenched open. I stiffened, expecting my own guts to fall into my hands. But no arrow came from his crossbow.

I heard the most horrible, penetrating sound – the splitting of ribs and sinew, the tearing of flesh. An awful gasp came from Stephen's mouth. But instead of words, a river of blood.

Anne pushed forward strongly. This time, the blade of the Lance pierced the base of his neck and came out before his very eyes. *'Have it, husband.'*

Then Anne put her mouth close to his ear and whispered, 'But know how worthless it is now, our Saviour's blood having mingled with your own.'

Stephen looked down. He stared disbelievingly at the Roman eagle and the blood-encrusted tip of the Holy Lance's blade protruding from his chest.

Then he fell over to the floor.

I stared at Anne, too dumbstruck to speak. She merely stared in return. Neither of us spoke. Then I saw a softening in her eyes, and a nod, as if we shared some kind of understanding, one that would never be put into words.

'I think it's safe to say,' she said, 'that when we pulled you from the ditch that day, such an ending would not have entered our minds.'

'Very safe, madame.'

I heard footsteps from down the hall. Emilie burst into the room, breathless. Our eyes met and my heart nearly exploded with joy. She looked at Stephen crumpled on the floor. Then at Anne standing over him. Then at me again, her eyes darting to the blood leaking from my side.

'You are wounded,' she gasped.

'And you are always nursing me back to health,' I said. 'Oh God, Emilie, you cannot know how it feels to see you now.'

'I do know,' she said.

She ran to me and flung herself in my arms. I lifted her off her feet and squeezed her as tightly as I have ever held anything in my life. I kissed her over and over, kisses of hope and gratefulness. For the first time, I actually realized that she was mine.

My eyes were moist, thinking of all that had taken place since I first set out from Veille du Père – all who had died. 'I have nothing. Not a sou to my name,' I muttered. 'Not even a living. How is it possible that I feel like the richest man in all the world?'

Emilie took my hand and whispered, 'Because you are free.'

Chapter One Hundred and Fifty-One

The Languedociens were the first to leave, early the following morning. Ox told me there was a saying in their part of the woods: no sense hanging around the wine cask when the party's over.

He and his men assembled at the gates at dawn, their horses loaded with sacks of grain, a few pigs, and hens fluttering behind. I went out in the early light to bid them farewell.

'You should stay,' I told him. 'Anne has promised to address all your claims. You deserve a lot more.'

'*More?* We are farmers.' Ox threw back his head. 'What else do we need? If we came back laden with gold chalices, our people would think they were to piss in.'

'In that case,' I patted him on the shoulder, and flashed him a glimpse of a plate of gold engraved with Stephen's crest that I intended to give him as a memento, 'no need to leave with *this.*'

Ox looked around and tucked it in his saddle pouch. 'I suppose I'll have to teach them some proper manners,' he grinned.

I embraced him, patting the warrior warmly on his broad back.

'Look us up, jester, if you ever have the urge to return that Lance,' he winked. He slapped his horse and signalled his men forward.

I watched until the last of them had disappeared through the city gates. Stephen was being buried later that day. That was one last thing I had to do.

A few of my men were there as the open casket was brought to the cathedral. It was not a service befitting a duke who had died in battle. Only Anne, two of their children, Emilie and I were inside the church with the bishop.

The duke's mangled body was placed in a marble sarcophagus and carried into a crypt deep inside the cathedral. We followed it down the narrow tunnel carved out of foundation rock. There was barely enough air to fuel a torch. In this dark, narrow space, well below ground, lay the remains of past bishops and members of the ruling family.

The blessing was simple and quick. What was there to say?

That Stephen had bargained his honour and title away for greed and power? That he had beaten his wife and been an indifferent father to his son. That he had plundered the Holy Land in search of loot.

The Bishop of Blois, the same who had excommunicated us, muttered through a quick prayer, his eyes continuing to dart towards the Lance. Emilie looked on, holding my hand. When the blessing was done, Anne bent over the casket and planted a dry kiss upon his cheek.

A final blessing was said. Anne led her sons out of the

crypt, the bishop stumbling close behind.

'Give me a moment,' I said to Emilie.

She seemed not to understand.

'I need to say something for my wife and son.'

She finally nodded and left me. *Just Stephen and me.*

I looked at his deep-set, hooded eyes, his turned-down hawk nose. 'If there ever was a bastard in this world, you were it,' I said. 'May you rest in Hell.'

I held the Holy Lance in my palms. It brought back memories of all those whose lives had been changed by it. Maybe years from now someone would find it, I thought. In a different time, when it would be celebrated for what it was. Something miraculous, close to God.

You were a hell of a good walking stick, I sniffed a smile, *but as a relic, you brought more blood than peace.*

I placed the Holy Lance inside the sarcophagus. Then I closed the lid tight and looked away.

The crypt attendant came back and I nodded for him to go about his duty. I stayed and watched, saying goodbye to Sophie, Philippe and the Turk who had spared me in Antioch.

The casket was sealed for good and pushed into the wall, speckled with mortar until it fitted seamlessly in the smooth stone.

To lie there for ever.

Or until it was needed again.

Chapter One Hundred and Fifty-Two

Church bells were ringing.

As I came out of the cathedral, Emilie rushed up, excited. 'We have visitors, Hugh! Archbishop Velloux is arriving at the gates.'

'Velloux?' I did not know the name.

'From Paris. He is the *highest* clergyman in France.'

Paris . . .! I did not know if this was good or bad. The Church had excommunicated us. If this was upheld, all we had fought for could be lost. No matter what Anne vowed to rectify, without the Church we were outcasts, more dead than alive. Without souls, we were without rights.

I hobbled into the courtyard. Anne stood by, expectantly. Bishop Barthelme too. From all about, my men gathered around the courtyard: Odo, Alphonse, Father Leo.

The highest clergyman in France! This was a humbling thing.

As the portcullis was raised, a column of soldiers in crimson surcoats galloped two by two into the courtyard, behind them an ornate carriage drawn by six strong steeds.

It bore the cross of Rome, insignia of the Holy See.

My heart was leaping out of my chest. Emilie squeezed my hand. 'I have a good feeling,' she whispered.

I wished I could say I did as well.

A captain of the guard jumped off his mount and placed a stool in front of the carriage door. When it opened, two priests with scarlet skullcaps emerged. Then, a moment behind them, the archbishop, about sixty by my gauge, his hair grey and thinned, a crimson robe and a large gold cross around his neck.

'Your Grace,' Bishop Barthelme exclaimed. He and his priests kneeled on one knee. Slowly, everyone around them did the same. 'This is a great honour. I pray you did not have too unsettling a trip?'

'We would not have,' the archbishop curtly replied, 'were it not that on your word we went first to Tours, expecting to find a rebellion there, "heretics and thieves". Yet instead, we found only peace and order. And remarkably, no lord. I am told there was a battle fought here.'

'There was, Your Grace,' the bishop said.

'Well, you look no worse for wear, Barthelme,' the archbishop smiled drily. 'Obviously, the Church still functions. Show me, where are all these dreaded lost souls?'

'Why, they are *here*,' the bishop said, stabbing his finger towards my men. 'And *here*.' He pointed towards me.

The archbishop looked narrowly at me. 'These men seem quite benign, for apostates and heretics.'

The bishop's face turned white. A few sniggers were heard around the square.

'The duke felt—'

'The duke obviously felt,' Velloux interrupted, 'that the Church's laws were available, as were you, to enact his personal bidding.'

For the first time, the tightened bowstring that was my chest began to relax.

'Your Grace,' Anne stepped forward and kneeled, 'your presence is most welcome, but there are matters of civil law that also need to be addressed.'

A voice called out from the carriage. 'That is why *I* came along, my dear . . .'

A stately figure emerged, wrapped in a purple cloak covered with gold fleur-de-lis. Each of the soldiers immediately dropped to a knee.

'Your Majesty!' Anne exclaimed, her face blanching. She immediately curtsied, eyes fastened to the ground. Gasps rippled through the crowd. Words I could scarcely believe.

'*The King* . . .'

The entire square dropped to one knee. *The King!* He had answered my call. I had to blink twice to make sure I wasn't dreaming.

Then I heard something that stunned me even more.

'*Father!*' Emilie exclaimed.

Chapter One Hundred and Fifty-Three

F ather? Did I hear right? I know that my jaw hung wide.
The King's eyes were drawn to her. I could not tell if
he was pleased or stern. 'Has your absence from the court
made you forget, child, who it is you address?'

'No, my lord,' Emilie stammered. She drew herself down
and averted her eyes. Then she lifted them, twinkling with
amusement. 'Father . . .' she exhaled and smiled.

'So,' the King signalled for us to rise, 'show me the
misguided fool who I am told is responsible for this
unrest.'

Emilie shot forward, clasping my arm. 'You are mistaken,
Father. It is not Hugh who is responsible, but—'

'Quiet,' the King elevated his voice. 'Anyway, I was refer-
ring to *Stephen*, the supposed duke, not to your damned
jester,' he said.

Emilie slowly rose again, her eyes moist and beaming,
and broke into a blushing smile. She took my hand.

'The duke is dead, sire,' Anne came forward. 'He died,
realizing his shame, by his own hand.'

'By his own hand . . .' The King glanced at the archbishop and snorted. 'Then it is *he*, after all is done, who is

withheld from God's grace. As for the rest of you heretics . . .' he turned to face my men, 'consider yourselves restored. I speak for Archbishop Velloux when I give you back your souls.'

A joyous cheer rose up. The men hugged each other and threw their fists in the air.

'Now as for *you*, jester . . .' The King turned back to me. 'You have made demands that, if granted, would throw half my country into disarray.'

'No demands,' I bowed my head, 'only the hope to return to our homes in peace, and some manner of law to redress ills perpetrated on us.'

The King sucked in a breath. For a moment, I thought he would go into a rage. Then he relaxed. 'My daughter has been talking about this very thing for years . . . Perhaps, it is time.'

The courtyard exploded in cheers, but he immediately put up his hand to stop them. 'The fact remains, you have risen up against your lords. Against those you were pledged to. The law of liege and vassal is not at bargain here. Some justice must be meted out.'

Emilie pushed me down. I took a breath and kneeled.

'You must be educated in the manner of the nobles,' said the King.

'Sire, I was a jongleur and an innkeeper. I am as far from highborn as one can be.'

'Yet you will *have* to be educated,' the King crooked his eye, 'if you intend to marry my daughter.'

I slowly raised my eyes. I looked about – a smile spreading on my face.

'Father!' Emilie gasped, and pulled me to my feet. Then

she ran to the King, and without so much as a curtsy, threw her arms around him.

'I know, I know. Fools are everywhere, even those who wear the royal robe. But first, I need a word with your boy.'

He came to me, evaluating me. Then he placed an arm around my shoulder and ushered me away. I felt some rebuke about to come.

'Not to seem ungrateful, son, for I know Emilie is in your debt . . . but in your letter you mentioned a Lance.'

I took a breath, then spoke. 'It was destroyed, sire. Hurled into flames, in the fighting here. I'm afraid there is nothing left.'

The King sighed deeply. 'It was the Lance that pierced Our Saviour's side? Such a relic was more valuable than my own crown. You are sure of it, lad?'

'Only sure that it has produced the most miraculous of outcomes. Look around you, sire.'

He looked – at the ebullient men, at his daughter's eyes wet with joy – then nodded wistfully. 'What a treasure that would've made. Still, just as well . . . In my experience, such things are better left the stuff of legends and myths.'

EPILOGUE

Chapter One Hundred and Fifty-Four

'**G** rand-père ...!'

My little grandson, Jacques, came up to me in the gardens. It was a bright June morning. I had just returned from the hill with a handful of sunflowers, as I did every morning in the summer. Though climbing to the spot was a little harder for me now.

Little Jacques, my daughter Sophie's son, who was five, threw himself in my arms and almost toppled me over. He pointed to the checked crest that hung above the entrance to our inn. (Of course, the inn was slightly larger than my first one, with, as my estate, a quarter of the land that once belonged to Baldwin. Some things do come with being married to the daughter of a king.)

'Maman told me you would tell me what our crest means. She said you were once a jester.'

'She said that?' I pretended to be surprised. 'Well, if she said that, then it must be true.'

'Show me?' Jacques insisted, his blue eyes twinkling.

'Show you?' I took his hand. 'Then first you must hear the tale.'

I took him to the bench that overlooked the town, where

we had lived these forty years, near where Sophie and Philippe were buried. Around us, the fields exploded with bougainvillaea and daffodils and sunflowers galore.

I took Jacques back to the time when all we had was a tiny inn. When an army marched through here, an army led by a hermit. To the battles near and far, and the holiest prize in the world, which for a short while was in my hands. To the fight of men to make themselves free, forty years before.

My little blond-haired grandson listened without as much as a breath. 'That was you, Grand-père? You did these things?'

'Me and Odo and Alphonse, and Georges the miller. When Uncle Odo was just a smith in town, and not our seneschal.'

'Let me see.' He screwed up an eye, as if I was joking with him. 'Show me what you learned.'

'What I've learned?' I jiggled his tiny, freckled nose. Then a thought flashed into my head. I sat him down on the bench and winked at him as if to say, *This is our secret. Whatever happens, don't tell your grandma.*

I sucked in my stomach and tensed my breath. I hadn't done this in thirty years. I tucked myself into a deep crouch. I prayed to God I would not kill myself. 'Watch this!'

And I sprang. Through the air into a forward flip. And in that fleeting second, a thousand memories flashed through my mind: Sophie. Emilie. Nico and Robert. And the Turk. I sprang for all of them. One last time.

With a thump, I landed on my feet. Every bone in my body seemed to rattle. But I nailed it! I was in one piece. Norbert would've been proud!

I looked at Jacques. His eyes glistened bright as the June

sun. I saw my beautiful Emilie in those eyes. Then all at once he started to laugh. A true child's giggle, like water rushing in a brook. It almost choked me, as I watched him. *Laughter*, the most beautiful sound in all the world.

'*That's* what I learned.' I tousled his long golden hair and smiled. 'That's what this crest is all about. That is *everything*.'

So I took my little grandson by the hand and led him back to the inn. Emilie, my queen, was waiting for me there. The hearth was roaring.

And I had sunflowers for her.

Afterword

The following books on the Crusades and the Middle Ages have been a source of information and background for both setting and characters in this book:

Armstrong, Karen, *Holy War: The Crusades and Their Impact on Today's World*, Anchor Books, New York, 2001

Bartlett, W.B. *God Wills It!* Sutton Publishing, Gloucestershire, England, 2000

Bishop, Morris, *The Middle Ages*, Houghton, Mifflin, Boston, 1968

Cantor, Norman, F., *The Medieval Reader*, HarperCollins, New York, 1994, including original works of: Song of Roland, William of Tyre, Peter Abelard, the Magna Carta, Goliardic Verse, St Ambrose, Gregory of Tours, Marie de France, Bernard Gui

Cohn, Norman, *The Pursuit of the Millennium*, Oxford University Press, New York, 1974

Connell, Evan, *Deus le Volt! Chronicle of the Crusades*, Counterpoint Press, 2000

Goetz, Hans-Werner, *Life in the Middle Ages*, translated by

Albert Wimmer, University of Notre Dame Press, Notre Dame, Indiana, 1993

Holmes, George, *Oxford Illustrated History of Medieval Europe*, Oxford University Press, New York, 1988

Joinville and Villehardouin, *Chronicles of the Crusades*, Penguin Books, London, 1963

Keen, Maurice, editor, *Medieval Warfare: A History*, Oxford University Press, New York, 1999

Konstram, Angus, *Atlas of Medieval Europe*, Checkmark Books, New York, 2000

Lacey, Robert and Danziger, Danny, *The Year 1000*, Little Brown and Co., New York, 1999

Ladurie, Emmanuel Le Roy, *Montaillou: The Promised Land of Error*, Vintage Books, New York, 1979

Read, Piers Paul, *The Templars*, St Martin's Press, New York, 1999

Tuchman, Barbara, *A Distant Mirror: The Calamitous 14th Century*, Ballantine Books, New York, 1978

Turn the page for a preview of another compelling thriller from master of suspense James Patterson.

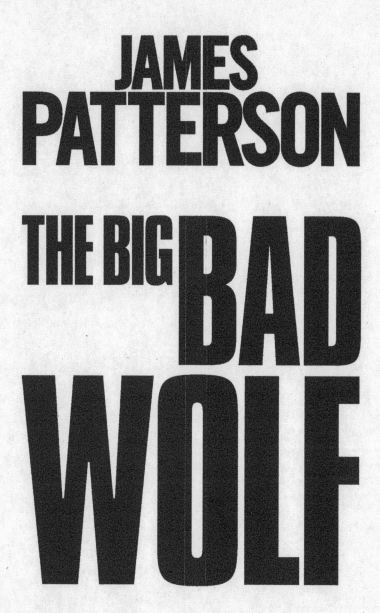

JAMES
PATTERSON

THE BIG BAD
WOLF

Chapter One

There was an improbable murder story told about the Wolf that had made its way into police lore, and then spread quickly from Washington to New York to London and to Moscow. No one knew if it was true, but it was never officially disproved, and it was consistent with other outrageous incidents in the Russian gangster's life.

According to the story, the Wolf had gone to the high-security supermax prison in Florence, Colorado, on a Sunday night in early summer. He had bought his way inside to meet with the Italian mobster and don, Augustino 'Little Gus' Palumbo. Prior to this visit, the Wolf had a reputation for being impulsive and sometimes lacking patience. Even so, he had been steadily planning this meeting with 'Little Gus' Palumbo for nearly two years.

He and Palumbo met in the Security Housing Unit of the prison where the New York gangster had been incarcerated for seven years. The purpose of the meeting was to reach an arrangement to unite the East Coast's Palumbo family with the Red Mafiya, thereby forming one of the most powerful and ruthless crime syndicates in the world. Nothing like it had ever been attempted. Palumbo was said to be skeptical, but agreed to the meeting just to see if the Russian could get inside Florence Prison – and then manage to get out again.

From the moment that they met, the Russian was respectful of the sixty-six-year-old don. He bowed his head slightly as they shook hands and appeared almost shy, contrary to his reputation.

'There's to be no physical contact,' the captain of the guards spoke from the intercom into the room. His name was Larry Ladove and he was the one who had been paid $75,000 to arrange the meeting. The Wolf ignored Captain Ladove's order.'Under the circumstances, you look well,'he said to Little Gus.'Very well indeed.'

The Italian smiled thinly. He had a small body, but it was tight and hard. 'I exercise three times a day, every day. I almost never have liquor, though not by choice. I eat well, and not by choice, either.'

The Wolf smiled, then said, 'It sounds like you don't expect to be here for your full sentence.'

Palumbo coughed out a laugh. 'That's a good bet. Three life sentences served concurrently? The discipline's in my nature, though. The future? Who can know for sure about these things?'

'Who can know? One time I escaped from a gulag on the Arctic Circle. I told a cop in Moscow, "I spent time in a gulag, you think *you* can scare me?"What else do you do in here? Besides exercise and eat Healthy Choice?'

'I try to take care of my business back in New York. Sometimes, I play chess with a sick madman down the hall. He used to be in the FBI.'

'Kyle Craig,' said the Wolf. 'You think he's crazy like they say?'

'Yeah, totally. So tell me, boss, *pakhan*, how can this alliance you suggest work? I am a man of discipline and careful planning, in spite of these humbling circumstances. From what I'm told, you're reckless. Hands-on. You involve yourself with even the smallest operations. Extortion, prostitution, stolen cars. How can this work between us?'

. The Wolf finally smiled, then shook his head. 'I am hands-on, as you say. But I'm not reckless, not at all. It's all about the money, no? The bling-bling? Let me tell you a secret that no one else knows. This will surprise you, and maybe prove my point.'

The Wolf leaned forward. He whispered his secret, and the Italian's eyes suddenly widened with fear. With stunning quickness, the Wolf grabbed Little Gus's head. He twisted it powerfully, and the gangster's neck broke with a loud, clear snap.

'Maybe I am a little reckless,' said the Wolf. Then he turned to the camera in the room. He spoke to Captain Ladove of the guards. 'Oh, I forgot, no touching. Now let me out of here.'

The next morning, Augustino Palumbo was found dead in his cell. Nearly every bone in his body had been broken. In the Moscow underworld, this symbolic kind of murder was known as *zamochit*. It signified complete and total dominance by the attacker. The Wolf was boldly stating that he was now the Godfather.

Part One

The 'White Girl' Case

Chapter Two

The Phipps Plaza shopping mall in Atlanta was a showy montage of pink granite floors, sweeping bronze staircases, gilded Napoleonic design and lighting that sparkled like halogen spotlights. A man and a woman watched the target – 'Mom' – as she left Nike Town with sneakers and whatnot, for her three daughters, packed under one arm.

'She *is* very pretty. I see why the Wolf likes her. She reminds me of Claudia Schiffer,' said the male observer. 'You see the resemblance?'

'Everybody reminds you of Claudia Schiffer, Slava. Don't lose her. Don't lose your pretty little Claudia, or the Wolf will have you for breakfast.'

The abduction team, 'the Couple', was dressed expensively, and that made it easy for them to blend in at Phipps Plaza, in the Buckhead section of Atlanta. At eleven in the morning, Phipps wasn't very crowded, and that could be a problem.

It helped that their target was rushing about in a world of her own, a tight little cocoon of mindless activity, buzzing in and out of Gucci, Caswell-Massey, Nike Town, then Gapkids and Parisian (to see her personal shopper,

Gina), without paying the slightest attention to who was around her in any of the stores. She worked from an at-a-glance leather diary and made her appointed rounds in a quick, efficient, practiced manner, buying faded jeans for Gwynne, a leather dop-kit for Brendan, Nike diving watches for Meredith and Brigid, a Halloween wreath at Williams-Sonoma. She even made an appointment at Carter-Barnes to get her hair done.

The target had style, and also a pleasant smile for the salespeople who waited on her in the toney stores. She held doors for those coming up behind her, even men, who bent over backwards to thank the attractive blonde. 'Mom' was sexy in the wholesome, clean-cut way of many upscale American suburban women. And she did resemble the supermodel Claudia Schiffer. That was her undoing.

According to the job's specs, Mrs Elizabeth Connelly was the mother of three girls; she was a graduate of Vassar, class of '87, with what she called, 'a degree in art history that is practically worthless in the real world – whatever that is – but invaluable to me'. She'd been a reporter for the *Washington Post* and the *Atlanta-Constitution* before she was married. She was thirty-seven, though she didn't look much more than thirty. She had her hair in a velvet barrette that morning, wore a short-sleeved turtleneck crocheted top, slim-fitting slacks. She was bright, religious – but sane about it – tough when she needed to be, at least according to the specs.

Well, she would need to be tough soon. Mrs Elizabeth Connelly was about to be abducted. She had been 'purchased', and she was probably the most expensive item for sale that morning at Phipps Plaza.

The price – $150,000.

Honeymoon

James Patterson and Howard Roughan

All writers have a book that they know is their very best, ever. James Patterson invites you along to his.

When FBI Agent John O'Hara first meets Nora Sinclair, she seems perfect. She has the career. The charisma. The tantalising sex appeal. The whole extraordinary package – Nora doesn't just attract men, she enthrals them. She's worked hard for this life and she will never give it up.

So why is the FBI so interested in Miss Sinclair? Mysterious things keep happening to the men in her life. And when Agent O'Hara looks more closely he sees something dangerous about Nora – something that lures him at the same time as it fills him with fear. And the more time he spends with her the less he knows whether he is pursuing justice or his own fatal obsession.

With the irresistible attraction of the greatest Hitchcock thrillers, HONEYMOON is a sizzling, twisting tale of a woman with a deadly appetite and the men who dare to fall for her. In his sexiest, scariest novel yet, JAMES PATTERSON deftly confirms why he is the world's bestselling thriller writer.

Praise for HONEYMOON:

'HONEYMOON is all pacy, sexy, high-octane stuff' *Guardian*

'O'Hara and particularly Nora stand as two of Patterson's most complex characters yet . . . This is one canny thriller and Patterson's millions of fans will be most pleased' *Publishers Weekly*

978 0 7553 0577 3

headline

Cradle and All

James Patterson

Cradle and All is megabestselling author James Patterson at the height of his creative power. A breathtaking combination of suspense, love and apocalyptic nightmare, it will keep his millions of fans on the edge of their seats.

Kathleen, from privileged Newport, Rhode Island; Colleen, from a poor, remote Irish village – two teenagers on opposite sides of the Atlantic whose lives are in great danger. Both girls are pregnant.

A private detective named Anne Fitzgerald suddenly has the case of a lifetime – she quickly finds herself caught between the certainty of science and the possibility of a miracle which could stop the terrible medical epidemics now sweeping the globe. Once a nun and now a private detective with a Masters in psychology, Anne's very belief in humanity is put to the ultimate test as she comes face to face with an unimaginable evil.

'The novel's considerable suspense arises as [Patterson] speeds the action from America to Ireland to the Vatican, sharpens it as supernatural forces come into play and spins it with a wicked twist' *Publishers Weekly*

'Compulsively readable' *Times Metro*

'A master of the suspense genre' *Sunday Telegraph*

978 0 7472 6698 3

headline

You've Been Warned

James Patterson and Howard Roughan

Internationally bestselling author James Patterson delivers the most haunting thriller of his career.

YOU'VE BEEN NICE, VERY NICE

Kristin Burns has lived her life by the philosophy, 'don't think, just shoot' – pictures that is. Struggling to make ends meet, she works full time as the nanny for the fabulously wealthy Turnbull family, looking after their two children and waiting for her life as a New York fashion photographer to begin. When her photographs are being considered at an elite Manhattan art gallery, it seems she might finally get the chance that will start her career.

YOU'VE BEEN NAUGHTY, VERY NAUGHTY

But Kristin has a major distraction: forbidden love. The man of her dreams is almost hers for keeps. Breathless with an inexhaustible passion and the excitement of being within reach of everything she wants, Kristin ignores all signs of catastrophe brewing.

NOW, YOU'VE BEEN WARNED

Fear exists for a reason. And Kristin can only dismiss the warnings for so long. Searching desperately for the truth through the lens of her camera, she can only hope that it's not too late. This novel of psychological suspense is a stunning new achievement for the man the *Sunday Telegraph* called 'the master of the suspense genre'.

Praise for James Patterson's bestselling novels:

'Pacy, sexy, high-octane stuff' *Guardian*

'A novel which makes for sleepless nights' *Daily Express*

978 0 7553 4956 2

headline

Now you can buy any of these bestselling books by
James Patterson from your bookshop or *direct from his publisher.*

FREE P&P AND UK DELIVERY
(Overseas and Ireland £3.50 per book)

When the Wind Blows	£7.99
Cradle and All	£8.99
Miracle on the 17th Green *(and Peter de Jonge)*	£7.99
Suzanne's Diary for Nicholas	£7.99
The Beach House *(and Peter de Jonge)*	£7.99
The Jester *(and Andrew Gross)*	£7.99
The Lake House	£7.99
Sam's Letters to Jennifer	£7.99
Honeymoon *(and Howard Roughan)*	£7.99
Lifeguard *(and Andrew Gross)*	£7.99
Beach Road *(and Peter de Jonge)*	£7.99
Judge and Jury *(and Andrew Gross)*	£7.99
Step on a Crack *(and Michael Ledwidge)*	£7.99
The Quickie *(and Michael Ledwidge)*	£7.99
You've Been Warned *(and Howard Roughan)*	£8.99

Alex Cross series

Cat and Mouse	£7.99
Pop Goes the Weasel	£7.99
Roses are Red	£7.99
Violets are Blue	£7.99
Four Blind Mice	£7.99
The Big Bad Wolf	£7.99
London Bridges	£7.99
Mary, Mary	£7.99
Cross	£7.99
Double Cross	£7.99

Women's Murder Club series

1st to Die	£7.99
2nd Chance *(with Andrew Gross)*	£7.99
3rd Degree *(and Andrew Gross)*	£7.99
4th of July *(and Maxine Paetro)*	£7.99
The 5th Horseman *(and Maxine Paetro)*	£7.99
The 6th Target *(and Maxine Paetro)*	£7.99

Maximum Ride series

Maximum Ride: The Angel Experiment	£7.99
Maximum Ride: School's Out Forever	£7.99
Maximum Ride: Saving the World and Other Extreme Sports	£7.99

TO ORDER SIMPLY CALL THIS NUMBER

01235 400 414

or visit our website: www.headline.co.uk
Prices and availability subject to change without notice.